THE HAEJU VIRUS
AN ASHLEY MORGAN JAMISON NOVEL

STEPHEN A ENNA

authorHOUSE®

AuthorHouse™
1663 Liberty Drive
Bloomington, IN 47403
www.authorhouse.com
Phone: 833-262-8899

© 2020 Stephen A Enna. All rights reserved.

No part of this book may be reproduced, stored in a retrieval system, or transmitted by any means without the written permission of the author.

Published by AuthorHouse 10/13/2020

ISBN: 978-1-7283-7172-6 (sc)
ISBN: 978-1-7283-7170-2 (hc)
ISBN: 978-1-7283-7171-9 (e)

Library of Congress Control Number: 2020944837

Print information available on the last page.

Any people depicted in stock imagery provided by Getty Images are models, and such images are being used for illustrative purposes only.
Certain stock imagery © Getty Images.

This book is printed on acid-free paper.

Because of the dynamic nature of the Internet, any web addresses or links contained in this book may have changed since publication and may no longer be valid. The views expressed in this work are solely those of the author and do not necessarily reflect the views of the publisher, and the publisher hereby disclaims any responsibility for them.

THIS BOOK IS DEDICATED TO
ALL THE MEN WHO WEAR THE NAVY SEAL TRITON
AND
TO THE FIRST WOMAN WHO WILL
SOMEDAY JOIN THEIR RANKS

A SPECIAL THANKS GOES TO THREE OF MY PALS
WHO TOOK THE TIME TO EDIT AND PROVIDE
ME WITH GREAT CONSTRUCTIVE FEEDBACK
MY SINCERE APPRECIATION GOES OUT TO
BILL CALDWELL
JOHN RAJALA
&
DENNIS WOOTTEN

CHAPTER 1
ATTACKED

It was almost dusk in Honolulu. The sun had yet to set and the streetlights and parking lights had yet to go on in Ala Moana Center. She hated shopping. So, when she did, she tried to do it all at once. As a result, she had way too many bags in her hands, but she knew she had less than a mile to walk to the Ala Wai Boat Harbor where her small apartment was located.

She left the Neiman Marcus Store which was the last stop on her quick shopping spree. The store faced directly at Ala Moana Blvd and the ground level exit door let her out not far from the boulevard.

Most of the parking for the Ala Moana center was built inside with up to three levels of customer parking. She did not have a car. She did not want a car and she looked forward to the short evening walk.

As she exited the store, she entered a small outdoor parking area that was designed for bus and taxi transportation. It was just outside the middle garage on the Makai or Ocean side of the shopping center.

She was carrying as much as she could as she began her walk. Her head was down but when she lifted her head up, she found herself facing two ugly men who were perhaps 20 yards in front of her.

While the light was poor, it was clear to her that each of them had a knife that was drawn and held in their right hands.

She barely noticed but she thought she saw a blue car parked on Ala Moana Blvd near the two men in front of her. Suddenly, she felt a huge push from behind which propelled her and her multiple packages directly at the men in front of her.

With little time to think she focused on the man on the right. He was momentarily distracted by her packages which went flying. The distraction was just enough to allow her to grab his wrist, and with one major twist it was behind his back and then she heard something crack. Then in an instant, her knee came up with full force hitting him directly in the crotch. He went down in a heap on the sidewalk. She turned to see his buddy starting for her with the knife held above his head. She did not even think as she reacted. Her right foot left her at a speed that would have rivaled the kicking motion of a 50-yard field goal kicker. Her right foot connected with his left knee and drove it completely sideways. It was not designed to bend in the manner it now did. The man dropped the knife and fell to the ground trying to grasp his knee. Two down and one to go she thought. Now the odds are a bit better.

The guy who had pushed her was now advancing even though he could see his two buddies were on the ground and disabled. He ran directly at her with the knife aimed straight for her. His momentum was such that he was carrying too much speed to control his movements. She simply stepped to the side as he approached and using her elbow, she aimed for a strike just below his nose and left eye. The elbow shot was perfect. As a result, blood gushed from his nose and mouth like a giant waterfall. She did not stop there. Using her right hand, she made a fist and then she hit him directly in his kidney area. He went down next to his two buddies. The three of them made on big heap of human flesh in the middle of the small parking lot.

She kicked the knives to one side and stopped for a moment to let each man know that if any of them so much as moved she would personally take great pleasure in slowly breaking another part of each of their bodies. They did not move. All they did was moan.

The blue car at the curb departed at a high rate of speed. By this time, she had attracted a small crowd, and someone had called 911. The police cars with lights flashing were suddenly lined up on the street where the blue car had once been. The first officer on the scene could not believe his eyes.

There, on the sidewalk, were three big ugly guys all with body parts broken and blood all over them.

With his gun out and aimed at them, he looked at her and said," Did you do this?"

"Yes officer, I did."

"These idiots apparently wanted to rob me of my Ala Moana Center purchases. They were waiting for me when I left Neiman Marcus. The guy with the short black hair pushed me from behind into the other two idiots who were standing in front of me with knives drawn. Obviously, I wasn't going to put up with it and you're looking at the result."

"Oh, and by the way. I think they had another buddy waiting in a blue car for them right where you are parked. That driver took off as soon as he could see his pals weren't going anywhere."

In no time there were at least 10 cops on site. The bad guys had been cuffed and the paramedics were on the way. One of the lead police officers asked her to please step to the side to give him a statement.

"Ma'am, I would like to get a statement from you if you don't mind."

"No problem officer. I would be happy to make a statement and file a formal charge against each of these idiots."

"Can we begin with your name, please?"

"Sure, my name is Captain Ashley Morgan Jamison, United States Marine Corp, Seal Vehicle Team 1 based at Pearl Harbor."

"Ashley Jamison? Are you the woman that was the first to earn the Navy Seal Trident?"

"Yes Sir, I am."

"Well that explains a few things right off the top.

"May I say that I have never seen anyone, man or woman, do to three guys what you just did? That was amazing"

"Excuse me officer, my name is Elma Witherspoon and I wanted you to know that I saw the entire thing from beginning to end. I am happy to make a statement if that is desired."

"Thank you, Ms. Witherspoon. Charlie, can you please take a statement from Mrs. Witherspoon for me?"

"Sure Boss, this way Ms. Witherspoon."

"Just a minute officer. Excuse me Miss, I wanted you to know that I gathered up your packages for you and put them on that bench over there."

Ashley looked at her and said, "Thank you very much."

"You're more than welcome young lady. It isn't often that I get to view a hero in action and you just provided me with that moment."

The lead officer then looked at Ashley, "Captain, my name is Sam Holland and I am the lead sergeant on the burglary detail for the Honolulu Police Department. I need to take a full statement from you but rather than go down to headquarters, would you allow me to buy you a cup of coffee?

We can get one at the small deli across the street."

"Thanks Sam that would be a much better plan for me." However, I need to get my packages."

"No problem, I will have one of our guys put them in my car and when we are done, I'll drive you home with them."

As they were about to leave there were several press vehicles now assembled and photos were being taken of everything, including the three guys in a giant heap in the middle of the parking area.

They crossed the street, ordered coffee and for the next hour Ashley took Sergeant Holland through the entire event from start to finish.

"I want you to know, Captain that you may have just solved a big problem for us. If I am right, and I am 90% sure I am, these guys have held up at least four other women in the same way as they tried to do to you."

"We have been looking for them for the last month and now I think you served them right up to us. In each of past robberies, they have used a blue car to get away. I am sure the car you saw was the getaway car. Now, with them in custody it is only a matter of time before we find out who the car's driver is and where we can find the car. It will not be long before one of them spills the beans."

When they were finished, Sergeant Holland drove Ashley and her packages the few blocks to her apartment and let her off in front with all her packages intact.

"Captain, are you going to be around for the next week or so?"

"Yes, we don't deploy for another few months so I will be here if you need me. I want to make sure that we formally charge those guys, so I will be around when you want me."

"Thanks, Captain."

Ashley trudged up the stairs to her small apartment. It was a studio apartment that faced directly out to Llikai Marina. Llikai Marina is one of the largest small boat harbors in Hawaii. It has 699 berths and 22 dry storage areas. It is home to the Waikiki and the Hawaii Yacht Clubs. It can handle a variety of different sailing vessels up to 85 feet.

Ashely was able to find the small apartment shortly after being assigned to Seal Team 1. She was the first woman to ever be granted the Trident and Navy Seal Certification and she was now the Assistant Officer in charge of Navy Seal Delivery Vehicle Team 1 based in Pearl Harbor. There was a second Seal Delivery Team which was Seal Delivery Vehicle Team 2 located in Little Creek, Virginia.

Once in her apartment she dropped her packages on the floor and fell onto the couch. She was exhausted and just laid there resting for about 20 minutes. When she felt better, she got up and picked up the phone to dial Captain Mark Price who was her boss and the head of Seal Delivery Vehicle Team 1.

"Hello, this is Mark, what can I do for you?"

"Hey Mark, its Ashley."

"Hi Ash, what do I owe the pleasure of this call to? Chief Johnson told me that you have been working extremely hard under water and were going to take two days off."

"That is still my plan, but I wanted to give you a heads up."

"Oh, what do I need to be on the lookout for?"

Ashley took Mark through the entire event from beginning to end and also told him that the press had shown up and she was sure that there would be something about it in the papers in the morning She was especially sure because of what Sergeant Holland had told her about the crime wave these guys seem to have caused.

Mark just told her not to worry and that any press calls should be referred to the base Public Relations Staff. He would call them and brief them. He told her not to talk to anyone from the press or anyone else except the police until the matter blows over.

Ashely was pooped. She poured herself a glass of Four Graces, Oregon Pinot Noir. It was good, not too expensive and a Pinot she always enjoyed. She carried her glass out onto her little balcony and watched the sun set behind the yacht harbor.

She had three glasses of wine while she sat on her little deck. It was a beautiful evening and at least she was able to enjoy part of it.

Her bed was a Murphy Bed that pulled out from the wall, so after a couple of hours of sitting she turned her attention to the bed and the next thing she knew she was sound asleep.

She woke up early. When she looked at the clock it said 6:30 AM. She was still tired but surprisingly she was not sore. She thought she might be, given the fight she was in the night before, but to her surprise, she felt simply fine and was nothing worse for wear.

At about 7 AM she got out of bed and headed for the bathroom. After a few moments she opened the door and headed for her kitchen.

Her Keurig Coffee Maker was on the counter and she put a K cup in it. It was a dark roast made by Peet's Coffee Company. She knew the company well as it was a Northwest based company located in Seattle, Washington. Ashley had grown up and gone through high school in Oregon, so she was a Northwest girl at heart.

While her Seal Team was in port, she had subscribed to the local Honolulu paper. The paper was the Honolulu Star Advertiser which is the largest daily newspaper in Hawaii. It was formed in 2010 with the merger of the Honolulu Advertiser and the Honolulu Star Bulletin.

She took her coffee and paper out on the deck. It was a beautiful morning. The temperature was already in the high 70's. She opened the paper and could not believe her eyes.

There on the front page was a huge picture of the three guys piled in a stack on the sidewalk. The caption over the photo said:

AND TODAY'S LESSON, LADIES AND GENTELMAN
IS
NEVER MESS WITH A FEMALE SEAL

CHAPTER 2
THE DAY AFTER

Ashley took a second look at the photo in front of her and began to read the story below it.

At 5:45 PM on Friday a woman departed the Neiman Marcus Store at the Ala Moana Center and headed out of the building to cross Ala Moana Blvd. Her arms were full of packages and according to eye witnesses she was carrying more than most do.

Suddenly a man, now identified as Ramon Ito, age 24, pushed her from behind into two men both with knives drawn. Mr. Ito's partners have now been identified as Ralph Signo, 23, and Scooter Miles, 26. All men are residents of Hawaii and hold the same address in Honolulu.

It appears from the facts released so far, that the police believe that this trio, plus a "get-away-driver," have been the group behind four recent attacks on women shoppers. The attacks at all the robberies are remarkably similar.

As our readers can see from the picture in our article, these men simply picked the wrong woman to try to rob. As it turns out, the woman attacked was Ashley Morgan Jamison. Ms. Jamison is a Captain in the United States Marine Corp and she is the Assistant Officer in charge of Navy Seal Delivery Vehicle Team 1, based in Pearl Harbor.

This name may be familiar to our readers as Ms. Jamison was the first woman, and we might add, still the only woman to qualify as a Navy Seal. As such she has earned the right to wear the famed Navy SEAL Triton.

Captain Jamison was not available to be interviewed for this article but according to eye witnesses she simply destroyed each of her attackers, one by one, until they were piled in a heap in the middle of the small parking lot. We might add that each of them, needed to be taken to the emergency room with at least, one broken body part.

According to Sergeant Sam Holland, head of the Honolulu Police Burglary detail, the three thugs were no match for the skills displayed by Captain Jamison. Sergeant Holland said, "I have never seen anyone, man or woman, display such a hand to hand, one on three, skill base. Captain Jamison not only served as a living example of what our Navy SEALs are trained to do but, in my estimation, the three thugs now in custody should thank God, they got out of that situation alive."

Sergeant Holland also indicated that they now have the name of the person driving the get-away-car and are looking for that person as this article goes to press.

Ashley took another sip of her coffee and smiled as she put the paper down in front of her.

The sun was bright, and the sky was clear. Ashley had the day off and was looking forward to a quiet day with some beach time on Honolulu's famed Waikiki Beach.

That thought went by the wayside as the first phone call came in. "Hello this is Ashley, what can I do for you?"

"Hi Ash, its Mark."

Hey Mark, what did I do to deserve this early morning call from my boss? As if I didn't know."

"Ash, have you seen this morning's paper?"

"Yep, I just read the article and thought it was pretty accurate."

"Well, all I can tell you is that it has already caught the eye of the top folks in the SEAL command as well as the Senior Officers here at Pearl Harbor. Everyone is over the top, on the moon so to speak, with the positive things that were said about you and the SEAL connection. You are going to be inundated with calls from everywhere today. Do not respond to any of them and if someone does get through to you, simply refer them to the public relations staff at Pearl Harbor."

"No problem Mark, I have no desire to talk to anyone about the incident."

I'm heading to the beach today, so I won't be around for phone calls or for that matter any personal knocks on my door."

Ashley no sooner hung up the phone when it rang again. She could tell by the caller ID that it was Ryan Joshua. Ryan was a Lieutenant in the Navy and he was a fighter pilot attached to the Yorktown. Ryan flies FA 18 Hornets off the carrier. He and Ashley went to school at the Naval Academy together. Ryan was Captain of the Navy Gymnastics team during the time that Ashley was setting NCAA swimming marks for the Navy. They had recently been reacquainted at the Officers Club in Pearl

Harbor and had begun what for Ashley, was the first serious relationship with anyone in her life.

"Hey Ryan, great to hear your voice."

"Hi Ash, are we still on for some beach time together today?"

"We sure are, what time are you going to come by. I thought about 11AM. We can grab some lunch at the Beach Bar and then spend the afternoon pretending we are tourists on Waikiki Beach."

"That sounds great. I will see you at 11 AM, Cheers."

Ashley got off the phone and thought, he has not read the paper and he does not know. This will be interesting to see how this all plays out.

Ashley made breakfast and put her bed back into the wall and then turned her attention to unpacking the packages she had purchased the night before.

The first package she opened was purchased at Neiman Marcus. She started to laugh as she pulled the contents out and began to put them away in her drawer. It was from the lingerie department. The first box contained panties. There were two types, which made her smile. The first were five pairs of sexy thong panties. These were for Ryan and for any other time she needed to feel sexy. Then there was the second box which contained eight more pairs. These were for her everyday comfort. They were not quite what would be described as old ladies' underwear, but they were clearly designed to be comfortable and practical.

The next box followed suit. They were bras. There were five sexy ones that matched the panties she had selected and there were four extremely comfortable, flexible ones for everyday use.

As she put the items away, she could not help thinking that there probably a bunch of women out there who only think about sexy and never about being comfortable and practicable. Oh well, she knew what was right for her and that was the way it would be.

The next box contained kitchenware and some utensils. She unloaded them and put them in the kitchen.

The phone kept ringing, but she just ignored it.

The last boxes were things she had purchased to make her small apartment more like home. One of the things she had purchased was a 15X15 framed photo of Mt. Hood. It was covered with snow and brought her right back to her roots in Portland, Oregon.

She also bought a few frames in which she could put some of her most treasured certificates. The first being her Navy Seal Triton certificate. The others she planned to display were her two Olympic swimming medals and her NCAA Champion recognition certificates. Last was her diploma from the United states Naval Academy.

When she finished her unpacking, she grabbed her swimsuit and a cover up from the drawer and put them on. Her phone continued to ring constantly but she just continued to ignore it and focused on her next event which was getting rays at the beach.

She was surprised when there was a knock on her door. At first, she thought she should not open it but she looked out the security peep hole and saw that it was the manager of her apartment, Mr. Piedmont, standing at the door.

"Ashley adjusted her cover up and opened the door. "Good morning Mr. Piedmont. How can I help you?"

"Hi Ash, I'm sorry to bother you but have you looked outside this morning?"

"Not really, I have been busy unpacking, why would you ask? I'm sorry Mr. Piedmont, please come in, the last thing we need to do is talk in the doorway."

"Thanks Ash. Look outside down at the street level."

Ashley peeked around the door and saw at least eight press trucks. All with radio antennas on them and a bunch of people milling around each of them.

"Holy Cow! I wonder what that is all about."

"Ash, have you seen this morning's paper?"

"Yes. Oh, now I get it. They want to talk to me about those idiots that tried to attack me when I left the shopping center last night."

"You got that right; one of them came up to my apartment this morning and asked if you lived here and in what unit. I told them that was none of their business and to get off the property immediately."

"Thanks Mr. Piedmont, I appreciate your effort and you're coming over here to advise me. However, I am not sure what to do. My friend is coming over at 11 AM and we were going to walk down the path to the beach."

"Looks like that might be a bit difficult to do now. I let my boss know about the press and he told me that all questions need to be referred to the public relations staff at Pearl Harbor. As such, I have not answered the phone. It keeps ringing off the hook. What would you recommend Mr. Piedmont?"

"Well first I would like to congratulate you on kicking the crap out of some really bad people. I am sure the entire community is grateful to you. I have an idea that I think will work. I will ask two of my cleaning staff to bring their cart to your apartment and to bring a set of cleaning clothes for each of you. Once they are into your unit, I would suggest that you and your friend change into the cleaning clothes and put your beach items in the bag on the cart."

"Once done, just leave the room with the cart and return to my unit. I will let you in with your cart. Once in, you both can change and head out my back door.

It will take you to the back of the building and from there you can pick up the path to the beach. When you return, come back the same way. If the folks are still there, we will just reverse the process. My guess, however, is they will be long gone by then."

At exactly 11 AM there was a knock on her door. She looked through the peep hole and saw that it was Ryan. On time as usual.

Ash opened the door and let him in. She greeted him with a kiss on the lips and said, "Ryan, it is great to see you."

"It's great to see you too Ash but what is going on outside? There must be six or eight press trucks in the street outside this building."

"Well to tell the truth they all want to talk to me. You obviously have not read this morning's paper yet. Here, before you ask another question, read the front-page story."

Ryan sat down on the couch and read the complete article. "Well, it looks to me like three guys made an awfully bad decision. Are you OK?"

"Sure, I'm fine. My Navy Seal combat training came in handy last night and this morning I am sure there are three thugs that wish they had picked on someone else. However, that was yesterday and today is today and I am really looking forward to spending it together with plenty of beach time."

"Me too but how do we get out of here without being harassed by the folks down on the street?"

"Mr. Piedmont, my manger, suggested an approach that should work. In fact, in a couple of minutes two members of his cleaning staff will be knocking on the door to clean. That my dear, is the key tour freedom."

Ashley was right. Within five minutes the cleaning staff knocked on the door and Mr. Piedmonts strategy worked like a charm.

Within 20 minutes they were seated at an outdoor table at RumFire Waikiki. They had a wonderful Oceanfront view of Waikiki and Diamond Head.

RumFire is Oahu's premier oceanfront restaurant and bar. It opened at 11 AM so they were seated on arrival at 11:30.

Ryan ordered a Jerry and Ginger. It was made with 92 proof spiced rum, ginger beer and fresh squeezed lime on the rocks.

Ashley ordered a Gidget's Crush which was made with Vodka, DeKuyper, watermelon liquor and sprite.

They looked at the menu and decided to split a Cold Sorba Noodle Salad. It was done with a soy dressing, mushrooms, edamame and cherry tomatoes.

No one noticed them or bothered them. It was a great start to the day.

CHAPTER 3
THE RELATIONSHIP

It had been a beautiful day. Ryan and Ashley spent the entire afternoon laying on the beach at Waikiki. They looked just like every other tourist laying on the beach with the exception that both were tan having already spent a lot of time in the Hawaiian sun.

At about 4 PM, Ashley said, "Hey Ryan, I'm feeling a bit baked are you ready to leave?"

"Sure Ash, whenever you want. What do you have planned for us next?

"Well, I think a cold gin and tonic sitting on my little deck looking at the yacht harbor might be a good way to start the evening off. What do you think?"

"Sounds good to me. Let's head back."

They walked up the beach and then turned off on the narrow path that headed to the yacht harbor and Ashley's studio apartment.

"I wonder if the press will still be there. I never dreamed that taking those three idiots down would cause this much commotion."

"Ash, in my eyes, and now I'm sure in the eyes of a lot of the residents of Honolulu, you are Super Woman."

"Oh come-on, Ryan, all I did was teach a few boys not to mess with a woman with packages in her hands."

They both laughed and continued their walk toward the apartment. As they got closer, they could see the front of the building and it was clear of all the press trucks. "Looks like Mr. Piedmont's strategy worked. Remind me that I want to give him a nice bottle of Oregon Pinot Gris."

"Will do. Sir"

"Ryan, what is your schedule for tomorrow?"

"I need to be back on the ship by 8 AM. We get underway at 9 AM and will be out to sea for the next two weeks. How about you Ash?"

"Well my schedule is not much different. I took two days off to rest, and as you know, that did not turn out quite like I had planned. I need to report to the sub by 8 AM tomorrow morning. We have a SEAL team meeting at 9 AM and then are in port for the day. On Tuesday, we begin a series of underwater exercises that will be particularly challenging. They will all be deep water exercises done from the submarine. I am looking forward to them. I still feel, I was born half fish and I am most comfortable when I am under water. I think we are out to sea for a week but after that I'm not sure."

"Ash, you know that being half fish is a bit weird."

"Yep, but it is what it is. Get used to it Mister. Look at it this way; you get to have all of this fish you want when it's out of water?"

"Now that is nice to know sailor. Do you want to go out to dinner?"

"No, I'm going to cook for you and then if you're up to it, I want you to experience what is like to play with a fish out of water."

"Now that sounds like a dinner to remember."

"I sure hope so."

They arrived back at the studio apartment and Ashley went right to work making them each a tall gin and tonic. She put a lime in each one and then served it to them on her patio. It was a perfect afternoon and would be a great sunset later.

"What do you have planned for dinner, Ash?"

"We are going to have barbequed Cornish Game Hens, with saffron rice and peaches with cranberry sauce."

"Wow that sounds great! Is there anything I can do?"

"There sure is, when you are ready, I want you to light the charcoal in our little hibachi barbeque I am afraid it is not a gas Webber, but beggars can't be choosers.

I measured it earlier and it will hold two Cornish game hen half's which is what I have prepared. All you must do is put the tin foil pan with the game hens on it in the BBQ. It should take 45 to 50 minutes. I have prepared the hens with salt and pepper and butter. That is, it."

"No problem let me finish my gin and tonic and I'll get right on it. Where in the world did you find fresh peaches? I'm not sure they are in season but even when they are, they don't seem to make it out to the islands very often."

To be honest, I saw them at Safeway yesterday and grabbed two of them. Then I started thinking what I would do with them and I decided I would keep it simple and just fill the pit opening with cranberry sauce. That led me to what goes good with cranberry sauce and suddenly, I had the Cornish game hen idea pop up. It sounds a little crazy, but I think it could turn out to be a good meal."

"Once I had the menu in my mind, I went to work on the wine, and I grabbed two bottles of Adelsheim Pinot Gris from the Oregon Willamette Valley. The Pinot Gris has the aromas of white peach which fits with the menu and is supposed to taste a little like pear blossoms, whatever that means. They say the wine goes great with oven roasted fowl. So, there you go."

Once he finished his gin and tonic, Ryan went to work on the barbeque and in no time, he had the game hens in their tin foil pan cooking away.

Ashley poured him a second gin and tonic but only about ½ of a glass. This worked fine and lasted him for the 50 minutes it took to cook the game hens.

At 50 minutes Ryan checked on the game hens and they were a perfect brown. "Ash, I think the birds are done."

"Great, here is a hot pad, bring them in and put them on the stove. They can cool there for a couple of minutes while I finish the rice and get the dinner plates ready. The table is set.

Would you open a bottle of the Pinot Gris and pour us each a glass? We should be ready to go momentarily."

They sat down to dinner and it was great. The wine went well, and they were full when they finished. They cleaned up the dishes and then had coffee on the deck.

The sun was starting to set. "I set the alarm for 6 AM. That should give us both the time to get to the ships by 8 AM."

At about 9 PM, Ash told Ryan that she had a bit of a surprise for him and that she was going to change and would meet him in bed in about 15 minutes. She asked him too to pull the bed down from the wall and get ready for bed.

He did what he was asked to do and stripped down to his boxer shorts and lay down on the bed. It was a beautiful evening and they left the deck door open so the breeze could filter through the room.

Ash came out of the bathroom and Ryan's eyes almost jumped out of his head. She obviously had her swimmers' body, with broad shoulders, tiny waist, small boobs and strong legs. That was not new to him but what she covered her body with was. Ashley had on an exquisite lace corded teddy that had a keyhole cutout in the front and lace up detail in the back. It was red, sheer and unlined. It had adjustable cross back straps and a back hook and eye closure. The bottom was a thong and from the back it looked like she had nothing on below her waist

Ryan could not take his eyes off her. "My God Ash, you look absolutely beautiful." She crawled in bed with him and from that point on they were two bodies in twisted total motion.

When they were done, they were both exhausted and just lay there looking up at the ceiling.

All Ryan could say was, "Wow Ash you were fantastic. I will never forget this night as long as I live."

"Thanks, big guy, you weren't so bad yourself."

Both wanted to do it again, but both were totally pooped and fell asleep in each other's arms.

The alarm went off at 6 AM and they were both up and moving quickly. Ashley had a Keurig Coffee Maker, so making coffee was simple. All she had to do was put a k cup in the machine and push the button.

She put a couple of pieces of toast in the toaster and they had their toast and jam on the deck and watched the sun come up. They called an Uber car and were headed to the base at 7 AM.

Once there, they gave each other a hug and headed their separate ways.

Ashley was dressed in civilian clothes. She headed down the pier to where the Nuclear Submarine USS Louisville SSN 724 was berthed. Ashley's SEAL Delivery Team was assigned to the Louisville and it had become her home away from home. When the sub was in port, so was she. When the sub was out, so was she.

She was met at the boarding plank by a First Class Petty Officer. His name was Freemont Abby. Ashley like him and he was one of the first guys she had met when she arrived on board. He was a real character and the name fit him well.

"Good Morning Sir" he said. "Welcome back."

"Thanks Freemont, good to see you."

"Sir, if I may say, I'm not sure that your two days off were as restful as you had hoped for."

Ashley just smiled and said" Yes, it was a quick leave with not much rest."

She headed for her cabin and changed into her Khakis. Her meeting was scheduled for the conference room on the base at 9:30 AM so she had a half hour to get herself together and make it to the meeting. As was her practice, she would be at the meeting and ready to go at least five minutes before the scheduled start.

Her SEAL team was part of Naval Special Warfare Group 1. It was composed of six platoons although her platoon was the only one attached to the USS Louisville.

Her team was led by her boss Captain Mark Price and was made up of 16 enlisted men

Ashley had trained with her guys for several months and had participated in a few key missions with them.

She hurried across the base and made it to the conference room with 10 minutes to spare. As she entered the room, she was surprised to see all the members of her platoon in place around the table with her boss Mark at the end of the table in the front of the room.

When she entered the entire group of men stood and gave her a standing ovation. Ashley did not know what to say or do, she felt her face getting warm and just looked at Mark as to say, "What the Hell."

The guys finally stopped clapping and sat down, at which time Mark said, "Hey Ash, welcome and congratulations. You have made all of us immensely proud."

She sat down but did not say anything. She was a bit embarrassed but knew that Mark was talking about the picture in the paper and the article that accompanied it.

"What do you have to say?" Mark asked.

"Thanks guys, I really don't have anything to say. What I did, all of you could have done in your sleep. Those creeps just picked on a SEAL and my guess is they will not do it in the future. In fact, I think that the ER staff is still trying to put them back together."

The entire group laughed and then they turned their attention to Mark at the front of the room.

"Tomorrow we get underway for one week of deep-water training. It will involve at least three-night dives and at least two island landings. It has been a while since we worked at night, so you should be prepared to spend a lot of time in the water with not much time to sleep after dark."

"The Captain has told me that he will be off loading us at 70 feet and at 150 feet. The 70 feet exercise you will use your front breathing packs. For the deeper dive we will use the scuba gear."

"We will be working in teams. I will lead team 1 and Ash will head up team 2. You will receive your team assignments later today. This training will be completed as drills so we will not have any live or armed obstacles to deal with. It is meant as a refresher so it should be easy for all of you" The group just laughed.

"You have the remainder of the day to check your equipment and make sure it is ready to go. Do any of you have any questions?"

With that the group disbanded and headed to Ash with 1000 questions.

CHAPTER 4
SEA TRIALS

The USS Louisville SSN 724 is a Los Angeles-class submarine. It was the fourth ship of the United States Navy to be named for Louisville, Kentucky. She was launched on December 14, 1985.

The Louisville became the first attack submarine to work up and deploy with a carrier battle group in the Pacific. She completed an extensive overhaul in Portsmouth, NH at the end of 2008 and then was home ported in Pearl Harbor, Hawaii in the spring of 2009.

Once she had established a new home in Pearl Harbor, she became the home of the SEAL Delivery Team 1. She was outfitted in Pearl to carry a mini sub that was used extensively by SEAL Team 1.

The ship was underway at 0800 and was totally submerged and headed out to sea by 0830. Captain Mark Price, who commanded SEAL Team 1 had called a meeting of his team to begin at 0900 in the small conference room. All members of the team were present and in their seats before the start time of 0900.

"Good Morning Ash and men, it is good to be underway again and to have the opportunity to brush up on our underwater skills.

As you know, in two months, on December 15th we will deploy to the South Pacific for a period of at least six months. I'm not sure what the actual deployment will entail but I can tell you, if the past is any indication of the future your entire skill base will be tested."

"I wanted to take this opportunity this morning to give you a glimpse of what we are going to experience this week. We will be out for 7 days and during that time we will have 2 deep water dives and 3 shallow dives with shore interventions."

"The deep-water dives will begin at about 150 feet and we will work down to 200 feet. This is well below the scuba limit depth for normal recreational dives so it will require your full attention to air supply, depth and surface procedures to avoid the consequences of not being smart at 150 feet and below."

"Our shallow dives will be with our front breathing packs and will be at 75 feet. They will all be at night and all will involve a land mission. You have been separated into two groups. Group I will be under my command and Group 2 will be under Ashley's command."

"I want to spend a few minutes now talking about our deep-water dives and to remind you of some of the things I want you to be cognizant of."

"Let us start with an overview of deep-water scuba diving. Less than ten people are known to have dived below 240 meters, or 800 feet, using a self-contained breathing apparatus on a recreational dive. More people have set foot on the moon than have reached the depth of the deepest scuba dive."

"We are obviously not going to go near that depth but at 200 feet we are in water that very few scuba divers have experienced. I can tell you from my own experience, that deep diving, even at 200 feet, brings a mix of fear and fascination to all of those who experience it."

"Now I am going to take you back to some of your early SEAL training lectures. I am going to do this because none of you have been to 200 feet either in training or since we have been together at SEAL team 1.

I want to begin at the beginning. I want to start there, not just to show you how smart I am, but to remind you of the things you will need to keep in mind in order to stay safe." The group laughed.

Captain Price then looked at the group to see if there were any questions. There were not any, so he continued. "Deep diving generally refers to recreational dives that go below the accepted safe depths agreed on by the diving community."

"Because of the limitations of our bodies, and the equipment used in diving, you can only dive to a certain depth for a certain amount of time. The deeper you go, the shorter your dive has to be for safety,"

"When people ask, "How deep can you scuba dive?" There is no short answer. There are many variables that affect the depths a person can reach."

"So, I want to talk to you about the risks we can encounter."

"Number 1 is nitrogen narcosis. Nitrogen narcosis is a state of altered consciousness that happens to your body when nitrogen gas is inhaled under high pressure. Some people call nitrogen narcosis the raptures of the deep. Nitrogen is always present in the air we breathe, and it usually passes through our bodies without issue. But when divers are deep underwater, they breathe in more nitrogen than usual because the air we breathe is condensed by the pressure of the water. This nitrogen excess saturates the nervous system in an intoxicating way. The deeper the dive the more severe the effects. Nitrogen narcosis begins with a sense of euphoria, light headedness or numbness. As it intensifies, divers lose some of their manual dexterity as well as the ability to make rational decisions. Anxiety, fear, or panic may set in. If it becomes too sever, nitrogen narcosis can lead to unconsciousness or death."

"The big problem is you may not even realize that you have been affected. I should add that at significant depths, the oxygen can also become toxic because it is so compressed. Breathing heavily compressed air for too long can be fatal even without nitrogen narcosis."

"So, the bottom line for all of you is to know what depth you are at, how much air you have left in your tank and how long you have been at that depth. Plan, accordingly, I do not want any accidents. Does anyone have any questions?"

There were no questions.

"OK then, the next issue I want to discuss is decompression sickness. As you may remember from your classroom training, the greater the depth, the greater the pressure, which means decompression sickness also becomes a threat on deep dives. You will need to take longer decompression stops. Your stops will keep gas bubbles from growing in your body as you rise from deep water. Since we will be working at 200 feet, you will need to take your time coming up."

"If you can gradually release the water pressure and let the buildup of gases in your bloodstreams leave naturally, it will reduce the likelihood of decompression sickness. Some call this sickness the bends. It happens when gas bubbles grow and cannot escape.

This sickness can affect the body in a variety of ways, but the most important fact you should know is the bends can result in paralysis or death."

"To put this into perspective, I want you to know that the world record for the deepest scuba dive is held by an Egyptian man named Ahmed Gabr. He dove to a depth of 1,090 feet four inches. He was able to reach this record-breaking depth in just 12 minutes but the important point to make to each of you is that it took him 15 hours to resurface to avoid negative effects from the dive. Thanks to his caution, he surfaced without any decompression sickness or other negative effects. Think about it gang. 12 minutes down, 15 hours up. Take your time."

"Last, I want to remind you that your air supply is the one you take with you. One major problem with deep dives is divers run out of air. During a deep dive, the high pressure means the air runs out faster. So, you will need to take extra air and carefully watch the supply, so your air supply lasts you until you return to the sub."

"Are there any questions? Yes Jimmy,"

"Sir, I have heard two things about deep dives. The first is that they are often referred to as technical dives and the second, that often there is a need to change the gas mixture in the tanks depending on how deep you go. Can you give me some information on that?"

"Sure Jimmy, thanks for bringing that up. First, technical diving encompasses any diving method that is used by divers to go beyond the depth and time limits of recreational diving. I'm not sure what those limits are today but generally I think they are about 130 feet."

"Technical divers often dive using special gas mixtures rather than air, which is better for breathing at great depths. Technical divers spend more time in deep ranges than other divers working on average in depths of 170 to 350 feet. As such, we will be using a special mix in our tanks that will account for our working at 200 feet."

"Are there any other questions?"

There were no other questions.

"OK, since there are no other questions, I want to turn this over to Ash to talk about the exercises that we will do towards the end of the week. It's all yours Ash."

"Thanks Mark. Good morning to all of you. I do not know about all of you, but I am really looking forward to getting back in the water. This shore leave is over-rated. I do not know why but I am glad to be back at sea and away from land. The group laughed and said in unison, "We hear you, Ash."

"OK, to the task at hand. We have planned two-night dives that will involve shore excursions. The sub will plan to let us out at a depth of 75 feet. As such we will wear our front breathing packs. Our goal will be to depart the sub at 2 AM, make our way to the shore of an island. This will require about a mile swim. We will surface and locate our target. Contact the target and photo it, then return to the sub. This entire exercise will be done in silence. While we do not anticipate any problems, should one occur, Mark or I will make a circle with our hands.

If we do that you should plan to form a circle around us whether we are in the water or on land. We will use our white boards to let you know what to do next. Any questions?"

There were no questions, so Ashley said, 'Back to you, Mark."

"OK gang, our first deep dive will be held at 10 AM tomorrow morning. We will complete our exercises at 150 feet. The sub will let us out at 100 feet, and we will then head down to the desired depth. If there are no further questions, I will see you at the in and out box at 0930 tomorrow morning. Cheers."

The next three days were spent underwater, day one at 150 feet, day two at 175 feet and day three at 200 feet. Each day the exercises involved the construction of different objects that could be used on a land exercise.

When day three was completed, Ashley asked Mark what he thought about the exercises that had been selected.

"I'm not sure Ash, but the orders came from SEAL headquarters in San Diego.

If I am right, they have something up their sleeve for our deployment in a couple of months. As I indicated before, I have never been on a deployment when we were not tasked with some live dangerous exercise. I would be surprised if that were not the case this time as well."

The first night dive with compass landing went well. Both teams departed the sub and returned on time with no problems.

On the second dive, Team 1 left first and was about 1 hour ahead of Team 2. All went well on Team 1's dive and they returned to the sub on time. As Team 2 moved in the dark waters toward the beach there was suddenly a commotion in the water behind the group. Ashley turned to observe what was going on and it was clear the last man in her group had been attacked by a Tiger Shark.

A struggle was in progress as she and the other members of her team moved to help the stricken diver. The diver was Jonnie Potts. Jonnie was swimming in the last position in a formation led by Ash with two divers following her on each side and Jonnie in the final spot following the group.

Jonnie was an experienced SEAL. Ashley quickly moved to Jonnie and grabbed him. She made the circular motion with her hands and her team moved to surround her and the stricken diver. Blood was everywhere in the water and it was clear that it was attracting other sharks.

Tiger Sharks are big and range up to 5.5 meters in length which means that a full-grown Tiger Shark can be as long as 18 feet. They are predators and are found in tropical and warm temperate warm waters worldwide. That includes the waters off Hawaii where Tiger Shark attacks have occurred over the years.

Tiger Sharks are present in a wide variety of marine habitats including those associated with continental shelves, oceanic islands and atolls and, they can be found extensively in the open ocean. Tiger sharks are opportunistic predators which means they consume a diverse array of food including other fish, other sharks, shellfish, reptiles, mammals and birds. Their diet changes as they grow and age.

In Hawaii, small tiger sharks feed primarily on reef fish and octopus, whereas larger sharks consume a variety of larger prey including other sharks, turtles, mammals and crustaceans.

Tiger sharks are one of the shark species most frequently implicated in attacks on humans although shark attacks are rare.

Ashley grabbed her white board and wrote. "We head for the beach. Keep the circle but move fast. I see three of them. Each about 13 feet long. If they come at you, hit them with your gun."

The team moved toward the beach with Ashley in the middle towing Jonnie Potts. When they reached the beach, Ashley had two of the men pull Jonnie up on to a tarp she had laid down. Blood was still coming out of his leg at a significant pace. She took her knife and cut his wet suit down from the top of his thigh to his ankle and pulled the suit away from the leg. The shark had bitten completely through the suit and bit down which was good. Tiger sharks are known to rip their victims from side to side. Ashley was sure that Jonnie had hit it as it attacked and that is what caused it to let go of the leg.

She put a tourniquet on his leg just below his groin and then worked on each of the teeth wounds to minimize the bleeding and cover each with an ointment that she had in her first aid kit. She could see that Jonnie had lost lots of blood and was weak, but he was still breathing and in significant pain.

To the surprise of all her men, she then pulled from her pack a large roll of gauze and a roll of silver duct tape. She placed gauze all over the leg and then began to wrap the entire leg from groin to ankle in duct tape. The tape stopped all bleeding. Once she had that completed, she placed the wet suit back in its original place and duct taped it together.

"OK guys. We now move him back to the ship as quickly as possible. We will move in our circle formation. We need to move quickly as Jonnie has lost a lot of blood. I will tow him in the center with me. Al, you take point and Charlie you take the rear position. Now let us get him home. Remember there were three of them and they may still be out their milling around."

They made great time moving back to the ship with no sign of the three Tiger Sharks. Once to the sub, Ashley took Jonnie immediately to the entry hatch and accompanied him into the ship. Once inside the sub, she told those meeting them what had happened and what needed to be done immediately. The doctor was called and Jonnie was moved to sickbay where the medical staff took over and went to work on him.

Team 2 had all their gear stowed within a half an hour and were back in their quarters and talking to each other. There were two subjects. The first was "How is Jonnie doing?" and the second was "Did you see the size of those things?"

The talk among the crew at dinner was all about sharks. To the submarine seamen they could not imagine doing what the SEALs do especially in the dark of night and underwater. They all kept trying to imagine three sharks that were 13 feet or longer. The thought was almost too much to bear for all of them.

That evening after dinner, the ship's Doctor, Lieutenant Scotty Morris, asked to see Mark and Ashley alone. They met in the officer's wardroom." Hi Mark and Ash, nice to see you again."

"Hi Scotty, it's good to see you too." Mark said."

"What can we do for you Scotty?"

"Well, actually nothing. I just wanted to give you an update on Jonnie Potts. The good news is he is going to make it. He lost a lot of blood but thanks to Ashley's quick thinking he will live and not lose a leg. The bad news is he required over 100 stiches and will require months of rehab once his wounds heal. Ash, I am not sure where you heard about the duct tape medical use, but I can tell you, from my perspective, that is what saved him. Once you applied the tourniquet and then layered the gauze over the wounds the tight duct tape wrap stopped the bleeding and as such it provided the time to get him back to us. I wanted Mark to know that if I could award a metal for smart thinking that you would be standing on the podium as I speak."

Ashley blushed a little. "Thanks Scotty, somewhere along the line I read about the multiple uses of duct tape and I have carried a roll with me ever since.

I remembered that I read that in the event of a large gash or wound it could be used as a seal until a doctor could stich up the gash. I knew it would not be a replacement for stiches but that it would reduce blood loss until medical attention could be obtained. I'm glad to know it worked"

"It sure did Ash, and it stopped the infection from becoming a real problem. Jonnie may never know it, but you, Sir, saved his life."

"Thanks Scotty, but as you can imagine it was a group effort."

Mark just turned and looked at her. "You my friend, never stop impressing me. Thanks for all your quick thinking."

The sub was headed back to Pearl Harbor and arrived the next morning at 1100. An ambulance was waiting and took Jonnie Potts off to the hospital.

CHAPTER 5
THE BLUE CAR

The USS Louisville was tied up at Pier 14 at Pearl Harbor Naval Base. Ashley had one more night on the ship before she had two days off. Ryan was out for another week, so she was not in a hurry to go anywhere.

She was standing on the outer deck just looking at nothing when her Platoon Chief, Mike Johnson, taped her on the shoulder. "Hey Captain, my sources tell me that you made headlines once again."

"Oh, come on Chief, I didn't do anything that you or any other member of this SEAL team wouldn't have done given the circumstances."

"Not what the men are saying, Sir. It sounds to me like you pulled a rabbit out of a hat and saved little Jonnie Potts' ass. In fact, based on what my sources tell me, Jonnie would not be walking around on this earth had you not been there and taken charge."

"OK Chief, enough is enough. As you well know, these are my guys too and I intend to do everything I can while I'm around them to be the best that I can be."

"Well, Captain, I for one can tell you that you don't have to prove that to anyone. Every one of these guys knows it."

"What I'm curious about is the shark. I heard there were three of them and they were pretty big."

"Yep, you got that right. I saw two of them clearly and the other one only from the rear. Do you remember when we were training on the delivery vehicle and a great white shark approached us?"

"Yep, I sure do. You popped it in the nose, and it took off."

"Well, the three sharks that we ran into were at least twice or maybe three times as big as that one."

"They say that Tiger Sharks can get as long as 18 feet. These weren't that big, but I know they were at least 13 feet."

"Wow, I have never seen any shark that large in my entire career as a SEAL. To see three of them all at once and underwater in a night operation could be the makings of a good horror movie."

"Yep, I was not scared, and I do not think the men were either, but the thing was big and aggressive. My guess is that once it hit Jonnie that he turned and popped it in the nose with the butt of his rifle. My feeling is it let go right then. As a result, it bit down but it didn't rip and tear which would have been exceedingly difficult to patch up."

I checked this morning to see if any of the sharks had been tagged but no luck. There were no tagged Tiger Sharks operating in that area yesterday."

"I'm curious because a number of years ago I read a study about them. As I recall they were referred to as swimming garbage disposals. They simply eat everything. As they grow, they eat bigger things like seals and in our case Jonnie's leg. As

I remember, they can weigh up to 1300 pounds and even more. Sounds like the ones you saw were in that category."

"Yep, based on what I saw I would say that all three of them had led pretty successful eating lives."

"As I remember they are the fourth largest shark known to man. They follow the Whale sharks, basking sharks and great whites."

"Chief, I think we were very lucky. These big fellows have notched teeth and they like to tear things apart. Because Jonnie hit it in the nose it did not tear. It simply bit down which made our recovery efforts easier. Had it ripped, the leg would have surely been lost and probably Jonnie as well."

"What did you think of the deep-water exercises Chief?"

"Well, I was a bit surprised that they had us down to 200 feet. It all went well but I have been a SEAL too long to not wonder why San Diego has us practicing this stuff. My guess is, it has something to do with our deployment but only time will tell."

"I think that's what Mark thinks as well."

"Well, once again, congratulations Ash, I'm off for a couple of days. I have a sweetheart waiting for me and I am looking forward to an ice-cold beer."

"See you later, Chief."

The next morning, Ashley gathered the few things she needed to take home with her and headed out to her apartment. She grabbed an Uber car and was there in less than 10 minutes. On arrival she saw something that caught her eye and she told the Uber driver to pull over.

There parked on the street down the block from her apartment, was a blue car. She was sure it was the same one she had seen the night she was attacked.

There was no one in it, which made her even more suspicious. She did not want to over-react, but she also did not want to deal with another confrontation. She pulled her phone out of her purse and dialed a number she had put in a couple of weeks before.

"Hello, this is Sergeant Holland, Robbery detail Honolulu Police Department."

"Hi Sergeant, its Captain Ashley Jamison."

"Hey Ash, it is great to hear from you. I am sorry about all the press, but it could not be helped. I can say this: you have a lot of friends in Honolulu."

"Thanks, Sergeant. I do not mean to be a pest and I do not want to seem to be overreacting, but I just got back from being at sea for a week and have just pulled up in front of my apartment. Everything from the street level looks fine but there is a blue car parked down the street that is identical to the one I saw that wanted to haul those thugs away."

"That is interesting, Ash. We have been looking for that car for two weeks with no luck. I will be there within 10 minutes with another car. We will be in unmarked cars and will pull up in front. My thought is we will go up and see if the manager is in and if so, have him let us into you unit to look around. Do not leave where you are at. This may be the lead we have been waiting for."

The uber driver looked at Ash and said, "Excuse me, ma'am but are you the Navy SEAL that kicked the crap out of those bad guys a couple of weeks ago?"

"Yes I am. I am afraid I would like you to stay here with your meter running. I am trying to avoid round two and I believe I will do so if we just sit her for another 15 minutes"

"No problem ma'am I'm glad to help."

In less than 10 minutes two unmarked cars were in front of the building. Three of the officers walked up to the manager's office and the other walked down to look at the blue car. Ashley watched Sergeant Holland knock on the door but with no luck. She noticed one of the officers was looking through a crack in the curtains into Mr. Piedmont's apartment. The officer said something to Sergeant Holland and suddenly he kicked the door of the manager's office in. The officers went immediately inside and found Mr. Piedmont tied up to a chair.

He told them that a single thug had come asking about Ashley. That he did not tell him anything but when he tried to close the door the guy hit him a couple of times and then tied him up to the chair. He told the officers that the thug wanted to know when Ashley would be home. He did not know for sure, but he did know that she would be coming home today and that she was in number 11.

Sergeant Holland thanked Mr. Piedmont and asked him for the key to Ashley's apartment. His plan was to open the door as if it were her coming home and take down anyone in the apartment waiting for her. Sergeant Holland walked down the outside hallway with the two cops with him until he reached apartment 11.

Sergeant Holland stood to the side of the door but rattled the keys in the lock to let anyone inside know that someone was about to enter. He then pushed the door open and stood to the side as the first shot rang out. There was almost no noise, but it was clear that a bullet had been fired. The guy in the apartment had been waiting with a loaded gun with a silencer on it with the goal to shoot Ashley as she entered her apartment.

It was a big mistake. Sergeant Holland responded immediately with one shot. It hit the thug right in the middle of the stomach. He immediately bent over and fell on the floor.

Sergeant Holland was into the apartment and had the guy cuffed while he was yelling and bleeding all over the place.

"Get the paramedics here and let headquarters know we had a shooting occur. Tell them to keep the airwaves quiet as I want to minimize the press coverage of this."

Ashley remained in the car until she saw Sergeant Holland leave the apartment. She thanked the Uber driver, paid him and then headed up the stairs to her place.

Sergeant Holland saw her and met her as she walked up the stairs. "Hi Ashley, your tip was right. The last of the brave men was waiting for you with a gun in your apartment. He now has a strong stomachache that will take a doctor to fix it up. I am afraid I cannot let you go into your place at this time. It is now a crime scene and our tech staff will need to go over it. Your carpet is also going to need to be cleaned."

"Well so much for my two days of time off. Is Mr. Piedmont alright?"

"Yes, the guy punched him in the face twice and then tied him up to a chair. He is in his apartment. You are free to see him if you like."

"Thanks, Sergeant."

Ashley turned and walked up to Mr. Piedmont's apartment. She knocked then entered. "Hi Mr. Piedmont, I am so sorry that his had to happen to you."

"No problem, Ash, I assume this was a buddy of the guys you beat up a couple of weeks ago?"

"Yes, it looks like he was the last of them. The police have been looking for him and his car for the past two weeks. I noticed the car when I came home and rather than go up to my place, I called Sergeant Holland."

"Looks like that was the smart thing to do Ash. I heard what I thought were two gun shots?"

"Your ears do not deceive you. There were two-gun shots. One was meant for me and the other is now resting in the bad guy's stomach."

"Based on what Sergeant Holland tells me, I can't go back into my apartment so I'm going to return to the base for the two days I wanted off. I will be back next weekend and hope to see you then."

"Ash, while you are gone, I will make sure the apartment is cleaned and ready for you next weekend."

"Thanks Mr. Piedmont."

Ashley called Uber and began to exit down the stairs. Sergeant Holland saw her and said, "Thanks again for the tip Ash, I think this ends this gang's history in Honolulu. I am sorry about your apartment, but things should be all back to normal when you're home next week."

Ash waived to him and said goodbye. The uber car arrived as she got to the bottom of the stairs.

"To the Pearl Harbor Naval Base, please."

Ashley returned to the Louisville and the first person she ran into was her boss Mark Price. "Hey Ash, didn't I see you leave here a couple of hours ago? I thought you were taking a couple of days off."

"Hi Mark, I was going to take a couple of days off, but my plans changed rather abruptly."

"What happened, Ash?"

"Well, you remember the problem that I ran into with the bad guys at the shopping center a couple of weeks ago."

"Sure, how could I forget?"

"Well what you may not know there was a blue car waiting at the scene to help the bad guys escape. Once it was clear they were not going any place except to the hospital and the police station the blue car took off. The police have been looking for it ever since. When I got home today, I noticed the blue car parked on the street not far from my apartment.

I thought it was strange so rather than go up to my place I called Sergeant Holland who was the guy in charge of my case and head of the robbery detail at the Honolulu Police Department."

"Sergeant Holland told me to stay put and within 10 minutes he was on scene and headed to my apartment. He stopped at the manager's office only to find my manager, Mr. Piedmont, tied up and bleeding from two blows delivered to his face by the blue car driver. Sergeant Holland and a couple of his buddies then approached my apartment. They opened the door and a shot was fired from inside directly at the door opening. Once the shot was fired Sergeant Holland fired back and put a bullet through the blue car driver who was waiting for me to enter."

"My God, Ash, you could have been killed."

"Yep, looks like the bad guys wanted to get even but they didn't. I can't go back to my apartment for a couple of days so here I am back again."

"Well, welcome home." I will say this about you, Ash you really do live an interesting life. I am glad to have you back and in one piece. Today makes your run in with the three Tiger Sharks look like child play.

CHAPTER 6
FLIGHT OPERATIONS

The Uber car let them out at the Pearl Harbor Naval Base Nimitz Gate. This is the gate that the military personnel use to leave from and return to their ships. He paid the driver gave Ash a hug and walked to the entry gate and showed the duty officer his identification. He was dressed in the same civilian clothes he picked up off the floor just one hour ago in Ashley's apartment.

His mind was not on his ship or his return to base. It was on the past 24 hours which may have been the best 24 hours of his life. He had never felt the way he did now or at any time in his life. He could see every inch of her body, every twist and turn and every muscle. She was clearly the most incredible woman he had ever met, been with and made love to. All he could think about as he walked toward the peer that the USS Yorktown CF-10 was tied up at was where would their relationship go from here?

It had been three, almost four years since he graduated from the United States Naval Academy. After graduation he went to Florida to the Naval Fight School. He graduated number one in his class and was now flying powerful jets off Naval Aircraft Carriers. He was a full Lieutenant in the United States Navy and assigned to the Yorktown.

As he walked down the pier, he could see the Yorktown well ahead. She was an old but huge Aircraft Carrier. She was one of 24 Essex Class aircraft carriers built during World War II for the US Navy. She was named after the Battle of Yorktown which occurred in the American Revolutionary War and was the fourth Naval Ship to bear the Yorktown name. She had a long and proud history and participated in several campaigns in the Pacific Theater earning 11 battle stars and the Presidential Unit Citation.

The Yorktown had been through several changes since her early commission. She had been modernized and served with distinction during the Korean War and later modernized again and served in the Pacific in the Vietnam War.

He knew she was on her last legs and that her decommission was coming up. He just hoped it would not be right away. He wanted to stay in Hawaii now, more than ever, and the last thing he wanted was news of a transfer back to the US Mainland.

As he neared the Yorktown, he could see the aircraft arranged on the flight deck. The placement of the aircraft on deck was no random act. It was all planned in detail by the aircraft handling officer. The aircraft handling officer was also known as the aircraft handler (ACHO) and he or she was responsible for the arrangement of aircraft on both the flight and hanger decks. The handler was charged with avoiding a locked deck. This occurs when too many aircraft are on deck and arranged in such a way that no aircraft can land prior to a rearrangement. The handler works in flight deck control, where scale model aircraft on a flight deck representation are used to represent the actual aircraft status on the flight deck.

There were a few helicopters on the deck but most planes that were topside were McDonnell Douglas FA -18 Hornets. Ryan had his eye on the Hornet since the first day of flight school. He was fascinated with the plane and with her overall power and capabilities but, like the Yorktown, she was slowly becoming a relic of the past. It was clear that the Navy was going to replace the Hornet with a new aircraft called the Super Hornet. Ryan loved the F-18 Hornet, but he had now flown the Super Hornet on a few occasions, and he was super impressed with the new aircraft. He was addicted to speed and power and the new jet promised to have plenty of both.

Ryan walked up the boarding gang plank and was met by the officer of the deck. "Good morning, Lieutenant Joshua. Welcome back, Sir."

"Thanks Ed," he said to the Petty Officer who was on duty.

"How was your time off?"

"It was great, and thanks for asking."

Ryan headed down below the flight deck to his stateroom He had made three cruises on two carriers since he had received his flight wings and thus his stateroom was now almost bearable.

The first stateroom he had on his first cruise was an eight-man stateroom. He shared it with seven others. They were all junior officers of similar rank. Some were pilots, some were not.

Officer sleeping quarters on an aircraft carrier vary. But all officers sleeping quarters are separate from all enlisted sleeping quarters. Officer sleeping quarters are in what is commonly called "officer country". The size and quality of officer berthing varies but is related to rank. Many are located below the flight deck, but others are much lower below the hanger deck.

His stateroom was not elaborate by any means. There were two bunk beds, a small fold down desk, a small safe and a wash basin. There was little storage but there was room to handle enough clothes to cover both military and civilian needs.

Ryan had been told that the Yorktown was scheduled to deploy to the Far East in November or December. The final date had not yet been set but that meant he had just a couple of months. The cruise was scheduled to last about six months, but no one knew what would happen to the ship after it was over. It was clear that it was on its last legs and was headed to decommissioning and perhaps a future role as a waterfront museum.

Ryan got to his room and threw his small overnight bag onto his bunk. His roommate was not there. Ryan bunked with Lieutenant Scotty Freemont. Scotty was from Oklahoma and was as close to a cowboy as one could be. He was a great pilot but walked like he had been raised on a horse and only got off occasionally to go to the bathroom. Ryan liked him and enjoyed his company.

Both Ryan and Scotty regularly flew the McDonnell Douglas F-18 Hornets. The F-18 is a twin engine supersonic, all weather, carrier-capable, multirole combat jet. It was designed to be both a fighter and an attack aircraft. The Hornet is also used by the air forces of several other nations. Since 1986 the Navy's flight Demonstration squadron, the Blue Angeles, had flown the Hornet. In fact, it was the Blue Angeles connection that peeked Ryan's interest in the F-18 Hornet the day he entered flight school.

Although he had never told anyone, it was his desire to someday be a member of the Blue Angeles demonstration team.

The F-18 has a top speed of Mach 1.8 or just under 1,200 miles per hour. It can carry a wide variety of bombs and missiles, including air to air and air to ground. They are supplemented by the 20-mm M61 Vulcan cannon.

The aircraft has excellent aerodynamic characteristics, primarily attributed to its leading-edge extensions. The fighter's primary missions are fighter escort, fleet air defense, suppression of enemy air defenses, air interdiction and close air support and aerial reconnaissance. Its versatility and reliability have proven to be an unbelievably valuable carrier asset and the pilots who flew the planes had the respect of the crews that serviced them.

Ryan learned long ago that the pilot was simply one clog in a wheel. The wheel had a lot of equal and important parts and it took them all working together to make for a successful mission. As such he valued his crew and was always most respectful of them.

He never forgot that when he graduated from flight school at the top of his class, he thought he was a big deal and a hot shot. That changed almost immediately when he received his first assignment and met his first Navy Chief. He will never forget what the guy said to him, Son, you might think you are something else because of those wings on your chest but you will soon learn that you are simply a grain of sand on the beach of life. If you remember that, and you learn to respect those below you as well as those above you, you will have success in this man's Navy. If you do not learn that you are going to go down in a heap of flames.

Ryan never forgot those words and let them guide him in his dealings with all Navy personnel, no matter what rank they were. In that regard, very few people know or understand what it takes in the way of a support team to put a F-18 through a successful mission. Ryan learned quickly that there were several critical clogs in the wheel and that they all need to function smoothly to make a successful flight mission happen.

First off, on an aircraft carrier flight deck, specialized crews are in a variety of different roles to manage the total air operation.

The different flight deck crews wear colored jerseys to visually distinguish their functions.

Yellow is reserved for aircraft handling officers, catapult and arresting gear officers and plane directors.

The color **Green** is reserved for catapult and arresting gear crews, visual landing aid electricians, air wing maintenance personnel, air wing quality control personnel, cargo handling personnel, ground support equipment trouble shooters, hook runner, photographer's mates and helicopter landing signal enlisted personnel.

White is reserved for quality assurance and squadron plane inspectors, landing signal officers and liquid oxygen crews as well as safety observers and medical personnel.

Red is reserved for ordnance handlers, crash and salvage crews, explosive ordnance disposal and firefighter and damage control party personnel.

Blue is reserved for plane handlers, chocks and chains entry level flight deck crews, aircraft elevator operators, tractor drivers and messengers.

Purple is reserved for aviation fuel handlers and brown is for air wing plane captains, squadron personnel and air wing line leading petty officers.

The only people wearing **white/black** are the final check inspectors.

So, it is a real rainbow of colors that depict the roles and responsibilities of those who make it possible for the F-18 to fly. When they are all called together, they are often referred to as the rainbow side boys.

There is one more color combination associated with flight deck. **Navy blue pants** are worn by junior sailors and petty officers. **Khaki pants** are worn by Chief Petty, Warrant and Commissioned Officers.

When a distinguished visitor arrives on the ship by air, a call to muster the rainbow side boys is made. Typically, two of each colored jersey stand opposite each other in front of the entrance to the ship to render honors to the distinguished visitors.

Ryan was about finished putting his few things away from his overnight bag when his roommate, Scotty, arrived. "Hey Ryan, how was your time with the "filly."

"Scotty, need I remind you that Ashley Jamison is not a horse and if she ever heard you say that, my guess is you would be unable to ride in a saddle for a year."

Scotty just laughed and said, "Sorry I was just letting my "Oklahoma" come to the surface."

"To answer your question, we had a great time. We spent some time on the beach, went to a great restaurant on the water which I would highly recommend by the name of RumFire Waikiki. We had a great dinner and then spent the rest of the evening together. What have you been up to?"

"Nothing like you, I am afraid. I played slow pitch softball last night with my team. We got beat seven to nothing. I then had an exciting time drinking beer with the losers, returned here and have not done much sense. Not exactly the bachelor in paradise story I would like to tell. Ryan do you know what time we get underway tomorrow morning?"

"Yep, 0800. We should be out in the open sea by noon and our first exercises are scheduled for the afternoon."

"Do you know what they are having us do? I think we are scheduled for some formation flying and some takeoff and landing exercises. Based on what my Chief told me, we should be done by dinner."

"How long are we out for?"

"Two weeks. I think the first week is devoted to daytime operations and the second to nighttime operations. I think we have a couple of destroyers accompanying us in plane guard operations."

"Are you talking about cyclic operations?"

"Yep, that is what I think we have scheduled."

"If I remember correctly, cyclic operations refers to the launch and recovery cycle for aircraft in groups or cycles. Launching and recovering aircraft aboard aircraft carriers is best accomplished non-concurrently, and cyclic operations are the norm. My guess is we will follow the normal pattern which means the cycle will be normally about one and a half hours long."

"We are carrying many aircraft so I doubt that we will have shorter cycles which only seem to occur when we have less aircraft. My guess is we will be launching two birds at a time."

"What's your plan for today?

"Well, I'm about ready for lunch and then I plan to spend some time this afternoon reading about advanced operations with the F-18. I understand it is going to be replaced soon with a super version and I want to understand all I can in advance of having to fly it."

"Sounds good to me. Let us head for lunch."

CHAPTER 7
AN UNEXPECTED MOVE

Ashley was back on the submarine and in her stateroom. She was lying on her bunk and trying to figure out what she was going to do for the next two days. She had planned to be in and out of her apartment, laying on the beach and completing the shopping that she started a week ago. Instead she was lying on her bottom bunk looking at the springs on the bottom of the mattress above her.

Her phone rang and she picked it up. "Hi, this is Ash, how can I help you?"

"Hey Ashley, this is Sergeant Sam Holland with the Honolulu Police Department."

"Hey Sam, nice to hear from you. Hope you are doing well after yesterday's meeting with the bad guy."

"I'm doing well, thanks Ash, I am calling to give you an update on the thugs that have suddenly become part of our lives."

"Let me guess who you're talking about? Oh yes, you must mean the four stooges, right? What's up?"

"Well, thanks to you, the entire ring of crooks is behind bars and probably will be for the next 20 or 30 years. We are charging the three that you dealt with directly with robbery, attempted kidnapping and attempted murder. The robbery charge covers all four of the incidents we know they were involved in. The kidnapping charge is the result of their trying to take an 80-year-old woman hostage in order to get to her daughter's jewelry and the attempted murder charges are related to the knife attack on you. We have enough evidence to call this a slam dunk, and in your case, it so happens that a woman videotaped the entire thing, which means they have no excuse."

"That sounds great, Sam, what about the guy yesterday?"

"Well, Mr. Blue Car, as we now know him, was after you in revenge for what you did to his buddies. He made a major mistake by thinking that you were at the door of the apartment instead of me."

"He has been charged with attempted murder of a police officer in the line of duty. He is going to be locked up for an awfully long time and I am happy to say that he will have a stomachache that should last him a lifetime."

"I'm sorry about your apartment: I know that we had to rope it off as a crime scene, so you won't have access for a few days."

"I do have one thing I want you to know. We told the press that we were investigating a home robbery and caught the guy in the act. We did not mention your name or that it was your apartment. My feeling is that it will make the papers tomorrow, but the article will leave you completely out of the picture. I don't think the press will put the two incidents together and I'm not sure that they really know what apartment yours is."

"Thanks, Sam, I appreciate that and I'm sure my boss will as well. Do you know how Mr. Piedmont is doing? I was worried about him. I'm sure that he never guessed that by renting to me it would end up costing him a fist in the jaw."

"I talked to him his morning, Ash, and he is doing fine. He is really happy that we shot the guy, and is pleased with the charge that is being brought against him. I know that he knows this was a random event and that he is sorry you had to go through the entire thing."

"Thanks, Sam, that is good to know. If you need me, you can reach me on this number. We are in port this week and I'm not going anywhere."

"Thanks Ash, I will be back in touch with you if anything changes."

Ashley hung up the phone and went back to staring at the springs on the bunk above her. Almost immediately her phone rang again.

"Hi, this is Ash, what can I do for you?"

"Hi Ashley, its Roger Piedmont."

"Hi, Mr. Piedmont, I was just talking to Sergeant Holland about you. Are you OK?"

"Yes, I am doing very well and thank you for asking.

I have a slight bit of swelling on my lip but other than that I am simply fine and cannot wait to file my personal charges against that guy. Ash, I'm calling to see if you might be interested in a change?"

"After yesterday's shooting one of our residents came to me and told me that they were giving notice. They have been looking for a larger place and I think the shooting just set them off and made them feel this was not the place for them. They have unit number 14 which is on the corner. It is a one bedroom with a much larger deck than you have, and it looks not only at the yacht harbor but also down Waikiki Beach. I would like to know if you would like the unit and I am going to offer it to you at the same price you currently are paying, with the same options included in your lease. You have been through so much and I think you deserve a break."

"Oh wow, Mr. Piedmont, that would be super and, of course, I accept. What do I have to do to make it happen?"

"Nothing, I will ask Sarah, our lead cleaner, to move you into your new unit over the course of the next couple of weeks. I'm sorry that it will take a bit of time before you can move into the new unit, but I will have them work as fast as they can."

"No problem, we are in port this week and then gone next week. I will be back in two weeks."

"That should work perfect Ash. When you return, just stop by and pick up the key and you should be able to walk into a brand-new place."

"Wow, that sounds great Mr. Piedmont. Do I need to sign or do anything at this point?"

"No, I just need your approval to make the switch and for you to allow Sarah to move your personal stuff."

"No problem, Mr. Piedmont, I don't have much and what I have isn't going to shock anyone."

"Thanks Ash, that is all the approval I need, I look forward to seeing you in a couple of weeks. Take care of yourself. Cheers."

SAN DIEGO SEAL TEAM HEADUARTERS

It was after work at the San Diego Headquarters of the United States Navy SEAL team. The enlisted bar was packed but the section that was reserved for senior enlisted men still had a few tables empty. At a corner table with cold beers in front of them sat Marine Gunny Sergeant Michael James and Master Sergeant Karl Reichardt. Both wore the Navy Seal Triton, and both looked like you should never mess with them.

"Hey Reichardt, I've got something to show you."

"OK, James, please no more nude photos of Ms. Columbia."

"No, Sarge, this is something that I know is going to interest you."

James pulled out a newspaper article and handed it to Reichardt. "Read this."

Reichardt looked at the headline first.

AND TODAYS LESSON LADIES AND GENTELMAN
IS
NEVER MESS WITH A FEMALE SEAL

Sergeant Reichardt then focused on the photo below the headline. He saw a picture of three guys piled on top of each other in a parking lot. Nothing registered yet so be began to read the article.

THE HAEJU VIRUS

At 5:45 PM on Friday a woman departed the Neiman Marcus Store at the Ala Moana Center and headed out the building to cross Ala Moana Blvd. Her arms were full of packages and according to eye witnesses she was carrying more than most people do.

Suddenly, a man, now identified as Ramon Ito, age 24, pushed her from behind into two men both with knives drawn. Mr. Ito's partners have now been identified as Ralph Signo, 23 and Scooter Miles, 26. All men are residents of Hawaii and hold the same address in Honolulu.

It appears from the facts released so far, that the police believe that this trio, plus a get-away-driver, has been the group behind four recent attacks on women shoppers. The facts released thus far indicate the exact same strategy was used in each robbery. As our readers can see from the picture in our article, these men simply picked the wrong woman to try to rob.

As it turns out, the women attacked was Ashley Morgan Jamison. Ms. Jamison is a Marine Corp Captain and she is the Assistant Officer in charge of Navy Seal Delivery Vehicle Team 1, based in Pearl Harbor.

This name may be familiar to our readers as Ms. Jamison was the first woman, and we might add, still the only woman to qualify as a Navy Seal. As such she has earned the right to wear the famed Seal Triton.

Captain Jamison was not available to be interviewed for this article but according to eye witnesses she simply destroyed each of her attackers, one by one until they were piled in a heap, in the middle of the small parking lot. We might add that each of them, needed to be taken to the emergency room with at least one of their body parts broken. According to Sergeant Sam Holland, head of the Honolulu Police Burglary Detail, the three thugs were no match for the skills displayed by Captain Jamison. Sergeant Holland said, "I have never seen anyone, man or woman, display such a hand to hand one on three, skill base. Captain Jamison not only served as a living example of what our Navy Seals are trained to do, but in my estimation the three thugs now in custody should thank God they got out of that situation alive.

Sergeant Holland also indicated that they now have the name of the person driving the get-away-car and are looking for that person as this article goes to press.

"Well, I'll be damned. Ash has done it again. That women has done more for the United States Navy Seal Organization than all their advertising combined. Wow, am I proud of her."

"Well, Karl, looks like she learned a lot from you and knows how to put it to good use."

"Thanks Mike, but we both know that Ash is something special and I know that while she learned from us, she has a natural ability that few will ever have."

"I think you should send this article to Roscoe Cook and Juan Sanchez at the YARD. My guess is they will not be surprised either."

"Good idea Karl, I will send an email off to them with the attachment in the morning. I wonder how SEAL command reacted to this article?"

"Good question, Mike."

"If I were them, I would make sure that her record reflected this event, in addition to all the other things she has accomplished in her young career. It is just another example of how this woman is beyond special."

"I only hope that the "good old boys:, who, Roscoe had to fight with just to get them to consider her as a SEAL candidate, now know that she is one of the best advertisements they have ever had."

"Boy, do I agree with you, Karl."

The next day, Mike James sent an email to lieutenant Commander Roscoe Cook and Master Gunnery Sergeant Juan Sanchez at the United States Naval Academy.

"Dear Sirs, it is with great pride that I pass this article on to you. May I wish you continued success in your decisions regarding who best in the future should wear the United States Navy Seal Triton. Sincerely, Master Gunny Sergeant Mike James."

"Good Morning, Sonny."

"Good Morning, Sir. I have an email for you that just came in. It is from Sergeant Mike James at Headquarters."

"Thanks, that is a bit unusual. I have not talked to Mike since Juan and I went out to San Diego for Ashley's graduation. Did you read it?"

"Yes Sir, and I think you're going to want to read it as well. I should also tell you that Sergeant James addressed it to Sergeant Sanchez as well, so he may have already seen it this morning."

Roscoe took the hard copy of the email that Sonny handed him and read it slowly. "Well I'll be damned, she did it again. Way to go Ash! This article has to have those old coots at Headquarters smiling with their heads held high."

"Yes Sir, I'm sure they have forgotten that they didn't make your life very easy when you were trying to convince them that she was worth the wait As I recall, she made them regret their hesitation and went on to make them and the United States Navy proud in the Olympic Games."

"You're so right Sonny. I am so happy when a plan comes together."

It was not long before the phone rang. It was Juan Sanchez and he was beaming just like Roscoe Cook.

CHAPTER 8
SHARK ATTACK IMPACT

Ashley had a light lunch in the wardroom of the USS Louisville. The place was empty. Most of the officers had taken the two days off to visit friends and families or to do what Ash had planned which was to catch up on beach time and errands.

The discussion with Mr. Piedmont had left her in a good mood. She could just vision sitting on her new apartment deck with Ryan. She had a glass of Oregon Pinot Gris in her hand and they were watching a beautiful Hawaiian sunset.

She finished her lunch and returned to reality. Ryan was gone for two weeks and she would be gone for all next week. Mark had told her that there would be a briefing for the SEAL team at 0800 when everyone returned the day after tomorrow and he indicated that the week at sea would be a big challenge. She did not know what that meant but decided to forget about it for now. She decided that she would take a walk over to the base hospital and check on Jonnie Potts.

She was worried about his leg and the potential for infection after the shark attack.

She arrived at the base hospital and went to the front desk. She was in her marine uniform on which the SEAL Triton was proudly displayed. The nurse at the front desk looked up and saw her and the Triton on her uniform.

"Good Afternoon, Captain. I am the lead nurse on this shift. My name is Sally Everlast. Let me guess who you are here to see? Would it possibly be a Navy SEAL by the name of Jonnie Potts?"

"Yes Ma'am. I am Captain Ashley Jamison and I was his commanding officer on the mission when the shark attacked."

"Oh yes Captain, I know of you and your accomplishments. Your reputation precedes you and I can tell you that you have set a standard that many women I know aspire to. It is a pleasure to finally have the opportunity to meet you."

"Thank you Sally. Where can I find Jonnie?"

Jonnie is in room 197 which is just down this hall and to the right. He has been resting but is now awake. His wife was here earlier but she left about ½ an hour ago."

"Thanks Sally."

Ashley walked down the hall, turned right and entered room 197. Jonnie was in bed with his leg elevated.

He was wide awake and when she entered a big smile came across his face.

"Hey Boss, it is great to see you. Welcome to my new home."

"Hey Jonnie, how are you doing?"

"Well, I have some good news and some bad news for you, so I'm really glad, that you came to see me today."

"What's up Jonnie? I hate bad news but would rather hear it and get it out of the way before I hear good news, so give me what you've got."

"OK, here goes. You probably do not know this, but I am up for reenlistment in two months and given this problem, that has been on my mind. The doctor here tells me that, thanks to you, I will not lose my leg and in fact, he told me that without your quick thinking I probably would not be here today talking to you. He also told me that he has the infection under control and believes that I should be ready to leave here and begin physical therapy in about two weeks."

"However, he also told me that I will never walk normally again. I will have a defined limp that all the physical therapy in the world will not be able to fix."

"As such, I have made the decision to put my Navy SEAL career and the United States Navy behind me and not re-enlist."

"Wow, Jonnie. That is bad news not just for me but for all our team. I understand and know that if you returned with the leg issue that it would at some point get in the way of your SEAL activities."

"What are you going to do?

"Well, this is the good news. As you know I am from the south. It is a small town in Alabama by the name of Clanton. It is near the center of Alabama and it has a population of a little over 8000. My folks own and run a restaurant there called "Greens Small Town Diner". I grew up in this town and so did my wife Jessica. I know, or at least my family knows, every person in this town. When I earned the SEAL Triton, it was a huge deal in my town and in fact they had a parade for me."

"Because of our SEAL medical training we are all Paramedics. When I decided to not reenlist, I contacted our local medical services company to see if there might be an opening. They offered me a job on the spot which I have accepted. I think I want to go to medical school, and this should help me with a good foundation."

"Then this morning, Jessica came to see me with more good news. It so happens she is now just about 1 and ½ months pregnant with our first child, so when we get home and settled, we will become new parents. She hasn't even told her folks or mine yet so there are going to be a few excited people in Clanton before this week is over."

"Jonnie, that is great news and I am happy for you. I will let Mark know this afternoon. I know he will understand as well."

"Ash, I do have to tell you, I can't get the size of those sharks out of my mind. I don't know if it is because one took a bite out of me, but I don't think I'm going back into the Ocean for some time."

"Jonnie, I want you to know, they were big and there were three of them. I believe that if you had not cracked that one on the nose with your rifle butt that we would not have been able to save you. So, you should know that it was your actions that helped save your life not just ours."

"Thanks, Boss that is good to know. I may never have the opportunity to say this to you alone again, but I want you to know that I not only speak for myself but also for most of the men I know. You are one hell of an Officer, Leader and Role Model. We all look up to you and admire you for who you are, what you represent and how you handle yourself. It has been my total pleasure to serve under you."

"Thanks, Jonnie. I'm leaving now, but I will be back in a few days to check on you."

Ashley left the base hospital and walked back to the ship. On the way she picked up the afternoon edition of the Honolulu Advertiser.

The front page carried the headline.

POLICE SHOOTING
AT HONOLULU APARTMENT COMPLEX

Ashley waited until she returned to her stateroom to open the paper and read the article. She sat at her desk and read.

This afternoon at an apartment complex next to Ala Wai Boat Harbor the Honolulu Police shot and injured a man who they say was in the process of burglarizing an apartment. The burglar, according to police, was wanted for questioning in the recent attacks on women. The police believe that this man was the same one that drove the get-away-car in several recent attacks on women leaving shopping centers.

Police, did not identify the man but did indicate that they located his residence and that it was the same residence used by the three men that were put in the hospital last

week by Captain Ashley Jamison, a United States Navy SEAL.

Police indicated that a search of the residence yielded several of the items that had been stolen in the recent burglary attacks.

Police also reported that the Ala Wai Burglar fired a weapon at police officers before being shot by police. The man will be charged with attempted murder of a police officer besides the charges associated with burglary.

No additional details were provided but police did say they now believe that they have all members of the burglary gang in custody either behind bars or in the hospital.

So, Sergeant Holland was right. Ashley was not mentioned other than in passing in the article and no one had put two and two together to figure out that the apartment in question was hers. For that she was incredibly grateful. Now, this incident could be put behind her and she could get on with her life.

Ashley buzzed Marks stateroom to see if he might be in. He was and answered the buzz by saying, "Hi, this is Mark, what can I do for you?"

"Hey Mark, its Ash."

"Hi Ash, what's up?

"Well I just left the base hospital where I had the opportunity to talk with Jonnie. The good news is his leg is going to remain a part of his body and the doctors have the possibility of infection under good control. The bad news is he will, in all probability never be able to walk normally again. He will have a limp forever."

"He told me that the Doctors have said that even with all of the physical therapy in the world that they will be unable to overcome the damage that has been done to the leg."

"He also told me that he was due to reenlist in two months and because of the injury he has decided to call it quits, not reenlist and head back to his hometown."

"He apparently comes from a small town in Alabama and his wife is from there as well. There is some good news to this story, he told me that he has contacted some folks in his town, and he has been offered and accepted a position as an EMT. He also told me he wants to use it as a jumping off point to go to medical school."

"The other piece of good news is that his wife told him this morning that she is pregnant and in about 7 or 8 months he will be a new Daddy."

"Well, I'm not surprised by this news and frankly I am a little relieved. I was worried about the consequences associated with his injury and what it might mean to his career as a Navy SEAL. This sounds to me like the perfect ending to an awfully bad story."

"Couldn't have said it any better myself, Boss."

"By the way, Ash, did you see this morning's paper?"

"Yep and I'm only glad the press didn't put the apartment together with me. Sergeant Holland told me they were going to try to keep me out of it and it looks like they did. Now perhaps I can move forward and not have to deal with this any longer. At least I hope so."

"So, do I, Ash."

"Are you still planning to hold a team meeting at 0800 the day after tomorrow?"

"Yes, that is the plan. I have some additional information that I received from San Diego and an outline of the training they want us to go through next week. I can tell you that I'm not looking forward to it, it looks like a lot and it won't be easy"

"Well, easy isn't what we signed up for when we put this Triton on, so I'm not surprised at all. To prepare for it, I think I will spend tomorrow lying on the beach, at Waikiki"

That made Mark laugh.

"Oh, by the way, Boss, this entire mess has not been without a small benefit to me."

"What does that mean, Ash?"

"Well, I got a call from my landlord, Mr. Piedmont, this morning. It so happens that one of his renters decided to give notice after the shooting and they will be vacating their one-bedroom apartment in the next week. Mr. Piedmont offered it to me at the same price I am currently paying for the studio. I'm told it has a large deck that looks out at the yacht harbor and that the view from the bedroom looks right down Waikiki beach."

"That sounds great, Ash. When will you be able to move in?"

"Mr. Piedmont said he should have it ready for me the weekend we get back from our sea training. He is going to move my stuff over for me while we are gone."

"Sounds like something good has come out of this after all. Talk to you soon."

CHAPTER 9
AIRCRAFT OPERATIONS

The USS Yorktown CV-10 was at sea for aircraft operations. Aircraft Carriers are often referred to as a city at sea. This term describes the Yorktown. Although she was old and had been through several updates, she was still capable of launching a significant strike force. She truly was a city of 5000 people working, relaxing, eating and sleeping on board.

But a United States Naval floating city is not like most cities you would think of. First, most residents have little opportunity to see the outside world. The flight deck, hangar and fantail all have wonderful views of the sea and sky, but they are so hectic and dangerous that only a handful of people are allowed access during normal operations.

The top levels of the island are safe enough, but sensitive operations and limited space means you cannot have a lot of people coming and going. A sailor who works below deck might go for weeks without ever seeing daylight.

Throughout the ship, conditions are much more cramped than in a normal city. To get from place to place, personnel must scale nearly vertical steps and squeeze past each other in narrow corridors. The berthing compartments are extremely tight. Enlisted personnel share a compartment with about 60 other people, all sleeping in single bunks, which are stacked together in groups of three.

Each person gets a small stowage bin and an upright locker for their belongings and everybody in the compartment shares a bathroom and a small common area with a television hooked up to one of the carrier's satellite dishes. Officers enjoy more space and finer furnishings, but their space is limited as well. Everybody on board must get use to tight quarters.

In that regard Ryan was incredibly lucky, but you often make your own luck which he had done by flying off two different carriers on his deployments since graduating from flight school.

The jobs on the carrier are highly varied just like in a normal city. Approximately 2500 men and women form the air wing, the people who fly and maintain the aircraft. The other 2500 make up the ship's company, which keeps all parts of the carrier running smoothly. This includes everything from washing dishes and preparing meals to handling weaponry and maintaining the engines or nuclear reactors.

The Yorktown has everything its residents need to live, even though it was not as comfortable as they would like. There are multiple galleys and mess halls, which collectively serve as many as 18,000 meals in a day. The ship also has a sizeable laundry facility, dentist and doctor's offices, various stores and access to phones where personnel can talk to their families.

Life onboard is undeniably difficult and exhausting but from Ryan's perspective it was also exhilarating. For him, and for many of the men and women on the flight deck, flying and bringing in planes on a tiny patch of runway, was like no other place on earth.

They had finished lunch and Ryan and Scotty headed back to their stateroom. They had been informed that the carrier would be underway at 0800 in the morning. All pilots and WSO's (Weapons Systems Officers) were to report to the main briefing room at 0900.

Who are you flying with tomorrow?" Scotty asked Ryan.

"Tomorrow I have a big guy with me, Commander Reggie Sanders. He is scheduled to be the mission commander."

"Have you flown with him before?"

"Yes, on a number of occasions. He is a great guy, knowledgeable, a good pilot and navigator and an expert when it comes to the weapon systems on the Hornet and Super Hornet."

"My guess is since I will have him that I will also be flying the new Super Hornet."

"Lucky you."

"I will have Jim Owens with me. He has been in my back seat on a number of occasions and I feel extremely comfortable with him, so it should be a good day."

"Do you have any idea what they have planned for us?"

"No, but my guess is that we will be launching two birds at a time and we will have formation drills with target practice using real bombs. I think we will be headed for that isolated island that the Navy uses for live ammunition training. If I am right it will mean about a 6-and-a-half-hour day. It that's the case and we are using the real thing, I'm sure it will mean that we will be judged on our performance."

The WSO's are Naval Flight Officers who are responsible for manning the weapons systems of the F-18 Hornet and the F-18 Super Hornet Strike Fighters. They are all knowledgeable of the Weapons Systems on Board and how and when to use them. In some cases, as in the case that Ryan was describing, the WSO is responsible for all phases of the assigned mission especially when multiple aircraft are involved. Ryan was sure that Reggie would be the Officer in charge tomorrow and probably for several the missions that were scheduled over the next week.

In a stateroom a fair distance from Ryan's room, Commander Reggie Sanders was sitting at his desk reading a novel by Stuart Woods. "Hey Reggie, what are you reading?" His roommate Carl Goodwin said as he entered the room. Goodwin was also a full commander and would serve as a mission commander on this trip as well.

"I'm reading book 11 in a series of some 55 books."

"You have got to be kidding me; this guy has written more than 50 books?"

"Yes, and I can't stop reading them. He has this main character Stone Barrington, who is an Ex NYPD detective and now a lawyer with a large New York firm."

"His wife was killed and left him with something more than a half billion dollars. He is a pilot and loves women who I might add also, love him. He loves good food and wine and lives in a great house in New York with a cook, driver and secretary."

"The guy lives the life that all of us just dream about. I just cannot get enough of it. He has his best friend Dino, who is the NYPD head of detectives. As you can imagine they get into everything."

"Sounds like something I might like to read as well. I assume that I can get them on Amazon on my kindle."

"Sure, no problem. I think each of them will cost you between 3 and 7 bucks."

"Who are you flying with tomorrow?"

"Well, this week I have the daylight group which I assume means you get the night groups. Am I correct?"

"Yep, I understand we get to switch the second week which I will look forward to. Night operations with two birds launching at a time is sometimes a bit harry."

"I know what you mean."

"To answer your original question, I am flying with Ryan Joshua. I requested him specifically. I have flown with him before and think he is one of the absolute best I have come across. I have him in a Super Hornet."

"I know Ryan as well. I agree, I have seen him in several situations, actual war and practice and the guy just does not get rattled ever. He seems to be one of the few that has ice in his veins."

"Yep, my understanding is he came out of the YARD. Placed first in his flight school class in Florida and would like to stay in and make this service a career. If he continues as he is, he could end up being one of the best pilots the Navy has ever produced."

"Wow, Reggie, coming from you that is high praise."

"Yes, I know. This mission is one that will be judged so we will see how he does and what kind of marks we can make together."

"Tell me the name of that author again?"

"His name is Stuart Woods."

"Thanks."

The next morning The USS Yorktown CV-10 was underway at exactly 0800. She was followed out of Pearl Harbor by two destroyers.

The USS Wayne E. Meyer was one of the two. The Wayne E. Meyer is a guided missile destroyer DDG 108. The Meyer was commissioned on October 18, 2008. Her original homeport was San Diego but after several trips she was home ported in Pearl Harbor Hawaii. She is an Arleigh Burke Class Destroyer capable of speeds up to 30 knots. She carries a complement of 275 officers and enlisted men and women. The Meyer is well armed with vertical launch systems capable of delivering several different war heads to their targets. She was assigned to the Yorktown for this two-week assignment primarily to handle plane guard detail.

The USS Wayne E. Meyer was accompanied by the USS Chafee DDG-90. The Chafee like the Meyer was also an Arleigh Burke class guided missile destroyer. She was named for Senator John Lester Chafee, a Marine veteran. The Chafee was also home ported in Pearl Harbor. Like the Meyer she had speeds capable of up to 30 knots. She carries a compliment of 350 officers, men and women.

The two destroyers will handle the plane guard duties. Plane guard duty occurs when a warship is tasked to recover the aircrew of planes or helicopters which ditch or crash in the water during aircraft carrier flight operations.

For ships, the plane guard position is typically 2000 yards astern and 2000 yards off the starboard bow of the carrier. When a carrier is launching or receiving aircraft the entire group of ships is moving at a maximum speed of between 25 and 30 knots. So, the operation is not without risk.

One of the destroyers has a boat prepared for launch and swung out over the side, but not placed in the water. If an aircraft ditches or crashes, the ship proceeds to the approximate position of the aircraft and the prepared boat is deployed to rescue the aircrew.

The plane guard role is dangerous for ships, as aircraft carriers must often change speed and direction to preserve optimum take-off and landing conditions for the aircraft.

Lack of awareness or any incorrect maneuvers on the part of either ship can place a plane guard ship under the bow of a carrier travelling at full speed.

At 0900 the pilots and their WSO's met in the main briefing room. They were addressed by Captain John Jacobs. Captain Jacobs was a Senior Naval Aviator and the head of Naval Flight Operations on the Yorktown. "Good morning Ladies and Gentlemen."

"As you are aware, we are scheduled for two weeks of flight training. We will be flying multiple missions with active ammunition. Your goal will be to attack the targets specified and then return to the ship. We anticipate that each mission will last approximately 6 hours. We plan to have you engage in both day and night operations."

"To simplify the matter, you have been placed in one of two groups. Group 1 will begin day operations tomorrow morning at 10 o'clock. The group will be under the command of Commander Reggie Sanders. We anticipate that all of Commander Sanders planes will be back safely on board by 4 PM. At 7 PM we will commence night operations with group 2. Night operations in week one will be under the command of Commander Carl Goodwin. We expect all of Commander Goodwin's planes will be back on board by 4 AM. After one week we plan to switch with Commander Goodwin's group working the daylight shift while Commander Sander's group works at night."

"We have distributed briefing books to all of you. As you will note, your missions will be judged, and you will be rated based on your performance."

"You will be using live ordnance so remember do not return to the ship with any bombs. Leave them on the island before returning."

"Each of you should follow your normal preflight procedures. Are there any questions? OK then, I want to remind you that we will be using Catapult assisted take off but arrested recovery. The CATOBAR system will be used as you all know to assist us with launch and recovery of your aircraft. We plan to use the launch assisted take off and will have you land using the arresting wires."

That evening Ryan and Scotty were in their stateroom after dinner. Ryan was reading a novel and Scotty was reading his briefing book for tomorrow's flight.

The phone in the room rang and Ryan picked it up off the desk in front of him. "Hi, this is Ryan.

"Hey Ryan, its Reggie. Are you looking forward to tomorrow?"

"Yes, this is the kind of training assignment I find the most challenging. Live ammunition and performance evaluations always get me peaked up. What can I do for you, sir?"

'Nothing really, I just wanted to ask you to be ready by 9:30 in the morning. Since we will be launching a lot of aircraft, I want to be in the air before they all start hitting the skies so I can be a good traffic cop and get them all moving in the right direction."

"No problem, sir. I will have completed my inspection and will be ready to go by 9:30."

"Thanks Ryan, have a nice evening."

"You to, sir."

CHAPTER 10
LIFE UNDERWATER

When she returned to her stateroom after breakfast there was a message from her boss Mark Price on her phone. It said "Ash when you pick this up, call me. I want to meet today to talk about our meeting tomorrow morning and to brief you on what I think we have ahead of us."

Ash picked up her phone and dialed her boss.

"Hi, this is Mark, how can I help you?"

"Hey Mark, its Ash. I'm returning your call."

"Thanks Ash, are you free this morning about 10 AM?"

"Sure am."

"Then plan to meet me in the Wardroom. I want to talk about our meeting tomorrow and what we have to look forward to next week while we are out to sea."

"I'll see you at 10. Bye Mark."

Ashley was in the Wardroom at five minutes to 10. Her standard practice had always been to be at least five minutes early to every meeting. At 10 Mark walked into the room. "Hi Ash, thanks for coming."

Mark poured himself a cup of coffee and sat down.

"What's up Mark? You look almost lost in thought."

"I guess I have been Ash. Our SEAL team was created to work with the Advanced SEAL Delivery System."

"Our mini submarine has been in use for a number of years with the goal of providing stealthy submerged transportation for our SEAL teams from the decks of nuclear submarines to targets that require clandestine special operations missions."

"In fact, I think the first design and prototype SDV's were developed in 1982."

"I was advised over three years ago that the ASDS would eventually be taken out of service. This was the primary result of cost overruns and reliability issues. If you will remember SEAL team 2 had a problem with a prototype sub that was destroyed by fire. We have not had to deal with any of the administrative and or cost problems that have plagued the ASDS."

"For a brief period of time I didn't know if the entire program would be cancelled but I was very happy to learn that the Navy awarded a contract to Lockheed Martin to design and develop a new shallow water combat submersible (SWCS)."

"The new SWCS has been in development for some time and I'm told that the Secretary of the Navy awarded the Safety Integration in acquisition category to the SWCS Team for developing systems safety specifications for the new SDV. The group that received the award had done a significant amount of testing of the underwater vehicle over the past two years and the reports that have been sent to me are all good as to its reliability and safety. So that brings me to the point."

"This week the first of the new submersibles arrived here in Pearl Harbor and we have been given the task of testing it underwater beginning with next week's at sea adventure."

"The ASDS was conceived to address the need for stealthy long-range insertion of special operations forces on covert or clandestine missions. It was designed to replace the wet SEAL delivery vehicle which exposed us to long, cold water exposures which hindered both our readiness and our underwater navigational capability."

"They simply didn't and still don't have the fuel or batteries to meet the needs of our missions. And frankly, we can only stay under water in the cold for so long."

"So, all of this background leads us to where we are today. The new Shallow Water Combat Submersible is a manned submersible and a type of swimmer delivery vehicle that is designed and equipped to get us to where we need to go but in a much more comfortable way."

"The new vehicle is 22 feet long and almost 5 feet wide. It can move at about 10 miles per hour or 6 knots. I'm told that it has an endurance of 12 hours and that it can operate at a depth of 190 feet."

"The thing carries a crew of 2 and up to eight passengers. That means that the new SWCS is almost a foot longer than the Mark 8 we are used to. It has a longer range and is heavier than the Mark 8. It has a more advanced computer system and a better navigation system with a variety of features including an electronical periscope and wireless communication between the crew and the passengers. It has a great deal of diversity in that it can be deployed from surface ships or from submarines. The sub option is the preferred option for stealth reasons."

"So why am I telling you all of this. The answer is simple. I'm not sure I trust the new SWCS and I know that using us as guinea pigs to test it out in the open ocean will carry with it dangers that at this point, I can only imagine."

"For purposes of our tests next week, you and I will be the crew. We will rotate our guys as we need to, in order that they all will have the opportunity to ride and work from it. I am giving you the manual today. You have about four days to read it. We will both pilot the thing and will be each other's navigator when we are not driving."

"I don't know why I am leery of this operation, but I am, so we should both take the time to really understand how this thing is intended to operate. Last time out, they had us working at 200 feet for a reason.

"This baby is designed to go as low as 190 feet. I know we will be asked to test it. If something goes wrong at that depth, we at least know that our guys have been trained to handle the swim up with scuba gear on."

"Well, we have always enjoyed the challenge of new adventures and this sounds like the beginning of a new adventure. All our men have been through the SWCC advanced training and all of them have a high level of training in tactical diving operations. I'm sure that they are ready for this type of challenge and any unforeseen problems that may face them."

"I will read the manual over the next few days and should be ready when we head out to sea next week."

"How do you plan to handle tomorrow's meeting?"

"Well, I want them all to know that we are guniea pigs of a sort and that there will be some danger associated with the trials. Between you and me, I also know that there is a bit of madness to everything that San Diego does. My guess is that the deep-water training last trip out coupled with this new shallow water submersible is getting us ready for something that we will be asked to do on our next deployment. I don't know what it will be yet, but my guess is these exercises are all playing into a future that we will be dealt."

SEAL MEETING PEARL HARBOR, HAWAII

The SEAL meeting was scheduled for 10 AM and everyone was in attendance and accounted for except for Jonnie Potts who was still in the hospital.

"Good morning men, you noticed I didn't say good morning men and women and the reason for that is I already said good morning to Ashley."

The men all laughed, and Ash blushed a little. "I want to cover a couple of things with you this morning. First, I want you all to know that Jonnie is going to come out of this with his leg still attached to his body."

"This is due primarily to Ash and the members of her team who managed to get him patched up and back to the ship while his blood lasted. For that we are all incredibly grateful. You have all talked about this before, but I wanted you to know what went in the official report. After talking with every member of the team I wrote that the attack was undertaken by three Tiger Sharks, all of which exceeded 13 feet in length and all of which weighed more than 1000 pounds."

"Based on what I have been told it is not uncommon for a group of Tiger Sharks to attack. To have three that were that large coming at once is very unusual. I am also told that because Jonnie used the butt of his rifle to hammer the shark in the nose that that probably more than anything saved his life. The bite was a direct bite and as such there was minimal tearing which Tiger Sharks are known to do because of the structure of their teeth."

I also want you all to know that the doctors have told Jonnie that while he will be able to walk on two legs, for the rest of his life he will have a limp which they can do nothing about and that his bad leg will never regain the strength it once had.

As a result Jonnie has informed Ash that he does not plan to re-up in two months but rather will leave the SEAL brotherhood and return to his home town where he already has a job as an EMT He told Ash that he plans to use that as a jumping off point to go to medical school. I also have learned that yesterday Jonnie's wife Joan told him that he is going to be a father in about seven and a half months, so he has a whole set of new challenges ahead of him, and we wish him the best."

"Jonnie will be in the hospital for at least the next two to three weeks so if you get a chance to stop by and wish him well, I'm sure he would greatly appreciate it.

"The second thing I want to cover with you this morning has to do with our current SEAL Delivery System. The ASDS has been around since about 2003. It was designed to provide us transportation from our sub base to the targets that we have been given in order to carryout covert and clandestine special operations missions."

"All of you have been through SWCC training and all of you are certified to deal with special warfare combatant craft."

"What most of you don't know is that the program has been plagued with cost overruns and problems since its inception. I am told that the Navy has spent almost $900 million on the program so far. I was advised about three years ago that the ASDS would eventually be taken out of service. I was not even sure that the Navy was going to keep the program going but a couple of years ago I was told that Lockheed Martin had been awarded a contract to develop a new Shallow Water Combat Submersible (SWCS). The new version is designed to keep us warm, as it features a dry interior, to go deeper, which I understand is about 190 feet, to go faster which I'm told is about 6 knots or a little over 10 miles an hour and to stay down longer which I'm told is up to 12 hours."

"The new SWCS has been undergoing a variety of tests for the past year and I am happy to say that it has met all of the criteria that the Navy specified. It is ready for sea trials and that is where we come into the picture. The new SWCS arrived this week and has been fitted to the submarine. We will be taking it out for its first sea trials next week. It takes two of us to drive the thing and I am told it will hold up to eight of you inside.

Because of its seating capacity we will be working in shifts. Ash and I will be taking turns driving the thing and we plan to rotate you all in and out."

To be honest, we are pretty much guinea pigs on this adventure. No one knows how it is really going to work in the open ocean. Based on what I have been told, the sub will be working in water that is no more than 200 feet in depth. Obviously, this is a safety issue. If we must leave the thing on the ocean floor we can do so and still reach the surface safely. Now you understand why we went through all of the deep-water scuba training."

"Safety and your lasting health are of great concern to me, so this mission will be taken with lots of caution"

"If we run into problems, we will deal with them as they occur, our problem will simply be the uncertainty of not knowing when, where or if a problem will occur."

"I can tell you this, we will be using he SWCS to get us close to our targets which will all be on land. So, we will be working off a couple of the islands that are not inhabited here in the Hawaiian chain."

"Are there any questions?"

No one raised their hands, so the meeting was adjourned. Ashley headed back to her stateroom with the operations manual in hand.

Ash spent the rest of the day learning about the SWCS. She learned that it was a foot longer and a half of a foot taller than the Mark 8. The SWCS has a longer range and higher payload capacity than the Mark 8. As such it is also heavier. It is about 4000 pounds heavier than its predecessor. The hull was made from aluminum and it has a much more sophisticated computer system. The navigation system is also better, and it has a new senor mast with an electro optical periscope. It also has wireless and wired communication between crew members along with sonar detectors and a sonar assisted automatic docking system. Like the SDV the SWCS can carry eight SEALs plus a pilot and a copilot/navigator. One of the key selling points was that it can move into much shallower water and thus get the SEALs much closer to their targets.

CHAPTER 11
SUPER HORNET

Scotty and Ryan were in their room when the phone rang. Ryan picked it up and said, "This is Ryan speaking, how can I help you?"

"Hey Ryan, it's Reggie. I just wanted to ask you to be ready by 9:30 in the morning. We have a group of experienced pilots for this trip, so we do not have to be concerned with any carrier qualifications. As such we will have a full flight deck in operation, and we will be launching a lot of aircraft. I want to be in the air before they all start hitting the skies. Our squadron will have 3 flights with each flight containing 8 aircraft. Each flight has a designated flight commander which role you will serve in the first flight. We will be launching the Hornets at a rate of two per launch. Our target is an isolated island in the pacific and, as you heard, we will be using live ammunition. Our target is about an hour and a half out so the total mission will be about four hours from start to finish. It will not be the 6 hours as originally stated. I will be evaluating our pilots take offs, landings and bomb drops. We will take a run first then watch the action by the others. You will be flying the Super Hornet."

"No problem Sir. I will have completed my inspection and will be ready to go by 9:30. Sounds like an interesting day."

Scotty then said, "Who was that, Ryan?"

"It was Reggie. He wants me to be ready to go by 9:30 so he can be in the air when the birds start to fly. He also confirmed what we talked about earlier. I will be flying the Super Hornet and the runs will be evaluated."

"Wow, lucky you. I know you have flown it a few times before, but I am still waiting for my chance. What have you found is the difference between the Hornet and the Super Hornet?"

"That's a good question Scotty. As you know they both look similar inside and out. In my opinion, the Super Hornet is a much-improved aircraft over the Hornet."

"It has more powerful engines and a much larger internal and external fuel capacity. It has two more weapons stations than the Hornet and it has numerous avionic improvements and is equipped with radar cross section reduction measures."

"Overall, I think that the design features not only make the jet look badass, but they enhance the jets' capabilities as well. One thing you will notice immediately is that the Up-Front Control Display (UFCD) is quite different. It replaces the old physical keypad for entering data. I think of it as it is like going from a flip phone with a physical keyboard and screen to an iPhone where the screen can show you anything you want. The cockpit displays are also in full color which is a lot better than the monochrome displays used in the Hornet."

"Some things are the same. For example, once you have entered your data and have the motors fired up, the high-performance nose wheel steering works the same as it does in the Hornet."

"But when you push the throttles past the MIL detent and into afterburner mode you get the full effect of the power that the

Super Hornet has. The takeoff performance is fantastic. It gets airborne in nearly 1000 feet less distance and nearly 20 knots slower than the Hornet."

"On the ship, the procedures are nearly the same as they are with the Hornet, except now the catapult launch is in full flaps and there is no selection of afterburner mid-catstroke. The sensation of the catapult stroke is still the same awesome feeling that you get in the Hornet, but the Super Hornet tends to leap off the flight deck easier than the hornet."

"There are a lot of other features that I haven't mentioned but the one real question is how the jet does in combat. I would argue that the Super Hornet beats the Hornet in air to air combat ever time. With the new radar system, the ability to fight out of visual range is unbelievable. The plane has extra gas which means it can fly longer and the new AIM 120 weapons it carries add an extra amount of fighting ability under the wings."

"Last, there is something the Super Hornet can do that the Hornet can't do and that is it can also be an aerial tanker.

"I personally have not flown one in that configuration, but I hear that the jet performs as a pig. That is no surprise with all the drag and 30,000 pounds of gas."

"Overall, the Hornet was my first love. I will always look back fondly on flying the F/A-18 Hornet and I am sure I will miss it. However, there is no doubt the Super Hornet is the jet I want to fly off the boat into combat."

"Well Ryan, you have just convinced me to move ahead and get into one of those babies as soon as possible. Now back to this manual."

The next morning Ryan was up early for breakfast. He was ready to go and headed for the flight deck right after breakfast. The flight deck was a frenzy of activity. The aircraft directors were all in active mode. They are responsible for directing all aircraft movement on the hanger and flight decks. They are colloquially known as "Bears" and those who work in the hanger go by the term "hanger rats." They all had on yellow shirts and all of them report directly to the handler.

The air officer for this mission was Commander John Adams. He was a former squadron commander and was known as the air boss. He is responsible for all aspects of operations and was housed in his perch in primary flight control.

The catapult officers were known as shooters and they are responsible for all aspects of catapult maintenance and operation. They ensure that wind direction and speed is sufficient over the deck and that the stream stings for the catapults will ensure that aircraft have sufficient flying speed at the end of the stroke. Ryan knew all the officers by name as they were the officers that signaled him that he could take off.

About 45 minutes before launch time, Ryan completed his walk around and then at 9AM the engines were started.

Once Ryan had completed a detailed check of his Super Hornet, he then reviewed the meteorological conditions for the daytime departures. It was a good day, with visibility around the carrier at about 5 nautical miles."

At 9:30 Commander Reggie Sanders arrived, and he boarded the Super Hornet.

They did their pre-flight checks together and when completed Reggie said to Ryan, "You ready to do this kid?"

"Yes Sir, ready when they say go."

The aircraft was then taxied from its parked position and spotted immediately behind the catapults. To assist the launch, the ship was turned into the natural wind. The wings on the Super Hornet were spread and a large jet blast deflector panel rose out of the flight deck behind the engine exhaust. Prior to final catapult hookup, final checkers made their final exterior check of the aircraft and the loaded weapons were armed by ordinance.

The catapult hook up was accomplished by placing the aircraft launch bar, which is attached to the front of the Super Hornet's nose landing gear, into the catapult shuttle. An additional bar, the holdback, was connected from the rear of the nose landing gear to the carrier deck. The holdback fitting keeps the aircraft from moving forward prior to catapult firing.

Ryan and Reggie then went into radio silence which is typically maintained for both launch and landings. Only in a case of emergency do they break that silence.

The preparation for launch was now complete and the final launch sequence began.

The catapult was put into tension whereby all the slack was taken out of the system with hydraulic pressure on the rear of the shuttle.

Ryan was then signaled to advance the throttles to full power, and he took his feet off the brakes.

Ryan checked the engine instruments and all the control surfaces.

When he was satisfied Ryan indicated that he was ready for flight by saluting the catapult officer.

The final checkers observed the exterior of the aircraft for proper flight control movement, engine response, panel security and leaks.

Once satisfied the checkers gave thumbs up to the catapult officer.

The catapult officer makes a final check of the catapult settings, wind, and then gave the signal to launch. He then pushed the button which fires the catapult.

Once that occurred, Ryan and the Super Hornet accelerated from zero to about 150 knots in 2 seconds. Ryan took control of the aircraft, raised the landing gear and performed a clearing turn to the right off the bow. After the clearing turn, he proceeded straight ahead paralleling the ships course at 500 feet until 7 nautical miles had been achieved. He was then cleared to climb unrestricted in visual conditions.

Reggie directed Ryan to a heading and altitude that he had given the flight commanders to rendezvous. All three flights of eight Hornets each joined up as directed and the 24 aircraft all followed Ryan's lead as they headed towards their target.

All the planes were equipped with 1000 lbs. of gBU-12 bombs. Each of the bombs would be guided by laser to its targets. Once the bombing runs were completed the group would then conduct a strafing run at low altitude. Each pilot and weapons officer would be evaluated on their performance which would all be calculated by computer. They would receive their rating after they returned to the ship. They would be evaluated on a variety of things including approach, accuracy and timing.

Ryan had the target on radar long before he could visually see it. Reggie gave each of the flight directors their goals which they in turn passed on to their aircraft pilots and weapons officers.

Reggie told Ryan he would want him to make the first run then to assume a holding position so Reggie could evaluate the performance of the squadron. Ryan made his first approach for the bombing run in perfect order. Reggie complemented him and then proceeded to evaluate the others. The strafing runs went well, and the group headed back to the carrier. With a couple of exceptions, the squadron performed well, and Reggie was pleased.

He then directed the squadron to return to the ship with Ryan leading in his Super Hornet.

The day's operation had gone well and with a group of experienced pilots he did not anticipate any problems with the landings. As it turned out the weather was still good, and the meteorological conditions were all favorable.

The carrier-controlled approach is analogous to ground controlled approach using the ship's precision approach radar. Pilots are told where they are in relation to glide slope and final bearing. The pilot then makes a correction and awaits further information from the controller.

The instrument carrier landing system is remarkably like civilian instrument landing systems. A bull's eye is displayed for the pilot, indicating aircraft position in relation to glide slope and final bearing. The pilot aims for the middle arresting wire, and immediately upon touchdown the pilot advances the throttles to full power so that a touch and go can be executed if all trap wires were missed. This did not happen to any of the squadron landings.

Reggie asked Ryan to take up the last landing position in order that he could allow an evaluation of the squadron's performance during the recovery aspect of the mission.

Once the group had successfully landed Ryan brought his Super Hornet down perfectly like he had done on several occasions before. The tail hook caught the target wire which abruptly slowed the aircraft from approach speed to full stop in about two seconds. As the Super Hornet's forward motion stopped the throttles reduced to idle and the hook was raised on the aircraft director's signal.

The aircraft director then directed the aircraft to clear the landing area. The few remaining ordinance was disarmed, wings were folded, and the aircraft taxied to the parking spot and shut down.

Reggie only said one thing to him on return. "Nice job kid."

When Ryan returned to his stateroom Scotty was there. "Looks like it all went well, Ryan. Did Reggie give you any idea what he thought of the squad's performance?"

Not really, I think he was pleased overall. He monitored each bombing run and had them all evaluated on that computer program he uses. I know he will give each pilot and weapons officer their evaluations tomorrow He did tell me that our next challenge will be a night run in a similar way we handled today's day run As you know when we have even a few pilots that are trying to gain and maintain carrier landing currency, everything slows down. At night, there are less things going on on deck and the whole process seems to move in slower motion. I know he does not like that and as such he was pleased that he had an experience squadron to work with today and he will have the same squad at night. I'm hungry, you ready for dinner?"

"Yep, let's go to the wardroom."

CHAPTER 12
THE NEW SUBMERSIBLE

Ashley spent three full days studying the operations manual for the new submersible. She wanted to make sure she was totally ready to field test the thing in the open ocean. She learned a lot about the new vehicle and how it differed significantly from the ones she had used in the past. It was officially called a dry combat submersible.

She was so used to the underwater sled that had been the standard SEAL vehicle for such a long time that this was going to be a whole new experience. The original vehicle was often referred to as a wet boat. To begin with, all the SEALs were used to riding the sled in full scuba gear, completely exposed to the water and often in freezing cold and pure blackout conditions. The longest Ash had spent on one of the sled missions was eight full hours. She often said it was like being locked in a cold, dark wet closet for eight hours.

She remembered that it took four hours on that mission to reach their target and after it had been destroyed it took four hours to get back to the sub.

She welcomed the fact that in the new vehicle she would be able to communicate with the other SEAL members of the team. In the past the only communication they had was looking at your buddy's eyes with a glow stick.

She also learned that the new vehicle came in a couple of different models. One was to be launched from a ship, the other from a submarine. The shipboard model was launched with a giant crane. The SEAL's entered the vehicle while on board the ship. They did not have to get wet at all.

The new vehicle they would be testing was about 39 feet long and was 7 feet in diameter. It has many of the same attributes as the old model. It has propellers, thrusters, ballast tanks, scrubbers, oxygen manifolds and a periscope. It differed in that it is battery powered instead of nuclear propulsion powered.

The new model also includes navigational technology that has a sonar doppler velocity log which bounces a signal off the bottom of the ocean to help provide essential mission relevant location information.

After bouncing off the bottom, a signal comes back to the device which tells the SEAL's how far and fast they are moving.

One key thing her boss had mentioned was that the new mini sub was designed to hold up to eight SEALs plus the driver and navigator. 10 SEALs meant it also had to carry all their gear. During their tests Mark wanted to staff the thing with the driver navigator and six SEALs.

The goal of the new vehicle was the same as the old one. It is designed to be used for shallow water infiltration and exfiltration of special operations forces, reconnaissance, resupply and other missions in high threat non permissive environments.

The idea with the dry submersible is to minimize risk and fatigue for special operations forces.

The actual vehicle consists of three compartments; a swimmer compartment where the SEALs will ride for the duration of the time, a line in and out compartment where they would exit and enter and the compartment that held the navigator and pilot.

Ashley noted that the swimmer's compartment was only about 12 feet long which did not make for much space if the submersible was carrying the maximum number of SEALs specified.

The most important element of the new submersible is that it was a dry vehicle which means no more freezing cold rides. However, as in the past, the SEALs would have to leave the submarine via the in and out hatch swim out to the vehicle and release it from the submarine before entering it. So, entry would still require that you get wet.

Ashley also got a feel for the expense associated with the new submersible. She noted that the Navy had ordered three. One arrived in Pearl Harbor, a second one was sent to SEAL team two on the east coast of the United States and a third one was still being developed. The cost to the Navy for the three was $236 million.

One thing that puzzled Ashley was that they were being asked to test the new vehicle in deep water when the thing was designed and developed for use in shallow water.

As Ashley thought about it, maybe that was what was bothering Mark. The tests ahead of them just did not quite fit the description of what the thing was designed for.

Just as she was about to be lost in thought her phone rang. "Hey Ash, its Mark."

"Hi Boss, what's up?"

"Have you been going through the manual?"

"Yep, I've been through it a number of times."

"Well, I think it's time for you and me to tour the thing before we get in it for real."

"I'm all for it. When can we do it?"

"How about right now."

"Sounds good to me. I'll meet you on deck and we will have our own private tour."

"OK, I'm on my way."

The new electric submersible had been mounted on the deck of the submarine in the same manner as the old one. It was larger and weighed more. Mark and Ash climbed inside it. They sat in the pilot and navigator seats and studied the controls. They were remarkably like what they were used to, and it did not pose a problem for either of them. They then moved into the swimmer's section, which would be dry.

It was a tight space and both felt that the six SEALs who would join them would be comfortable but they both felt that if it was holding the maximum number advertised that it would not be a comfortable ride for the full complement.

"Well, what do you think, Ash?"

"I think our guys are going to like being dry and warm. I do not think it will be difficult to drive or handle. But I am a bit puzzled by the fact that we are being asked to test it in deep water and not in shallow water when all of the things I read about it says it is designed to be used in shallow water."

Mark just smiled and said, "You have just hit on my worry. Why are we taking this thing deep when it is designed for shallow?"

"Have you looked at the topography maps of the area we will be testing it in?"

"Yep, I noticed it is a pretty flat part of the ocean bottom with depths about 200 feet but I did notice that at one end of our training area the bottom drops off and looks like it goes down to about 2000 feet."

"Yep, I noticed that trench as well and I plan to stay away from that drop off. The thought of dropping off that cliff in this new rig just doesn't do it for me."

"I hear you on that, Boss."

After their tour they returned to the Wardroom. Mark explained to Ash that they would have three dives in the new submersible during the week. He had spoken with the Captain and that orders had been received from San Diego were that they wanted three dives. One at 100 feet, a second at 150 feet and the last at 200 feet. Mark had divided the SEALs into three groups. Each group would have six SEALs in it. So, all members of the team would get experience. He also explained that each

SEAL would be asked for their observations on the experience and all comments would be included in the evaluation. He mentioned that all dives would be made in daylight instead of at night which would take one risk element out of the picture.

The SEALs were to test the vehicles mobility, reaction at depth and the ease of entry and exit. Since they would be working a great depth, they would be using a compound oxygen mixture instead of the normal air tank mix.

The next two days were a whirlwind of activity. The SEAL Team members spent a lot of time making sure they understood how the new vehicle was attached to the sub and how to release it. They also made sure that they knew what needed to be done once the mission was completed to remount it on the submarine in a way that avoided it from falling off the sub deck.

At least most of the procedures outlined matched what they had been using in the past so at least there was not a great deal new to be learned.

Each SEAL group toured the space and did so with full scuba gear on. The group of six was comfortable and it was clear that they were all looking forward to a dry and warm experience. No one was bothered about the wet entry, but all were looking for the dry warm ride.

The submarine was ready to go on time. It was a Sunday morning at 8 AM and the lines were released, and the sub was underway and heading out of Pearl Harbor. Once they cleared the harbor entrance the Captain gave the order to commence the dive process and it was not long before they were down to 150 feet and heading out to sea.

Ashley and Mark met again that evening to go over the first of the vehicle launches. It would be completed in the daylight beginning at 10 AM.

At the appointed time, the first SEAL team met in the in and out chamber room of the submarine all dressed in full underwater combat gear. The team consisted of Mark and Ashley and six of their SEAL team members.

The exit from the submarine went flawless as usual. The sub was in about 100 feet of water and it was 10 in the morning so there was plenty of light for the team members to work releasing the vehicle from it mounting on the deck of the submarine. Ashley and Mark were first to get into the vehicle and took their positions as the driver and navigator. They adjusted the controls and the mini sub lifted off the deck surface of the submarine. Mark then moved the mini sub to a position away from the sub and the six members of the team loaded one by one.

Once everyone was aboard and their gear stowed in the designed compartments, Mark took over the controls and the new special warfare craft was underway. Mark maneuvered the vehicle to about 500 yards from the sub before he began to work the controls putting the new vehicle through several turns and moves both up and down. To his surprise and relief, the new mini sub moved easily in the directions he asked it to. Eventually he took it down to 150 feet which it handled with no problems.

Ashley asked the members of team how it was to ride in the back, and all responded that it was dry, comfortable and very functional. No issues with the exception that the team of six noted that if they were to put two more men in the compartment it would be extremely tight and limit their movement.

The return trip to the sub went just as smoothly. The team exited the new mini sub as Mark and Ashley positioned it for placement on the submarine. Once in position the team latched it down to the deck of the sub and Mark and Ashley exited it as well. Everyone was back on board the submarine and the mission was viewed as a success by everyone.

The second day of trials went just as well as the first day with the second SEAL team joining Ashley and Mark. The dive to 200 feet was smooth with no problems at all.

The third day trial had the goal to take it down below 200 feet and test it.

All went well with the test and as they had discussed both Mark and Ashley could see the giant trench that had shown on the map. It was almost 2000 feet deep, but they could only see far enough down as the light would let them. Mark and Ashley had discussed the fact that they had no intention of getting close to that drop off and Mark made sure he stayed away from it as he maneuvered the sub through its various turns.

Mark began his assent back to the submarine as planned but suddenly Ashley noticed that the sub was beginning a decent rather than the assent that was planned. She first called out to Mark but got no response. She then saw that Mark was very white and slumped over the controls of the mini sub in front of him.

Ash knew immediately that something was wrong, but she did not know what and Mark was not responding. She did what she was trained to do and that was to take control of the vehicle. She managed to push Mark off the control panel and then took control. However, that took a couple of minutes and by the time she was able to stop the decent her depth gauge showed that they were at 450 feet. She was able to level out the mini sub and some relief came over her as she was now stable instead of headed right down the canyon.

She stabilized the thing and then began a slow assent. She had no idea about the pressure that was being placed on the sub, but she felt that it would be no different than a diver coming to the surface from a deep dive.

Take it slow each step of the way. Once she was on the assent, she told the team in the back that they had an emergency on their hands and that something had happened to Mark. She told the team that they would be returning immediately to the submarine and that she would need help from them to get Mark out of the vehicle and into the submarine as soon as possible. She indicated that her plan was to approach the submarine and then hold it still while two SEALs exited with Mark. The goal was clear to everyone. Get him into the submarine as soon as possible. Once that happened, she would bring the new mini sub on to the platform and have the remaining four members latch it down before she exited.

She notified Captain Miles that they had an emergency on board and that the medical staff should be ready. She did not know what the problem was, but Mark was not responsive, and she suspected a heart problem.

She obviously didn't have a navigator, but she knew where she was going and located the submarine with no problem. Once she had it in sight, she brought the new mini sub into position. Two of her team got gear on Mark and then attempted to buddy breath him into the in and out chamber of the submarine. Once that occurred Ash maneuvered the mini into its target landing position and the four remaining team members lashed it down.

Ash was the last to leave the mini and the last to reenter the submarine.

The news she was greeted with was the worst possible. Mark had died of a heart attack and based on the doctor's assessment it was a blockage of the widow maker artery. His death had occurred instantly. The ship's doctor told Ash that there was nothing she or her team could have done about it. Mark died instantly.

Ash did not know what to say but a tear formed in her eye and she could not make it go away.

CHAPTER 13
THE LONG WAY HOME

Ashley left the doctor and the Captain and headed to her stateroom. Both of her eyes were filled with tears. Mark had been such a supporter of hers and had taught her so much she just could not believe that he was gone, and he was gone in an instant. No symptoms, no warning, just gone.

She contacted the SEAL team and told them there would be an emergency team meeting in the Wardroom at 1900. The meeting was mandatory. She knew that the word would already be out among the SEAL team, but she wanted to let them know the facts as she knew them.

She also knew she would be required to make a full report to SEAL team headquarters, so she sat at her desk with tears still in her eyes and began to write.

The report would be twofold. The first portion would be to let headquarters know the facts about Mark as she understood them. She knew that there would be an autopsy conducted when they returned to Pearl Harbor and that the results would be provided to headquarters, so she kept only to the facts as she knew them. The second portion of the report dealt with the mission itself. In that portion of the report she noted that the new vehicle reached a depth of almost 450 feet before she was able to stabilize it and begin the return trip to the submarine. To her knowledge, this would be interesting to the SEAL command as no SEAL vehicle had ever been that deep before and the new mini sub seemed to handle the depth with no problem.

She finished the report before dinner but did not feel like going to eat anything, so she remained in her stateroom until it was time for the all SEAL meeting to take place.

She arrived at the wardroom five minutes before 1900. To her surprise the entire team was there and sitting in silence. She went to the head of the table where Mark would normally sit and addressed the group.

"Good Evening. It is with the greatest of sadness that I must inform you that our Leader Captain Mark Price passed away today while on our morning mission. I know most of you are aware of this, but I wanted to hold this meeting this evening to make sure that you all are aware of the facts surrounding Mark's death."

"First, my thanks to those of you on this mission for helping return him to the ship and for your professionalism in restoring the vehicle topside. You were all a big help as usual."

"Mark passed away while at the controls of the mini sub. It is important for you all to know that his death had nothing to do with our mission or the new vehicle we have been testing. The doctor on board told me that he believes that it was a heart attack caused by a blockage of his widow maker artery. This will be confirmed when he goes through an autopsy at Pearl Harbor Hospital on our return."

"For those of you who do not know the left anterior descending artery is a branch of the left coronary artery. This artery is also known as the widow maker artery as it is associated with an extremely high death risk and often triggers death with no warning. I believe this was the case with Mark's death. To me, he showed no signs of a problem. When I noticed that we were dropping in depth I looked over and he was bent over his console and not moving. I now know that it was at that point he passed away suddenly."

"I have completed a report to SEAL headquarters and I'm sure that we will hear back from them very soon. Mark was a confirmed bachelor and for that I am grateful, so we do not have to deal with children or family regarding his death. SEAL headquarters will notify his parents who I understand are still living on the East Coast."

"As to our unit, I have talked with Chief Johnson and together we intend to run the unit as normal until we get word from SEAL command on who will be assigned to replace Mark."

"I am personally incredibly sad about this loss. To me, and I know to a lot of you, Mark was not only a leader but a supporter and defender of all of us. I'm going to really miss him, and I know you all will as well."

Tears welled up in Ashley's eyes, but she finished by saying. "I guess we have all been taught that SEALs are tough and not supposed to show much emotion. Well, this one has taken a toll on me and if my eyes reflect emotion then screw anyone who might take issue with it."

With that she said "dismissed."

There was silence and then there was clapping, and the entire team stood up.

Once the clapping stopped the guys left the room in small groups. Chief Johnson stayed behind and said "Sir, you are one tough lady and everyone in this room just gave you all the respect you deserve. We can do this together and we will."

With that he left the room. He did not tell Ashley that Mark's death had also taken a toll on him. He had mentioned to her briefly that he was seeing a woman in Honolulu but he did not tell her that he had asked the woman, whose name was Sarah Miles, for her hand in marriage before they left Pearl on this mission. He had planned to tell her after the mission.

He knew now was not the time to mention it and, as such, he decided he would wait for the dust to settle before he told her and gave his official retirement notice.

The news hit SEAL command hard. Mark Price was a very valued SEAL leader and was destined for a major assignment in the future. The news quickly spread throughout SEAL Headquarters in San Diego. Over drinks one-night Sergeant James and Sergeant Reichardt were talking and James mentioned that Mark's death was a shock to those in SEAL command. He was not only respected but was viewed as a major future leader.

"Who do you think they will replace him with Sarge?"

Reichardt said, "Your guess is as good as mine, but it will have to be someone special. That is the command that Jamison was assigned to. As if it isn't tough enough to be a SEAL and a SEAL leader but when your mentor and leader is suddenly taken away from you it has to present a bunch of unknown challenges."

"Yep, I hadn't thought much about that. Ash is, however, one tough lady and even though I know how much she respected Captain Price I do not think this will get in her way. I have bet on that woman for some time now and I am not changing my bet yet. She will succeed. Rumor has it she took control of that new vehicle which normally takes two to drive it. She stabilized it and brought it back to the sub herself. Not to mention the fact that it had descended to more than 450 feet and was headed further down the trench before she reversed its course."

The USS Louisville SSN 724 returned to Pearl Harbor and tied up at the submarine peer. Within an hour Captain Mark Price's body was removed from the ship and taken by a waiting military ambulance to the base hospital for autopsy.

Ashley watched as the ambulance moved away from the ship pier and thought never in her wildest dreams did, she expect this to happen. Mark was young and vibrant and appeared to always be in great shape. How could one crummy artery change everything in a matter of seconds?

Ash had almost completely forgot about her new apartment then remembered that Mr. Piedmont had said that it would be ready for her on her return. She went down to her stateroom and called him.

"Hello, Mr. Piedmont, it's Ashley Jamison."

"Hi Ash, welcome home or rather I should ask if you are home?"

"Yes Sir, we pulled in this morning. I called to see if my new place was ready to go. I believe you thought it would be ready when I returned."

"Yes Ash, the cleaning staff finished with it yesterday and just today my head cleaning lady moved your items over to the new apartment. When do you think you will be able to pick up the key?"

"Well, I'm going to take a couple of days off beginning tomorrow. So, if it's OK with you I will plan to come by about 10 o'clock tomorrow morning."

"No problem, I'll be here with your key"

"Thanks, Mr. Piedmont, I look forward to seeing it. See you tomorrow."

Ashley spent the next couple of hours packing some of her things that she wanted to take to her new place. She was excited to see it but was still depressed by the loss of Mark and she hoped that the new digs would help get rid of some of the pain she felt.

She walked back up to the submarine deck and watched as the sun began to set. What a day and what a week it had been. She was about to leave when Chief Johnson joined her.

"Hey Chief, good to see you."

"Thanks Captain, I'm glad I found you. How are you doing?"

"Well, I wish I could tell you well, but Mark's loss has been difficult. I just got off the phone with my apartment manager and am going to see my new place in the morning. I am looking forward to it and hope it helps get rid of this sadness I feel."

"I'm sure it will help. I feel somewhat the same way but during the last 27 years in this Navy I have had some great leaders like Captain Price and lost some of them along the way. It takes time but healing does occur, and it will for you as well."

"I have some news for you as well. From my perspective it is great news but from your perspective it may not be so great."

"What's up Chief?"

"Well, you know before we left on this last training exercise, I told you I was meeting a woman and was looking forward to a cold beer."

"Yes, I remember that."

"Well, the woman's name is Sarah Miles. She is a retired schoolteacher and I have been seeing her for the past three years while stationed here. I did have the beer, but I also asked her to marry me."

"Wow, Chief, that is great news, I hope she said yes."

"She did and we plan to get married next month. Mark had planned to be my best man and he was excited to stand up with me."

"Obviously, that is not going to work any longer, so I have a question for you. Would you please be my best man so to speak? I have enormous respect for you, and I would be more than proud if you would stand with me."

"Chief, I'm not sure that a woman has ever been a best man, but I would be more than proud to stand with you in my best dress blue and white uniform."

"Now that we have that piece of business out of the way there is something else, I need to tell you. I advised Mark before we left that after 27 years, I am going to retire from the SEAL brotherhood and the Navy. My plan is to do so just prior to our deployment so I will not be leaving until the SEAL command has made the staff changes to replace both of us."

"Well Chief, I am a little disappointed, and frankly, a bit scared to think what SEAL life will be without the two of you next to me but I'm ready for whatever comes next and that includes standing by you at your wedding. 27 years is a long time and in SEAL life it probably equates to about 50 years. Thanks for letting me know."

SEAL COMMAND
SAN DIEGO, CALIFORNIA

At the SEAL Command Center in Coronado, the Senior Officers were discussing the loss of Mark Price when they learned that Chief Johnson had given his formal retirement notice. "Well, one of the officers said, our Ashley Jamison must be feeling a bit weak in the knees with these one two punches."

"I'm sure your right Jim, but Ashley has proved over and over that she is one unusual and tough SEAL.

My guess is she will have no problem adapting to whatever we throw at her next. How do you think we should handle the replacements?"

"I've thought a lot about that in the last week since we learned of Mark's death and now with the Chief's decision it makes the pieces of the puzzle, I have been thinking about start to come together. I think I have the perfect solution."

"OK, I'm ready to hear it. What have you got?"

"Well, now that Lieutenant Commander Roscoe Cook and his pal Sergeant Juan Sanchez have spent five wonderful years at the YARD, I think it will do them both a world of good to go on vacation in Hawaii. Both were involved in Ashley's selection and both are SEAL combat veterans. I think it will be a perfect fit for both and I know they both have the total respect from Ashley."

"Brilliant if I don't say so myself, Sir."

CHAPTER 14
FLIGHT OPERATIONS

The first week of flight operations went smoothly for Ryan and Reggie. The squadron performed well with no problems. Ryan's ratings from Reggie were as high as they could be. The second week would be night operations which Ryan knew would be more difficult for some of the younger pilots that had not had much night experience.

"Reggie. Did you look at the latest meteorological conditional report? Here we have been cruising along at a case one level and based on what I read this morning we could be facing a case three level this week."

"I saw it Carl and I didn't like it. At least you have days this week. I'm not extremely high on night operations with a level III."

"As you well know, when we are not anticipating needing to use instruments it makes our operations much less complex. It has been good this past week to have visibility clear below 3000 feet and five nautical miles. With the case three rating we are expected to encounter instrument conditions during both departure and recovery where visibility could be lower than 1000 feet and three nautical miles."

"I seem to have a number of experienced pilots in my squadron this trip but I'm still a bit nervous about them with poor visibility in night operations. I remember my first night operation like it was yesterday. Everything was dark and I felt like a five-year-old hiding under the covers to avoid monsters in the dark."

"Normally with level I there will be a few stars in the sky and maybe a partial moon above a thick layer of clouds but with a level III, most of these guys will be flying only with their instruments."

"What's that old Naval aviator term that is often used to describe flying at night?"

"It's called alone and unafraid."

"I remember it now. It was coined to describe how a naval aviator feels during night operations. I think it amply describes that certain haunting loneliness that only a few of us have experienced."

"Yes, it is no simple task to land a multimillion-dollar aircraft onto a moving vessel when it is daylight let alone at night during bad weather."

"Do you know who will be in night traffic control?"

"I think it is Bud Fremont."

"I hope you're right because that guy is as good as they get. The carrier air traffic control center or CTC is lucky to have that guy. He is one of the most competent sailors on the ship and he is exactly what the civilian air traffic controllers want. He could name his job if he decided to leave the Navy."

"Yes, and he is one of those guys who can tell an officer of any rank what to do and they do it without hesitation."

"Reggie, given the weather report are you going to change anything about your cycle?"

"Good question, Carl. Normally, I like to have 12 aircraft up in each cycle. This is my standard practice. But as I told you, I have some experience pilots on this trip, but many have not had much night experience. So, if the weather holds at a three, I am going to reduce the cycle by 50%. That would mean I have three squadrons of six to deal with instead of three squadrons of 12."

"As you know space is a premium on the carrier surface and anything, we can do to acquire more of it will help the guys. The bad weather, and especially at night, less is better than more."

"Reggie, are you going to fly with Ryan again?"

"Yes, I'm going to ride that horse this entire trip. I want to see him in action as much as possible."

"As I told you, I think he is one of the best and I want to make sure. After our next deployment he will be ready for reassignment and if he continues to demonstrate the skill level I have observed, I may be recommending him for the Blue Angel Team."

"You really do think highly of him, don't you?"

"So far I really like what I see. I asked him to take the new pilots through a basic reorientation with attention to night landings in bad weather today. I know the guys think this reminder session is unnecessary, but I have found over the years that the refresher is important especially during bad weather night operations. He is actually giving the session as we speak."

PILOT BRIEFING SESSION

"Good evening Ladies and Gentlemen. My name is Lieutenant Ryan Joshua. I was asked to talk to you tonight by Commander Reggie Sanders who you all know. This pilot briefing session will be repetitive to all of you but, having been through it myself a number of times over the years; it will provide you with a few reminders that are critical when conducting night operations and particularly, when the weather is bad which it looks like it's going to be."

"My goal tonight is not to bore you to death but rather to take you through a few of the things that are important to a successful night operation. We will all be carrying live ammunition and thus it will add an additional complication to our mission."

"Let us begin with a brief discussion of wire positions. You all know the most aft wire on the ship is the number one wire. The most forward wire is the number four wire. Your target is the number three wire. It is easier to hit number three during the day than it is at night. You all learned this early on in flight school that you want to try to avoid the number one wire because it is uncomfortably close to the back end of the ship and, that more than one Navy pilot has lost his life because he misjudged and hit the back end of the aircraft carrier."

"The goal however is to catch a wire, any of them will work and be considered a success. You will all be graded on both your takeoff and landing. Your goal should be to do both successfully and not to worry about how pretty it was. Once you are safely stopped on board you can reflect on the things you may want to improve on next time."

"Night operations can result in a lot of problems that are harder to deal with than in the daylight. For example, if you fail to take off properly or slide off the deck on landing your harder to recover at night then during the day. As such, I want you to always remember that when landing you need to set the throttles of your aircraft to full military power which is full power without afterburner. Obviously, you do this just as you touch down on the landing area of the deck."

"When you do so, it greatly increases your chance of a touch and go if you miss the wire and gets you airborne to try again. If that happens, you know that you have become a bolter and will need to reposition your aircraft."

"If you fail to catch a wire and cannot get airborne again, you'll have to eject and determine when to do so. Our hope is that your ejection is timed in such a way that the carrier does not run over you and that you end up in a position where one of the plane guard destroyers is able to pick you up. Everything just gets more difficult when it is dark."

"Okay. Let me remind you that you will be using live ammunition and to make sure that you do not return to the ship and try to land with live bombs on board."

"If you bolt on landing and are running low on fuel you must conform to the bolter pattern above the ship. It is a pattern that is like a level oval racetrack pattern above the ship."

"If you need to get gas, control will ask you to elevate to the tanker pattern which is located above the bolter pattern. If this occurs, air operations designates an airborne tanker to hawk or monitor the situation and will place you in a position to provide you with aerial refueling."

"Last, I want to talk to you about adverse weather conditions. During adverse weather conditions we will need to take the Marshall stack formation."

"The easiest way to describe the Marshall stack is to visualize this pattern as if there were a stack of pancakes above the ship. Each pancake is a plane in a separate pattern. Altitude between patterns is the primary method of separation.

To keep track of all this flight control reflects in real time the location of every aircraft that is airborne."

"When an aircraft checks in with the Marshall controller you must provide a fuel state and a side number. State is the term used to define how much fuel you have left in the tank. Instead of saying your tank is half-full, you must express your fuel remaining in pounds, which is shortened to two numbers for example 301 state 6.5."

"Okay, the last thing on fuel. Remember aircraft fuel state is one of the most critical pieces of information. Fuel states are tracked by AIROPS and you will be asked to update state every 10 minutes. This is standard practice and sometimes I know that it seems like overkill, but it is not and should be taken seriously. Remember, that your fuel state is an indicator of weight and as such prior to each landing the tension for the arresting gear is adjusted to the maximum weight for your aircraft."

"Last, just a reminder that your every movement is live on TV. AIROPS is the carrier's hub for all night flying activity. There are two status boards in AIROPS one that tracks every plane launched and one that tracks every plane that is about to land.

Fuel states, aircraft mission, pilot names, aircraft side numbers, landing attempts and any miscellaneous information is displayed on these boards, which is then piped through the ship's internal TV system for everyone to see."

"For those of you have not seen it on the ship's internal TV, there's also a platform camera that shows a view from the landing area looking back to the stern of the ship. This channel is always on throughout the ship, including the bridge, AIROPS, and primary flight control where the air boss sits. So, you are all an open book and trust me there will be a lot of people watching you."

"Are there any questions?"

There were none so Ryan dismissed the pilots and headed back to his state room. He no sooner got to his room and sat down when the phone rang. "Hi, this is Ryan, what can I do for you?"

"Ryan it's Reggie."

"Good evening sir. What's up?"

"I want to know how tonight's briefing session went and I want to briefly talk about tomorrow's night operation."

"The briefing session went well. It is not news to most of the pilots, but I did have their full attention due to the night operation and the weather report. There are a couple of them that have made very few night landings and with the added weather element they paid close attention."

"Great Ryan, thanks for doing that. I would like to get tomorrow's operation underway at 1900. I would like you to be ready to go a half hour before our first group takes off. I want to be up in the air before the fun begins to watch and evaluate the group. We will be flying with six planes in each group.

That will mean half as many as we did during days last week. Our route will be the same, so I expect that we will be out in a little over three hours and back in the same time. When we return, we will Marshall Stack. You and I will be the top of the stack so we will be the last plane in."

"No problem, sir. What do you expect for whether?"

"Right now, there is broken layer of clouds at about 2000 feet above the water with scattered layers all the way up to 15,000 feet. We also have thunderstorm activity nearby and I expect it will be the same or worse by the time we launch tomorrow night. On dissent I will want each plane to begin their dissent to 5000 feet which will be our platform altitude. I don't want anyone below the platform I do not think that, for the most part, any of our pilots will be able to follow the guy in front of them so there will be no opportunity to see blinking lights against the darkness. I believe that all our planes will need to make a full instrument approach to landing. That should test the skills and abilities of all of them and I know it will require their full attention."

"Ryan, how do you feel about night landing in bad weather?"

"Sir, I have done it on many occasions I am totally comfortable with it. I will be nervous for some of the new pilots, particularly if there is a strong crosswind that will make it difficult for them to hold it steady until they have touched down but I have confidence in all of our squad leaders and I know they will have their pilots ready. My hope is that we take on the night and come out of the experience as well as we did during the daylight. I will see you tomorrow evening."

"Thanks Ryan and good night."

CHAPTER 15
THE NEW DIGS

Ashley was up early. She had breakfast in the wardroom with some of the submarine officers. All were sad about Mark, but there just was not much to say. He died of natural causes and he died immediately doing what he loved to do.

Ashley listened to the conversations, but she did not say much. She did think however, that in one sense, Mark died a death that was not a bad way to go but he still was only 38.

So, Ash was sad but at the same time she was excited to see her new apartment. She had told Mr. Piedmont she would be by at 10 AM to pick up the keys and, as was her practice, she would be on time or perhaps five minutes early.

It was a beautiful day at Pearl Harbor. She could tell that the temperature would end up being about 88° because it was well over 70 and it was only 8:30 in the morning yet. She had some time to kill so she went up topside and looked out at Pearl Harbor.

She thought how lucky she was to be stationed at the headquarters of the United States Pacific Fleet. It was a long way from Kodiak Alaska where she did her cold temperature training and she hoped she would never have to see that place again.

She was surprised by the number of ships that were in port. She had not noticed all of them on arrival, probably because she was preoccupied with Mark's death. She knew that the Naval

Station provided birthing and shoreside support both to both surface ships and submarines and that a lot of maintenance work and training was also conducted on the base. She also knew that Pearl Harbor could accommodate the larger ships in the fleet.

From her perspective, it looked like a lot were in port for the weekend ahead. Because Pearl Harbor was the only intermediate maintenance facility for submarines in the middle Pacific, it served as host to many visiting submarines. From her position, on deck of the Louisville, she could see seven other subs in port.

Her mind was wandering but she thought, given the day and the number of ships in port that it must have been similar to Sunday, December 7 1941 when the Imperial Japanese Navy under the command of Admiral Chuichi Nagumo began bombing Honolulu and the Pearl Harbor base.

She remembered from her Naval history classes at the YARD that the Navy was not completely surprised by the attack. Through earlier code breaking activity, the Americans had determined that an attack was likely to occur. However, the Americans failed to discover Japan's target location. They thought that the Philippines were the most likely target. That was until 6:05 AM on December 7, when six Japanese carriers launched a first wave of 183 aircraft composed mainly of dive bombers, horizontal bombers and fighters.

The Japanese struck American ships and military installations at 751 in the morning. The first wave attacked the airfields of Ford Island. At 830 a second wave of 170 Japanese aircraft, mostly torpedo bombers, attacked the fleet anchored in

Pearl Harbor. The battleship Arizona was hit with an armor piercing bomb which penetrated the forward ammunition compartment, blowing the ship apart and sinking it within seconds, killing 1177 crew members.

The overall death toll was 2467. Five United States battleships were sunk and the other remaining three were severely damaged. Overall, nine ships of the US fleet were sunk, and 21 ships were severely damaged. Three of the 21 were not repairable. 188 US aircraft were destroyed, and 159 others were damaged. Japan only lost 29 out of the 353 aircraft they used in the attack.

Ashley was surprised how much of the history she remembered. Then her mind stopped wandering and she began to think about the new apartment she was about to be introduced to.

She left the submarine at about 915 in the morning and began her walk down the peer. She had called Uber and knew they would be waiting for her just outside the gate.

The ride to her apartment took about 10 minutes. She thanked her Uber driver and headed up the stairs to Mr. Piedmont's apartment. She rang the bell and he answered immediately.

"Hi Mr. Piedmont."

"Hey Ash, it's good to see you and to have you back on dry land, safe and sound. Are you ready to see your new place?"

"I can't wait."

"Then let me grab your key and I will show it to you."

They walked down the outside walkway past her old unit until they reached the end of the building. No need to turn the corner because the front door faced directly out to the boat Harbor. Mr. Piedmont put the key in the lock and opened the door for her.

"Welcome home, Captain." He said.

Ash walked in and could not believe her eyes. The living room was twice as big as her studio apartment and there was a deck off the kitchen that looked directly out to the boat Harbor. The deck was also twice as large as the one she had before. The kitchen was great and much larger than her studio apartment one was. The place was furnished nicely and the things she had in her old living room were also added to this one.

One of the doors in the living room was open and she could see that it led into the bathroom.

The bathroom was a full bathroom with a tub and shower combination and double sinks. There was a second door leading out of the bathroom which she opened, and it led into her one-bedroom.

The configuration was perfect. Guests could use the bathroom from the living room without going through her bedroom and she would have direct access from the bathroom to her bedroom.

She walked into the bedroom. It had several windows and a lot of natural light. The windows along the wall provided a perfect view down Waikiki Beach.

"Mr. Piedmont, this place is perfect. I can't thank you enough for thinking of me and for giving me the opportunity to live here."

"Ash, I assume that means you like it. Correct?"

"Are you kidding me, I love it! Thank you so much."

"You are more than welcome Ash. I am happy you like it and I like having you around. Here is the key, make yourself at home and let me know if you need anything."

"Will do, sir."

Mr. Piedmont left and headed for his own unit. Ash just stood in the middle of the living room with a big smile on her face.

Ash grabbed a pen and paper and began in the kitchen. She made a list of everything she thought she would need to both furnish it and have the basics she would need for cooking. Then it was on to the living room, bathroom and bedroom. Last was the deck where she added three items to her list. They were two comfortable outdoor chairs, a small table, and a gas Weber barbecue.

Her plan was simple. Spend the afternoon at the shopping center. Finish furnishing the apartment and go to bed early.

The next day she planned to spend the entire day on the beach working on her tan. She wanted to take her mind off Mark and decided that there was nothing she could do about his replacement, so she was just going to roll with whatever happened.

0800 UNITED STATES NAVAL ACADEMY

SEAL TEAM OFFICE

Roscoe opened the door to his office and was greeted by his assistant Sonny Miller. "Good morning, Ms. Miller, how was your weekend?"

"To be honest sir, it was just great until I walked into the office this morning."

"Why Sonny? What's wrong?"

"I put a package from SEAL Team Headquarters on your desk. I opened it and put it in your reading folder. It will probably please you, but it didn't please me."

"Well, let's see what's bugging you."

Roscoe walked into his office and picked up the reading folder that was placed in the middle of his desk. Facing him on top of the pile where his new orders to take command of SEAL Team 1 in Pearl Harbor, Hawaii. He could not believe his eyes. He had heard about Mark's death but orders to replace him came as a total shock.

"Okay, Sonny, I'm starting to get the picture."

"Well, boss, your one-of-a-kind and I am selfish, and I just don't want to lose you. I know it's what happens in the Navy but just for this one morning I'm going to be a moody bitch and I hope you understand why."

"I understand, Sonny. I will miss you as well."

The phone rang and Sonny picked it up. "SEAL Team office. Sonny speaking. How may I help you?"

"Hi Sonny, this is Juan Sanchez is the boss around?"

"Sure, let me get him for you."

"Sir, Sergeant Sanchez is on the phone for you."

"Hi Juan, what's up?" Well, I should ask you the same thing. I tried on my bathing suit and it does not fit as well as it once did. I guess I need to buy a new one for Hawaii."

"You're kidding me; did you get orders to go as well?"

"Guess they think we make a good team and didn't want to split us up."

"We'll all be damned. We have been at this together for the past five years and I was wondering how much longer it would be before something came up. I guess with Mark's death they felt it would be right for us. My guess is that they also had Ashley in mind and felt that we might make the transition easier for her."

"I didn't even think about that, but you could be right. This is going to be an interesting assignment."

"My orders say we must report by the end of the month. That gives us about three weeks to get our act together. My orders have me heading out via SEAL Team Headquarters. They want me there to do some orientation so it looks like we will meet in Pearl Harbor at the end of September."

ALA MONA CENTER
HONOLULU

Ashley spent the rest of her day shopping at Ala Mona Center. By 6 PM she had everything on her list and was back in her apartment. To complete her list, she needed to go to the local Ace Hardware which she decided to do immediately. She needed to furnish her new deck. She took off and found the Ace Hardware. It was only a couple of blocks from the Ala Mona Center. She found just what she wanted at the store and the guys from the store said they would deliver the barbecue and chairs the next day and set them up for her.

Ashley arranged with the guys from the Ace Hardware to notify Mr. Piedmont when they arrived, and he would let them in to do the assembly.

She did not have the energy to fix dinner, so she stopped at the Makai market food court and picked up some sushi at the Honolulu Sushi Company. Ashley ordered a few of her favorite items to go which included a spicy tuna roll, one order of crab, one order of cooked shrimp and for a vegetable she chose an order of edamame.

She still had a bottle of Oregon Pinot Gris in her refrigerator and it had been moved over by the cleaning staff when they moved her, so she was all set. She dumped all her household purchases in the middle of the living room. Opened the refrigerator and took out the bottle of ice-cold Pinot Gris. She took one of her kitchen chairs out to her new deck along with her takeout and sat with her wine and dinner looking at the yachts in the harbor. It was a beautiful evening and she could tell she would have many more of them in this place. She hoped that many of them would be with Ryan. In fact, she could not wait to show it to him. He would be home at the end of next week, so she was already looking forward to next weekend.

For the next hour she just sat and had her wine. She really did not think much about Mark, but she did think about how he had impacted her career and for that she would always be grateful. She did think about who might replace him and she hoped that it would be someone she could relate to.

She slept great that night and headed for the beach early the next day. She would plan to be home by midafternoon to unpack and then would be back on board ship the next morning by 0800.

CHAPTER 16
THE REUNION

Ashley spent the day at the beach. It was about 88° and perfectly clear. Waikiki Beach is Hawaiian for sprouting water. It is host to more than 4 million visitors each year. It is 2 miles long and the sand is as white as it gets. The two-mile stretch is full of hotels, restaurants, bars and shops. The place contains something for every tourist desire.

Ash just laid on her towel in the sand and watched people. Part of the time she slept, part of the time she just looked up at the sky, and part of the time she thought about two guys. Mark, who was now gone from her life and Ryan who was rapidly becoming a much bigger part of it.

The day was a lazy day and she enjoyed every minute of it. She headed back to her new apartment about three in the afternoon. Her goal was to finish her unpacking, have a light dinner and go to bed early. She needed to be back on the ship by 0800 so she would be up early and gone.

When she got back the first thing, she noticed was the new Weber gas grill on her deck and the two comfortable deck chairs with a small table in between. The Weber that had been set up as planned and the chairs and table fit perfectly.

She changed out of her suit and into a pair of cutoff jeans and an exceptionally light top. For dinner she planned to eat the leftover sushi she had from the night before, so she was not worried about fixing dinner. She had another bottle of Oregon Pinot Gris in the refrigerator, so she was all set.

By 630 she had all her purchases put away and she poured a glass of wine and headed for one of her new deck chairs that looked directly out at the boat harbor. The temperature was perfect, and she was totally relaxed.

She poured a second glass of wine and grabbed her leftover sushi and returned to her deck chair.

She finished her meal and watched the sunset as she finished the bottle of wine. It had been a good day and she was happy that her mind was slowly returning to normal and pushing Mark further and further back in her memory.

She was up early and headed back to the base. She was in her stateroom by 0730. She was surprised to find a message in the middle of her desk. It was dated this date at 7 AM. The message was from Admiral Ralph Omark, US Special Operations Command.

Ashley could not believe her eyes. Admiral Ralph Omark was the head of the Navy Special Operations Command. He was the first Navy SEAL to ever be appointed to a four-star flag rank and he ran SEAL operations from the base in San Diego.

The note on the message was clear. Please call as soon as possible.

Ashley sat down at her desk and took a deep breath and then she dialed the number.

"Hello, you have reached the US Special Operations Command, Admiral Omark's office. May I help you?"

"Hello, my name is Captain Ashley Jamison. I am the AIOC of Navy SEAL Team 1 located in Pearl Harbor Hawaii. I received a message this morning to call Admiral Omark as soon as possible."

"Yes Captain, Admiral Omark is expecting your call. Please hold and I will put him on the line."

"Thank you."

Within a minute a voice on the other end of the line said "Good morning, Captain Jamison. This is Ralph Omark."

"We have never met but I can guarantee you that I know more about you than you do about me. You have made me and our entire SEAL team immensely proud on more than one occasion."

"Thank you, sir. How can I help you?"

"Well there are two items I would like to cover with you this morning. The first is regarding Mark Price. We were shocked and very saddened by Mark's death. He was an exceptionally good man, an outstanding SEAL and a real leader. He was also a huge supporter of you and thought the world of your abilities. I want to take this opportunity to thank you for the actions you took to get him back on board the submarine after his major heart attack. It is my understanding; you were with him testing the new underwater vehicle when he was struck by the heart attack. I understand that when it happened, he fell forward on the driving control panel. This resulted in the vehicle taking a nosedive into the Miles trench which I know is over 2000 feet deep."

"I also understand that you were able to take control of the vehicle, level her out at over 450 feet and return it to the submarine with all your men. That, sir, was a significant performance and one that not only saved the lives of the number of Navy SEALs but also saved the Navy the cost of the new vehicle."

"We are very grateful for your effort and I wanted to let you know personally that it is been noted in your file."

"Second, I have a surprise for you and one that I think you're going to like. I want you to know who we have selected to replace Mark and Chief Johnson."

"Yes, sir, that is of great interest to me."

"Well, Ashley, your new boss is going to be none other than Lieutenant Commander Roscoe Cook. As a bonus, we are replacing Chief Johnson with your friend and mentor Gunny Sergeant Juan Sanchez."

"Wow sir, that is absolutely great news. I have so much respect for them and they are two of the reasons that I now proudly wear the Navy SEAL Trident."

"Yes, Captain, I am aware of your list of supporters and they, like Mark, are at the top of the list. Well I have some work to do now so I will leave you in Hawaii to work on your tan. Cheers Captain."

The phone went dead, and Ashley just sat at her desk with a huge smile on her face.

She then picked up the phone and called Chief Johnson.

"Chief Johnson, speaking."

"Hi Chief it's Ashley." "What's up boss?"

"Well, this is been quite a morning so far. I just got off the phone with Admiral Omark at Navy Special Operations Command."

"Wow, that's the big boss. What did he want?"

"Well he said some nice things about Mark and thanked us for getting him back to the ship and for not losing the new vehicle in the process. He also wanted to inform me who they have decided will replace both you and Mark."

"Now that is some news I would like to learn."

"I'm going to tell you and all of the team this morning. Would you please call a meeting of our team for 11 o'clock? Participation is mandatory."

"I'll do it. Are you going to spill the beans to me before the meeting?"

"Yes, the new replacements are extremely high on my list. They are both coming to us from the YARD"

"Mark will be replaced by Lieutenant Roscoe Cook and you will be replaced by Gunny Sergeant Juan Sanchez. I also think this will be a good time to let the gang know that you are going to retire at the end of October. Are you okay with that?"

"Now that is really good news. Both of those guys are well known and very experienced. They have also been a team for some time and know each other very well. I have met both and have a high degree of respect for them. I agree that we should tell them about me. In fact, it will be a relief for me. I will get the meeting set up and will not say a thing."

"Thanks Chief. I'll see you at 11 AM."

1100
SEAL TEAM CONFERENCE ROOM

Ashley arrived at the conference room at 1055. She was not surprised to find everyone present and already seated. She took her place at the head of the table and addressed the group.

"Good morning guys. Thank you for coming on such short notice. I talked with Chief Johnson this morning and he agreed that a communication meeting was important given the news we have to pass on to you."

"This morning I received a call from Admiral Ralph Omark. As all of you know he oversees our naval SEAL command. The purpose of his call was to let me know who SEAL command has chosen to replace Mark. I also wanted to let you know that my pal and one of my mentors, Chief Johnson has fallen in love and has decided to retire at the end of October."

Everyone looked at the Chief and started to ask him questions. "What's this about love, Chief?"

The Chief then said, "Okay, what Ash said is true. I'm going to get married in October to the retired schoolteacher I have been seeing for the past three years."

"A number of you have met her but for those of you who have not, her name is Sarah Miles. This October I will complete my 27th year with the Navy and it is finally time for me to hang it up. As Ash said to me recently, 27 years as a Navy SEAL is probably the equivalent of about 50 years in the regular Navy."

The entire group started to laugh and suddenly the group began to sing "for he's a Jolly good fellow."

Once the group settled down, Ash took control of the meeting again. "Okay so who's going to replace Mark and now Chief Johnson? Well, I am happy to tell you that I know both replacements very well and both have played a real role in my journey to becoming a Navy SEAL. The two are Lieutenant Commander Roscoe Cook and Gunny Sergeant Juan Sanchez. Both are very experienced Navy SEALs, and both have a real record of working together for a long time."

"Both are currently stationed at the United States Naval Academy where they have been in charge of SEAL recruiting and selection for the past five years. Before the YARD they were operational SEALs, and both have been through many years of SEAL operations."

"I am told that they will report by the end of September and so they will overlap with Chief for about a month before our next deployment. This will allow for a seamless transition."

"You should also be aware that Mark and Roscoe were very close, and both went through SEAL training together."

"I got to know both Roscoe and Juan from the moment I entered the Naval Academy. Both played a real role in coaching me towards the goal of becoming a Navy SEAL. I have complete respect for both, and I know that you are going to be happy to have them as a key part of our team."

"I also am happy to tell you that I have agreed to stand in for Mark as the "Best Man" at the Chief's wedding."

"I'm not sure if a woman has ever played that role but I dare anyone to challenge me as I fill out that role and the responsibilities that go with it."

The entire room broke out in laughter.

"I'm not sure about this but I think I am correct in saying that we will remain in port during the months of September and October. We will not conduct further test with the new vehicle until Roscoe and Juan are in place."

"I will tell you, as you know, we had that baby down to over 450 feet which SEAL command was most interested in. They obviously didn't like the reason we went that deep, but they were happy to know that the vehicle made the journey safely."

"I should also mention that the Admiral was very complimentary of those of you who helped get Mark back on board and the new vehicle back in place."

"I talked to Captain Miles and he told me that he will be taking the sub back out a couple of times during the remainder of September and October. We will not go on those missions due to our upcoming change in command. So, when the sub is out to sea you will have the opportunity to take a few days off. I will let you know as soon as I do know when those dates have been set."

"I checked on Jonnie on our return. He is doing well with no signs of infection. I am told that he will be released from the hospital next week and that he will begin his rehabilitation at the physical therapy facility on base. If you have not had time to see him, you might want to check in with him this week. As you know, once this rehab is completed, he will be leaving the Navy, so his time is running out."

"Are there any questions or do any of you have any objection to me standing up as the Chief's best man?"

The group just laughed. "Okay then, you're dismissed."

Everyone gathered around the chief with a lot of congratulations.

CHAPTER 17
HOOK SKIP BOLTER

Ryan had completed his inspection by 1815 so he was in the pilot seat of the Super Hornet when Reggie arrived to board at 1830. Once he was settled in Reggie gave Ryan the okay to begin the flight process. Ryan had already completed the preflight checks before Reggie was on board. The live ammunition had been placed on the aircraft, so they were good to go.

The weather was miserable. It was raining hard and the wind was blowing across the deck. The crew moved the Super Hornet from the park position to the catapult ready position. The wings on the Super Hornet were spread while the blast defector rose from the flight deck.

The catapult hookup was accomplished, and the holdback bar was connected from the nose landing gear to the carrier deck.

Ryan and Reggie went into radio silence and Ryan prepared to launch. He received a signal to advance the throttles to full power and took his feet off the brakes. One last check of the instrument panel let him know all was good and ready to go. He saluted the catapult officer and waited as the catapult officer made a final check of the settings and then Ryan watched as the catapult officer gave the signal to launch and the super hornet accelerated from zero to about 150 knots in less than two seconds.

Visibility was terrible so Ryan flew totally by instruments. He was soon at the altitude and heading that Reggie had given him. They were now positioned to watch on radar as the three squadron of six aircraft each took flight.

The sea was much rougher than it had been. Normally because of the size of the carrier the ship did not pitch or roll but the sea was rough, and the ship was pitching with slight rolls which Ryan knew would make the landings on return even more difficult.

The three squads formed up and they all followed Ryan toward the bombing target they had been to on the daylight runs. Flying at night is vastly different especially when the cloud layers keep getting in the way of visibility. The squad stayed together, and Reggie was pleased with the launch.

It took about three hours to reach the target island. Reggie and Ryan made the first bombing run which he did with no problems. Visibility was much better at the target location so while they were still flying on instruments and using their radar control systems to align with the targets it was easier than it would have been with no visibility at all. The stars were out so the island profile was easy to see.

Reggie evaluated each pilot and their bomb drop performance. For the most part he was pleased. Everything went well and the planes lined up and hit the target in sequence with precise accuracy.

Each squad lined up in a conga line and each pilot could see the night lights blinking softly against the backdrop of darkness. Ryan knew that this was lucky because on return if the weather had not improved the layers of clouds would impair the vision the pilots would have and make their landings difficult even with full instrument help difficult. It would take all their skill and attention to land safely.

At 10 miles out Reggie gave the word to each quadrant head to line them up and to descend to 1200 feet. He reversed the order from takeoff, so the last aircraft to depart the carrier would be the first to return. By doing this, he kept Ryan in the air until everyone else had landed. This provided Reggie the opportunity to evaluate each pilot.

Reggie notified each squad that at 8 miles out he wanted each aircraft pilot to change into landing configuration.

The landing configuration required that landing gear and flats come down along with the arresting book. Pilots were taught and each did so by double checking all their instrument settings and fuel state. It is important to note that when a Hornet is 6 miles from the aircraft carrier it means that they will be making their first pass at the carrier within two minutes.

Reggie had each squad increase the distance between planes. He wanted extra time given to landing in the bad conditions.

He asked Ryan to leave the formation and take a pass so he can see what the conditions were at the carrier level. He notified AIROPS that they would make a pass to check out conditions before allowing the first of the three squads to begin the landing process.

It was clear to Ryan and to Reggie that this night would not be an easy night to land. The carrier was pitching up and down in the rough seas. Reggie asked AIROPs if they had a tanker up. He received an affirmative to his question.

Reggie and Ryan knew that in the case of a Bolter that fuel would become especially important and if you missed a second time you would need fuel before coming in.

On the carrier, AIROPS had become an intense place. Luckily, the Captain of the carrier was able to keep the ship moving directly into the wind and did not need to change course to find the proper wind conditions. Simply stated the planes cannot land if the ship is turning.

The landing signal officers were in place and ready to wave off any aircraft if for some reason or another they had a safety concern.

At three miles from the ship each plane picked up the instrument landing system ILS or as it is referred to by the pilots as the bull's-eye. This is an aircraft system that receives glide scope, azimuth and elevation signals that are converted into fly to indications on the pilot's display. There is a second system called the ACLS or automatic carrier landing system that locks onto the aircraft and provides similar information.

The main difference between the two systems is that the ACLS is a two-way communication from the ship to the aircraft and back while the ILS is only a one-way communication ship to the aircraft. The ACLS is more accurate and thus is relied on more by the pilots.

Both the CLS and the ILS are used in conjunction to place the pilot in his plane in a good start position meaning on centerline, intercepting the glide scope at approximately three quarters of a mile behind the ship at 360 feet above the water with a 650 to 750 feet per minute rate of dissent and a controlled speed.

The optimum rate of dissent will vary with the glide scope angle, approach speed and headwind component and timely corrections to the rate of dissent will be critical if a pilot is to catch the hook properly.

Each pilot knew that the runway in front of them was a moving target and thus a good start was a must. They would have little time to make corrections once they got closer to the ship. At three quarters of a mile from the ship, CATCC hands off control of the aircraft to the landing signal officers.

As the first of the squadron aircraft made their approach Reggie listened as the CATCC said "101 on course, on glide path, three-quarter mile call the ball."

The first pilot responded "101 hornet ball, 5 you're a little high."

"Roger, adjustment made."

The carrier was pitching when the first aircraft arrived but as the plane came in and the pilot gave it full acceleration the hook caught the number three line in the plane was down safely.

The landings continued without a problem until the last plane in the second flight was due to land. Just as the pilot was about to set down on the deck the carrier pitched in the rough sea and suddenly the pilot was looking directly at the end of the carrier with no landing deck insight.

The stem of the ship had pitched up and remained at its highest point for about a second before it sank back down to normal level. The pilot went to full throttle and heard a slight ping sound but felt no change in speed. He had missed the arresting wire. Suddenly over the radio the LSO said "Bolter, Bolter, Bolter. Hook skip Bolter."

The hook had bounced over the arresting wires and as a result the pilot would have to move to Bolter position and check his gas before getting a second shot at the landing.

Reggie watched until all aircraft except the Bolter were safely down and then he directed the Bolter to assume landing position. The second attempt went well and then it was Ryan's turn.

The weather had done nothing but get worse and the crosswind was horrible. Ryan, however, was a steady and unnerved by the situation as anyone could be.

He positioned the Super Hornet and had a good start. From this position there was only about 20 seconds to go to touchdown. The ship had very few lights on it, just a small outline of a box in the landing area and a few lights off to the starboard side near the tower. Darkness was the theme; Ryan stayed focused on the ball and listened to the LSO give him the power call. He adjusted his throttles and found an angle of attack to keep the aircraft just above the glide scope. Precision is the master key to success, and it could have been Ryan's middle name. As his plane approached final touchdown things started to move faster in his brain and he had a feeling that seemed to almost take over all his senses. The plane descended over the stern of the ship and down into the landing area. At the moment of touchdown, he could feel the landing gear thud into the carrier deck. His throttles were full military power and then the hook caught, and he put the baby down on the third wire. "Perfect unquote is all Reggie said.

The two-plane guard guided missile destroyers were really bouncing around. Ryan could only imagine what it must be like to be on one of those in a storm like this. Must be like riding on a toothpick in a toilet that has been flushed. No thanks he thought.

Ryan then retracted the arresting hook and flaps and taxied out of the landing area to the spot he had been directed to. He never tired of the feeling he got from a good landing. The aircraft tugs on the wire and pulls it out like a rubber band, bringing the pilots to a violent but very welcome stop. Initial feeling was always a sense of relief, but it was always followed by a sense of pride in what you have just accomplished.

He stepped down from the plane and for the first time felt the power of the wind and the rain. It was a terrible night for flying and he was happy now to be home and headed for the state room. It was 02:30 in the morning.

He walked into his room only to find his roommate sound asleep. He dropped his clothes in place and crawled into bed with his boxers on. His thoughts were with him for about a minute before he was sound asleep. But for that one minute he thought only about one thing, Ashley.

Ryan was awake by 9 AM. He dressed and headed to the Wardroom for breakfast. When he arrived, he saw that Reggie was talking with his roommate commander Carl Goodwin.

"Hey Ryan, nice job last night. I think you know my pal, Carl Goodwin."

"Yes sir, I know commander Goodwin, but I have never had the pleasure of flying with him. Good morning, sir."

"Ryan, Carl and I have decided to cancel today's flight operations. We talked to the Captain and learned that this weather increases our risk and as such we think we will hold off for a day. Would you please inform our squad commanders that they have the day off and we will reevaluate tomorrow?"

"Yes, sir. That should be a relief to many of them."

After breakfast, Ryan returned to his room and let his squad commanders know that today was a day off and the flight schedule for tomorrow would be determined based on the weather. The next day turned out to be clear and the seas were calm. There was wind and there was enough to fly so both the day and the night operations went on as scheduled with no problems for either of them.

Reggie and Ryan did run into one problem with one plane who bolted and had to refuel at night which turned out to be a new experience for the pilot and not an easy procedure.

The pilot who missed the hook had moved into the bolting position, but his fuel was running low. He was told to fly the wave off bolter pattern until he received a vector to the tanker. The weather was still an issue, so the tanker had to fly above the cloud cover to find clear air. It made it more difficult for the pilot to find the tanker.

He spotted the flashing lights of the tanker and switched to the tanker common frequency. He extended his aircraft refueling probe out to meet the hose and basket that the tanker had displayed. The basket was now just 5 feet from the nose of his jet, but the strong winds were creating turbulence that had everything bouncing around. The probe caught the side of the basket which caused a miss on the first attempt. The second attempt was a success and the green light illuminated which indicated that he was now getting the fuel he needed.

Once he had enough fuel, he returned to the bolting pattern and landed safely.

The mission was completed, and the carrier headed for Pearl Harbor. It was Thursday and they would be tied up to the peer by noon on Friday. Ryan was like a kid in a candy store. All he could think about was an open weekend with Ashley.

CHAPTER 18
SECRET PLANS FOR MAJOR DISRUPTION

PYONGYANG, NORTH KOREA
KUMSUSAN PALACE OF THE SUN

Kim Jong-un sat in his office at the Kumsusan Palace of the Sun. It was a warm day in the spring. His secretary buzzed him. "Yes Chloe, what is it?"

"General Fong Ho is here to see you, sir."

"Please show him and Chloe."

"Good morning, Supreme Leader."

"Good morning, Ho, how is our special project coming along?"

"Well sir that is the purpose of my visit. I wanted to give you an update on project V. It was almost 3 years ago when we kidnapped three chemical scientists from China. We took them from three different areas in China and we did not take them all at once. They simply disappeared one by one. To my knowledge, China has not yet figured out what happened to the three and with all the problems they currently have with the Coronavirus their focus has been on many other things. The three scientist's disappearance seems to have been placed on the back burner. The onslaught of problems with the Coronavirus worldwide has only helped us with our cause."

"Our secret facility in Haeju has provided the Chinese scientists with all of the resources they need to both educate and work with our best chemical experts in the quest to develop a virus we can release and control as desired. The Coronavirus outbreak has given our scientist much needed information on how best to target and control a virus for use against our enemies."

"The three scientists were unwilling to provide us with assistance in the beginning. But, over time we have managed to bring them into the fold. The six women we selected to provide them with pleasure services have done their jobs and each scientist has now realized that they have never had it so good. We are housing the three Chinese scientists along with our own six scientists and the six ladies on a barge in the middle of Haeju Bay."

"We not only provide them with an excellent place to work, the best Korean food and drink, and an excellent living space, but they have more sex than they might have had in an entire lifetime."

"What progress are you making on the development of the specific virus desired?"

"We have isolated a virus that we call "VIPER". The "VIPER" appears to have the power to immediately kill those infected. We are now working on how to control it. Our goal is to develop it so it can be specifically targeted to either an individual person or an entire population. We are also working on how it can best be delivered.

Coronavirus is an example of what we do not want it to do. Coronavirus is out of control and even our experts are uncertain how it is being spread."

Haeju is the perfect location for our research facility. It is in South Hwanghae Province right on Haeju Bay. The population of Haeju is now about 273,300 and I can guarantee you that no one in that town has any idea where our facility is located. Haeju is a strategic port and has several chemical-related enterprises. As such, we were able to redirect the services of some of our best chemical experts to work on project the."

"The port of Haeju provides us with the opportunity to replenish our facility needs from the sea rather than risking the chance of being noticed by a land operation. The port is small, but the channel is 25 to 50 feet deep so our supply ships can anchor in 21 to 25 feet of water. It is also to our advantage that the port is the only port on the West Coast of North Korea that does not freeze over in the winter."

"We were careful to select only scientists who were not married and did not have families. They were all volunteers and they all receive the same benefits as the three Chinese. As such, our volunteers are incredibly happy and very satisfied."

"Our facility was built on and in an old dock building. From the outside it looks like it has never been in use. On the inside it is as modern as one can build, and the facility is rated as excellent by our scientists. It is self-contained. Our staff and scientists are all housed off the property on a large barge. All their needs are met so they have no need to leave the facility when they are working. We have a state-of-the-art security system surrounding both the research facility and the barge. Our security system uses both electronic and manpower. So, we have actual guards stationed 24 hours per day both at the research facility and on the barge."

"So, to summarize, our project continues. We are working as fast as we can, but we still have a lot of work to do with control and delivery. My estimate is within one year we will have a new weapon that the world is not ready for. So, my report this morning is to inform you that we are well on our way to our goal."

"Thank you, General Ho. I am pleased with your report. I look forward to your updates in the future. You are dismissed."

"Thank you, Supreme leader."

NAVY SEAL SPECIAL OPERATIONS COMMAND
SAN DIEGO, CALIFORNIA

Roscoe's plane arrived on time at San Diego international Airport. He carried only an overnight bag as he had arranged to have all his personal things sent directly from the YARD to his new station in Pearl Harbor, Hawaii.

He grabbed a cab from the airport and directed the driver to the US Special Operations Command Center at the Naval Amphibious Base on Coronado Island.

Once there he paid the driver and headed for the US Special Operations Command Office of Admiral Ralph Omark.

He found the office easily as he had been to it on several occasions in the past. He was a bit surprised that he was asked to come to the office in San Diego before reporting for duty in Hawaii, but he did not think much about it. He knew Admiral Omark well and he always enjoyed being with him.

He walked in and was greeted by an attractive woman sitting behind a huge desk. He looked at her and said, "Good morning. My name is Lieutenant Commander Roscoe Cook. I have orders to go to Pearl Harbor, Hawaii to take command of SEAL delivery team 1 but I was asked to stop by headquarters in route to meet with Admiral Omark."

"Good morning, Commander, Admiral Omark is expecting you. I will let him know that you have arrived."

"Thank you."

A few moments later the door opened, and Admiral Ralph Omark appeared. He had a huge smile on his face and he warmly greeted Roscoe.

"Roscoe, how the heck are you?"

"I am fine sir and I must say you are looking well."

"Thanks, but I feel fat and get little exercise in this job. I think it is the easiest job a SEAL could ever have. I assume you have met my assistant, Ms. Marcia Abelson. I think if they would ever let me out of this desk job that she could replace me. She is simply the best and I view her as a real talent."

"Why thank you, sir."

"Come on in, Roscoe, I have a number of things I want to discuss with you. Marcia, please hold my calls for the next hour."

"Yes sir."

"Well Roscoe, I want you to know that I feel the loss of Mark deeply."

"He was a great guy and his death took us all by surprise. I know you were close to him and that it must have hit you hard as well."

"Yes sir. Mark and I went through all our SEAL training together. He was a great friend and a real SEAL brother. He will be missed by me and many others I'm sure."

"I know that the two of you both thought that Ashley Jamison was something special and as it turns out you were right. I still kick myself in the butt and a few others here do as well when we could not make up our mind on whether she or for that matter any woman could meet the challenge of the SEAL program. Not only did she do it, but she exceeded beyond everyone's expectations. I know that Sergeant Reichardt and a few others around here who tried to test her to the limit are in total admiration of her abilities."

"So, when Mark passed away it was not hard for us to determine that you would be the logical replacement. We also were unaware that his Chief, Chief Johnson was ready to retire. Once we learned that, it allowed us the opportunity to fill his spot with Juan Sanchez and keep the two of you together."

"Thank you, sir. Yes, I hold Ashley in high regard and so does Gunny Sanchez. We watched her from the summer of her first year in the YARD until she graduated. Not only was she at the top of her class in almost everything but she also went on to become an NCAA and Olympic swimming champion representing the United States Navy."

"You are so right, Roscoe. It takes a lot to admit we were wrong but in Ashley's case we were. Since she has been in the field, she is also excelled on several occasions and we know that her men think she is one hell of a leader. What you may not have known is when Mark had his heart attack he died instantly and collapsed on the control panel of the minisub. Ashley was able to get him off the controls and stabilize the thing while it was slowly descending into a trench that dropped 2000 feet."

"She stabilized the thing at 450 feet and resurfaced it with Mark. No easy feat and it also proved that the new vehicle can go as deep as 450 feet which is 200 feet deeper than it has ever been tested."

"I did not know that sir. I had heard from Mark about the rescue of the Chinese freighter sailors and the shark attack, but I did not know about the deep dive problem."

"That brings me to the reason I wanted you to drop by on your way out to Hawaii. You are scheduled to deploy to the South China Sea in a couple of months. Your team has been training in the new drive vehicle and has been working at 200-foot depths. At this point, I cannot tell you much, but I can tell you that you may have a mission ahead of you that will require the deep-water skills and the drive vehicle. I can also tell you that if the intelligence I have received is correct you in all probability will have one major task ahead of you."

"I don't know much about it yet but the information I have received and I'm about to tell you, is top-secret and for your ears only. It is not to be shared with anyone until authorized. Do you understand?"

"Yes sir. I understand."

"Well then, here is what I know. Our South Korean intelligence folks believe that our friend Kim Jong-un is up to no good again. We believe that he has set up a very secret research facility in a small North Korean port by the name of Haeju. We are not sure yet, but we think the scientists at the facility are focused on the development of a new virus that can be used as a weapon. The widespread fear associated with Coronavirus has only increased our interest in what he is up to."

"The Port of Haeju goes back to the Neolithic period. The waterway is fed by the Yellow Sea which is an inlet of the Pacific Ocean that lies between mainland China and the Korean Peninsula."

"If this turns out to be real then my guess is the research facility will become a SEAL target and will require all of our skills to deal with it. I will keep you informed but for now I would only advise that you continue to work with the new vehicle and practice deep diving."

"If I am right, a mission like this could involve the submarine letting you out in deep water and then using the dry delivery vehicle to move up and into the mouth of the Bay of Haeju. The new vehicle is designed to get you into much shallower water than the old ones could. I have looked at the bay and the depth charts and it looks like we could have to operate in shallow water, about 25 feet deep."

"As I understand it, Ashley is also fluent in Chinese which could come in handy on this assignment. Very few people are aware of this, but about three years ago; three top chemical research scientists disappeared from mainland China. They were all located in different parts of the country and they all disappeared at different times. The Chinese were all over it and have yet to determine what happened to them."

"Our guess is they were kidnapped by the North Koreans and are being used to help develop this virus project. With the horrible problems associated with the Coronavirus, the Chinese have simply shifted priorities and stopped their search for now. So, this operation could also involve a rescue of sorts. At this point, I just don't know."

"So, Roscoe that is what I wanted you to know. Do you have any questions before you leave me and head out to Hawaii?"

"No sir. Juan and I are both looking forward to getting back out in the field, so I look very much forward to the challenges ahead of us thank you for the opportunity."

"My pleasure Roscoe and best of luck to you and all of your team."

"Thank you, sir."

With that Roscoe left the office. Said goodbye to Ms. Abelson and headed into San Diego. He planned to stay the night downtown and then get a flight out to Honolulu in the morning.

CHAPTER 19
GETTING TO KNOW YOU

It was Saturday morning. The sun was out, and the temperature was going to be 85 degrees. Ashley was up early and was on her second cup of coffee sitting out on her deck looking at the boat harbor when the phone rang.

"Hello this is Ashley speaking."

"Hey sunshine how would you like to go to the beach?"

"Ryan, you are back. It is so great to hear your voice. It is hard to believe that it has only been two weeks. You've been missed, big guy!"

"Ash, I've missed you as well. I am off for two days. What is your schedule?"

"Well, I'm off for three days and I have a lot to tell you. When can you come over?"

"Well if you put up with me, I can come over now."

"That would be great. I'm just sitting out here looking at the yacht harbor waiting for you."

"I'm on my way."

"Ryan, bring an overnight bag and come to unit 27 instead of my old place."

"Will do, see you soon."

Ashley went into her bedroom, made the bed and put her clothes away. Then it was into the bathroom for a quick shower. Once that was done, she put on a pair of cutoff jeans and a loose-fitting shirt and sandals. She did not wear a bra. She would never be known for having large breasts and she simply did not care. God gave her a swimmer body and it served her very well during her 20 plus years of life."

In about a half an hour there was a knock on her door. She looked through the security peephole and smiled as she looked at Ryan on the other side of the door.

She opened it and almost jumped into his arms. She was so excited to see him, she did not even notice that in one hand he had his overnight bag and in the other he held a bunch of flowers. She grabbed hold of him around the waist and gave him the longest kiss she had ever given anyone.

"Wow! All I can say is wow! That was the best kiss I have ever experienced. It is great to see you, Ash. How did you pull off this beautiful place? I happen to know what your rank is, so I know how much you make, and I know that it is not enough to afford this great place with a view to die for."

"Welcome home big guy. That is but one of the many stories I have to tell you. Two weeks feels like a lifetime has passed; a lot happened while you were playing in the clouds. Come on in and let me show you around." Ryan followed her in, set his bag down in the living room while Ashley took the flowers and put them in a vase in the kitchen.

"As you can see, we now have a living room that is large enough to sit in and entertain in. Off the living room is your space which as you can see has a new barbecue for you to learn to use and two chairs and a table for wine at sunset."

"Through that door is the bathroom which also connects to the bedroom. Follow me to the bedroom."

It was much larger than Ryan expected and had a full view right down Waikiki Beach. "So, what do you think?"

"I can't believe it. It is a perfect apartment and I hope you will have me over as a frequent guest."

"You can count on that big guy."

"So, Ash, without further ado, did you win the lottery or something while I was gone?"

"Nope, but I guess you could say that I have been incredibly lucky. You remember when that idiot broke into my studio apartment and made the mistake of trying to shoot me when he thought I was at the door. To his surprise he shot at a Honolulu police officer and ended up with a bullet in the stomach and the charge of attempted murder on a police officer which will put him away for a long time."

"The incident didn't bother me a bit, but I had to stay out of the unit for a couple of days for the crime scene to be cleared. During that time, the couple that rented this unit came to Mr. Piedmont and let him know that they had found a larger place and were going to move out right away. We will never know for sure, but we think that they were a bit freaked out by the shooting and that that was the straw that broke the camel's back."

"I got a call from Mr. Piedmont shortly after they gave notice. Mr. Piedmont said that he was sorry for all of the hassle that I have had to go through since those guys attacked me at the shopping center and then he asked me if I would like the larger unit at the same price I was paying for the studio. He also told me that I could have it with the same terms he had given me on the studio which means that he will sublet it for me when we deploy in a couple of months."

"What a sweet deal. This is a real find. Mr. Piedmont seems like a genuinely nice man and a fan of yours as well. In fact, I am sure that besides Mr. Piedmont there are a whole lot of women in Honolulu that are fans of yours. I'm also sure that there are four thugs that are very sorry they decided to pick on you."

"Thanks, Ryan, those are very nice words to hear."

"Where do you want me to put my stuff? Put it in the bedroom. I plan to kidnap you and make you stay in that room for hours while you're here."

Ryan returned. Ashley handed him a cup of coffee and they both headed out to the deck and sat in the new chairs looking out at the yacht harbor. When they were settled in Ash turned to Ryan and asked him how his two weeks at sea were.

"The weather was terrible. We had flights scheduled most days with live ammunition. The day sessions were fine but the night sessions in rough weather were a bit hairy. We also had several pilots on board that had not flown in conditions like we experienced which made our night operations difficult."

"I flew with Commander Reggie Sanders. He was one of the two flight commanders on board. All the pilots were evaluated by him. So, he rated each of them as they took off and landed and he rated them when they made their bombing and strafing runs on the target island. For the most part, the group did well. We had a couple of guys miss the wire on the night runs which can scare you a bit, but they recovered, and all went well."

"How did you get assigned to fly with the Commander?"

"Who knows? He sets the schedule and determines the flight pairings. Why he chose me I will never know. It did mean that I was always first to take off and last to land. Each mission was over four hours so there were some long days."

"Enough about me what else happened in your life last week?"

"It wasn't an easy couple of weeks. In fact, it was a horrible couple of weeks now that I think about it. The first and most important thing that happened was my boss Mark Price died of a heart attack. It happened on a deep dive with our new mini submarine. It now has been confirmed that it was a blockage of his widow maker artery and death was instant. It makes me sick to think about it. He simply slumped over the controls of the mini sub."

"The next thing I knew we were headed down when we were supposed to be going up. In fact, we were headed down a trench that drops off to more than 2000 feet in depth. I was able to get him off the controls, level the thing out at about 450 feet and bring it back up. It was not fun, and I am glad I'm here to tell you about it. The scariest part of it was the new mini sub had never been tested below 200 feet."

"My God, Ash, that is terrible. I feel so sorry for his family."

"That, at least, was the better news. Mark was a bachelor and had no family. His parents are still alive and live somewhere in the eastern United States. The entire event was a bummer and one that I will never forget. He was not only a great guy, but he was an extraordinarily strong supporter of me, and I learned so much from him."

Ryan finished his coffee and asked if he could have another cup which Ash got him immediately.

"After that story, I'm afraid to ask what else went on in your life."

"Well there is more to tell you, but I think I will hold off, so I have something to talk to you about at dinner. The thought of just sitting here staring at you dumbfounded with nothing to say scares the hell out of me."

Ryan just laughed, put his coffee cup down and gave her a noticeably big smile and an incredibly soft kiss on the lips.

"How did you say it? I think it went like this. WOW."

"So, we have the rest of the day ahead of us, what you want to do?" Ryan asked.

"I have food for dinner, and I hope you can figure out how to use that Weber over there. My thought is, we head to the beach. We can have lunch at a new place I found and then enjoy the sand and sun for a couple of hours before we head back here for dinner. After dinner, I plan to capture you and force you into isolation in the bedroom."

Ryan laughed, "speaking of isolation I guess this Coronavirus outbreak is really getting bad."

"Yes, it still hasn't had much of an impact here in Hawaii yet but from what I can gather from the news it is just a matter of time. This virus stuff gives me the creeps. They say that folks can carry it around and not even know they have it while they pass it on to others."

"So back to your original question. What do I have planned for the rest of today? Well I think we should change into her suits and beach tops and head down the path to Waikiki. I thought we can start the day with a lunch/brunch in the lobby of the Hilton Hotel. There is a restaurant on the lobby level that is called M.A.C 24 /7. It was voted the People's choice for the best breakfast on this island. I have my heart set on trying their stuffed French toast. It is filled with lemon cream cheese, strawberries, bananas and guava jam. Then it is topped with whipped cream. They also have something called Mochi pancakes which look something like you might like."

"After that it's off to the beach for a couple of hours in the sun and perhaps a dip or two in the ocean."

"Once we finished that, we will come back here for a shower and then it will be on to dinner. You have a major role to play with dinner. I got a half slab of baby back ribs and some bull's-eye barbecue sauce. You will need to cook them on low heat for about an hour basting them every 10 minutes. The ribs will go with the Caesar salad and a great Oregon Pinot Noir. The wine is from Dundee, Oregon and it is called Four Graces."

"Ash, that sounds like a very full day in a number of ways let's head for the beach I'm hungry."

They changed into their suits and put on beach shirts and headed for the Hilton. They were seated at a great table. It was not outside, but they had a view of the water.

The service was excellent. Ashley had the French toast. When she ordered it, she asked for the diet Hawaiian stuffed French toast. The young woman who waited on them wrote it down like she said it, then turned to her and said, "in your dreams, honey." They all laughed.

Ryan had the Mochi pancakes. They were huge and he could barely eat three of them. They both had a bloody marry and they left the restaurant feeling like to beached whales.

They found a great place on the beach, spread their towels next to each other and settled in for a rest in the sun. After two hours they were both up and, in the water, Ryan was just as amazed as he was when he saw her swim for the YARD. In the water Ashley was as close to a fish is a human could be. Ryan was a good athlete but next to Ashley he always felt like he was in second or third place. After about three hours they called it good and headed back to the apartment. It had been a great day for both. However, the night was still young and there was more to experience. It was on both of their minds as they picked up the trail that led to the apartment.

CHAPTER 20
AND THE BEAT GOES ON

Ashley and Ryan held hands as they worked their way up the path from Waikiki Beach to the apartment at Llikai Marina. The boat harbor was one of the largest small boat harbors in Hawaii. With the temperature around 85° and the sun starting to move down, the reflection off all the boats was really something to see.

On the way back to the apartment, Ashley told Ryan that she had a couple of additional stories that she wanted to share with him about her difficult week. She said they all have a happy ending but when you add them all together it was one hell of a week.

When they arrived at the apartment Ashley said to Ryan. "Ryan, you grab the shower first and then I will have you focus on the barbecue and your cooking skills."

"Will do." Ryan dropped his shirt and suit in the bedroom and turned on the shower. When the water was just at the right temperature he hopped in and let the water run over his head and shoulders and down onto the rest of his body.

He had his eyes closed and was thinking about the day and Ashley when the shower door opened and suddenly, he had company.

He opened his eyes to find a completely naked Ashley rubbing him down with a big bar soap.

"Wow, what a great surprise," he said. He could feel the excitement building quickly in his body.

"Well Ryan, you know me, where there is water you can find Ashley."

"Now that I know that, I may never get out of the shower again."

"He was hard as a rock by the time Ashley had soaked her way down to his legs."

"Looks like you're enjoying our shower, Ryan."

"Are you kidding me? I'm in heaven right now and I'm loving it."

They both laughed. Then Ashley said "don't get too excited. The best is yet to come. But now you're going to have to get out of the shower and start to focus on your task with our dinner."

"Do I really have to get out?"

"Yep, save your strength because you're going to need it later" Ash just giggled rinsed off and hopped out. She grabbed a towel and headed for the bedroom leaving Ryan standing in the shower with the water running down his body. The excitement he had just experienced disappeared like the water running down the drain.

Ashley put on a pair of short shorts and a loose top that left little to the imagination. With her short hair and always in the water lifestyle she never dried her hair. She felt great, slipped on her sandals, and headed for the kitchen.

Ryan smiled, grabbed a towel and headed for the bedroom. He grabbed a pair of shorts from his bag and an underarmor breathable T-shirt. He put his sandals on and then joined Ashley in the kitchen. He gave her a hug and an exceptionally soft kiss and said, "I think that was the best shower I have ever had. You are really something else."

"Thank you, sir I try my best. There is a cold can of bikini blonde lager in the refrigerator. I thought you might need a cold beer to help you learn how to use our Weber grill. The instruction book is on the counter. The side of ribs will take about an hour or perhaps a bit more so you should get started now."

"Thanks Ash, the beer sounds great. My folks had a Weber barbecue, so I think I am going to be up to the task. I will get started right away. Cheers."

Ryan grabbed the instruction manual and the beer and headed out to the deck. He really did not even need the manual. The guys from Ace Hardware put the thing together which was the hard part. He turned the gas on at the tank and then set the first of the three burners to start and push the button the grill suddenly came to life. He then turned on the second and finally the third burner. The grill worked perfectly. He let the grill heat up to 500 in order to ensure that the new grill grates were clean. He then reduced the heat to low on all three burners.

Once he had accomplished that he walked back into the kitchen and asked Ash for the half side of ribs and the bull's-eye barbecue sauce. He had finished his beer and put the bottle in the recycling bag and returned to the deck.

Ashley was busy in the kitchen. She had made up the Caesar salad but did not dress it. She wanted to ensure that it was not soggy when it was served. She had purchased a baguette of sour French bread from the store which she now removed from the bag and cut into inch slices all the way down the baguette. She then filled each cut with butter and garlic powder. When she had the loaf sliced and filled, she wrapped the loaf in tin foil and put it in the oven on low.

Next on the agenda was to open a Pinot Gris from Oregon and poor two glasses. Ashley selected and Eyrie vineyards Pinot Gris from Dundee Hills Oregon. She had not had it before but had read about it. It was dry and light and had the taste of pear and citrus, so it was perfect for a warm evening on the deck in Hawaii.

She carried the two glasses out to the deck and set them on the table. Ryan was doing as he was told. Every 10 minutes he was basting the ribs. He finished and sat down. Ashley lifted her glass to him and said, "To a great day and a great guy. Cheers."

Ryan said "cheers" and they touch their glasses. "Wow, this is really light and refreshing wine. What is it?"

"It is an Oregon Pinot Gris from Eyrie vineyards. They were one of the first vineyards in Oregon to begin producing a Pinot Gris. I have not had it before, but it got great reviews. How do your ribs look?"

"Not bad if I don't say so myself. I am doing what you said, and I am basting them every 10 minutes to make sure they stay moist. They should be done in about 45 minutes. Hey Ash, you mentioned that a couple of other things happened while I was gone. What were they?"

"Well both are positive. The first is that my Chief, Chief Johnson, announced that he is going to retire. That hit me by surprise. First Mark up and dies and then my right arm Chief Johnson announces he is retiring. It was a one-two punch. It so happens that the Chief got engaged just before we headed out to sea and he plans to retire before we head out on our deployment. He also asked Mark to be his best man at his wedding. Obviously, that cannot happen now so, to my surprise he asked me to be his best man at his wedding. Not sure if such a thing has ever happened before but I considered it quite an honor and agreed to stand up with him."

"Wow that is great. When is the wedding?"

"I am not sure, but it will happen before we deploy in November. I'm looking forward to it."

"What else happened, I think you said a couple of additional things?"

"You're right I saved the best for last. You remember when we were at the YARD that I had a couple of SEAL recruiters and trainers that kind of took me under their wing."

"Sure, I remember. We used to run into them at the gym from time to time. As I remember the officer was a full lieutenant. I think his name was Roscoe Cook."

"Great memory my dear. Roscoe was one of my strongest supporters and the one who gave me advice on how to get through SEAL training. His gunny Sergeant was Juan Sanchez. Juan was also a trainer and I always felt he kept an eye on me and was a strong supporter. I think both of those guys backed me with SEAL command when I had the opportunity to go to the Olympics."

"I know that SEAL command wasn't sure about a woman in the first place nor were they ready to give me a break on my start date. As it turned out Roscoe and Juan were right. The Navy benefited from my Olympic participation and the SEAL command was pretty proud when a woman successfully completed their program."

"Okay, so what does this have to do with last week?"

"Well a lot. Roscoe is about to become my new boss and Juan our new chief. I could not have been happier when I heard the news. In fact, I got a personal call from Admiral Omark himself. Admiral Omark is head of SEAL Operations Command in San Diego. He called me to thank me for my efforts with Mark and to let me know who would replace him."

"Ash, you got a call from the Admiral himself?"

"Yep, you're dating one hot mama!"

"I'll say. What a week you had."

Ryan put the last of the bull's-eye sauce on the ribs and they finished the bottle of wine. He let Ashley know that the ribs would be done in 10 minutes Ash set the little table on the deck and opened another bottle of wine.

The ribs turned out perfect and the salad was crisp. Ashley had dressed it lightly and then added croutons at the very end.

They ate their dinner, had their wine and enjoyed the sunset.

Ryan helped Ash with the dishes and then it was time for bed. Ashley told Ryan to get ready for bed and leave the side bed light on. She told him to get comfortable and that she would be in in a couple of minutes. Ryan had no problem getting ready for bed. He slept in his shorts, so he was ready in one minute.

He laid in bed thinking about Ashley, the day that they had had, and all the accomplishments Ashley had achieved. How could he be so lucky?

In a little over 10 minutes the door to the bathroom opened and out stepped Ashley. Ryan's eyes almost popped out of his head.

Ashley was wearing a fitted garter corset set that was purple. It was beautifully detailed in loose mesh. She had on a low-rise thong with it, along with thigh high stockings. The corset had a padded foam line plunge cup which provided Ashley with a lift making her boobs look twice as large as they really were. The back had adjustable stretch straps which gave her a customized fit. It had a hook and an eye back closure along with the side front and nonremovable garter straps that linked up with the long thigh-high stockings.

Ryan could not take his eyes off her. She was just beautiful and beyond anything he had ever wish for.

"Well what do you think?" "I think you are incredible. That is the sexiest outfit I have ever seen and on you it is perfect. I wish I had a picture of you to put in my wallet."

"No pictures please. Just enjoy the moment in memory."

With that she got in bed beside him. They made love three times that night and both were totally exhausted when they finally fell asleep.

They slept in until 8 AM. Ryan was first up and into the bathroom and out. He went to the kitchen and made a cup of coffee and headed out to the deck. It was going to be another warm day in Hawaii, and he wondered what Ash had planned.

In about a half hour Ashley left the bedroom. She had on cutoff jeans and an extra-large sweatshirt. She still looked beautiful but not in the same way as she had the night before.

"Good morning, sunshine. You were fantastic last night, and I want you to know I will never forget it. Can I get you a cup of coffee?"

"Yes, please, and I might add you weren't so bad yourself."

Ryan grabbed her a cup of coffee and they both sat there looking at the boat harbor. Some pleasure boats were already getting underway, but most were still moored and swayed gently in their respective slips. "What do you have planned for us today?" "I thought I would try something different if you're up for it". I found this tour that is called "Kevo's Beach Bus." It is a tour for those who do not like tours and says that it is designed to spend minimal time on the bus and maximum time off the bus. I am told we can catch it at the Ala Moana Center and then we can spend the rest of the afternoon doing whatever they have planned. The two guys who run it are named Bo and Daniel. I am told they are both funny and informative. What do you think?"

"I'm up for anything as long as it includes you."

"Okay then, let's have breakfast and head over to the shopping center. I'm told we can pay there, and they will return us to the shopping center when the day is over."

"Your wish is my command."

CHAPTER 21
TOGETHER AGAIN

Gunny Sergeant Juan Sanchez arrived at Honolulu international on a direct flight from Los Angeles. He had flown from Washington DC directly to Los Angeles on United and then boarded a red eye continuing flight to Honolulu International. It was 10 AM when he arrived, and the temperature was already 80°. What a difference from the cold, wet rain he left behind on the East Coast.

He wore his United States Marine Corps short sleeve dress khaki shirt with the Navy gold Triton pin over his left breast pocket. Below the pin were four rows of ribbons signifying the special operations he had participated in. He was super glad he had on the short sleeve shirt the minute he left the confines of the international airport. It was hot but it felt so good.

He caught a cab to Pearl Harbor and was let off at the active-duty service entrance. He had shipped his large duffel bag over earlier, so he carried only an overnight bag.

Once through the gate he asked for directions to SEAL delivery team 1 operations. He was given directions and headed to the building to report in for active duty. He was glad to be back with SEAL operations and away from the YARD and the business of recruiting. The assignment had been interesting, but he was an operations guy and he much preferred to be in the field and dodging bullets.

He arrived at the SEAL team facility and immediately saw a familiar face. "Well, I'll be damned if it isn't Master Chief Mike Johnson."

Chief Johnson saw him walk in and greeted him with a huge hug. "Great to see you Juan. You look good. Are you ready to get back at it?"

"I'm as ready as I'll ever be. Mike, you look great as well. I hear that you have made a big decision or rather I should say a couple of big decisions."

"Yes. Number one is I am retiring, and number two is I am getting married. It has been a great 27 years but now that I have met the right woman and Mark's past on, it's time for me to go."

"I understand. We were all sick when we heard of Mark's passing. He was a great guy and I know my boss thought of him almost as a brother. I guess I should ask you how's Ashley doing?"

"The woman is unbelievable. She is not only a skilled SEAL in every respect, but she has earned the respect of everyone in this unit including me as the AOIC. I cannot tell you the number of times she has impressed everyone. We are lucky to have her and I am sure the two of you, who had something to do with her being here, will never regret that she is a part of your unit. I think so highly of her, I asked her if she would stand in for Mark as my best man."

"Wow, Mike that is saying something."

"Juan do you know when Roscoe is due to check in?"

"I think he will be here in a couple of days. SEAL operations in San Diego wanted to see him before he headed out. I have no idea what they wanted to talk to him about, but my guess is that it has something to do with our upcoming deployment."

"Let's get you checked in first and then I'll show you the bachelor officer quarters where you will stay until you decide where you want to live. Then I'll take you to the ship and show you around your new mode of transportation."

Chief Johnson checked Juan in and then took him to the BOQ where he found his room. His duffel was already stored in the room and there was a bottle of Oregon Pinot Noir on his desk with a note that said, "Welcome home sailor" it was signed "Ash."

He looked at the bottle of wine and then looked at Chief Johnson. "She doesn't miss, much does she?"

"I told you the women is pretty well thought of and this is just another example of why that is. We are in port for the next two weeks so you will have time to settle in. Most of us live off the base in apartments. Hawaii is expensive but deals are out there, but you must look for them. I would recommend that you take some time this week to orient yourself to Honolulu and then start looking for a place you can call your own."

"I am getting married so, I will be giving up my studio apartment. Once you have looked around you may want to check it out. I would be happy to pass it on to you if you want. Most of the team has housing off base and we all head for our places once the workday is over. When we are at sea our home is the USS Louisville SSN 724. She is under the command of Captain Jason Miles. He is a great guy and has been a pleasure to work with. Mark got along with him well. Our unit has worked with Captain Miles and his team for several years now and we have never had even the slightest of problems. Once we leave here, we will go over to the ship together."

Chief Johnson took Juan on a tour of the facility and showed him where to eat and where the gym was and then they headed over to the Louisville.

"Well there she is Juan. The USS Louisville SSN 724. She is pretty old and I expect she will probably be decommissioned after your upcoming deployment, but she is solid as a rock. She has taken us everywhere, we needed to go including a couple of hairy situations. Remind me over beer to tell you about the Chinese freighter story."

"I see the new vehicle mounted on her deck. Is that the dry one everyone has been talking about?"

"That's it. I am told it can be launched two ways. It can be put in the water with a crane from a freighter or similar ship or it can be launched from the submarine.

Unfortunately, the sub launches underwater, so we still must get wet to get her underway. But once you're inside it's pretty cozy and sure beats the heck out of hanging on and being towed underwater."

"Let's go aboard. I think that Ashley is aboard, she had some paperwork to do and some follow-up from our last trip out.

When Mark had his heart attack, he collapsed over the control console and the thing began to dive. Ashley was able to stabilize the mini, and level her out before bringing her up but not before she reached 450 feet in depth. I should add that there were six of us aboard when that happened. If she had been unable to handle it, we were headed down to about 2000 feet."

"I thought the thing only went to 200 feet?"

"That is what we were told and that is where we tested her, but we now know that it's capable of a much greater depth. Not that I want to ride her down to that depth again, but it is nice to know she is able to go deeper safely.

They crossed the gangplank and were greeted by the deck officer. They each saluted each other, and Mike Johnson asked for permission to come aboard. The deck officer said "granted."

"Juan, I want you to meet Petty Officer First Class Ramon Castro. Ramon, this is Gunny Sergeant Juan Sanchez. Juan will be replacing me as the Chief of the SEAL unit."

"Glad to meet you sir and welcome aboard."

"Thanks Ramon."

"Ramon, is Captain Jamison aboard?"

"Yes sir. She has been in her state room all day doing paperwork."

"I don't even think she's been out once for air. Would you like me to let her know that you are on board?"

"Yes, that would be great. If she is free, tell her I would like to buy her a cup of coffee in the Chief's dining room."

"Will do sir." They headed below deck and seated themselves in the Chief's dining room. "I'll give you a tour of the ship once we have coffee. As I said, it's an old submarine but one that has proved to be very functional." The door opened and in walked Ash. She had a huge smile on her face and gave Juan a big hug.

"I'm not sure that's official protocol Gunny, but I'm so happy to see you."

"Welcome to SEAL delivery team 1."

"Captain, I've been a Navy SEAL for almost 18 years, and I have never had a welcoming hug by a beautiful woman. You are a genuinely nice addition to the welcome party."

They all laughed and Chief Johnson poured Ashley a cup of coffee. "Nothing in it. right Captain?"

"Yes, just black. Thanks Chief."

"Are you tired Juan?"

"Yep, I left the YARD about 20 hours ago. Flew direct to Los Angeles and then grabbed a redeye to Honolulu international. It is been a long day."

"You will have some time to catch up. We are in port for two weeks and then will be back at sea for two weeks. When do you expect Roscoe to arrive?"

"My guess in a couple of days. He was headed for San Diego first."

"SEAL command wanted to meet him before he took command of SEAL delivery team 1."

"How did he handle Mark's death?"

"As well as one could expect, it was a total shock to both of us as you might imagine. He and Roscoe were almost like brothers and they go back all the way to Buds together."

"I knew that, and I'm sure that connection had something to do with my getting this great assignment."

"Captain, how have you adapted to SEAL life?"

"I think okay. Chief could probably give you a better answer than I would. It has been both a learning experience and a challenge. I should also add I have been tested on a couple of occasions."

Mike Johnson started laughing and said, "That is the biggest understatement I have ever heard." He then turned to Ash and said, "how was your weekend off?"

"It was as close to fantastic as I could imagine. Juan, do you remember Ryan Joshua?"

"Yes, I do. He was captain of the men's gymnastics team at the YARD and I remember him working out with you in the gym on weekends."

"Great memory, Gunny. Ryan went on to flight school, graduated at the top of his class and now has completed two deployments. He flies the F-18 Super Hornet off the Yorktown which is home-based here in Pearl Harbor."

"Do I sense some sort of relationship Captain?"

"I hope so, because he is one of the nicest men, I have ever known present company excluded." That caused both to laugh.

"We had a great weekend. Cooked ribs: Drank great Oregon wine and even played tourist.

We found two guys who pride themselves on giving a tour where you spend as little time on the bus as possible. It was great and we were in the water a lot. But now it is back to normal. I have been doing paperwork all day. SEAL command is really interested in our deep dive in the new toy."

"I'm sure they are. The spec said the baby was designed for 200 feet. You leveled her off at 450 feet which doubled their pleasure. Have you heard anything about our next time at sea?"

"Yes, and I talked to Jason about it. We are going to be out for two weeks. They want us practicing with the mini from 200 feet to 25 feet with scuba gear and they want us to practice bringing the vehicle into very shallow water. They said they want us to be able to rest her on the bottom in 25 feet of water. Seems a bit strange but who knows what they are up to. Okay, got to get back to the paperwork. Juan it is great to see you and to have you as a part of the club. I want to finish this work and head home to a glass of Oregon Pinot Gris and a view of the yacht harbor. Cheers to both of you."

"Okay Juan, let's get you a quick tour of this sub and then get you back to the BOQ for some rest."

Mike gave Juan the quick tour and Ashley finished her paperwork and headed home. Once home, she dumped her uniform in the bedroom and slipped on her loose over shirt and cutoff jeans. Then it was to the refrigerator for a glass of Oregon Pinot Gris. Time to relax on the deck.

CHAPTER 22
GETTING TO KNOW YOU

Ryan and Ashley left the apartment at 7:15 on Monday. The weekend had just flown by and they were both happy and exhausted. They were each due back at 0800. The driver let them off at the active-duty entrance. Ryan paid the bill and gave Ash a kiss on the cheek before he headed toward the aircraft carrier. Ash headed the other way to the submarine pier.

Ash had tons of paperwork to do so her day was already planned out in advance. Ryan was not quite sure what he would be doing. His ship was in port and would not go back out to sea for another week.

All he could think about as he walked toward the peer was Ashley. It had been the best weekend of his life. The woman was everything to him. He just could not believe that she could be so tough and driven yet so fun to be with, easy to talk to and even more fun to look at. Forget the fact that she was also super organized and a great cook.

As he walked back his mind started to drift and he focused on where he was and what he had to look forward to in the future.

While he was assigned to the Yorktown his life had followed a normal pattern. He normally went to sea every month for up to two weeks for training purposes and when back in port he was either inspecting the aircraft he would fly or sent to training sessions. His deployment pattern was predictable as well. Every 18 to 24 months he deployed which allowed him to visit ports around the world. All his deployments had been for six months or slightly less.

The Navy had a policy that allowed personnel returning from deployment to have at least as much time at home as they spent on deployment. He had been home for about a year and thus it was about time for his ship to deploy again.

Ashley was set to deploy at the end of November, and he assumed that he would not be too far behind.

As he walked aboard the carrier, he realized that he had just spent time trying to figure out how he could continue his career as a Naval Fighter Pilot and at the same time continue to maintain his relationship with Ashley.

At one point they both realized that a relationship was just not possible. They were both beginning their naval careers, and both were extremely focused on how to begin with the right platform for the future. However, now they were both established. Ryan was a full lieutenant in the Navy and Ashley was a captain in the Marine Corps. Both were at the 03-pay grade level and both were well respected by both subordinates and superiors.

It was complicated but he was bound and determined to make it work and not let their careers get in the way of their newfound relationship.

He arrived at his stateroom and his roommate Scotty Fremont was reading at the desk. "Hi stranger," how was your weekend? Don't tell me you spent it in that tiny studio apartment of yours in the heart of bustling Honolulu."

"Hey Scotty. I had a great weekend. I spent it with Ash, and we had a blast. We ate great food and drank great wine. We also spent a lot of time in the sun and water and became tourist for a couple of hours. It was a super time. How about you?"

"Well, mine was not nearly as exciting as yours. I spent it right here in this stateroom. I ventured out to the officer's club last night but found no one to talk to so I had a couple of beers and headed back to the ship. I've been thinking of starting to look for a small place off base like yours but with the deployment looking us straight in the eyes I think I'll wait until we return."

"Oh, if you're wondering what we're going to be doing for the next two weeks the answer is sitting on the corner of our desk. Here read this."

Ryan picked up the paper and read that he and Scotty were assigned to attend class for the next two weeks on the Super Hornet. Classes would be held on base from 0900 to 1600 each day. Flight officers were then free each day after 1600. Ryan had already been to one school on the Super Hornet and since he had flown them on training runs, he felt that he had just gotten a two-week pass to see Ashley every night.

He looked at Scotty and said, "Well this looks like it will be interesting. I have been to one school on the beast, but more information cannot hurt. I think this will set you up for your desire to fly one of these which I think you want. Right?"

"Yes, I was pleased to get the class. Several pilots were not selected to attend. They tended to fall into two categories, those that did not get high grades on our last timeout and those who were just too junior. So, my decent grades paid off.

I knew that you would be an automatic given your experience and time spent with Commander Reggie Sanders. Rumor has it that he gave you the highest marks of everyone evaluated."

"Who knows? I am glad I can spend two weeks on shore and in class. I am hungry. Do you want to head to lunch?"

"Let's do it."

The rest of the day went by quickly. Ryan reviewed the paperwork he had to complete to attend the class beginning in the morning. At about 2000 he called Ash.

She picked up on the second ring. "Hi, this is Ash."

"Ash, it's Ryan." "Hi big guy. What's up?"

"First I just want you to know that this last weekend was the best weekend of my life and I think you are wonderful. In fact, I'm having a hard time not thinking about you all of the time."

"That is nice to hear. I thought it was a great weekend as well and my feelings for you mirror those you just expressed. To what do I owe the call?"

"I got my schedule back today. I have been ordered to attend a two-week class on the F –18 Super Hornet. I have already been to school once on the plane and I have been flying it on a regular basis so it should be an easy two weeks for me. I go to class from nine in the morning to four in the afternoon, so every evening is off. Have you learned anything about your schedule yet?"

"I spent the day doing paperwork and I was happy to see Juan Sanchez. He checked in today so my plan will be to spend quite a bit of time with him and Chief Johnson to ensure that we have a smooth transition. We are in port for the next two weeks as well so I will be home every night. "My new boss Roscoe Cook should arrive in a couple of days and once he is here, I'll be spending some long days with him. I am curious to know why they stopped him off at SEAL headquarters on his way out. My guess is it had something to do with our deployment."

"So, I would suggest that if you are free, you plan to spend Tuesday, Wednesday and Thursday night here. We can cook, drink wine and talk. Once Thursday is here, we will have a much better idea what to plan next. So, if that is okay with you, I will plan to see you around 1800 for dinner tomorrow night."

"I can't wait. I will see you then. Good night Ash."

"Good night Ryan."

Ashley hung up the phone and sat for a minute watching the last of the sunset. Hawaii was a beautiful place and she knew she was incredibly lucky to be stationed there. She picked up the phone and dialed a 503 number that she knew by heart the phone was answered immediately. "Hello, this is Sarah."

"Hey Mom, it's Ash."

"Ash, it is so good to hear your voice. How are you?"

"I'm great; actually, I'm more than great."

"Aren't you worried about the Coronavirus that has taken the country over and for that matter the world?"

"To be honest, I think about it but here in the islands it has yet to make a great impact. The governor keeps bringing it up as an issue but at this point, we have had a lot of freedom to do what we want. How about you?"

"As you probably know the thing hit the state of Washington like a ton of bricks. We in Oregon have not had it as bad, but we are confined to our homes unless we perform a service that is essential, and we must maintain a social distance of 6 feet from others which keeps everyone separated. So, your Dad's been home for the past week working on his computer. We haven't driven each other nuts yet but we will see how it goes as we move ahead in the weeks to come."

"Tell me what's going on in your life."

"Well, there are lots of things to tell you about. Let me begin with a negative and end with the positive. The most significant thing that has happened in the past couple of weeks is my boss Mark Price had a major heart attack and died while we were out at sea. Then when we returned my Chief, Chief Johnson, who I rely on for just about everything told me he's going to retire."

"Ash that is really bad news I hope the good news helps to offset it."

"The good news is Roscoe Cook and Juan Sanchez, both of whom you have met when I was at the YARD and when I completed SEAL training, have been assigned to replace Mark and Chief Johnson. I am thrilled with the news. Juan arrived today and I think Roscoe will arrive in a couple of days."

"The second bit of news is my landlord Mr. Piedmont had a one-bedroom apartment come available with a view to the yacht harbor and all the way down Waikiki Beach."

"He offered it to me at the same price and terms he had given me on the studio. I am now in it and I could not be happier. In fact, when this virus thing passes over, I want you and Dad to come out and visit before we deploy in late November or early December."

"The last piece of good news has to do with my relationship with Ryan. We are now seeing each other on a very steady basis and to be honest with you I think I have fallen for him big time. It is hard to describe how I feel when I am with him but so far, I couldn't be happier."

"So enough about me. How is John doing?"

"Your brother is fine. Like Dad, he is working from home. He has moved into a very contemporary apartment that looks out over the Willamette River and onto Mount Hood. I am not a real fan of total contemporary houses, but it fits John to a tee, and he is incredibly happy with it. Like you, he seems to have found the new love of his life. Her name is Tiki Rodriguez. She is a PhD microbiologist and graduated from Oregon Health Sciences. I am afraid John has not seen much of her of late. She, like everyone else in research is totally focused on this virus. The bottom line is right now all is good with John."

"Mom, I had better run, I have a big day tomorrow. Please give my love to Dad and John if you ever get close enough to talk to them again. Don't forget when this virus thing passes over, I want you guys to come and visit me at my new digs." Ashley got off the phone and then started thinking about what to do for dinners the next three nights. She needed to plan for Tuesday, Wednesday and Thursday. Friday was up in the air but it was part of the weekend so she felt that she and Ryan would plan that together. She grabbed the pen and paper and began to think. She wrote down the following:

- Tuesday – fish tacos with special sauce.
- Wednesday – shrimp scampi – Jasmine Rice.
- Thursday – barbecued chicken with bull's-eye and Caesar salad

She knew each of these dinners would be easy to make so they would not take a lot of time or effort. She would need to get to the store after work tomorrow and be home before 1800 when Ryan would show up. She would use the leftover marinade from the ribs on the chicken and the croutons she had saved would be good for use in the salad. She then made out her grocery list. It read as follows:

FOR THE FISH TACO'S

- green cabbage
- tortillas for soft tacos
- mayonnaise and sour cream for the taco sauce
- fresh limes for the sauce along with garlic powder and siracha sauce
- mahi mahi

FOR THE SHRIMP SCAMPI

- linguine noodles
- shallots
- garlic
- raw shrimp
- red pepper flakes
- chicken stock
- white wine
- lemon juice
- parsley and Parmesan cheese

FOR THE BBQ CHICKEN

- two boneless chicken breasts
- romaine lettuce
- Caesar dressing

She also added wine to the list and then put it next to her bed so she would not forget to bring it with her in the morning when she left for work. That being done she put on her PJs and jumped into bed. She was asleep in a matter of minutes.

CHAPTER 23
THE GANGS ALL HERE

He had not been to San Diego since Ashley completed her SEAL training and was awarded the Triton. He called ahead and booked a room at the San Diego Marriott Marquis and Marina. He had stayed there before and liked the location.

It was a four-star hotel, located in downtown San Diego and offered a great view of the waterfront. He asked for a room with the deck and a view of the water. He also booked a massage at the on-site spa. He had one night to rest and that is what he intended to do.

He could not stop thinking about what Admiral Omark had told him. If he was correct and the SEAL mission would be to destroy the virus research facility, then he knew that the team would have their work cut out for them. He understood, but he was disappointed he could not share the information with the team until SEAL command told him too.

Roscoe had been a bachelor all his life. He enjoyed looking at and being with attractive interesting women, but he never found one that he thought he would want to spend the rest of his life with. He was for the most part, wed to the SEAL team and that is the way it had been for a long time and perhaps would be in the future as well. On the other hand, he thought, Hawaii was known for its beautiful women and beaches. Who knows what the future has in store, he thought?

He arrived at the hotel and put his travel bag in his room. He changed into a swimming suit and headed for the pool. He did

32 links of the pool and then headed back to his room. He had 45 minutes to kill before his massage appointment, so he took a long hot shower and then laid down to rest until he had five minutes to make the appointment.

The massage was great. It was a full hour and a full body massage. Tina was his massage therapist and she knew what she was doing.

Roscoe was in his late 30s, but he was built like a tank and still in great shape. More than once Tina remarked what good shape, he was in. In fact, she mentioned it enough that it crossed his mind that a dinner date might be in the offering. He thought about it again and with his early departure in the morning he did not need the complication of a relationship of any kind.

At 7:30 he headed down to dinner. He picked Roy's which was in the hotel. He knew Roy's well. It was founded by Roy Yamaguchi in Hawaii and was known for its blend of classic French techniques with the bold flavors of the Pacific rim. What better restaurant to begin his tour in Hawaii with?

He was given a table that looked directly out to the harbor and he ordered a bottle of Cakebread Sauvignon Blanc. He looked through the menu while he enjoyed his first glass of wine and was ready to order when the young waitress appeared at his table.

"Have you made any decisions, sir?"

"Yes, I have. I would like to start with the crispy wak fried shrimp tempura. I think it comes with peppers, mushrooms and a curry aioli."

"Yes, that is correct. It is one of our most popular starters. In fact, it is my favorite."

"Great. I would like to follow it with the blackened island Ahi with the spicy soy mustard butter sauce and then I would like to order the kaffin lime tart for dessert."

"The lime tart comes with a graham cracker crust and whip cream. Is that okay?"

"You bet. Bring it on."

After an hour and 15-minute dinner, he finished his wine and ordered a cup of coffee and just looked out at the boat harbor. It was a perfect night in San Diego.

He was in bed by 9:30 and up at 5:30 to catch an 8:30 flight to Honolulu International.

He dressed in his Navy officer summer white uniform. His shoulder stripes reflected the fact that he was a U.S. Naval Lieutenant Commander. He had four rows of ribbons on his left breast and above them was the gold Navy seal Triton. His belt buckle was gold and his shoes were white.

It was another great day in San Diego and the temperature was perfect. His flight left on time and he rode coach out to Hawaii.

He arrived on time at Honolulu International Airport and, like Juan, he was super glad he had on a short sleeve shirt the minute he stepped out of the airport terminal. He grabbed a cab and asked the driver to take him to Pearl Harbor.

He was all eyes as they drove from the airport to the naval facility. The sky was almost royal blue and there were no clouds in it. The ride took no time at all and just like that he was at the active service gate. He asked for directions to the SEAL Operations Building and was given directions.

He arrived 10 minutes later and was greeted by Chief Mike Johnson.

"Well, look what the cat dragged in. Commander it is great to have you aboard." The Chief put his hand out and they shook hands.

"I think I'm supposed to tell you that I'm reporting for duty, but I gathered you knew that already."

"You bet sir. We have been waiting for you. Juan arrived two days ago and has already been introduced to the team. Ashley handled all of the introductions and I know she's anxious to be back with you and Juan again."

"Yes, it's funny how things turn out. We were both sick to learn of Mark's death, but we are both thrilled to learn we would have the opportunity to replace you and him."

"Mark's death has had an impact on all of us. However, if ever someone stood in and up at the right time, it was Ashley. The woman is just something else. I have got to tell you sir, that in 27 years as SEAL, I have met very few leaders who could hold a candle up to her. She has really earned the respect of the team and has proved to all of them that, in the field, she is second to none. Everyone calls her Ash but believe me they all know who the boss is, and they have total respect for her."

"That is great to hear Chief. Both Juan and I had a feeling from the first day we saw her that she would turn out to be something special. It is good to hear that that appears to be happening."

"Sir let me show you to your quarters in the BOQ. Almost everyone here has a place of their own off base. Hawaii is expensive but good places can be found. I am told our unit will deploy in late November so you will have two months to check the places out and decide if you want to stay here until we return or get your own place now. Your bag should be in your room. I will show you where the gym and officers club is on the way to the submarine."

"I'll leave you for an hour to unpack and then I'll be back to give you the five-cent tour. When we finish the tour, we will meet Ash and Juan for lunch. I have scheduled a meeting for you with Captain Jason Miles at 1500. Captain Miles is in command of the USS Louisville SSN 724. He is a great guy and I'm sure you will get along with him very well."

"So, I'll leave you now and then be back in about an hour."
"Thanks, Chief."

Chief Johnson was back in an hour. "Commander, are you ready for your tour."

"Lead the way, Chief."

Chief Johnson took him to the officer's club, the gym and the pool and then headed to the submarine pier.

"Well there she is. The USS Louisville SSN 724. She's pretty old but she is in great shape and is commanded by a great guy."

"I assume that what I see on her deck is our new vehicle."

"Yes, that is the one that Mark died in and it's the one that dove to 450 feet before Ashley straightened it out and brought us back up to the surface. From what I understand, it is designed to be launched from either a freighter like vessel or a sub. From the sub we obviously get wet before we get the benefit of the dry ride. I'm told that from the freighter it is a dry entry and trip until we get out to go about our business."

The deck officer was waiting at the end of the gangplank when Chief Johnson walked up. He saluted the deck officer and asked for permission to come aboard. "Granted Chief."

"Commander let me introduce you to Petty Officer First Class Ito Yamaguchi. Ito was born here in the islands and is our senior enlisted weapons officer. Ito, this is Lieutenant Commander Roscoe Cook. He will replace Mark as the ICO of SEAL Delivery Team 1."

"Welcome aboard, Commander. We have heard a lot of positive things about you and look forward to having you part of our team."

"Thanks Ito, I look forward to being a part of the team as well."

"Ito do you know where Ash and the Gunny are?"

"Yes, sir they are in the chief's mess quarters. They said they would be meeting you there for lunch."

"Great we will head down there now. Thanks Ito."

"Chief, I sense informality here. Am I right?

"Yes sir, first names are used but everyone knows where they stand, and it makes things a lot less formal especially when we are under some stress. Which I might add is not an infrequent experience."

"Follow me sir."

Roscoe followed Mike to the Chief's mess quarters. They entered and there sitting at the table was Juan and Ashley. Ashley jumped up and gave Roscoe a big hug. "It is so great to see you sir."

"Thanks Ash, that was some greeting." They all laughed and sat down. Lunch was served and the conversation hummed along. There was no talk of shop but rather what it was like to be stationed in Hawaii and what to do when you were a SEAL out of water.

They talked until about 1430. Ashley and Roscoe agreed to meet at 9 AM the next morning to talk about the team. They asked both Mike and Juan to join them in the conference room at the SEAL team facility on land.

Roscoe and Mike then headed for their meeting with the Captain in the Wardroom. They were five minutes early which was the SEAL strategy. At 1500 Sharp Captain Miles entered the room. Roscoe stood and introduced himself and shook hands with the Captain.

"Please sit down, Roscoe, and welcome to the USS Louisville. She is an old sub, but she can still perform at a high level. We miss Mark a lot, but I have heard nothing but great things about you and Juan and I look forward to working with you. Ashley has already proved herself to every man and woman on this ship. She is one hell of a SEAL. I'm sure you're not surprised to hear that."

"No sir. Ashley has never surprised me; in fact, she has overachieved every expectation I ever had for her. You're right about Mark, he was like a brother to me and together we had a little to do with Ashley's assignment with SEAL Delivery Team 1."

"Chief, I would now like to ask that you leave us alone. I have a couple of things I need to talk to Roscoe about and, unfortunately, I need to do it in private."

"Yes sir, I'm out of here. Roscoe I will see you and Juan at 9 AM tomorrow morning."

"Thanks Mike, I'll see you then."

After the Chief left Captain Miles looked at Roscoe and asked him if he had met with Admiral Omark.

"Yes sir, I met with him yesterday in San Diego."

"Then I'm sure he briefed you to the extent he could on our North Korean friends and what we are now referring to as the Haeju virus."

"Yes sir, he briefed me on it and asked that I not discuss it with anyone until such time as there was a need to know."

"I have been briefed and if our intelligence continues to show that Kim Jong-un is trying to develop a targeted virus that he can use as a weapon we will be destined to take it out."

"We will get underway at the end of next week and we will be out for another week. I have been told that I need to take your team down to 200 feet for the exercises outlined. They want you to be comfortable at that depth in releasing the new vehicle, boarding it and then taking it up to 25 feet where they want it to rest on the bottom. I have been studying the depth charts around Haeju harbor and now understand what this could be about. We are scheduled to deploy at the end of November, and they want you extremely comfortable with the vehicle before we depart."

"If I am right, they do not want the Submarine to let your team out in water levels above 200 feet. I am sure, given my review of the depth of the Yellow Sea, that this is a caution to avoid being detected. The depth in Haeju harbor gets very shallow and it is only about 25 feet. If the special operation takes place, the exercises I've described will all come in handy."

"That fits with what the Admiral briefed me on. So, I will need to learn how to drive this baby quickly. We look forward to challenges and this may just be a big one coming up in the future."

"Roscoe, I will let you know if anything else comes up but at least you have a general idea about the skills we are trying to develop."

CHAPTER 24
THE NEW TEAM BEGINS

It was 1600. Ash was done for the day and headed home. She asked her driver to stop at Safeway and let her off. She needed to pick up the items on her list for dinners this week and she could easily walk home from the store. She was in her summer khaki uniform and the gold Triton was mounted above her left breast pocket. Unlike Juan and Roscoe, she had only three ribbons below it. Her service medal and two ribbons she had been awarded for her rescue efforts with the Chinese Freighter. She knew in time that the rows of ribbons would come to her but for now she did not care. It was all about the Triton and it stood out for all to see.

Tonight's dinner was fish tacos, so she focused on that first. At the seafood counter she grabbed a three-quarter pound piece of fresh mahi-mahi. She also picked up a ½ pound of fresh Argentine prawns that were shelled. She would use them in the shrimp scampi on Wednesday night.

She would have Ryan cook the mahi-mahi on the barbecue with olive oil, salt and pepper tonight. Next, she headed for the vegetable aisle and grabbed a head of cabbage. Then she was off to the bread aisle for the soft flour tortillas and then to the spice aisle for the garlic powder and siracha sauce. She had mayonnaise in the refrigerator, but she needed sour cream. Once she had those items she was set for the evening. She had a few bottles of Duckhorn Sauvignon Blanc, so she did not need wine.

She then focused on Wednesday's dinner. It was shrimp scampi. She had the prawns, so she headed to the pasta section and picked up some linguine noodles. She had garlic but she needed chicken stock and red pepper flakes. She also picked up a couple of lemons, parsley and Parmesan cheese.

Last, it was to the poultry section. Thursday night would be chicken breasts. She had the makings for the Caesar salad, so she grabbed two chicken breasts and headed for the checkout line.

As she waited in the checkout line, she had someone behind her tap her on the shoulder. She turned around to see who had tapped her. It was a small woman who said, "Excuse me, officer, are you Ashley Jamison?"

"Yes I am. What can I do for you?"

"Nothing really, my name is Elma Witherspoon and I wanted to thank you for kicking the crap out of those guys outside the Ala Moana Center. I saw the entire thing and could not believe my eyes. You were fantastic and all the women in Honolulu are indebted to you for taking those crooks off the street."

"Well thank you Ms. Witherspoon. Let us hope they stay off the street for a long time."

Two other women standing in line heard Ms. Witherspoon's comments and both started clapping. Ashley was totally embarrassed but she just smiled at the women, paid her bill and headed home.

She was home by 1700 which gave her an hour to change and get ready for Ryan's arrival. She changed out of her uniform and put on a pair of yellow short shorts and a Hawaiian men's shirt. She looked great and was ready for him when he arrived.

As usual, he was right on time and greeted her with a kiss and a bouquet of Hawaiian flowers. It was made up of yellow hibiscus and bird of paradise. The bouquet made the entire apartment smell like you were walking through a Hawaiian garden.

Ryan was in uniform but carried a small overnight bag with a change of clothes in it. He changed into shorts and a underarmor dry fit T-shirt.

Ryan came out of the bedroom and said, "Okay boss, what you want me to do?"

"First, please open one of those bottles of Duckhorn Sauvignon Blanc. They are in the refrigerator. Then pour us each a glass.

Tonight, we are having fish tacos, so I need you to cook the mahi-mahi on the Weber and a heat up a couple of the flour tortillas as well. I coated the mahi-mahi with olive oil, salt and pepper so it should be good to go when you are ready."

Ryan opened the wine and they toasted each other.

"Ryan let's sit on the deck and enjoy our wine before you begin to cook. I have the sauce for the fish tacos ready to go so will not take any time to put dinner together."

"Sounds like a plan to me. How was your day Ash?"

"My day was good. Roscoe arrived and is getting settled in. We have a meeting with the SEAL team at 0900 tomorrow to introduce he and Juan to the gang. We all miss Mark, but Roscoe will be the perfect replacement. He has a strong record and his reputation precedes him. It is amazing to me how quickly people in the service learn about others. I can't imagine what the guys thought when they learned that they were going to get a woman as their AOIC."

"How about you?"

"My day was easy. I sat in class all day. Most of today was a repeat of what I have learned before. The next two weeks is all about the F 18 Super Hornet. It comes in two versions. One is a single seat aircraft and the other is a dual seat aircraft.

I have been flying the dual seat aircraft on all our training runs. Our flight commander likes to ride with me so he can evaluate how all the others are doing from his perch in the second seat. Most of the guys are flying the single seat plane."

"Does it make you nervous to have the boss sitting right behind you?"

"Not at all, Reggie is a good guy and I have flown with him on a number of occasions. I am totally relaxed and assume he likes the ride because he sets the pairings and I am always the one he flies with."

"What is the F 18 Super Hornet look like?"

Ryan grabbed his phone and handed it to Ashley. There on the screen was the F 18 Super Hornet.

"Wow, that looks like one mean machine."

"Yes, the Super Hornet has an internal 20 mm M61 rotary cannon and it can carry air to air missiles and air to surface weapons. It also has five extra fuel tanks so it can serve as a refueling plane when needed in fleet operations."

"Ryan, it is hard for me to imagine you flying that thing and landing it on a postage stamp in the middle of the ocean."

"I admit that my first landing was pretty scary but now it is become just very natural. When I think of what you do, I cannot imagine being 200 feet underwater in the pitch dark. Frankly, it gives me the creeps."

"What is it they say? Different strokes for different folks." They both laughed.

"Okay it is time for you to go do your magic on the grill." Ashley gave him the mahi-mahi and let him go to work barbecuing the fish. She chopped up the cabbage and added some green onion and tasted the sauce. The sauce was a combination of sour cream and mayonnaise with a tablespoon of lime juice, garlic powder and hot sauce. It had a real kick to it.

The fish did not take more than five minutes. It was fresh and was done after 2 ½ minutes on each side. He added three flour tortillas to the grill while the fish cooked for the remaining 2 minutes. He then delivered the food to Ashley in the kitchen. She assembled the tacos and poured each of them another glass of wine. They sat at the little table on the deck and ate while the sun set over the yacht harbor.

After dinner they talked at length over coffee. She told him about her call with her Mom and her hopes that they would be able to make the trip out to Hawaii before they deployed.

They also talked about the Coronavirus. It was really on the move, and Hawaii was now directly in its path. There was talk that all the tourism was about to come to a halt which would kill the economy. Neither of them knew what to make of it but it was clear that it was a major problem worldwide and as such it probably would not be long before Hawaii was exposed to it.

When it was time they headed into the bedroom. Ashley told Ryan she would be in in a minute. She closed the bathroom door and slipped into a pair of black thong panties. She did not wear a bra. It was just one more thing that Ryan would take off. When she was ready, she came out of the bathroom and Ryan's eyes just popped out.

"You are one beautiful woman Ashley."

"Thank you, sir. You are not bad yourself."

"Hey Ash before I attack you, I wanted you to know if you want me to use any protection."

"No need for a condom, I have been on birth control pills for the past month with no side effects."

With that in mind Ryan went to work and after two times they were both sound asleep. The alarm went off at 6 AM and they both were up, showered and in uniform. The Uber driver picked them up at 7 AM and they were at the service gate at

7:15. They kissed lightly and said in unison, "See you tonight about six."

"Bye for now."

0900 NAVY SEAL TRAINING ROOM
PEARL HARBOR, HAWAII

The entire SEAL team was in the conference room and seated five minutes before 0900. The room was set in a U shape. Ashley and Juan sat on either side of the center chair at the head of the table.

The entire team sat across from each other on either side. At 0900 Roscoe Cook walked through the door and headed for the empty chair at the end of the table.

Ashley stood and addressed the team. "Good morning, men. It is my pleasure to introduce you to our new OIC. His name is Lieutenant Commander Roscoe Cook. I know that you have all have done your homework on him and I know that he has checked positive in the boxes you are concerned about. Let's be frank. Mark was a great guy, a mentor to me and to most of you in this room. He will be missed but like all of us he is replaceable. The guy selected to replace him has a lot to do with my being here and I hold him and for that matter Gunny Sanchez in the highest regard. Let me introduce you to our new boss Roscoe Cook."

There was a brief applause and then Roscoe took control of the meeting.

"Good morning. As Ashley has told you my name is Roscoe Cook. I want you all to call me Roscoe. I know that it has been informal around here and I want it to stay that way. Both Gunny and I have been on shore for the past five years recruiting potential SEALs at the United States Naval Academy. Our only concern with this assignment was whether we would remember how to swim or not. To that point I want you all to know that on my way out here stopped in San Diego and jumped in the hotel pool. I am happy to tell you I can still swim." The group laughed.

"I am not sure about Gunny? So, once he gets in the water here, I would like a couple of you to stay close to him. I will tell you that in the past he does a mean dog paddle."

That pleased the group, and everyone got a great laugh out of it.

"I was asked to stop in San Diego to meet with Admiral Omark on the way out. He heads up SEAL command. He confirmed what most of you already know, we will deploy to the Far East at the end of November. We anticipate that the tour will be about six months and I can guarantee you that we will have a few missions that we will have to undertake."

"I frankly do not know what they are but I do know they want us to be ready to deal with our scuba gear at 200 feet and they want us to be able to move the new vehicle around and operate it in very shallow water. Perhaps as shallow as 25 feet. I met with Captain Miles yesterday and he told me that we would be in port for the next two weeks and then we will be training at sea for two weeks. That is all I know about our schedule so far so please let those that need to know what your schedule will be."

"During the two weeks we are in port will be training each day at the range with small arms and automatic weapons. We will also spend a day in class reviewing our underwater demolition skills. Once the classroom day is over, we will spend two days practicing placing explosives on the bottom of a ship. The schedule will be posted by Chief Johnson later today so each of you will know when you need to be at the range or in class."

"You should also be aware that both Juan and I have known Chief Johnson for years. He is a man to be respected and he will be missed when he formally retires before we deploy."

"I know I am not out of school by saying this, but the Chief has told me that you all will be invited to his wedding. He has also told me who his best man will be, and that will be none other than our AOIC Ashley Jamison." Everyone clapped.

"So that is about it for now. Are there any questions? If not, you are dismissed."

CHAPTER 25
PRACTICE MAKES PERFECT

Roscoe asked Chief Johnson, Gunny Sanchez and Ashley to meet with him following the meeting. They all stayed behind as the room emptied. Once it was clear, Roscoe said to both the Chief and Ashley, "I have a roster here of our team. I would like to go down the list one by one and get your opinion of each of them. I am looking for your opinions and observations so what you tell me will not be written down anywhere it is only to help me and Gunny to understand what we have to work with. I have a picture roster here, so I want to see what each of these guys looks like as you described them to me. I would like to go through the first half today and continue our discussion with the rest of them tomorrow morning at 0900 if that will work for you?"

"Chief, let us start with you. Give me a brief overview of the structure and size of our SEAL team."

"We have a total staff of 18 and that includes you, Ashley and me. Of the remaining 15 we have one lead petty officer whose name is Samuel Franklin Pierce. He is called Sam, by all of us. He is a Petty Officer First Class and has served as my assistant so to speak. Below Pierce we have 2 SEAL teams each with 7 SEALS. Mark liked to have them grouped as he felt they would know each other better and overall would work together like a well-oiled machine."

"Let us start then with petty officer Pierce. He has been with this SEAL delivery team the longest of any of us. He has 24 years in the Navy, is single and has a small apartment in the city of Honolulu. He is one tough son of a bitch and from what I can tell he is not afraid of anyone or anything. He is also an excellent swimmer and was one of the swimmers Mark selected to swim with Ashley when we rescued the Chinese sailors that were about to go under in one hell of a storm. I should add that I have complete confidence in Pierce. He does what he is told, and he is quiet as he goes about it. I should add that it was Pierce who came back to Mark after Ashley's first major test to tell him that Ashley not only could out swim him, but she beat him up the rope ladder and on to the sinking ship before anyone else was halfway up. He made it clear to Mark that Ash was a real leader. He said there was no doubt who was in charge of that mission."

"Sounds to me, Ash, that you may have earned a real fan in Mr. Pierce."

"I think the world of him Roscoe. We are lucky to have him and I would want him alongside me on any mission."

"Okay then, let us start with the first seven enlisted men. Petty officer second class Jim Martinez."

Ashley spoke up first. "I have led this SEAL team of seven on a number of exercises. Our normal practice is for me to lead one team and Mark the other. We did not always lead the same team, but we kept the team together no matter which of us was leading. Martinez is the senior member of the team in rank. I have seen him in action on several occasions and believe he is the SEAL through and through. He was with me when we had the tiger shark attack on one of our men and he was both calm and collected and he helped me get our man to the beach where we applied first aid. He was also the guy that took Mark back to the sub after the heart attack. He is well respected by all members of the team. I should also add he was with me when we swam to the Chinese freighter. He is a great swimmer and was a real asset on that mission."

"I agree 100% with what Ashley just said." the Chief responded.

"Thanks, Chief."

"Okay, let's keep going down the list. Tell me about Rick Johnson."

"Rick's been with us for about three years. We got him straight out of BUDs. In the beginning, my observation was he thought he was something special. He had passed the SEAL training and wanted everyone to know it. It did not take long for is star to fall. He suddenly found out that everyone he was talking to knew more than he did and was just as strong and tough. Once the chip was knocked off his shoulder he really settled down."

"From what I can tell he has become a valued member of his team. I know that Jim Martinez has confidence in him."

"I have had no problems with him. Given his past, one would have thought that reporting to a woman would have been a problem for him. Not so. He does what he is told, and he has been humbled by the SEAL team experience.

"Charles Chan?"

"We call him Charlie," Ash said. "He is our only Chinese SEAL. Charlie is noticeably quiet. He goes about his business without fuss or bother. When you think of the Chinese people you think of people who are, for the most part, shorter and smaller than normal people. Charlie is not like that at all. In fact, he weighs about 190, swims like a fish and prides himself on being the best marksman of his team. From what I have observed, he is everything I just described. He also speaks fluent Chinese and some Korean. As such he has been a great person for me to stay current with my Chinese language skill. He is American born. His parents were the first of his family to immigrate to the United States. He is proud to be an American and lets you know it in a variety of different ways."

"Chief, anything to add on Charlie Chan?"

"No, the boss said it all."

"Next we have Ricky Wise. Is his real name Ricky?"

"Yes, his parents were real fans of the golfer Ricky Fowler. Ricky grew up in Florida and his dad used to play practice rounds of golf with a much younger Ricky Fowler. Our Ricky is not only a solid SEAL, but he is one hell of a golfer. When he has a day off, he is out on some golf course somewhere. He has the body of a professional golfer in that he is tall, about 6'2", and he has a strong upper body. In fact, he looks like he has the body of a competitive swimmer."

"Roscoe, I have spent a lot of time in the water with Ricky and I can tell you he is comfortable, knows what he is doing, and is a team player."

"Next we have Michael Jones."

"I will take this one" Chief Johnson said. "Mike Jones is the all-American boy. He is about 6 feet tall, weighs about 180. He is strong as an ox and single. He has the looks of the movie star and puts those looks to good use when around women.

He is our lady's man and as near as I can tell, he has women in almost every port we have visited.

"He, however, is a real SEAL at heart. He takes his job seriously and is never distracted by his hobby which I think is women. He is a team player and is actually a lot of fun to be around and have a beer with."

"Okay, tell me about Jackson Strong."

"Obviously, Jackson is black. He is from Charleston South Carolina. His Dad was a career Navy enlisted man who retired as a Master Chief Boson Mate. Jackson was raised by his mother Betsy. This was because his Dad was always out to sea. He grew up in a Navy family and never wanted to be anything other than a SEAL. He accomplished his goal and I believe he wants to stay with this for a full career and retire out just like his dad did. He is married and has two small kids. His wife is Chinese, so he and Charlie have become great friends."

"That brings us to Peter Gomez."

"Peter was our token Hispanic until Juan showed up this week. He rounds out our United Nations group. He is quiet, takes orders well and is an expert with underwater demolition. I think he really likes to see things blow up. He is good at what he does and is a valuable member of the team. He is single as well and spends a lot of his free time with Ricky and Mike. He is never in need of a date."

"Last we have Kermit Fox." Chief Johnson took the lead on Kermit.

"Kermit Fox is our quiet one. He rarely talks; he has no real buddy that he hangs around with. He is a voracious reader and always has a book in his hands."

"I have never been able to figure the guy out. He is super smart and a SEAL through and through, but he is also a loner that does not seem to need anyone to be happy and content. He rarely goes out with the guys and he spends most of his free time reading."

"What does he read, Chief?"

"It is all over the map. One day he will be reading war and peace and then the next time I see him he has a romantic fiction novel in his hands. He follows orders and can be relied on to get his assigned job done but he is a total enigma to me."

"Okay, we covered half the team. We will get to the rest tomorrow. I have to meet with Jason Miles this afternoon so I will see you both later or tomorrow morning." Ashley and the Chief headed over to the SEAL operations facility. They would work on a schedule together and post it later in the day.

Today was Wednesday so they had two days remaining this week and five days next week to arrange the training schedule. They decided to have the Jim Martinez group, accompanied by

Juan Sanchez, head to the range on Thursday and the second group accompanied by Ashley to head to the range on Friday.

The plan was for the SEALs to spend the morning working with their standard weapon of choice which was the Colt M4 A1 Carbine Assault Rifle and the afternoon would be spent practicing small arms fire. All SEALs need to be able to use a wide variety of weapons including sniper rifles, shotguns, grenade launchers, mortars and handheld rockets. The Chief and Ashley, however, wanted the weapons training to only focus only on the two.

The following week they would all work as a group underwater and focus on their UDT skills. They had a practice freighter that was anchored in the bay and they would use it to train on the proper placement of underwater mines.

Both the Chief and Ashley felt that the underwater training session would work and then they would follow it with two more days of handheld arms training.

When they were done it was about 1500. Chief Johnson said he would post the schedule as requested then he would meet Ashley at 0900 to continue with the staff briefing to Roscoe.

Ashley did not return to the ship. She headed off base to her apartment. Once there she hung up her uniform, took a shower and changed into a Hawaiian print dress with spaghetti straps. It was short, sexy and with her sandals that matched she looked great.

Tonight, was her scampi dish so she began to do the prep as soon as she was cleaned up and dressed.

Ashley took the Argentine prawns out of the refrigerator and put them in a bowl, then she got her wok out and put a couple of tablespoons of olive oil in it and heated it up. She sprinkled the prawns with salt and pepper and then when the wok was hot, she put the prawns in it and turned them often until they were cooked through. Once that was done, she took them out of the wok and put them in a bowl and set them aside.

She then heated water in a saucepan until it was boiling. She added the linguine pasta noodles to the boiling water and let them boil for four minutes. She tested them to make sure they were done and then dumped them into a colander in the sink. Once they were cold, she put them in a separate bowl. With the two main parts of the scampi prepared she did the final prep work. She peeled and thinly sliced a shallot, added a couple of cloves of minced garlic, and a touch of salt. To that mixture she added red pepper flakes and a zest of one lemon. She chopped up some parsley and grated the parmesan cheese.

She was now ready, and it was almost 5:45. She poured two glasses of wine and put them in the refrigerator and waited a few minutes for the doorbell ring. It did and Ryan as usual was on time and greeted her with a big hug and kiss.

"Hi you. Do I have time to get a quick shower and change?"

"Sure, have at it. I have your wine ready when you are."

Ryan was out in no time. He had on khaki shorts and a Hawaiian golf shirt.

"You look beautiful, my dear."

"Thanks, big guy here is a glass of wine. Let sit outside and you can tell me about your day." "They talked until about 7:30 when Ashley said, "it is time for me to go to work."

"Anything I can do?"

"No, I will have dinner ready in 10 minutes. We are having shrimp scampi tonight."

"That sounds great. Ash, your meals are really starting to spoil me."

"All you have to do tonight is make sure you keep our glasses full."

"I can handle that."

Ashley took the wok and poured the mixture of shallots, garlic and red pepper flakes into it. She then added a quarter cup of chicken stock, some white wine and the lemon zest. She added butter and a little olive oil to the mixture and then heated it until it was simmering. Then she added the shrimp and the pasta and let the entire thing simmer for 10 minutes. After that she put the contents onto plates and topped each with parsley and the parmesan cheese. She served it on the deck, and it was over the top delicious.

They talked until 9PM and then did the dishes. They were in bed shortly, thereafter, and made love before they both fell asleep. All Ashley could think about as she fell asleep was, "so far so good."

CHAPTER 26
TEAM PROFILES

At 0855 Ashley and Chief Johnson sat in the conference room ready to continue their briefing with Roscoe. Yesterday they covered eight of the men on the SEAL team and today they would brief him on the other seven.

At 0900 sharp Roscoe walked into the room with 3 cups of coffee. "Good morning. I brought you coffee but passed on the donuts. The thought of having my staff fat just does not fit with the image I want to project."

Both Ashley and Chief Johnson laughed. Then the Chief said, "I can tell you that I feel like I am right on the border but my wife to be, thinks my love handles are just fine, so I am going to stay the way I am at this point. I can tell you this however, my AIOC sitting here doesn't have an ounce of fat on her and from what I have heard I don't think she ever has had."

"Thanks Chief. I try" Ashley said with a smile on her face.

"Okay, yesterday we covered Sam Pierce, Ricky Wise, Charles Chan, Juan Martinez, Mike Jones, Jackson Strong and Kermit Fox. Who do we have on the agenda this morning?" Chief Johnson spoke up.

"Since I started yesterday, I will kick it off again today. First up is Terry Lund. Terry is a second-class Petty Officer and has been a member of the SEAL team for the past five years. He is experienced and respected. He is known for his marksmanship skills but is not the strongest swimmer of his group. He is liked and has good social skills. He gets along with everyone and I should add he has the ability to take charge when asked to."

"Next up is Albert Fineman." Ashley said.

"I am not sure if Al is an American Indian, but my guess is, he is. He is from Oklahoma and is built like a fireplug. He is only 5'8" but he has the strength of an elephant. I have watched him in the water and have had had him on missions with me. He is steady, always in control and a good member of the team."

The Chief then said, "Let me take the next one."

"Next up we have Harold Toomont. The gang calls him "Old Weird Harold." The guy is not old, but he is strange. He has been a SEAL for three years and, frankly, I am surprised he is still one. He seems to always be a step behind everyone on the team. He is a slow swimmer, a poor shooter and not the quickest man I have ever met. I think he is the one you will have to watch. I have been on missions with him and he has been okay, but I can tell you I would not want him with me for going into a risky situation."

"Thanks Chief sounds like I will need to focus on him. Based on what you have said, I am not sure he should be here now. I will make my own judgments over time but if what you say appears true to me "Old Weird Harold" will need to find other work."

Ashley then said "Next up is Raymond Odemier. Ode is an all-around great guy. He is well-liked and is a proven SEAL. He is an excellent swimmer and a good marksman. He never seems to get rattled and my prediction is he will be a career SEAL. He is married, lives off basin has two twin girls. His wife is a Navy held at a small chapel close to Diamondhead. He explained that the wedding would be small with about 100 invited guests. Guests would include on her side, family and friends and on his side the members of the SEAL team. There would also be a few guests who knew both the bride to be and the groom. However, there were not many that fit in that category. The Chief also told Ashley that his wedding day would be his last day as a SEAL, He would move into his new wife's place after the wedding and officially retire.

Ashley made a note to save the date and then spent the rest of the afternoon cleaning her weapons and getting ready for the range in the morning. At 1600 she left the SEAL facility and headed home.

Tonight, was the last of the three meals she had planned, and it was the simplest. She would ask Ryan to barbecue the two boneless chicken breasts and to marinate them with the remaining bull's-eye sauce. In the meantime, she would wash the romaine lettuce for the Caesar salad. She had the dressing but would hold off dressing the salad until the last minute. She did not want a soggy salad and wet croutons.

She checked her wine supply and it was still good. She pulled out two bottles of Oregon Pinot Gris for the evening and put them in the freezer to get super cold. The wine she selected was a 2011 Tori Mor Pinot Gris from the Willamette Valley. She had read about the wine and it was described as "summer in a glass." It smelled of mineral, pear and dried citrus peel with a touch of ginseng and honeycomb. She thought it would go perfect with both the chicken and the salad.

The targets began at 20 yards. Then they were moved back 5 yards after each firing session. The final handgun target range was 40 yards.

Overall, the group's training went well. The morning handgun marks were high, and Juan was pleased.

That afternoon he switched the instruction to assault rifle training. He asked the instructors to have the guys tested and practiced both in standing positions and prone positions on the ground. The SEALS standard weapon of choice is the M4 A1 Carbine Assault Rifle. All the men had their weapons and lined up in the afternoon as they had in the morning.

The two instructors went down the line and inspected each weapon. The group did well, and no one got chewed out.

Targets began at 50 yards and then were moved back in 25-yard intervals until they were at 150 yards. The instructors reminded all the SEALs to remember the lollipop method. Sight the rifle right where the stick joins the lollipop and chances are good you will hit the target.

The group was far better when lying on the ground in a prone position than they were standing up. Overall, they performed well, and Juan was pleased.

At 1600 they were done. The second group would follow in the morning.

It was Thursday. Ashley had lunch with Chief Johnson. He told her that they had set the date for the wedding. It would be on November 10. It was a Saturday and the wedding would be

PEARL HARBOR NAVAL FIRING RANGE

HONOLULU, HAWAII

Gunny Sergeant Juan Sanchez met the two SEAL weapons instructors at the firing range. He had Sam Pierce with him and the team that was led by Jim Martinez.

"How do you want us to handle the training today, Gunny?"

Juan told him he wanted to use the morning to work on small arms training. He wanted the focus to be on accuracy and safety. He was not sure how long it had been since the team had had small arms training, so he wanted the basics to be covered in detail. He also told them he wanted them men to practice from an upright standing position.

The instructors took over from there. They asked Jim to get his boys lined up so they could do a weapons inspection. Each man had in his possession the SEAL handgun weapon of choice. It was a Sig Sauer P226. Jim arrange the guys down the line. He put Ricky Wise in position one, Charlie Chan in position two, Peter Gomez in position three and Mike Jones in position four. Mike was followed by Jackson strong in position five and Kermit Fox in position six.

The weapons instructors went down the line and looked at each of the SEALs guns. It was a reminder to all of them that once you are a Navy SEAL your training is never over. Two of the guys, Mike Jones and Kermit Fox, were barked at for not having their weapons as clean as they should have been.

All the others passed inspection with no problem.

nurse and works at the Naval Hospital. I have evaluated him on several occasions and he always comes out toward the top of my list. I think he is a real keeper."

"Next up we have Sam Olson. Sam is one of the strongest swimmers we have on the team. He was a competitive swimmer in college and lives to try to beat me in the water at anything. He is an extremely competitive guy. He is strong and always has a smile on his face. I like him and I have seen him operate in terrible conditions. He handles most everything well."

The Chief then said, "That leaves us with two to go. To make it simple they are identical twins. Ron and Mattie Forkman. They grew up in a small town in Iowa and they are real Cornhuskers at heart. You can tell by their bodies that they spent a lot of time on the farm lifting hay bales for their Dad. Neither of them went to college. They graduated from high school, enlisted in the Navy and applied together to be SEALs. They went through all their training together and once it was completed, they asked to be stationed together. They are real pair of bookends."

"They have the respect of everyone and work exceptionally well together."

"Mark relied on them for many things and to my knowledge they never let him down. I felt it was odd to have brothers together in the beginning but having watched them for the past three years I think the Navy would be foolish to separate them with different assignments. I think there is an old Jack Johnson song that says, "we are better together" and I think that is the case with these two."

She had changed from her uniform and put on a pair of short white shorts with a tight light blue top that was cut incredibly low in front. She looked in the mirror and thought Ryan is going to like this look.

At 1800 a knock came to her door. She opened it and the next thing she knew she was in the middle of a big hug and a long kiss. "Wow, do you look great."

"You are just prejudiced." She knew, however, that the look she had hoped to achieve was a success. "Okay, let me get a quick shower and then I can help you with dinner. What are we having tonight?"

"Tonight, it is simple, we are having barbecue chicken breast with bull's-eye sauce and a tossed Caesar salad."

"I assume I am in charge of the chicken."

"You got that right sir."

Ryan was in and out of the shower in no time and into his standard shorts and dry fit T-shirt.

Ashley asked him to open a bottle of wine and to pour two glasses. They would sit on the deck with a glass of wine before he went to work on the chicken.

When they were settled down, they toasted each other and said "cheers."

"How was your day?" Ashley asked.

"It was okay but a bit boring. I am starting to really understand this airplane and as a result almost everything I have listened to this week I know. I realize it is important, but I am not finding the class challenging."

"How is it for the other guys in the class?"

"Well they are not all men, there are three women pilots in the class as well. I think for most of them it is a challenge. They have been used to flying the single seat Hornet and now they are being exposed to the Super Hornet and the possibility of having someone else along for the ride."

"How about you, Ash?"

"Chief Johnson and I spent the morning briefing Roscoe on the SEAL team and then I spent the afternoon cleaning and checking out both my pistol and my assault rifle. Tomorrow I will spend the day on the range and see if I still am an okay shot or not."

"Why do you think they are putting you through the small arms refresher training?"

"Who knows, but SEAL command has a reason for everything they have us do, so my guess it has something to do with his upcoming deployment."

"I have to say I hope you do well. The last thing in the world I want is to have you return from deployment with a hole or two in you."

"I hear you on that, my dear."

"Okay, let us get going on the chicken."

The chicken took about 20 minutes. Ryan basted it every five minutes and it came out moist and with great smoky flavor. The Caesar salad was great. They ate as usual at the little table on the deck and finished the first bottle of wine. Ryan opened the second and poured each of them another glass.

"Tomorrow is Friday and with the weekend ahead of us. What you want to do?"

"Well we have cooked in all week so I thought it would be fun to go out. There is a restaurant that I have heard great things about, and it is in the Waikiki Beach Marriott Hotel which is an easy walk from here. The restaurant is the Sansei Seafood Restaurant and Sushi Bar."

"I have been to that one a couple of times and it is great."

"What did you have?"

"We shared small plates. The restaurant has won several awards and we tried most of the winners. Let me see. As I recall we had four different things. They have this dish called shrimp dynamite that is fabulous. We also had Asian shrimp cake and a Panko crusted Ahi roll and a Japanese calamari salad."

"Those things sound perfect. Now I am excited to try it. It is almost 9 can you help me with the dishes? I am pooped and have a big day ahead of me tomorrow."

"Sure."

They cleared the dishes and headed for the bedroom. Ash told Ryan to get into bed. She changed into a peach color transparent teddy with lace unlined cups that provided push-up without padding. It had a thong bottom and when she stepped out of the bathroom and into the light Ryan could hardly believe his eyes.

They made love for about 30 minutes and then they were both sound asleep. Tomorrow is a workday and they would be up early and gone by 0700.

CHAPTER 27
BACK IN THE WATER

At 0855 Ashley was lined up with the members of the team that were due to go through the small arms and automatic assault rifle training at the range. She had cleaned her Sig Sauer P226 and her M4 AS1 Carbine Assault Rifle on Thursday afternoon so she felt comfortable that both weapons would meet the instructor standards.

Chief Johnson was at the range as was Juan and Roscoe. They were not there to train only to observe. Lined up next to Ashley were Terry Lund, Albert Fineman, Harold Toomont, Raymond Odemier and Sam Olson.

Like they had done the day before, the two weapons instructors moved down the line inspecting each weapon. Ashley went first. Her weapon was deemed to be clean which she expected. Instructors proceeded down the line until they got to Harold Toomont. The first instructor had taken "Old Weird Harold's" weapon apart and called the other instructor over to look at what he had found.

The second instructor then said, "When was the last time you cleaned this weapon sailor." Toomont just looked at him and said, "I do not remember, sir."

"Sailor from what I can see this thing has not been cleaned in months. This is unacceptable. You will not be able to participate in today's training. In fact, if it were up to me, you would not be training here again. If I were one of the men counting on you to have my back in a small arms fight, I would be royally pissed off at your lack of preparation. I am not sure, given the shape this weapon is in, if either of us, who, I might add, are paid to instruct how to use the weapon, could hit anything with it. You are dismissed. If I were you, I would spend the rest of the day cleaning your weapons."

Toomont left the line and started to head back to the SEAL training facility. He did not get two steps beyond the group when the Gunny grabbed him by the arm and said, "You are going to go for a walk with me, son."

"You know Chief," Roscoe said, "if there is one thing, I have learned in this man's Navy it is to never, and I do mean never, have a Marine Gunnery Sergeant who is also a SEAL mad at you. Our friend, **"Old Weird Harold"** is about to get his butt kicked big time."

"I hear you sir."

The small arms training went well. As expected, Terry Lund and Raymond Odemier stood out as excellent marksman. From a standing position they both did exceptionally well. Ashley was not disappointed with her performance she was in the top third but was never going to be the marksman that Lund and Odemier were.

The afternoon training with the rifles went well. Ashley surprised herself and beat Odemier from the prone position. Lund still took top honors.

Juan took Mr. Toomont behind SEAL headquarters and ripped him verbally in a way he had ever been talked to before. The Gunny finished his lecture by saying "One more time with anything having to do with the safety of our brothers and you are out of here. Do you understand?"

Toomont just kept his head down. He only responded at the end by saying, "yes sir."

Later that afternoon Juan met with Roscoe, Ashley and Chief Johnson. "I am not giving that kid much of a chance of lasting with us. He is one strange dude and does not seem to care much about anything. I am not sure if he is naturally depressed or what, but his head is not where it needs to be. It will be interesting to see him underwater next week."

At 1600 her day was finished, and Ashley grabbed a Uber car home. She was in and out of the shower in no time and spent some time getting ready for Ryan and their trip to Sansei.

She had picked a very cute and short Hawaiian yellow dress with spaghetti straps. She wore flats so she could walk easily to the restaurant. Her legs were tan and extraordinarily strong. With the outfit she had selected she would get a few looks on the way to the restaurant.

As usual Ryan was on time. It was 6 PM when he knocked on the door. He was in uniform and needed to shower and change. He brought his overnight bag with him. He gave Ash a hug and kiss and headed to the bedroom. He was ready to go in a half an hour which gave them 30 minutes to walk to the restaurant. It was another typical Hawaiian evening. The temperature was about 80° and the walk to the restaurant took only about 15 minutes. As they walked along Ryan asked Ashley how her day had gone.

She told him the story about **"Old Weird Harold"** and his problem with the gun instructors. She also told him that Juan had taken him by the arm and delivered a message no one would ever want to be on the receiving end of. Ryan just laughed and said, "No thank you. Gunny's are not my favorite people in the first place and a mad one is more than I can imagine."

Ash laughed as they walked into the restaurant. They were seated in a larger room with mostly tables for four. There was no view of the water, but they were given a table for two by the window which they were happy with.

Their waitress came over and gave them menus. She told him what the specials of the day were and about the award-winning dishes that Ryan had described to Ash the night before. "Could I please have a wine list?"

She brought the wine list and Ryan selected the Cakebread Sauvignon Blanc.

"Well, you are going with the good stuff tonight."

"Yep, you are my date and you deserve nothing but the best. I am also buying dinner. Tonight, we do not split."

"How nice. I accept your offer and will try to repay you in some way, shape or form before the evening is over."

The waitress returned with the wine and chilled glasses. She poured a small taste for Ryan to sample. "That is fine. Thanks", he said.

"Have you made your mind up what you would like to have?" The waitress asked them both. Ryan responded, "Tonight we are going to sample a number of your small plates. I would like to start with an order of Shrimp Dynamite and an order of the Panko crusted Ahi."

"Great choices, I will get them going right away. I will leave the menu for you to look at so you will be ready to order other items when those dishes arrive."

They enjoyed their wine while they waited for their first order to arrive. "Ash, what is up for you next week?"

"We have a week of training in the water. A lot of UDT training and then we head to sea the next week for two weeks. How about you?"

"We are still scheduled for class next week and then head to sea for two weeks of flight operations. My only hope is that the weather is a lot better than it was the last time out."

The Shrimp dynamite arrived, and Ashley took her first bite.

"This is out of this world. I think I could eat a whole bucket of these."

"Glad you like it, here comes the panko crusted ahi. It is a sushi roll of sorts."

"This dish looks unbelievable, and as you know, I love Ahi especially when it is just seared which this looks like it is."

"Try it and let me know what you think?"

Ash took one of the rounds off the end and put it in her mouth once. "This taste is over the top delicious. It almost melts in your mouth."

The waitress gave them some time to work on their orders and then was back to ask if they would like anything else. Ryan took the lead and said, "I think now we would like to have an order of the Japanese calamari salad and an order of the Asian shrimp cake."

The waitress wrote the order down on her pad and then said to Ryan, "you have to have been here before. You have now ordered the four most popular award-winning dishes we have."

"You are right. I have been here before and these are just as good so far as they were the last time."

The next two orders arrived, and they were just as good as the first two. As they neared the end of the shrimp cake, Ash looked at Ryan and said, "I am stuffed. I cannot eat anymore even though I do not want to stop."

"I hear you; I am just as full."

The waitress stopped by to ask them if either of them wanted dessert, but she could tell by the way they were shaking their heads that no dessert was needed tonight. She brought Ryan the bill and wished them a good evening.

The walk back to the apartment was a slow one full of low-key conversation. When they were back, they each changed into their normal apartment dress, grabbed another glass of wine and headed for the deck.

"What do you want to do tomorrow, Ash?"

"I have planned an interesting day for us. One of my team told me about a guy that has a nice yacht here in the harbor. He takes small groups of 2 to 10 people out toward Diamond Head. He parks his yacht in cove somewhere around Diamond Head, serves lunch, allows time to snorkel and then brings them back to the harbor. I called him this week and we are scheduled to go with him at 10 tomorrow morning. He said just wear a bathing suit and sandals. He also told me that he had no one booked for the day so we may have the yacht all to ourselves."

They went to bed early, made love only once and fell asleep in each other's arms. At 10 the next morning they were down on the dock and boarding a 46-foot new lagoon catamaran. "Good morning" a voice came from the top deck.

"Please come aboard." By the time they were on board the Captain was down to greet them. "Hi, I am Sam Owens; you must be Ashley and Ryan."

"You got that right" Ashley said.

"Today is your lucky day as you two will be our only passengers. My wife Esther is in the galley and will be ready to serve you as soon as we get underway. My plan is to take you around Diamond Head to a cove on the other side of the island. We will anchor in the lee of the island and you will have the opportunity to swim if you wish. We will also have lunch there before we return so I will leave you now and we can get underway."

The yacht was beautiful it had three bedrooms and three bathrooms as well as a galley and a salon. Sam's wife, Esther, was up to meet them shortly after they were underway. She introduced herself to them and then offered them Mimosas or Bloody Mary's. Ashley went with the Mimosa and Ryan the Bloody Mary.

They learned a lot on their way around the island. Sam and Esther were quick to point out several facts, most of which neither Ashley or Ryan knew anything about.

They also learned that Sam and Esther lived on the yacht. They were transplants from Newport Beach, California where Sam had been in the yacht business. They were finally sick and tired of California, the tax structure and all the people. They sold their small home in Long Beach for 1.3 million and bought the yacht for $900,000. They explained that they were just getting their business started and they hoped it would catch on with locals who wanted a day away.

Ash and Ryan were sold before they anchored on the other side of Diamond Head. There was no question in either of their minds that they would be back. The day was spent snorkeling around the reefs. The water in the cove was crystal clear and the fish were abundant. Ryan had not spent much time in the water so for him it was a real treat. For Ashley it was almost another day at the office, but she did not care.

If she was in the water, she was happy. Esther made them a great lunch, so dinner was not something they were really thinking about.

They were back in the apartment at 4 o'clock. They decided to make dinner simple and so it was a quick trip to Safeway. Dinner was simple. They had turkey burgers with swiss cheese and a cold beer.

Sunday was spent just lounging around. They woke up late, had a long leisurely breakfast and then went for a long walk on Waikiki Beach.

They were home at 4:30 and decided to order take out for dinner. They found a Thai restaurant that they liked and ordered a mango salad which was made up of shredded fresh mangoes with prawns, fresh mint and onion mixed with Thai spices and seasoning. They also ordered an order of chicken satay which came grilled and marinated on skewers and one order of Pad Thai which was made with fried rice noodles, tofu, egg and bean sprouts. Door Dash delivered the order within an hour. They opened a bottle of Grgich Hills Fume Blanc to go with it.

It had been a great weekend. They both had busy weeks ahead of them, so they decided to focus on their jobs until Thursday and then they planned to spend Thursday through the weekend together. The following week they would both leave for at sea training and they would both be gone for two weeks.

They were tired but not too tired to roll around for an hour. They did so and fell asleep right away.

CHAPTER 28
OPEN OCEAN SWIM

Ashley was back on the base and in her stateroom by 0730. Roscoe had called a SEAL Team training meeting for 0900 and as usual, she planned to be there early. She knew today's meeting would be all about the training this week. The training she knew, for the most part, would be under or at least in the water. It was what she lived for and she was happy to get on with it.

She walked down to the wardroom and grabbed a cup of coffee and took it back to her desk. Her mind was still focused on the weekend and the relationship that was developing with Ryan. She had no idea where it would go or how it might end but for now it was as good as it gets, and she only hoped it would continue.

At 0845 she left the sub and headed over to the SEAL Team meeting room. She was 10 minutes early but was not surprised to see almost everyone on the team already seated. There was one noticeable exception, however, **"old weird Harold"** was not at the table yet. Something was wrong with that guy and she was beginning to think she knew what it was. She made a mental note to talk to Roscoe about it later.

At 0900 Roscoe entered the room and took his position at the head of the U-shaped conference table. "Good morning," he said to the group. In unison they all replied.

"Good morning sir."

"Lady and gentlemen, today we get back in the water where we belong. My plan is for us to be in the water each day of this week. Next week we will begin two weeks of training with the vehicle. I have talked to Captain Miles and he told me that he has orders to put us down to 200 feet and to work with the vehicle at that depth during the first week. The second week we will be working in very shallow water off one of the Hawaiian Islands.

"I do not know which one. The first week at sea we will be working with scuba gear on and the second week we will be working with the LAR V Draeger rebreather that you are all familiar with."

"This week we will be reviewing and refreshing your underwater demolition team training. I would like to give you a bit of history in order to put you all in the right frame of mind. The UDT special forces units were established by the United States during World War II. They came to be considered more elite and tactical during the Korean and Vietnam wars. Their primary function began with the reconnaissance and removal of natural or man-made obstacles on the beaches prior to amphibious landings. They were later assigned to assist in the recovery of space capsules and astronauts after splashdown in the Mercury and Apollo spaceflight programs. The UDT teams were pioneers in underwater demolition, closed-circuit diving, combat swimming and midget submarine operations. Commando training was added making them the forerunner of the Navy SEAL program that exist today."

"I say this to set the stage for a training this week. We will be working on underwater demolition and closed-circuit diving.

Our work with the delivery vehicle will begin next week in the open ocean."

"Back to a bit of our history." Roscoe stopped talking as Harold Toomout entered the room and took a seat at the table. "Mr. Toomont you are late for our meeting which is in my book unacceptable. Do you understand that?"

"Yes sir, I just seem to have lost track of time. It will not happen again, sir."

"I hope not Mr. Toomont, after yesterday's performance you, sir, are running out of time to get your act together."

"Yes sir, I understand."

"Okay back to our history discussion. In the mid-1950s the Navy saw how the UDT mission had expanded to include a broad range of unconventional warfare skills. This clashed with the traditional role of the UDT's and set up the birth of our SEAL operations today. The goal the Navy had was to build on the UDT elite qualities and waterborne expertise but to add land combat skills, including parachute training and guerrilla counterinsurgency operations. So, it is from that point that the acronym for sea, air, and land otherwise known as US Navy SEAL's came to be. Our SEAL delivery vehicle team 1 was an outgrowth of SEAL team 1 which was headquartered in San Diego. In fact, our unit is an outgrowth of UDT unit 12. Under the restructure, UDT 12 became SEAL Delivery Vehicle Team 1. All the way along our SEAL team has been involved in a variety of operations."

"Chief Johnson is a perfect example of that. If you look at the four rows of ribbons, he wears below his Triton you will get an idea of the wide variety of SEAL team clandestine operations he has been a part of. I bring that to your attention today because Chief has advised me of his retirement date which is November 10. I am told that this is his wedding date as well. I mentioned this to you before, it is my understanding you will all receive an invitation to the wedding. Obviously, you are not required to attend but if you do not you will have to explain to the Gunny why you missed the party." The entire group broke out laughing.

"Okay I am not going to bore you with more history today. I will tell you that we will begin working with bomb placement techniques tomorrow. We plan to use the training freighter as our target. Small craft will shuttle us out to the site, and we will work in teams as we have in the past. You should plan to be at pier 2 for small boat boarding at 0900 tomorrow morning. Please go through your gear and come dressed for full underwater training."

"Today, it is a beautiful day outside and, as such, I think it is a great day for a swim. I told Chief Johnson that my wedding gift to him is he does not need to participate in this event. However, Ashley, Juan and I will join all of you. We have a nice mile swim scheduled out to the buoy and back beginning at 11 AM. It is a little over a mile and will be done with no fins. You may wear swimming goggles if you like. Are there any questions?

"If not, you are dismissed. I will meet you at pier 2 shortly before 11 o'clock."

Ashley was looking forward to the swim. It had been a while since she had had a good mile ocean swim and it was something she always enjoyed. She smiled when she thought about it, because she knew that Sam Olson would be trying his best to beat her. He was an extremely competitive guy and wanted nothing more than to say he beat an Olympic champion.

Ashley waited until almost everyone had cleared out of the room before she went up to Roscoe and said, "Roscoe, can I have a moment with you?"

"Sure Ash, what's up?"

"Have you got a couple of minutes?"

"Sure, let's just sit here."

"I want to talk to you about Toomont. When we briefed you, we told you that he had been a SEAL for about three years. I went back through his service record this morning before our meeting. He has been with the delivery vehicle team for two of the three years. Right out of Buds he went to Afghanistan. Based on the record, it looks like he was involved in a terrible firefight while there. It looks like three of the men in his SEAL unit were killed. I have been watching his behavior for the past month and I am now starting to believe that he may have posttraumatic stress disorder. As you may be aware, it is a mental health problem that some people develop after experiencing or witnessing a life-threatening event. Combat is an example of an event that can trigger it."

"It is normal for most of us to have upsetting memories, feel on edge, or have trouble sleeping after a traumatic event. I am told however, that this disorder may make it hard to do normal daily activities, like go to work or spend time with people you care about. Most people start to feel better after a few weeks or months. However, if it has been longer than that it is very possible that one has PTSD. For some people symptoms may never stop.

"If I am right, Toomont has PTSD. His symptoms were just delayed and are now coming to the surface. I do not know how he feels but we know he is a loner. I don't know if he may feel on edge or if he may have trouble sleeping but it is pretty clear to me, he is not right."

"I think that he is a potential disaster in the making and that to avoid a problem now or in the future we should have him take a full physical now. If he does have PTSD it will have to be dealt with medically. We certainly do not need someone who is carrying that kind of baggage around on our team."

"You know, Ash, I never even thought about it. You were supersmart to look at his jacket and I think your observations make all the sense in the world. I will call the medical staff now and see if I can get him in for an observation while we are swimming in the blue Pacific. Good job and thanks."

Ash then said, "See you in a couple of hours. Do you and Juan still know how to swim?"

"Watch yourself young lady, those are fighting words."

They both laughed and Ash headed back to her state room on the submarine.

Roscoe called the mental health unit of the base hospital and introduced himself to the nurse on call. "Hi there. My name is Lieutenant Commander Roscoe Cook and I am the officer in charge of the Navy SEAL vehicle group 1 attached to the USS Louisville SSN 724."

"How can I help you, Commander?"

"I would like to make an appointment with one of your doctors to evaluate one of my men. His name is Harold Toomont. He is a second-class Navy Seaman and he has been a Navy SEAL for the past three years. His first year as a SEAL was spent in Afghanistan where he was involved in a major firefight in which a few members of his team were killed. He has been with our unit for the past couple of years and my staff has noticed some major changes in his behavior."

"He does not seem focused and my concern is he may have delayed PTSD. I would like to have a complete evaluation done on him before I put him in any additional stressful situations."

"When would you like us to see him?"

"If possible, I would like to have the evaluation begin this morning."

"Let me check the schedule and see if we can get him into one of the doctors later this morning. Anyone can develop PTSD at any age. There are several factors that can increase the chance that someone will have PTSD, many of which are not under that person's control. For example, having a very intense or long-lasting traumatic event can be a real factor. PTSD is quite common after certain types of trauma, like combat, for example. Stress can make PTSD more likely and lack of social support can make it more so. I have a doctor they can see Mr. Toomont at 1130 will that work for you?"

"Perfect, I will have him there."

Roscoe called Chief Johnson and told him about Ashley's observation. "Makes sense to me, Roscoe. I do not know why I did not think about it myself."

"It did not even dawn on me either Chief so don't beat yourself up. I would like to ask you to get hold of Toomont and explain to him we are concerned about his behavior and want to see him evaluated for PTSD. Make it clear he does not have a choice in the matter. This is about his safety and the safety of our team. Then please escort him to the 1130 appointment. I want to make sure he gets there. Let them know I would like to know the results of the evaluation once they have drawn their conclusions."

"Will do, Roscoe. Thanks for letting me out of the swim. I know I can do it, but I am not sure at this point that it would be good for me or the team. I will talk to you later."

At 1045 the SEAL team was milling around the pier.

Roscoe and Juan were not there yet but Ashley was. Everyone had on Navy issue swimming suits. Ashley had a swimming cap and her goggles as well. Everyone was in good spirits and having a good time. Petty Officer Pierce was an excellent swimmer and he had a big smile on his face when he said to Sam Olson and Ray Odemier, "Hey you guys, is today the day you have your dream come true and beat the a AOIC in the mile swim?"

They both turned to him and smiled which he knew meant they were both thinking about how to do it. Pierce was an excellent swimmer himself, but he knew that while these two guys may have dreamed that they were in the same swimming class as Ashley, it was just that....... a dream. When it came to the water, she was in a class by herself.

Ashley heard the conversation and just smiled. She said nothing to either of them. She was focused and could not care who was trying to beat her. As was her normal strategy, she would stay with them and let them reach the halfway buoy first then she would pull up next to them and pour it on for home.

Roscoe and Juan arrived, and Roscoe told everyone to get the water, which all of them did. "Okay gang when I say go, it is out to the buoy and back. Have a good time. On your mark, get set, go."

The SEALs took off like a herd of turtles. As she expected, Sam and Odie were leading the pack and setting the pace that she knew would kill them both. Ash stayed with them but made sure they knew they were in the lead. The rest of the team fell in line almost as expected with Albert Fineman bringing up the rear.

Ash could see the competitiveness of Sam. He was really pouring it on and slowly moving ahead of Odie. Ash set a smooth pace and stayed in third place. After the first quarter of a mile she could tell Odie was getting tired.

He had gone out extremely fast and was now slowing. She moved up on him and passed him as though he was standing still. Sam would round the buoy first which was fine with her. She kept her eye on him but did not change the pace. Her arms and legs were moving in perfect sync and she knew that whenever she asked her body to increase the speed it would respond.

She let Sam go around the buoy first and watched him as he headed back toward the pier. She was not that far behind at the turn and decided to move up on him a bit. Her plan was to put it in high gear at the three-quarter mile mark and that is exactly what she did. She went by Sam as though he was no competition at all. He saw her coming and tried his best to increase his speed, but he was finished, and he knew it. When she went by, she was moving so smoothly in the water he could hardly tell she was swimming. All he could do was to put that big smile on his face and think, this woman is something else.

Ash finished first and purposely jumped out of the water and was drying herself off when Sam arrived. "Hey Sam, nice swim."

"Right boss. You win again." They then both started to laugh. The rest of the gang arrived in small bunches. Roscoe and Juan were in the middle and as she expected Albert and Charlie Chan brought up the rear.

When everyone was finished and dried off Roscoe dismissed the group and told them to meet at pier 2 at 0900 in the morning dressed for UDT training.

CHAPTER 29
UDT PRACTICE

Roscoe changed the time overnight. He now wanted the team to meet in the SEAL classroom at 0900. He called Ash and let her know he wanted the team to have some class time before they went underwater to practice their underwater demolition skills.

At 0855 the team was in place, that is all except one. Harold Toomont was missing. Everyone noticed his absence, but no one said anything.

"Good morning everyone. I am sorry for the change in plans but after thinking about it a bit I felt it would be wise for all of us to get a brief refresher on underwater demolition. I have asked Rick Fellowes to join us this morning. Rick is fondly known as the mad bomber in the circles I run in." The group laughed and so did Rick.

"He is an expert UD guy and probably has forgotten more about bombs and underwater weapons than we will ever know. Welcome Rick.'

"In the next two days we will be underwater. We will be reviewing the proper placement of underwater explosive devices and the various types that are available to us. This is not to be taken lightly. How we handle it, place it and explode it is all-important unless you want to blow yourselves up. In that case, do not worry about learning anything." Once again, the SEAL team got a good laugh.

"Okay, Rick, they are all yours until we break for lunch at 01130."

"Thanks Roscoe and good morning to all of you. As SEALs you have been trained in a variety of skills. I am a UDT specialist and thus I do not know half of what you all know but I do know underwater weapons and how to safely use them to get the bad guy."

"To begin with this morning, I intend to talk to you only about limpet mines."

"These are the mines that are designed to be placed on the hull of a ship. They are designed for underwater use only. The mines are triggered with a timing device. The timing devices vary but they are all designed to go off as set and create an explosion that will ultimately sink the target."

"There are lots of different types of explosive devices. For purposes of our discussion I am going to focus only on those that would apply to you and that work with the limpet mines. So, I will not talk about nuclear explosives at all."

"Let's begin by saying an underwater explosion is designed to take advantage of water.

Water has a much higher density than air which makes water harder to move. It is also relatively hard to compress when under pressure in a low range. As a result, the two combines to make water an excellent conductor of shock waves that are generated when an explosion occurs."

"Underwater explosions are categorized by the depth of the explosion. Shallow underwater explosions are those where a crater is formed at the water surface that is large in comparison to the depth at which the explosion occurred. Today we are only going to focus on shallow water explosions."

"We use what is called a limpet mine to help us sink tankers and other ships. The mines are typically attached with magnets. The mine is named limpet because of its superficial similarity to the limpet, a type of sea snail that clings tightly to rocks or other hard surfaces."

"The swimmer or diver may attach the mine, which is usually designed with hollow compartments to give the mine just slight negative buoyancy, making it easier to handle underwater."

"Usually limpet mines are set off by a time fuse or they may have an anti-handling device. This is a device that makes the mine explode if removed from the hull by someone other than the guy who put it there. Sometimes limpet mines have been fitted with a small turbine which would detonate the mine after the ship had sailed a certain distance."

"I am not going to bore you with limpet mine stories, but I will give you one example of how they helped us in World War II. In September 1943, allied commandos from the Z special unit raided Japanese shipping in Singapore harbor. They paddled into the harbor and placed limpet mines on several Japanese ships before returning to their hiding spot. The resulting explosions, seriously damaged seven Japanese ships comprising over 39,000 tons between them."

"Most recently in May of 2019, some oil tankers in the Emirati port of Fujairah suffered damage from what appears to be limpet mines. Preliminary findings of the investigation by the UAED, Norway, and Saudi Arabia concluded in June of 2019 that limpet mines were placed on oil tankers to explode as part of the sabotage operation."

"Okay, so how do we handle these things? Well you will be using your rebreather breathing set. We now have one that is supplied with a keeper plate to clip the limpet mine to your chest."

"These mines are not heavy. They attach with extremely powerful magnets. The mines you will be training with are blanks but other than that they are for all practical purposes real in both looks, weight and size. Believe me the real ones can pack a real bang for your buck."

The lecture went on. At 01030 they took a break then resumed until shortly before noon. The focus of the lecture was on the mine itself and how to safely detonate it. Rick also spent a great deal of time with diagrams of the hulls of various types of ships and where best to attach a bomb for maximum effectiveness.

At 01145 Rick finished, took questions and turned the meeting back over to Roscoe.

"Thanks Rick. I think we all learned something this morning. I appreciate your taking the time."

"Happy to do it, Roscoe."

"Before I dismiss you, I have two brief announcements to make. The first is we will meet at pier 2 at 1330 dressed for UDT work with your LAR V Draeger rebreather on. Second, you may have noticed that Harold did not attend this morning's meeting."

"We have sensed over some time that his behavior has been somewhat unusual so yesterday Chief Johnson took him to be medically evaluated. What you may not know is Harold was with his SEAL team in Afghanistan for one year before he joined us. During that year he was involved in several significant firefights and 3 of his brothers were killed. I am sorry to say that Harold has a delayed version of post-traumatic stress and as such he will need significant treatment over a long period of time. As a result of this treatment, he will not be returning to our team.

The good news is he has been evaluated and will get the treatment he needs. It is unfortunate but it could happen to any of us. I am told that he can have no visitors for some time. When that changes, I will let you know. You are dismissed."

"Hey Ash, stick around a minute will you."

"Sure boss. What is up?"

"As you just heard you were right, and it was a good thing you noticed. Chief told me on the phone that Harold has a profoundly serious case of PTSD and without treatment he would have surely endangered his own life and probably those of others who were around him. Chief told me it may take years to get him to somewhat normal but who knows. So, thanks for your observation."

"No problem, just doing my job. See you at 1330."

Ash left and headed for the submarine. At 1330 she was at pier 2 with the rest of the team. They spent the next two hours underwater learning how to place and arm the lipid mine models. Ashley watched each of the team members work through the exercises.

As the afternoon went on it became clear to her that two guys really stood out at the top of the heap when it came to the placement of bombs. Odie, Raymond Odemier, was good at placing the explosive packs. He never rattled and had nerves of steel. Ashley was also incredibly impressed with Petty Officer Jim Martinez. She had watched Martinez during the shark attack. He was cool, calm and collected. Those were the same skills he was using to place and arm the limpet mine models.

When the afternoon ended, Ash headed back to the sub to shower and change. On the way back Roscoe asked her for her observations. She told him about Odie and Martinez.

"Good to know, Ash. Thanks."

Once showered and changed, Ash headed down the peer and grabbed an Uber to her apartment she was tired when she arrived home but not too tired to pour a glass of Oregon Pinot Gris and take a seat on her deck. She had not even thought about dinner, but she had a Swanson's chicken pot pie in the freezer and that would be dinner tonight.

She was in bed early and back in the water the next morning by 0900. Each day Roscoe had them swimming at least a mile with more practice on bomb placement underwater.

On Wednesday night she headed home but stopped at Safeway on the way. Tomorrow Ryan would return, and she wanted to have something special for him. She decided she would have dinner in for them on Thursday and Friday nights and then go out on Saturday night. Sunday would be another night at home as they were both underway on Monday. She decided on the following menus:

Thursday night – French cut lamb chops with Maggie Ginns stir fry sauce.
    Green beans with bacon and iceberg wedge salad
    Oregon Four Graces Pinot Noir

Friday night – Indian dinner – chicken with bangle Marsala rub
    Nan bread with dipping sauce
    cucumber and yogurt salad with cumin and cayenne pepper
    Duckhorn Sauvignon Blanc

Sunday night – tostada bowls with refried beans, chicken and guacamole.
    Mexican beer.

On the way to Safeway she made out a grocery list. When she checked out everything fit into two bags, so she just walked home carrying her grocery bags. Once back in the apartment she put the food and wine away then poured a glass of Four Graces Pinot Noir from Dundee Oregon and sat in her chair looking out at the Yacht harbor. She could see Sam and Esther's catamaran from her deck. What a great memory that would always be

CHAPTER 30
A GREAT WEEKEND BEGINS

Thursday was another day in the water. Roscoe continued to work on the placement of bombs on the bottom of the trainer freighter. He constantly evaluated the performance of the men. Odie and Martinez were the best, and clearly, they would be the two he would use should the skill be necessary in the future.

After the third day of underwater training Roscoe said to the group, "Good job, gang. I am giving you Friday off. Enjoy the weekend. See you Monday when we get underway. Be on the sub at 0800. Cheers."

Ashley had not expected this, and it gave her a bonus day. She was pumped when she left the sub at 1600 and headed home. She knew Ryan would be on time at 5 PM and she secretly hoped he would be able to get Friday off.

When she got home, she hung her uniform up and jumped in the shower. The warm water felt good given the fact that she had been swimming in the ocean for the past three days. She stayed in a long time until all her muscles were relaxed. She then dried off and picked her outfit for the evening. She selected a pair of tan short shorts and a sheer Hawaiian blouse. She did not need a bra and she was sure that the look would be just about right to hold Ryan's attention. She also did not need any makeup.

She put the bacon on. She planned to use it both with the beans and the iceberg wedge salad. She cut the iceberg lettuce into two wedges and then put the pickled onion she purchased on top along with a few sliced cherry tomatoes. She had a light blue cheese dressing that was cold, and she knew it would work well on the salad along with the bacon chips. Once that was done, she blanched the green beans and put the French cut lamb chops in a dish and poured the Maggi Gins stir fry sauce over them. There were three for Ryan and two for her.

Once that was all done, she looked at the clock and she had 15 minutes to spare. She used the time wisely by opening a glass of Prosecco and taking a seat in her chair on the deck. She poured a glass for Ryan as well and put it in the refrigerator.

As usual he was right on time and had another Hawaiian bouquet of flowers in his hand. She opened the door and jumped in his arms. He was in uniform but had his overnight bag with them.

"Wow, what a great welcome," he said.

"These are for you. If the lady I bought them from his right, they should make your apartment smell like you live in Hawaii."

"I'm sure they will Ryan. Why don't you grab a shower, change and then meet me on the deck? I have a glass of Prosecco waiting for you."

"I won't be long," he said as he headed for the bedroom.

Ryan was out in no time and joined her on the deck. She got up, grabbed the Prosecco she had poured for him from the refrigerator and then handed him the glass. "Here's to the start of a great weekend. Cheers."

"Ash, you're forgetting it's only Thursday night. We have one more day to go until the weekend is officially here

"Not me. We have tomorrow off. Do you have to work?"

"I'm not sure what you would call what I've been doing for the past two weeks but it isn't exactly work. To answer your question, I do have to go in but it is only for a half day so I should be back here by noon tomorrow. These two weeks of classroom training have been about as boring as it gets. I will be so happy when it is over tomorrow. By the way, Ash, you look unbelievable in that outfit. Not only does it look great on you, but it's pretty sexy if that is an acceptable thing to say."

"I take that as a compliment. It may in fact be the first time in history that anyone thought a Navy SEAL was sexy and said so." Ryan just laughed

"This Prosecco is great, it's super cold and hits the spot."

"What did you plan for dinner? And what do I need to do to help?"

"Dinner is pretty simple. We are having French cut lamb chops, with green beans and bacon and an iceberg wedge salad."

"That doesn't sound simple to me. How do I cook a French cut lamb chop?"

"It's easy. I have them marinating already. You will just need to heat the grill up and cook them for 3 ½ minutes per side. You will need to baste them once when you flip them. That's it. I have everything else under control."

"I'm not surprised. I don't think there is anything that you can't do."

"Oh yes there is. I have no desire to or even want to think about landing a jet, like the one you fly, at full speed on a postage stamp bobbing around in the ocean. I will leave that to the real men on this planet."

Ryan just laughed. He then raised his glass and said, "Cheers to the most beautiful and complete woman I know."

"Okay enough. I am going to put the beans on and mix the bacon in with them. I have the lamb chops ready. Why don't you turn on the grill? When it is up to 500 degrees turn all the burners on low and put the lamb chops on for 3 ½ minutes then baste and flip. Another 3 ½ minutes and we will be ready to eat. When you have time, please open this Four Graces Pinot Noir. It should be perfect with the dinner."

Ashley then set their little table. Finished off the iceberg wedges with bacon and blue cheese dressing and put them on the table. Ryan did as he was told and it seven minutes, he took the lamb chops off the grill. They were done perfectly at medium rare.

They sat at the table and poured the wine. "Cheers to us," Ash said

"Well I'm pretty curious. What is our plan for our last weekend together for a while?"

"I have purchased a surprise for you that will take up our Saturday. We are going to the North Shore Keana Farms Zipline Venue.

We need to grab and Uber to get us up there and back. We need to be there by 10 in the morning. We have a three-hour guided zipline tour which includes Oahu's longest ziplines ranging from 500 feet to over a half a mile in length. I am told the ziplines are world-class and they are dual so we will be going together at the same time. I am told the views are out of this world and that the farm is a real working farm which will allow us to bring home some things for dinner. I was a little worried you might be afraid of speed but then I figured since I would be with you, you would macho up and be okay."

"That sounds like a blast, Ash. What a treat to look forward to."

"Tomorrow while you are in school, I am going to head to the beach to our normal spot. I have a key to the apartment for you, so when you get back just change and join me at our normal spot. We will find some place to get lunch once you arrive."

"Tomorrow night we are having dinner and you're in for a special treat and I hope it all comes out as planned. I am taking you to India for dinner. We are having barbecued chicken with bangle marsala rub, nan bread with dipping sauce, cucumber and yogurt salad with cumin and cayenne pepper and a surprise Indian dessert. You will have to wash it all down with a Duckhorn Sauvignon Blanc."

"Ash, you are spoiling me to death. I have never eaten this good in my entire life. I've got to make sure that I don't evolve from being called Ryan to being called Bubba."

Ash just laughed. "Don't worry pal; I will not let that happen. Even if I don't have a gym to drag you to, I will figure out another way to keep you active until you're ready to drop or just can't breathe anymore."

"Now that sounds like a workout I would really enjoy. Cheers to you and your creativity."

The evening was over almost before it began. They went to bed early and when Ryan looked up to see Ash come out of the bathroom he was blown away once again.

Ash had on a Victoria's Secret very sexy bombshell necklace bra and panty set. It was in red lace and the color against Ash's tan body was over the top. Ryan was beside himself and all Ash could think about as she lay exhausted in his arms was Victoria's Secret did the trick. With that thought in mind she fell sound asleep.

As usual they were up early. Ryan showered and put his uniform on while Ash made him a cup of coffee and went to work on her nan bread dipping sauce. She knew that when she was done her entire apartment would smell like an Indian restaurant, so she planned to leave the window open when she headed to the beach.

She grabbed a recipe book and looked up "Sanaa's Jalapeno Lime Pickle dipping sauce. She had first tasted in on a trip to Disney animal kingdom. It was one of the dipping sauces served with the bread at the villas where she and her brother had stayed with her parents.

It called for ¾ cup of canola oil and one and a half cups of shallots along with 3 tablespoons of salt. The recipe also required 1 tablespoon of chili powder, 2 tablespoons of paprika, 2 tablespoons of curry powder and 1 ½ tablespoons of cayenne pepper. It then required 1 cup of white sugar and 1 cup of white vinegar along with ½ cup of lime juice and 2 tablespoons of lime zest. Last it required 2 cups of fresh jalapeno peppers.

Once she had all the ingredients ready to go, she heated the oil and cooked the shallots with the salt until the shallots were translucent. She then added the spices and continued cooking while stirring in order not to burn the spices. Then she added the sugar vinegar lime juice and zest.

She let it heat to a boil then reduced the heat to low and cooked it for 10 minutes. She then turned off the heat and added the jalapeno pepper and let the whole thing rest for 30 minutes. During the rest. She opened the kitchen window and jumped in the shower.

When she was done, she put her swimsuit on and packed her bag for the beach. When she was ready to go, she poured the dipping sauce into a quart glass jar and put it in the refrigerator. Now it was time for the beach.

At about 1 PM Ryan met her at their place at the beach. "Hey Ash, my class is over, and boy am I glad. What a pain that two weeks was. I changed at your place and it smelled just like an Indian restaurant. You must've been pretty busy chef after I left this morning?"

"Remember tonight is Indian night at the apartment. Are you hungry?"

"Starving, have any ideas?"

"Yes, I have a plan. Look over your shoulder past the path and what do you see?"

"I see a food truck."

"But that is not just any food truck. That is Ken's kitchen food truck. It is a one-of-a-kind and they serve the best shrimp plates you will ever taste. They come in four different choices, garlic butter, Thai basil, spicy garlic and spicy red curry. You just have to pick your poison."

"Sounds great. Let's go."

The food was great. They just relaxed on the beach until about four in the afternoon and then they headed back to the apartment for dinner.

They got home and jumped into the shower together. They were giggling like two teenagers as they soaked up every part of their bodies. When they were done, they were out and dried off and changed into their normal weekend wear. For Ryan it meant shorts and an underarmor breathable T-shirt with sandals.

For Ash it was short shorts and a top that was cool. No bra was the norm for her on weekends and she matched the shorts with a pair of new sandals.

"Okay, what do I need to do for dinner?"

"I need you to baste the chicken breasts with the rub I have on the counter. It is called bangle marsala rub. Then once you have them coated on both sides; I need you to barbecue them for about 11 minutes on each side. When they are done, I will want you to come in and slice the chicken into narrow long pieces and add a bit more rub where you make the cuts to ensure we get the full flavor. While you are doing that, I will get the cold cucumber, yogurt and sour cream dish going.

To keep us in the spirit I need you to open a couple of bottles of Duckhorn Sauvignon Blanc and pour each of us a glass. That should help us work properly."

"Now that sounds like a plan. You told me earlier that were going to have something special for dessert. Can you tell me now?"

"Sure, but I can't take credit for it, I bought them at the Indian market. They are Balushahi. They look like small donuts. They are made with Maida flour, yogurt, oil and sugar. They are to die for but do not eat more than two or you're going to feel like you are going to explode. They are in the refrigerator."

They ate their dinner on the deck. It was perfect and Ryan could not get enough of the Nan bread with dipping sauce. By the time they were ready for bed Ash was exhausted. She did not surprise Ryan with anything but her nude self. It worked just as well and afterward they fell sound asleep. It had been two great days with the best yet to come.

CHAPTER 31
THE WEEKEND ENDS

They were both up early looking forward to their Saturday together and to their Keana Farms north shore zipline tour. It was another perfect Hawaiian day. They both dressed in khaki shorts, breathable T-shirts and sandals. At 8 AM they called an Uber driver to pick them up at 8:30. They did a MapQuest on their phone and saw that it was about 35 miles to the farm. It was in the town of Kahuku. They packed a small backpack, and each put a sweater in it along with their running shoes. They walked down the stairs to the street from the apartment. The Uber guy was waiting for them at the curb.

"Where to?" He said.

Ash told him that they wanted to go to Keana Farms in Kahuku.

"I think the best route is Highway 83. It should take about an hour I think?"

"Oh yes, you're going to the zip line farm."

"I know it well. You are right Highway 83 will take us to it. I have been out to it several times and when I pick people up on the return all the reports have been great. It should be a good day for it."

They did not talk much on the way out. The drive was easy and there was not much traffic, so they just watched the beautiful scenery as it passed by.

They arrived with over one-half hour to spare. They found the entry and registered at the welcome desk. Ashley had paid for the three-hour tour in advance and she had the receipt so there was no problem checking in. The temperature was about 80° but only predicted to reach 85 later in the day so it was not too hot. They were met by their guide, who was a young woman who looked like she had spent every day of her life in the sun. Her name was Wiki Manu. She was born in a small town on the north shore and she had never been anywhere else.

She went to grade school and high school in Kahuku and her family including her grandparents all lived on a plot of land that it been in the family for years. She told them that this was where she wanted to be and nothing else interested her. In fact, Ryan could not believe it when she said she had only been to Honolulu five times in her entire life.

She told them that she would be their personal guide for the three hours. She also told them that, because of the fear of Coronavirus, their business was dropping off and thus what would normally be a group of six was today a group of two. Both Ryan and Ashley were happy to hear that.

The day was great. They zip lined on all eight tracks and both were amazed how fast and how high they went. A couple of the runs went right over the tops of trees which frankly made both have second thoughts. The views from the top of each line run were amazing. They could see the entire north shore and look out over massive amounts of green land.

They were taken by Wiki on a four-wheel drive excursion through the jungle and they both rappelled down a fairly good size wall.

It was a great day and a great tour. When they finished Ryan gave Wiki a $50 tip which made her incredibly happy.

Ashley knew that Keana Farm was a working farm and as such she asked Wiki where they could purchase some vegetables grown on the farm. Wiki pointed out a food stand to them. Ash bought lettuce and tomatoes before they headed back to the apartment. Tonight, would be Mexican night and she could use both for dinner.

The three-hour tour along with the commute to and from had gone by fast. It was almost 4 o'clock when they arrived back at the apartment and they were both tired from their active day in the sun.

As they walked up to the apartment Ash said to Ryan, "I don't know about you but I'm tired, thirsty and in need of a long hot shower."

"I feel the same way, Ash, that was one great day."

"Ryan, tonight's Mexican night and were going to have tostada bowls but I have a suggestion. In the refrigerator I have a six pack of Mexican beer. I would suggest we each grab one and sit out on the deck and relax before we shower and start our dinner prep. What you think?"

"You talked me into it. What kind of Mexican beer did you buy?"

"I bought Dos Equis. It should be ice cold. It is a Mexican beer made by the Cuauhtemoc Moctezuma brewery. It was originally called 20th century. It is a pale lager in green bottles."

"Oh yes, I know it and think I've had it before. It should be great."

They put the bag on the floor of the living room, went straight to the refrigerator grabbed two Dos Equis and headed for the deck.

They just sat and looked at the harbor and sipped their ice-cold Dos Equis. After half an hour Ashley said, "Okay time for a shower. You want to go first, have me go first, or just jump in together?"

"That my dear is a no-brainer. See you in the shower."

When they were out, dried off and in their evening cloths, Ryan asked what he needed to do for dinner.

"There are two tostada molds on the kitchen counter. Take two of the large burrito size tortillas and put one in each mold. Then put them on a cookie sheet and put them on the barbecue until they firm up and brown. You will need to watch them because we do not want them to get too done. We will use the shells to put our tostada salad stuff in. Once you have the shells done, put this boneless chicken breast on the grill and grill it for about 11 minutes per side at low temperature. When the chicken is done please shred it for me."

"What are you going to put in the tostada salad?"

"I'm making a bunch of things and then you'll make your own. Let's see, I have nonfat refried beans, chopped tomatoes and chopped iceberg lettuce. In addition to that I have black olives, the chicken breast you are cooking and homemade guacamole. You can top that off with taco sauce and salsa. Dessert tonight is vanilla ice cream if you have room for it. We are having another beer with our tostadas."

"It's a good thing I'm going out to sea for two weeks on Monday. If I continue with this incredible food I'm going to turn into a balloon."

They finished dinner and it was as described, fantastic. They were both too tired and full to think about dessert so they both had a cup of coffee and watched the sunset.

"Well I hate to bring this up, but tomorrow is our last day together for a couple of weeks. What do you have planned for us, Ash?"

"Almost nothing. I do not want to cook in because I do not want food around for the two weeks we are gone and we are going to need an early start on Monday morning. I need to be on the sub by 0800. My thought for Sunday is a day to sleep in. A late brunch on the beach followed by people watching and a couple of ocean swims. Home by 4 PM clean up then off to dinner."

"What treasure house have you picked for dinner?"

"I really asserted myself on this one. I not only picked the dinner place, but I picked the menu. Here is what you must look forward to. We are going to 53 by the sea. It is an all seafood restaurant that gets a solid four stars. It has sweeping views of Waikiki, Diamond Head and the surf at Kakaako. For dinner we are going to split the chilled seafood tower which is an exceptionally large dish made up of lobster, shrimp, abalone, oysters, fish and a few other things I can't remember."

"Following that were going to split a Meyer lemon aioli baked mahi-mahi with King crab. That should all go down with a couple of bottles of great white wine. How does that sound?"

"Sounds perfect but it is a bit hard for me to focus on more food at this moment."

"Our dinner reservation is for 6:30 which should allow us a great view of the sunset, plenty of time for dinner and then home and in bed by 9 PM. Anyway, that is the plan."

That night Ash surprised him with the black lace bra and panty set. It worked well. It was not the first time she had worn it for him, and the second time was a charm.

They slept in until 8:30 and then showered and changed into their beach clothes. Then it was down the path and onto brunch. They walked to the Outrigger beach resort to have brunch at the Hula grill. They had both heard of the brunch menu and looked forward to the view.

They got a window table. Neither of them wanted anything with alcohol to drink so they both ordered papaya lemonade which came in a huge glass with lots of shaved ice. Ashley ordered the banana mac pancakes and Ryan had the breakfast BLT which was made with eggs over easy, spinach and tomatoes.

They were on the beach by 1 PM. Both took a couple of dips in the ocean during the afternoon. They were home at 4 PM and took the time to get ready in order to walk to dinner. They left the apartment at about 6:10 and walked to the Outrigger resort. They had no problem with the reservation and were given a great table.

The waitress came over and said "I see you both preordered. Can I get you anything to drink before we start with your dinner?"

"Yes, I would like to see a wine list," Ryan said.

The waitress was back in a minute and gave the wine list to Ryan. He took a brief look at it and ordered a bottle of Dry Creek Sauvignon Blanc from Napa Valley in California.

The waitress returned with the wine. Ryan sampled it and it was fine. She poured two glasses for them and then asked them if they would like to begin with the seafood platter they had ordered.

They both were ready to eat so they asked her to bring it out.

When she arrived with the dish it was huge. "My gosh, this is a lot of seafood," Ashley said, "too bad were leaving tomorrow we could have taken some of it home."

Ryan dug in beginning with the lobster. "This is excellent."

Dinner lasted almost 2 hours, which was longer than Ryan thought they would take. They did not have dessert, but they did have coffee after they finished all they could handle. The mahi-mahi was excellent and had a nice Macadamia crust on it. It was a good thing they had split both orders because it was clear to them that even with a half order, they had more food than they could handle.

They walked back slowly and were home by 9 PM. They were both tired and had an early start in the morning. Ashley cleaned the house a bit and Ryan helped by doing the bathroom. When it was all done it was about 10 o'clock? They made love very slowly and were sound asleep by 10:30.

Both were up at 6 AM, showered and dressed in uniform and grabbed their Uber car to the base. Once there they gave each other a hug and a brief kiss goodbye and headed to their respective ships.

They were both on board before 0730. Ashley's submarine was set to go at 0800 and Ryan's aircraft carrier would be underway at 01030.

Ryan walked into his state room and seated at the desk was his roommate Scotty. "Hey Ryan, how was your weekend?"

"Mine was great Scotty. We had a blast, went zip lining, ate and drank too much, but I would not have changed a thing. How was yours?"

"Nothing like yours I'm afraid. After two weeks of school I guess I am ready to get back in the air. Those two weeks were almost too much for me to take and most of the information was new to me. You must've been bored because I know you've been through it all before."

I was so happy they let us out at noon on Friday, otherwise I'm sure I would've gone nuts."

"At least you had Ashley to look forward to. Guys like me had nothing to look forward to other than their stateroom each evening."

"Yes, Ash is special, and I simply can't get enough time with her to ever satisfy me, but I'm like you. I'm ready to get back in the air." "Hey Ryan, have you been following the Coronavirus news. It seems to be getting worse and while it doesn't seem to have quite reached us in Hawaii it certainly is coming our way?"

"I have been reading about it. I just hope it stays away from us and this ship. How about breakfast?"

"You're on, let's go."

CHAPTER 32
DEEP DIVE

Ashley was alone in her state room. When she first came aboard the Louisville, she had a roommate. Her name was Misty Fremont and she was the Chief Weapons Officer. Not long after her arrival Misty was promoted to Lieutenant Commander and transferred out to the east coast of the United States. Misty was replaced by a young Lieutenant by the name of Peter Frake. Peter was a great guy and Ashley liked him, but she lost her roommate in the transition and now had the state room to herself which was both good and bad. Good in that she had it to herself, bad because she rarely had another woman to talk with.

The submarine was about to get underway when her state room phone rang. "Hi, this is Ashley." She said.

"Hey Ash, it's Roscoe. Can you join me for a cup of coffee in the word room? I would like to talk to you about the next couple of weeks and what we are scheduled to do. I heard from SEAL command over the weekend and I talked to Captain Miles yesterday. We are all in sync with what needs to be accomplished so I would like to bring you up to speed."

"No problem boss, I'll head to the wardroom now. See you in a couple of minutes."

Ash was sitting in the chair when Roscoe arrived. The submarine was underway, and the dive officer was going to take her down once they reached the outer harbor. Until then the submarine was rolling back, and forth which was not what she was designed for.

"Hey Ash, great to see you. I assume you had a great weekend with your Navy pilot."

"We had a great weekend and it included some really fun things like zip lining and repelling."

"Based on what I know about you, you were made for those kinds of activities. I assume you were tested beyond your ability." They both laughed.

"So, what do we have to look forward to this time out?"

"Well, I have to get used to driving the new vehicle and I will want you by my side navigating and sharing the joy with me. We both need to become proficient in driving the thing. Our first week is going to be spent in deep water. The Captain has orders to let us out at 200 feet. We will need our teams to get used to entering and exiting the sub and the new vehicle at that depth. I'm not 100% sure why but I know it has to do with our upcoming deployment."

"Our second week we will be working in very shallow water. I'm told that the captain will let us out at 200 feet, and we will work our way to and island where we will put the vehicle on the bottom at 25 feet'.

I'm not sure why but they also want us practicing loading the vehicle while on the surface. Should be really interesting trying to hold it steady while guys go in and out of the hatch."

"Now that is a really weird request if you ask me." Ash said.

"They also want us to be fully armed during all of our exercises. The Captain told me that he has some weapons practice that he must complete with the submarine crew so it looks like our SEAL team will be underwater about four days of the seven each week. On the days we will have off the Captain will put the sub and his crew through their weapons exercises."

"I want us to continue to work in two teams like Mark designed and I want to keep the teams together. I think it works best and gives everyone a little bit more confidence. We will plan to make our first dives tomorrow. You and I will drive the vehicle. We will take one team out in the morning and the other in the afternoon. Then we will have Wednesday off. We will dive again on Thursday and Friday and then not again until the following Monday."

"Roscoe, I'm not sure if you have paid much attention to this but we may be fortunate that we are spending the next couple of weeks underwater. This Coronavirus thing is really something that looks like it will likely hit Hawaii like it has so many other states."

"Yes, I've been paying attention to it. I just can't imagine how someone can carry that virus, pass it on and not even know they have it while the other person they passed it on to can become extremely ill and possibly die."

"In any event, it seems like we are pretty safe underwater as long as no one on the crew or one of our teams gets the darn thing. Let's keep our fingers crossed."

TUESDAY MORNING 0900

The Captain had the submarine down to 200 feet and the first SEAL team met in the in and out chamber. Team one consisted of Petty Officer Sam Pierce, Rick Johnson, Charlie Chan, Rick Wise, Mike Jones, Jackson Strong, Peter Gomez and Kermit Fox. That meant that the vehicle would have 10 SEALs fully dressed on board.

Ashley knew from her previous dives that that would be the maximum particularly with full gear on. Roscoe had spent a great deal of time studying the operating instructions, but he was more than happy that Ash was along to help if needed. He explained to the team that they would exit at 200 feet with full scuba gear on and then release the vehicle from the sub and board it one at a time.

He explained that once everyone was on board that he and Ashley would be taking them on a tour and letting them out along the way. He would let them out at 150 feet and at 100 feet. They were to exit and once everyone was out to reenter the vehicle with full combat gear on. When they had completed the drills Roscoe and Ashley would take the vehicle back to the sub and all would exit, remount the vehicle to the sub and reenter the submarine.

As they all exited the submarine, Roscoe was surprised at how clear and light the water was. For some reason he expected it to be much darker than it was. It was a sunny day and the sunlight kept the water clear to way below 300 feet.

Once they were all out, Ashley and Roscoe entered the vehicle and took their positions up front in order to drive. The team went to work detaching it from the submarine. The process went smoothly as they had all been through it before.

It was clear that Sam Pierce was the leader of the group. Using hand signals, he was able to have the group work together almost as though they were one. When the vehicle was safely detached from the submarine, Roscoe gently lifted it off its platform and moved it to a position that was safe distance from the side of the submarine. Once he had it in position Sam gave the hand signal to begin the entry process. One by one the SEALs in group 1 entered the vehicle. Roscoe was amazed how easy it was to hold the vehicle steady while the entry process occurred. He talked to Ashley about it as the entry process was taking place. He also explained to her that he would plan to drive the vehicle for the first two days to get used to it then he would switch seats with Ashley on the third and fourth day of practice.

Once everyone was in, Roscoe and Ashley took the mini sub on a tour. They practiced up and down and side to side turns eventually arriving at 150 feet. Once there, Roscoe told Sam to move them out which he did with no problem. The entire process went well and was performed again at 100 feet.

Once that was done, Roscoe moved the mini sub back to its position above the submarine deck and Sam and his team went to work attaching it. Ashley was the second to last to leave followed by Roscoe. Everyone reentered the submarine using the in-and-out box. Before noon, the team was all back on board.

Roscoe and Ashley had lunch together in the wardroom. Roscoe was pleased with the morning group exercise and he was also impressed with the operating performance of the new vehicle.

At 1400 the second team of SEALs assembled in the in and out hatch room. This team was led by Jim Martinez. It included Terry Lund, Albert Fineman, Ray Odemier, Sam Olson and Ron and Mattie Forkman. This team was missing one man, Harold Toomont. This meant there would only be nine in the vehicle, so Gunny Sanchez joined the group. It was a tight fit, but everyone settled in.

Once everyone was out of the submarine, Ashley and Roscoe boarded the vehicle and Jim gave the hand signal to the group to begin the detachment process. Like team one, team two did well. They had all been through it with Mark and Ashley and their experience showed. Roscoe lifted the vehicle off the submarine and moved it away for a safe boarding distance. When he was positioned, Jim gave the signal to the team to begin the boarding process. Once on-board Ashley and Roscoe followed the same path that they had chosen with group 1. At 150 feet it was everyone out and then back in and the same thing occurred at 100 feet.

At 100 feet the water was warm, above 70°, and with the sunlight from above everything was clear and light.

Suddenly everything turned dark. Ashley and Roscoe noticed it from inside the mini sub immediately and so did the SEAL divers that were all outside in the water. Jim Martinez looked up and motioned to the team to do that as well. Ashley saw the signal and mentioned Roscoe that Jim was pointing at something that was above the vehicle.

Roscoe maneuvered the vehicle so they could see through the small windows they had. Both were amazed at what they saw. There, moving slowly above them was the largest shark any of them had ever seen. At first, they could not believe their eyes, but it was not long for them to realize that a whale shark had taken a position about 50 feet directly above the mini sub.

Roscoe knew immediately what it was as he had seen one before. He said to Ashley, "Ash it's a whale shark. I am a bit surprised to see it this close to Hawaii. They normally they like tropical waters where it is very warm.

They live in the open sea but not in great depths of the ocean, although they are known to occasionally dive to depths close to 6000 feet. They are primarily seasonal feeders and they know where to go at what time of the year. One of their favorite spots is Bahia de Los Angeles in Baja, California. That is where I saw my first whale shark."

Once the initial shock was over, Jim and his team just watched the thing as it stayed in one position. It seemed to just hover above the vehicle. Jim tried to estimate its size. It was clear to him that it was over 60 feet long. He knew a bit about whale sharks, but he had never seen one. The whale shark holds many records for size in the animal kingdom most notably being by far the largest living non-mammalian vertebrate. He also knew that the whale shark was found in open waters but mostly in tropical oceans. It was odd to see one this close to Hawaii but with the water temperature over 70° at 100 feet it was not unheard of.

He could not believe the size of its mouth. He knew that the team was in no danger as whale sharks feed almost exclusively on plankton and small fish and pose no threat to humans.

Jim got permission from Roscoe to take the team up for a closer look at the giant. As he got closer, he could see that in its mouth it had over 300 rows of tiny teeth which it used to filter feed. The mouth appeared to be more than 5 feet wide. It had large pairs of gills. The head was wide and flat with the two small eyes at the front corners. It was dark gray with a white belly. The skin was marked with pale gray and white spots and stripes.

It had three prominent ridges along its sides, which started above and behind the head and ended at the caudal peduncle. The skin was thick and looked like it would be very rough to the touch. Seals are tough but, in this case, no one wanted to go and pet it with one exception. The group did not know it but Gunny Sanchez had seen a number of whale sharks over his years and to demonstrate his familiarity with it he swam up and petted it on the stomach. The shark did not seem to mind or for that matter notice. After about 10 minutes the shark started to move slowly swimming off into the distance. The light came back as the huge shark departed the area.

Once the shark started its movement, Jim signaled to the boys that it was time to reboard the vehicle. They rejoined the vehicle at 100 feet and one by one they entered. Once inside, they were all talking about shark. None of them had ever seen one before and the size of it was unbelievable. It was much bigger than a whale which they had all seen on many occasions and they could not get over the size of its mouth nor the fact that Gunny petted it.

Roscoe turned the mini sub back towards the submarine and gradually took her down to a depth of 200 feet. Once there, he centered it over the sub and Jim and the SEAL team exited the mini sub and secured it to the submarine. Once that was done Ashley and Roscoe followed them.

One by one they entered the submarine through the in and out chamber. Once inside all the talk was about the whale shark. It certainly grabbed the attention of the sailors on board. No one had ever seen one and most of them could never imagine getting in the water with one let alone swimming up to it so close that they were able to touch it if desired. Ashley met with Roscoe after dinner to talk about the day. Both were pleased with the team and with the operating performance of the mini sub.

They would be back in the water again in the morning. Group one would go out at 1000 and group 2 at 1400. The mission would be the same. The idea was to practice until it became the new normal.

Both Roscoe and Ashley were tired and by the time they hit their racks they were sleeping before their heads hit the pillows.

Tomorrow Roscoe planned to have Gunny lead team one.

Everything else would remain the same. He also planned to change the depths again. Tomorrow, they would start at 200 feet and would then move to 150, 100, then 50 feet. They would all use full military gear and scuba lungs.

Each training day went well during the first week. Ashley took her turn at the controls and had no problem with the vehicle. Roscoe could tell she was totally at ease and in complete control. Once again, she made him smile.

CHAPTER 33
SHALLOW DIVE

It was Monday morning of week two. Roscoe had asked Ashley to meet with him after breakfast at 0900 and the wardroom.

"Good morning, boss."

"Good morning, Ash. How did you sleep?"

"Great, I think being back in the water just makes me relax and when sleep time nears, my body seems to be trained to take advantage of it."

"What is your friend Ryan doing while you're out at sea swimming with whale sharks?"

"Well, I never know for sure, but my guess is he's flying a mission per day. He flies off the USS Yorktown CV 10. The last time they were out they had horrible weather and for some of the less experienced pilots I guess it was a real test. I told Ryan; it is hard for me to imagine trying to land a jet at full speed on a postage stamp in the middle of the ocean when the landing strip is moving all over. I'll take our undersea adventures anytime over that."

"Do you know if he flies alone or does he have someone with him?"

"He flies the F–18 Super Hornet. Most of the time he is asked to fly the flight commander. I think his name is Commander Reggie Sanders. Apparently, all the pilots are judged on each mission and Reggie is the judge. He always asks Ryan to fly him."

"I know Reggie Sanders. He was at the YARD a couple of years before me. I have not seen him in a lot of years, but I know that he is very valued pilot and that the Navy thinks very highly of him. My guess is your pal Ryan is one hell of a pilot."

"That would be my guess too, boss."

"Well, I wanted to talk to you about this week's training. I met with Captain Miles yesterday. He has located a small island in the outer Hawaiian chain that is unoccupied. The island is well protected by coral reefs but there are two channels that provide access to it. Captain Miles has been instructed to drop us off at a depth of 200 feet. We are to drive the mini sub to the island and up the channel. I am told that the channel moves gradually upward as it nears the island but there is a flat area where the water not far from shore is only 25 feet deep. We are to put the mini on the bottom there and have the men exit, swim to the island and then return.

On return, we have been told that we are to bring the mini sub up to the surface and that the men are to board the mini sub while we are on the surface not underwater. Once we complete that exercise, we are to return to the submarine. We will take group 1 out tomorrow morning and group 2 in the afternoon I know it seems like one strange exercise and I'm not sure how we keep the mini sub on the surface to board the men but we will have to cross that bridge when we get there."

"Well, we are rarely without a challenge. This will be interesting. I assume we are in full fighting gear like we were last week?"

"That's the plan."

Group 1 met at the in and out compartment shortly before 10 AM. Roscoe and Ashley were there to meet them and make sure everyone was present. With everyone present they were ready to go and they left the submarine one by one. Roscoe was out first, followed by Ashley and the rest of the team.

Roscoe and Ashley boarded the mini sub first, while the team worked to release it from the submarine. Once that was completed Roscoe lifted the minisub off the surface of the sub and moved it away to allow the team to load.

Once everyone was in, Ashley gave Roscoe the headings needed to move to the island channel. Roscoe moved the vehicle up as he kept it on its heading. At 100 feet he asked Ashley to calculate the distance remaining to the island channel. They were still 1 mile away but headed directly for the channel.

At 50 feet in depth Roscoe could see the channel that would lead them through the coral bed and to the island. Roscoe could see a flat area and he knew that is where he would move the vehicle down until it rested on the bottom. The water was 25 feet deep when the minisub settle on the bottom.

The team then exited the mini and proceeded to swim up the channel until they were able to step out of the water and onto a nice beach. Sam phoned Roscoe to tell him they were on the island and were about to head back to the vehicle. He also confirmed with Roscoe that they were to board from the surface not as normal.

Roscoe affirmed that and he and Ashley began the process of moving the mini sub up to the surface. There was some wave action but for the most part the mini sub remained pretty stable. The team was back in no time and began the boarding process. It was clear that to achieve the goal they would need to remove most of their fighting equipment. Sam went first and following him each man removed their gear and handed it in prior to boarding. The process took twice as long as normal, but they were able to accomplish it. It was clear to everyone, however, that both cover and efficiency were to be sacrificed it boarding on the surface was necessary.

Roscoe did not like it and believed that if it had to be used it would keep his team out in the open for longer than he would like. It took the stealth out of the mission.

Once everyone was in and loaded, they headed back to the submarine and all boarded successfully. The afternoon session went exactly as the morning session without problems. However once again it reaffirmed that if a surface loading was to be necessary men were going to be put in harm's way.

NIGHT FLIGHT OPERATIONS USS YORKTOWN CV 10

They were in their second week of training and it was a night landing exercise. Ryan was flying with Reggie like he had on so many other occasions when the call came in from one of the squad commanders.

"Big sky, this is Arrow over."

"Reggie responded, "Go ahead Arrow. What's up?"

Radio silence had been broken so Reggie knew there was some sort of a problem brewing.

"Big sky, I have bird number three with an instrument problem. He is telling me that his instrument readings are not working and thus his ability to call the ball will be impossible. Over."

"Roger Arrow. I will advise flight operations of the problem and wait for their advice. Please have bird number three move to a holding pattern and land the rest of the squad."

"Flight operations this is Big Sky, over."

"Big Sky, I read you, what's up Reggie?"

"We have a plane with an instrument problem which is giving the pilot a bunch of bad data. As such, he will be unable to call the ball in the normal manner. How do you want me to handle it?"

"Big Sky clear all birds then position yourself so the hurt bird can follow your lights to the deck. Bring your plane in as though it is going to land but without the hook down. Have the hurt bird follow you in with his hook down. It will require extremely low approach for you but if the hurt bird follows your lights with the hook down, he should be able to land safely. It will take some skill on your part, Big Sky, to make it happen."

"Roger, will do."

"Okay, Ryan, you heard what flight operations said. Are you ready to do this?"

"Yes sir, I'm ready when you give me the word."

"Okay bring the hurt bird in and up behind you. Tell him exactly what you are going to do. He is to follow your lights exactly."

Ryan contacted the other pilot. He was not very experienced, and he was extremely nervous. Ryan calmed him down and told him to fall in behind him and to stay close. He wanted him close enough to follow exactly but he knew at the speed he would be traveling that things were going to happen extremely fast and there was no room for error. Reggie gave him the word and Ryan headed for the carrier. Before he began his approach, he reminded the pilot to follow him and to engage his landing gear and drop the hook. The pilot affirmed that he had done so. Ryan checked to make sure his landing gear was in the up position.

Word had spread throughout the carrier that there was a bird about to land with a major problem. The emergency teams were all scrambled and the destroyers in the plane guard positions were notified of the potential problem.

Ryan accelerated the Super Hornet and headed for the deck of the carrier. The pilot behind him did exactly as he was told. Ryan buzzed the deck of the ship with about 3 feet of clearance. He passed over the deck of the carrier in an instant and pulled up. He and Reggie looked back and were relieved. The pilot had caught the hook on the number three line and made a safe landing.

"Hey Ryan, that was nicely done. I must admit it gave me a bit of the creeps when you dropped so low. You executed that perfectly. Now let us go home."

"Yes sir."

Ryan called the ball and had his super hornet on the deck in no time. When they finally exited the plane, all the men on the deck of the carrier were clapping for them.

The next morning Reggie was in the wardroom having breakfast when Captain John Jacobs, the Senior Naval Aviator and Director of Naval Flight Operations, came in and sat down.

"Reggie that exercise was something to watch. I have got to tell you that my stomach was tight, and my shorts were riding up. I am sure glad they stayed dry when you guys made that emergency run over the deck.

That was one hell of a piece of flying. I do not think your Super Hornet was more than 3 feet off the deck when you made that run. Who was flying it?"

"It was Ryan Joshua Sir."

"Oh yes, I remember him. I would say that it was as fine a piece of flying that I have seen in years. In fact, I would venture to say it was a Blue Angel quality."

"Yes sir, I agree. It's funny you should say that because when we complete our next deployment Ryan will be up for reassignment and the Blue Angels have been on my mind."

"If you need additional support with your recommendation you've got it for me."

"Thank you, sir."

TWO WEEKS DOWN AND HEADING HOME

It was Friday night; the USS Louisville would be back home in Pearl Harbor by noon on Saturday. Ashley asked Roscoe for a couple of days off which he approved. So, beginning on Saturday afternoon, she would be home free until Wednesday at 0800. She did not know when Ryan was due in on the Lexington, but she thought it would be sometime on Saturday as well. She knew he would call when he was free, so she set about planning her time off.

First things first. She wanted to call her Mom and Dad and see if they might be free to spend a week with her in the next couple of weeks. She was not up to speed on the Coronavirus, but she hoped it wouldn't get in the way of her folks joining her in Hawaii.

The Louisville arrived in Pearl Harbor on schedule and as soon as she was tied up Ashley was off and on her way home. She arrived home to find it just as she had left it, she put her uniform away, changed into shorts and a loose top and grabbed the paper and pen to make some notes.

Since she did not know what Ryan's plans were, she decided to make the dinner tonight amazingly simple and flexible.

To accomplish that she wrote down, cheeseburgers with potato salad. She did not want to make any additional meal plans until she knew what Ryan's plans would be. She grabbed her bag and walked to Safeway. There she picked up two thirds of a pound of ground sirloin, some hamburger buns, Clawson's dill pickles, a tomato and a red onion. Then she went to the deli and got a pint of German potato salad. With those things in hand she went to the wine section and grabbed a bottle of white and a bottle of red. She selected a Dry Creek Fume Blanc and a Shea Wine Cellars Pinot Noir. With that done she headed home.

It was about four in the afternoon which meant it was seven in the evening at home in Portland. She had not heard from Ryan, so she decided to call her Mom and Dad. "Hello, this is Jim."

"Hey Dad it's me."

"Ashley, we've been thinking about you. It's great to hear your voice. How have you been?"

"Well for the last couple weeks I've been literally underwater which always makes me happy. I got back today, and I am going to take a couple of days off before I must go back to the ship. How are you guys doing?"

"To be honest we are not doing anything except staying in the house. As you may have read this Coronavirus is really bad. The state of Washington had it bad for a while so here in Oregon, we are being cautious and told to stay home stay inside and stay away from other people. We take walks when we can and in general, we isolate from others. Everyone here wears masks and keeps a social distance which is six feet apart."

"I've been totally out of touch for two weeks, so this is new news to me. I was so hoping you could fly out and spend a week with me before we deploy overseas next month."

"Doesn't look like that can happen, Ash. Everything here is frozen, and we are being told flights everywhere are being canceled. I know the viruses is traveling fast so I am sure it must be in or about to hit Hawaii.

It seems like it has hit everywhere else in the world. I heard today that 600 people died of it in New York alone yesterday."

"Wow am I out of touch. How is Mom and John doing?"

"Here, I'll put mom on. I think John is in love or so it seems. Not sure if I'm right and God only knows he will never tell what he is thinking but my guess is there will be a Jamison wedding within the next year."

"Wow, that is exciting."

"Here's mom."

"Hi Ash, how's my baby SEAL?"

"Hi Mom, Dad was just filling me in on the Coronavirus. I've been at sea for the last two weeks so I know nothing about it but it sounds like it's bad enough that neither of you will be able to make it out here before we deploy next month."

"I'm afraid that is the case. This thing is worse than anything we have seen before. Not only is it killing lots of people, but it is tearing this economy apart. There are so many businesses that are closing and so many people out of work it makes me sick."

"Dad tells me John may be getting serious about the girl you told me about."

"Yes, I think so, but you know John. I will probably be the last to know when he asks her to marry him. Men are hard enough to understand but your brother is right up there at the top of the list."

"How was your time at sea?"

"It was a lot of drills and a lot of time spent underwater. We are working with a new dry ride vehicle which seems to work well. Oh, and I saw something the other day I have never seen before."

"What was it?"

"We had a 60-foot whale shark hover over us for a while in the middle of the ocean. The thing was just huge."

"Did you say 60 feet?"

"I can't imagine being in the same ocean with one of those things let alone having that hover above my head."

Ashley talked to her mom for another half an hour and then hung up. No sooner had she hung up when the phone rang again. "Hey sailor, would you like a date for tonight?"

Ashley just smiled as she thought the weekend is about to get started.

CHAPTER 34
PLAY TIME

The knock on the door came at 6:30 PM. As usual he was on time. Ryan was in his uniform. His wings were above the two rows of ribbons he had earned on his past two deployments. Ashley was dressed in a normal evening attire which consisted of short shorts, a loose-fitting top and sandals. She had no makeup on and did not need it. She was tan and fit with her swimmer's body she looked like something out of a magazine.

She jumped into his arms and gave him a long and meaningful kiss. He did not say anything. He just enjoyed the moment. When it was over, he said "I missed you."

"Me too," she responded.

"Why don't you grab a shower and join me for a glass of wine on the deck. Tonight's dinner is simple. We are having barbecue cheeseburgers and potato salad with a great Pinot Noir."

"Sounds great. I will be out in a couple of minutes."

Ashley was parked in her chair with her glass of wine when Ryan joined her.

"I put your wine glass on the counter. Grab it and join me."

He did so, touched her glass with his and said, "cheers to you."

"How was your two weeks on the carrier?"

"It was pretty routine. I did have one thing that required more concentration than normal."

"What was that?"

"One of our guys had a problem with his landing instruments which meant he needed to make the carrier landing without instruments at night."

"So how did that involve you?"

"Well, as you know, I've been flying Reggie the last few times out and I was this night as well. He was the flight commander and had to make the determination with the carrier operations command on how to deal with the situation. He decided that we would need to get all the planes landed safely and then we would lead the plane without instrument controls in for a landing. The pilot was instructed to follow me and the lights on my plane with his landing gear down. My landing gear was up but I needed to bring him in low enough to catch the hook on the wire. So, I did just that, I took my super hornet in for a landing with no landing gear and crossed the deck landing surface with about 3 feet of space between the bottom of my plane and the deck of the ship."

"You've got to be kidding me, Ryan. That sounds like you were really playing with wildfire and if anything went wrong it wouldn't be good for a whole bunch of folks including you and Reggie."

"You're right, but I felt like it wouldn't be a problem and, as it turned out, it wasn't. Our guy landed on the first try. It was kind of strange. When we finally landed ourselves, Reggie and

I deplaned, the carrier crew on deck waited until we got down from the plane and then they started clapping as though we were something special."

"My guess is you impressed quite a few people."

"Who knows, it was just another day at the office for both of us. All Reggie said was good job kid." "How was your two weeks under the sea?

"Like you, it was pretty uneventful other than we have been conducting some exercises that are being driven by SEAL command in San Diego that are pretty weird."

"I'm not sure and I don't know what Roscoe knows but I think they're getting this ready to do something when we are out on deployment."

"They've been training us at 200 feet down and then at 25 feet down. I just cannot figure it out. Oh, there was one other thing of interest that happened this week."

"We were training in warm water at about 100 feet. The water was clear, the sun was out so it was easy to see when suddenly it was like someone turned out the lights. We looked up to see that a 60-foot whale shark had taken a position about 50 feet above our vehicle. He just stayed there for about 10 minutes. Roscoe and I were driving the mini sub, but our guys were outside right below the thing. They decided to go up and look at it closely. The thing had a mouth that was more than 5 feet wide. It was interesting to watch. The guys swam up to it and Gunny Sanchez actually petted it on the stomach."

"Ashley that just gives me the creeps. I cannot imagine being in the water with that thing even if I were told in advance it wouldn't hurt me. Just the thought of looking up and seeing that thing makes my stomach turn over."

"You have your challenges and I have mine. Now before we start dinner and before a second glass of wine I would like to ask you a favor. Would you please kiss me again like you did on arrival?"

"With pleasure ma'am."

"That was perfect, now it's time for burgers and potato salad. I have made up the patties and have the mild cheddar slices ready to go. The burger should take about 10 minutes on the grill. I would flip them in five minutes, then put the cheese on. Add the buns to the grill with about two minutes to go. I will have all the other condiments ready as well as the potato salad."

The burgers are great and so was the wine. When everything was cleaned up, they sat outside watching the lights on the marina. It was so peaceful and perfect.

Ryan broke the silence and said, "Have you thought about what you want to do this weekend?"

"Funny you should ask. I planned tonight's dinner but that was it. I wanted to see what you wanted to do before I set a schedule in place. What would you like to do?"

"I would like to spend the next 60 hours in bed with you."

"What a nice thought but having viewed our combined performance in that area we would not have the stamina to do what you have in mind. Any other thoughts?"

"I've been reading a lot about this Coronavirus and it is pretty clear it's headed towards Hawaii. It seems to be making a mess of the states and the rest of the world for that matter. Looks like many of the states are now requiring sheltering in place and bars and restaurants are closing. So, my thought is let's go someplace now that we may be unable to go to in the near future."

"On this trip out my roommate, Scotty, told me about a restaurant that I would like to try. It is expensive but it sounded like great fun. The name of the restaurant is Senia. It is located at 75 North King St. in Honolulu. I am told that the way to best enjoy the restaurant is to get a seat at the chef's counter. They have only one seating at the counter and it is at 6:30. There are only eight seats available at the counter so I am not sure we can get in but if you're up to it I would like to try to get us in for Sunday night. It will be my treat."

"Is there a menu?"

"No, the Chefs change it all the time and all the dishes are original. I looked it up on the Internet and was able to see pictures of the small plates they prepare. They look amazing. Would you be up for it?"

"Sure, especially if it's your treat. I'm not sure how I could ever repay you, but I'll try to think of something."

"Great. I'm going to call now and see what they say."

Ryan called and there were only two spots left for Sunday night. He booked them.

"Okay. Sunday night is booked. That leaves us with an open day tomorrow, I vote for a late brunch. Followed by a day of sand and surf. Then I would recommend dinner at home of your choosing and a roll in the hay after dinner. How does that sound?"

"It sounds great. I want to try the Loja kitchen. It is on Ena Road just around the corner from the Ala Moana Center. I'm told that they make great eggs Benedict, have a dish called Loco Moco and serve a Diamond Head souffle pancake.

"We can sleep in if that's possible. Go to brunch around 1030. Stop at Safeway on the way back, change and then head for the beach. For dinner I want to do a filet of sole with a potato chip crust with spicy catchup and steamed broccoli."

"Ashley, how do you come up with this off the top of your head? You really are amazing."

"Keep talking like that and it will get you everywhere you want to go. Oh, by the way, I forgot to tell you that I have Monday and Tuesday off. Any chance you can get free on one or both of those days?" "I don't see why not. We are in port for some time now and most of the time will be spent checking out the aircraft. I will call Reggie and see if he has a problem with me taking a couple of days off."

"Great, that would be super if we both were off."

Saturday went just as planned they arrived at the Loja kitchen around 1045. Got a table and they both had eggs Benedict. The food was good but no view. They told themselves they would come again but they favored the view of the beach and the ocean over a restaurant on a side street.

They stopped at Safeway on the way back to the apartment. Ashley ordered three quarters of a pound of filet of sole and made sure that it had no bones in it. She also picked up a bag of baked potato chips and some eggs.

Along with that she grabbed two bottles of Willakenzie Pinot Gris from Oregon and some Thai chili sauce. She also got some baby broccoli at the produce counter. She put the groceries away when they got home and then they headed for the beach. It was a great day. They were home by 5 PM, showered and changed into their normal evening wear. Ashley put the chips in the blender and then she dipped the fish in flour, egg mixture and then covered them with the blended chip crumbs. She made up a sauce using catchup and spicy chili sauce. She put the filet in a skillet on the stove and cooked it in butter until it was crisp on both sides. When served they dipped the sole in the spicy catchup mixture and ate the steamed broccoli.

The dinner was great and so was the wine. They made love and fell asleep in each other's arms. Sunday was there before they knew it and the day passed quickly. At 6 PM their Uber car showed up and they headed for Senia restaurant and their 630 reservation.

They were seated at the counter with the other six customers. Everyone was about the same age. The dinner was outstanding. All the courses were small plates, and each looked like a work of art. Wine was served with each course and the entire dinner took over two hours. They left both full and happy. It had been a great evening and was well worth the money.

Ryan heard back from Reggie and he was off for Monday and Tuesday so with nothing on their agenda they had one glass of wine before they went to bed.

On Monday morning they slept in. They were up and showered and having coffee on the deck around 1015. Ashley was reading the paper and said, "Hey Ryan get this. There is this company called URB-E Hawaii. They have tours all over the place, but they are based in Honolulu. They are a scooter company. We see people riding their scooters all the time. We can book a tour that takes us with a guide, out to Diamond Head and then have a hike before we return. Looks like it would cost us about $100 each for three-hour tour. Do you want to do it tomorrow?"

"I'm up for just about anything, Ash. That sounds like great fun. Let's give them a call and see if we can book something for tomorrow morning. I don't think it is going to be superhot, but I'd rather go in the morning than in the afternoon."

Ashley called and booked a trip for them the next day

"Okay here's the deal. We are booked for the 2 ½ hour Diamond Head ride and hike express. We leave downtown Honolulu at 9 AM tomorrow morning."

"The cost is $129 per rider. They tell me the ride and hike express is meant for those who are trying to pack as much in as possible in their time on Oahu. We start out at Waikiki;

we ride along Kapiolani Park and ascend to Diamond Head Crater."

"We stop at a few photo spots along the way so we should take a camera. We then enter the Diamond Head Crater. They tell me we lock the bikes up at a bike rack inside the crater and then we climb to the peak of Diamond Head for the view. It is supposed to be one of the most popular rides especially for those who want to get the Diamond Head experience."

"Sounds like a great plan to me. Any thoughts on dinner for tonight and tomorrow night?"

"I want you to continue to become a real grill master. So tonight, it will be teriyaki steak with a Japanese seaweed salad and tomorrow night it will be Cornish game hens with Jasmine Rice."

"I thought you might have something up your sleeve. Looks like we better make a Safeway run."

"Let's make a list. It should be simple. We can split a filet mignon. We will need to get some teriyaki sauce to use on it. The seaweed salad we can just pick up and the sushi bar section. They have it already made up. We will get one Cornish game hen and have them cut it down the middle and then we can pick up a box of Jasmine Rice that will go with it. We will also need to grab a peach if they have them and some cranberry sauce. That, plus wine, should do it."

They made the Safeway run, made a wonderful easy Japanese dinner and followed their normal evening routine. They were up early and took the tour. The weather was super, and the trip was well worth the money. Dinner was again simple, and their time together ended with both of them smiling.

CHAPTER 35
INTERCEPTED COMMUNICATION

SEAL COMMAND, SAN DIEGO CALIFORNIA

Admiral Omark's phone buzzed. "Yes, Marcia, what is it?"

"Admiral James is on the phone from Naval Operations in Washington."

"You mean Admiral Peter James, Head of Naval Operations?"

"Yes sir, it is one in the same."

"Thanks Marcia, I will pick it up."

"Pete, how are you? I can't imagine you're calling me to wish me a happy birthday, but I do remember birthday that both of us would like to forget."

"Ralph, how the heck are you? And no, I am not talking about your Subic Bay birthday party where none of us could catch the hook in the officers' club because it was physically impossible in the shape, we were in. Vietnam was a long time ago my friend."

"Okay, then I assume this is not a social call."

"You got that right. I am afraid we have a real problem brewing and it looks like it is a problem that was meant for the Navy SEALs. Do you remember when I told you about Kim Jong-un and our worry about a special project he might be working on?

"Yes, that was scary news."

"Well our friends in South Korea intercepted a communication today that was between a General named Fong Ho and a scientist who is working on a special project in someplace called Haeju Bay. It was clear from the communication that the North Koreans are working on the development of a virus that can be targeted at individuals or communities and it's so deadly that it kills everyone infected."

"You've got to be kidding me, Pete. This takes our problem with the Coronavirus to a completely different level."

"That is what we're dealing with. We are working with all our intelligence agencies at this point to identify as much as we can, and we are using every bit of our satellite technology to give us a picture of what is going on.

I should have more to tell you in a day or so, but it looks to me like your SEAL team out of Hawaii may have a very delicate job on their hands. Do not talk to anyone about this until you hear back from me and we've given some thought to the problem and what our approach should be."

"Will do Pete. Talk to you soon. Goodbye."

FOUR DAYS LATER

Admiral Omark was sitting in his office at 6:30 in the morning having his first cup of coffee. Marcia was not in the office yet so when his direct line rang, he picked it up and said, "Admiral Omark, may I help you?"

"Ralph it's Pete; I'm glad you're in early."

"Hey Pete, good to hear from you, I hope this call is a lot more positive than the last one we had."

"Unfortunately, Ralph, it is worse, so grab your notepad because I have a lot of ground to cover with you. Please put your phone on secure."

"No problem, you're good to go at any time."

"Okay, when we talked last, I mentioned that South Korea intelligence and picked up a communication between a North Korean General whose name is Fong Ho. The communication was coded and was between General Ho and a North Korean research immunologist by the name of Hong Ye. Apparently, Mr. Ye is the lead scientist on a project that North Korea is calling **Project V**."

"We now know that **Project V** is the codename for the development of a death virus that North Korea is trying to create so they use it as a bargaining tool to get whatever they want on the world stage. I'm told that the virus is already developed but they have yet to fully understand how to deploy it or to contain it."

"Our sources and satellite photos have told us that the research is being conducted in what looks to be, a broken-down warehouse on a dock in the small port of Haeju. To get to the bay where the dock is you must enter down a narrow channel from the Yellow Sea."

"As you may recall, the Yellow Sea is a marginal sea that is part of the Western Pacific located between mainland China and the Korean Peninsula."

"It is our understanding that the research facility is kept completely isolated from the population surrounding it. All supplies are brought in by ship through the narrow channel and the facility is provided whatever it needs with weekly night transfers."

"We aren't completely sure about the staffing, but we know that the facility itself is not that large and that there are six or eight guards that surround it at night. We also assume that it is alarmed as one would expect but there is no way for us to determine this."

"The research staff include six Korean scientists led by Mr. Ye and three other scientists that we believe are Chinese. They work a normal workday which begins at 7 AM and ends at 4 PM. The scientists are housed on a barge which is anchored a short distance from the warehouse facility. The scientists are transferred to work and back each day by a small battery-powered boat which limits the noise factor."

"We believe that the three additional scientists are from China and they serve as the lead research biologists. We believe that the three Chinese scientists are the three men who disappeared almost 3 years ago from their residences in China. It now looks like they were kidnapped by the North Koreans. The three Chinese scientists are also housed on the barge."

"We don't yet know how they convinced the Chinese to cooperate, but we assume it was with a variety of tools including force and some sort of bait and switch process."

"We also know that there are six or eight women on the barge. They are probably used to provide sex services. They never leave the barge and were probably used to convince the Chinese to cooperate."

"Okay, so now that I have given you the details of what we know it boils down to now I will give you my thoughts on what we need to do about it."

"And....that's where you come in. The only way we think we can disrupt this project is to do it with a clandestine operation that is conducted from the water. This is SEAL Team territory. Your SEAL team 1 is scheduled to deploy with the nuclear submarine USS Louisville next month. We think that timeframe needs to be moved up by at least two weeks. I know we sent Roscoe Cook out to lead the team recently and I know Roscoe's record so I feel comfortable that we have the team in place that can handle the operation."

"I also know that SEAL Team 1 has been testing the new mini sub and if I'm right it may get it's first operational test soon."

"So Ralph, I'm passing the ball to you and will leave it up to you to put a plan and timeline in place. Please give me a call back when you have your plan together and, Ralph, there is urgency to this operation. Talk to you soon."

The phone then went dead and all the Admiral could do was look at the four pages of notes he had taken during the conversation.

It did not take him long to decide what to do. Marcia was in, so he had her put in a call to Captain Jason Miles.

"Admiral, I have Captain Miles on the phone for you."

"Jason, how are you?"

"I'm fine, sir. To what do I know the pleasure of your call? It isn't every day I get a call from an Admiral in San Diego."

"Well, Jason, I'd like to tell you I think you could use a rest in San Diego, but unfortunately that is not the reason for my call. I need to see you here in my office on Friday. I am also inviting Roscoe Cook and his AOIC Ashley Jamison to join us. The meeting will be held beginning at 0900 here. It is totally confidential, and no one is to know what you are going to San Diego for or who you are going to be meeting with. You can discuss travel with Roscoe but I'd rather that you all come separately."

"I understand Admiral. I will be in your office at 0900 on Friday morning."

Admiral Omark then buzzed Marcia and said, "Marsha would you please get Lieutenant Commander Roscoe Cook on the phone for me?"

"Yes sir, right away."

"Admiral I have Commander Cook on the phone for you."

"Thanks Marcia." He picked up the phone and said, "Roscoe are you all settled in?"

"Yes sir, thank you for asking."

"Well I hate to disrupt your vacation, but I need to see you in San Diego on Friday morning at 0900. I have talked with Jason Miles this morning and asked him to be there as well. I would also like you to bring along your AOIC, Ashley Jamison. I don't want anyone to know where you are going or who you are meeting with and I would prefer that you all traveled separately."

"Yes sir, we will see you on Friday morning at 0900."

"Thanks Roscoe and good day to you."

Roscoe picked up the phone and dialed Ashley's room. "Ashley speaking, how can I help you?"

"Ash, it's Roscoe."

"Hi boss, what's up. Well I just got off the phone with Admiral Omark in San Diego. He wants to see us in his office at 0900 on Friday morning. He asked Captain Miles to be there as well. Whatever is going on he wants to keep it very confidential. He also said that he wanted us all to travel separately. So, you are on your own to get to San Diego. No one is to know where you are going or who you are going to see. I am going to stay at the Marriott Marquis and Marina Hotel. It is nice. You may want to book in there as well. We can have dinner together on Thursday or Friday night. If we do not meet up, I will see you at 0900 at SEAL team headquarters in San Diego. Have a safe travel."

Ashley called the airlines. She could get a flight out on Thursday morning direct from Honolulu International to San Diego. It leaves at 0700 and arrives in San Diego about 1000 West Coast time.

That would give her the afternoon and evening in San Diego which she could handle. She booked the flight and the return as well. The return would leave San Diego on Saturday morning at 0700 arriving Honolulu at 1500 Hawaiian time. She then booked a room at the Marriott Marquis and Marina for two nights, Thursday and Friday.

She called Ryan but he was not in, so she left a message. "Hey Ryan, it's Ash. Unfortunately, I have been called away on business and I will not be back until Saturday afternoon. If you can, plan to have dinner with me on Saturday night. Leave me a message if that works for you. See you at my place at 6 PM Saturday night. Cheers Ashley."

That night she got a call back from Ryan, but she did not pick it up. She didn't want to be in a position to tell him where she was going or who she was meeting with, so she just let him leave a message. He would be there on Saturday night. She caught her flight out early on Thursday morning and flew in uniform directly to San Diego. She carried only an overnight bag with a change of clothes. She also threw in her bathing suit on the chance she could use the pool at the hotel.

She grabbed a cab from the airport and checked into the hotel. It was a nice hotel and located right on the water.

There was a message waiting for her at check-in. It was from Roscoe. He would meet her for dinner at 630 at Roy's restaurant in the hotel. She knew Roy's well and looked forward to a dinner of Asian fusion.

Roscoe met her at 630. He was in uniform as well. In downtown San Diego they fit right in. There were naval and Marine officers coming and going all the time the only difference was, very few of them wore the SEAL Trident designation above the ribbons on the left side of their uniforms.

They had a nice dinner together but there was not much shop to talk about. Roscoe told her he was in the dark and they would both learn together in the morning what SEAL command had in mind. They agreed to cab it over together and meet at 0815 in the lobby.

Roscoe told Ashley he arranged to fly back on Saturday morning as well so they would have the evening to talk about whatever they were about to learn.

They caught a cab from the hotel and were outside the Admiral's office at 0845. At about 0855 Captain Miles arrived and the three of them were ready to meet with the Admiral.

Marcia met them and escorted them to the conference room. "The Admiral will be with you shortly. Please help yourselves to coffee." They thanked Marcia, poured coffee and waited for the Admiral to arrive.

CHAPTER 36
THE BRIEFING

They each had a cup of coffee and were sitting at the conference table when Admiral Omark arrived at 0900. They all had notepads in front of them and were ready to take notes. They all stood as he entered the room.

"Please sit down and thank you all for coming on such short notice. Jason and Roscoe, it is good to see you again and this must be Captain Jamison."

"Yes sir, I am Ashley Jamison. It is a pleasure to meet you."

"Thank you, Ashley, if I may please call you by your first name?"

"No problem sir, everyone just calls me Ash."

"Okay then I will as well. I must tell you Ash that these two guys have pretty solid performance records with the Navy and I expect that they both have very good careers ahead of them but I must tell you that neither of them has the reputation you have earned. You are a real SEAL superstar."

Ashley just blushed a little and did not say anything. "Roscoe was all over me about you from the first time he saw you perform during plebe summer and he has to go down as one of your strongest supporters."

"Yes sir, I am very grateful for his help and guidance along the way."

"Yes, but advice and guidance is one thing, performance is quite another. I cannot tell you how many times your name has been brought to my attention by a bunch of tough guys who would never ever before mention a woman's name in a SEAL performance discussion. Every time your name comes up you have done something that they once thought was totally impossible. I guess the point is you are viewed and looked up to by many."

"In any event it is a pleasure to finally meet you. Now let me get down to the mystery behind this meeting."

"First, I asked you to travel apart out of concern for the absolute confidentiality of what we will discuss this morning. The data I'm about to share is of significant concern to our overall national security and as such, the information I'm going to pass on to you must stay with the three of you until you are underway and on to the mission were going to talk about this morning. Is that clear?"

"Yes sir," they said in unison.

"Okay. Jason you are scheduled to begin a deployment to the far east beginning at the end of November. It was designed to be a six-month training exercise with a few ports of call thrown in to break up the trip.

That deployment has been moved up to the second week in November which is three weeks from today. You will have to notify your men that you will be departing early but you will be unable to tell them why. Roscoe, that goes for you as well. Your team will be departing with Jason. You can tell them the deployment has been moved up, but you will be unable to tell them why."

"So, let's talk about the why first. I have now been briefed by the Secretary of the Navy that our friends in South Korea have intercepted several communications that indicate Kim Jong-un is up to no good again. We now know that he has been working for at least the past two years to develop a virus that will kill humans instantly. We know that he has completed the work on the virus itself, but his research team is still trying to perfect how to control it. Our feeling is they want to be able to target a small target, like a single individual or a large target like an entire city. So whatever their goal is we know they are playing with wildfire and it is extremely dangerous and must be taken seriously."

"We also know that a little less than three years ago three key research scientists were taken out of China. They did not disappear all at once but individually over the course of six months. We now know they were kidnapped by the North Koreans and are being used to advise and assist on this virus project. The project by the way is known as "**Project V.**"

"We think the V stands for Viper. The lead Korean scientist on the project is a guy named Hong Ye. He communicates with a Korean General by the name of Fong Ho."

"The research is conducted in a small broken-down warehouse which sits on a peer in a place called Haeju. We now know that the warehouse inside is a state-of-the-art research lab. It is well guarded on the outside by at least six or perhaps eight armed men 24 hours per day and we're sure at night it is secured with electronic protections as well."

"There are six Korean scientists plus the three Chinese that work each day on a regular schedule from 0700 to 1600. They are brought to and from the research lab by a boat with an electric motor. The scientists are all living in isolation on a barge which is anchored in the middle of the Haeju Bay. The barge is designed to provide them with all the services they need including women.

We now believe that there are at least six or perhaps eight women whose job it is to keep the men happy in any way desired."

"All provisions going to the barge or research lab are brought in by boat once per week on Tuesday. We have reason to believe that those living in and around the town of Haeju have no idea what is going on in their backyard."

"The barge also has security protection 24 hours per day. We've noted that there are at least three armed men on guard on the barge at all times."

"Access to the harbor is via the Yellow Sea. Jason, at its deepest point, the yellow Sea is only 500 feet deep, so it makes it a bit tough for a nuclear sub to penetrate that body of water without being detected. The channel that leads into the harbor rises quickly and where the barge is anchored the water depth is only 25 feet."

"So, here is what we want to accomplish. We want to enter the harbor, completely blow up the research facility, capture and return the three Chinese scientists, kill the North Korean research scientists, free the women and sink the barge."

The Admiral then stopped the conversation for 15 seconds. He wanted it to sink in and it did to all three of them.

"Now, how you pull that off is up to you, but I have every confidence that you will be able to do it. My understanding Ashley is that you are fluent in Chinese and my guess is that skill will come in handy during this exercise. Jason, you will also have aboard, a team of three of our Chinese interrogators. It will be their job to find out everything the three scientists have been doing for the North Korean since they were taken by them. We will then arrange a drop off point for you to return the scientists to China. I am not sure when or where that will be. It, probably won't be decided until the mission is accomplished, and you are back out in international waters."

"Jason once you are underway, you'll be heading for the Yellow Sea and directly to the point where the mission launch will occur. This will be a direct in and out mission. Once you have accomplished the goal, we will decide what the next steps will be and how long and where you will go next."

"To say that this mission is dangerous is a gross understatement. We not only have the complexity of dealing with the bad guys, but we have a virus to deal with that is designed to kill instantly and no one has figured out how to contain it yet. We have some of our best minds on that part of the puzzle and Roscoe you will have the right tools in place to deal with the issue before you get underway."

As you can now assume, I have had some idea that his was coming down the road and that is why you have been conducting the training exercises you have. My review of the Yellow Sea and Haeju Harbor charts made it clear that you were going to have to work in 200 feet and 25 feet of water and it was going to require the use of the new mini.

"Do any of you have any questions at this point?"

Jason said, "I know a little about the Yellow Sea, but I want the best oceanographic charts we have on it and all the bottom survey charts that lead to the channel. I also know that the sea lies between both Korea and China and both are constantly watching that body of water with everything they have. The only way this is going to happen is it must be completed in silence and it must be a lights out night operation."

"I agree with you Jason. The last thing I want is for the submarine to be detected while our team is in the middle of the operation."

"Roscoe, once you and Ashley have designed your approach, I need you to provide me with a list of any special items you may need to pull it off. I will be working on what we can use to destroy the virus but you two are going to have to figure out how you want to handle everything else. I also do not want you to forget that if this all goes well you will be bringing back three additional people in the mini sub on your return to the Louisville."

"Yes sir, we will develop a resource list and a plan and will be prepared to go over all of the details with you. Would you be able to get us copies of the satellite photos of the research facility and the barge in the harbor?"

"Roscoe, I have asked for them already and I'm told that I will have a packet of information ready for you by noon today.

Jason, I should have all the topographical ground maps of the Yellow Sea for you by noon as well. Please check back with Marcia about noon to pick up the packets. Do any of you have any further questions?"

No one said anything, so Admiral Omark dismissed the group and said, "good luck lady and gentlemen."

Once they were outside of the Admiral's office, they all looked at each other. Captain Miles was the first to speak, "Roscoe, I think I just heard we are to pull something off that might be almost impossible."

"Jason, this is going to be a real test on a lot of fronts. If you can get us to a point where we have access to that channel, then we can pull this off. It isn't going to be easy, but I think with the right resources we have the skill base to pull it off."

"We have about an hour before we are to be back here to pick up our packets. I've got a couple of people I want to look up so see you both back here in an hour."

"Ash, you're free for an hour. I'm sure this place brings back memories."

Ashley knew exactly what she wanted to do. She headed for the SEAL operations checkin building.

Once there she looked in the window and could see a staff sergeant with a SEAL Triton over his left pocket and a bunch of rows of ribbons below it. He was busy looking at a computer screen so he didn't see her as she entered the office. Once in she said, "Hey sailor I need to talk to someone who knows something about becoming a SEAL but it looks to me like you're not smart enough to be able to help me."

Ashley could see the impact her opening statement made, and she knew that it had really hit a nerve with the Sergeant. As he turned around, he looked like he wanted to kill someone. Once he saw her a huge smile appeared on his face.

"Well I'll be God damn, if it ain't the most beautiful SEAL I have ever seen." He came out from behind the desk and gave her the hug of her life.

"Captain, you look great. I can't believe you're here."

"Thanks, Sarge, I'm here with Roscoe. We had a meeting to attend to this morning and I got free for an hour so there are only two people on this base I want to see, one is named James and the other one's name is Reichardt."

"Well my name is James and I'm really happy you looked me up. I happen to know where Reichardt is now; he is training the new group of Buds candidates. If you have a couple of minutes we can walk over to where they are working and perhaps surprise him."

"Let's go."

"Okay. On the way I want to understand a couple stories that have circulated about you. I should add that they are all good in your reputation has skyrocketed around SEAL country."

"Can you briefly give me the facts about the Chinese freighter, the shark attack and the thugs you beat the crap out of in Honolulu?"

"Sure, I will give you the cliff notes version as we walk over to the training area." Ashley told him about the events he had asked about and she also told him about Mark's heart attack. She did most of the talking and he just listened attentively."

The Buds trainees had just finished a timed run and they were all lined up. They were all wet, sweaty and exhausted. Reichardt had them standing at attention. He was facing them, so he did not see Ashley or the Sergeant approach. He noticed some of the trainees looking past him, so he turned around and saw his pal Mike James and Captain Ashley Morgan Jamison.

"Well I'll be damned!" He said. Ashley walked over to him and gave him a great big hug and a kiss on the cheek. Good to see you Sergeant Reichardt. I see you are still trying to make grown men cry. Are you having any success?"

"Yes sir, I'm doing my best." The men in line just could not believe their eyes. Reichardt, was one of the toughest men they had ever been exposed to. He was also the person that each of them was slowly learning to hate. They just could not believe that he had just been kissed by a woman in front of all of them and, if their eyes were correct, she wore a Navy SEAL Triton.

He turned and faced the group. "Hey, you slugs, I want you to meet Captain Ashley Jamison. She is one of the toughest SEALs I have ever known and furthermore, based on what you've shown me so far, she could easily beat all of you at anything you would choose with one hand tied behind her back and that includes the rope climb. I do not think any of you will ever look like her, but I can tell you that you should do everything in your power to strive to be like her. You are dismissed."

"Wow it is great to see you. We have heard so many stories about you that you're becoming somewhat of a legend around these parts." "Thanks, Sarge, I briefed Mike on a couple of the stories he had heard about on the way over here, I'm sure over a beer or two he can fill you in on the details. As I told him, I only have an hour and there were only two guys I wanted to see while I am here, and you guys are the two.

I have now achieved what I wanted to do so I completed that task and now need to get back to meet Roscoe. It is great to see you as well. Take care of yourself."

"Thanks for taking the time Captain, you just made my day."

Ashley was back at the Admiral's office with 10 minutes to spare. Roscoe and Captain Miles were already there and each of them had a packet in their hands. "Okay Jason, we will talk on Monday on board. Have a safe trip home. Ash, let's catch a cab back to the hotel."

CHAPTER 37
THE PLAN EMERGES

Pyongyang North Korea
Kumsusan Palace of the Sun

It was early in the morning and the Supreme Leader was sitting in his office enjoying the morning sunlight when he was buzzed. "Yes Chloe, what is it?"

"Sir, General Ho is here for your morning briefing."

"Please send him in. Thank you."

"Good morning, Supreme Leader."

"Good morning Ho what news do you have for me today?"

"Well sir, our project is moving ahead. We believe were making progress and should have a solution to our target containment issue within six months."

"That is six months faster than you had told me before."

"Yes sir, we have made good progress, particularly since the Chinese scientists have grown accustomed to their routine. We have also dangled a possible return date for them to China. We told them it would be one year from now if the project continues to make progress. What we did not tell them is that they will never return but that one year from now they will all be dead and forgotten."

"We did have one problem this month, but it is not had any effect on our progress."

"What problem do you speak of Ho?"

"Well it seems that one of our own scientists gradually became very homesick and decided one night to leave the barge."

"He was not able to untie the dinghy for his escape before he was shot to death by one of the guards. So, we are now down to five of our own scientists and the three Chinese specialists."

"How have the others taken the result of the guard's action?"
"It seems to have reinforced the importance of following the rules. Of course, we do not know what they say to each other when they are alone, but I care little as long as the project continues to move forward. We have told the other five that their goal is to finish this project and then they will all return home. Of course, that is never going to happen as well. Once we have everything completed, they will suffer the same fate as their Chinese counterparts."

"Thank you for the briefing Ho. Please monitor the others closely and keep me advised if anything changes or if our progress begins to stall."

"Yes, Supreme Leader, I will ensure that you are informed and advised of any issues we have or think we will face. Good day sir."

Marriott Marquis and Marina
San Diego, California

Roscoe and Ashley grabbed a cab and headed directly to the hotel. They were both hungry, so they decided to grab a sandwich and some potato salad to go from the hotel deli. They decided to reserve a private conference room and headed there with their sandwiches, potato salad and diet cokes.

Neither of them had said one word about the operation from the minute they left Admiral Omark's office. Once they were in the room, Ashley looked at Roscoe and said, "Well boss, it looks like we have our work cut out for us."

"You got that right, Ash. At least we now know why we were practicing deep dives and shallow water landing work. This is going to be one complex clandestine operation and as you heard it will not be without a huge danger factor."

"Let's take a look at our package of photos."

They spread the contents of the package out on the table. There were at least eight satellite photos of the broken-down warehouse and another eight photos of the barge. There was also a detailed map of the entry channel with depth marks all the way along it. The photos of both were date and time stamped. Some were taken during the day and others at night.

They both studied the warehouse first. From the photos it was easy to see that there were armed guards posted at all four corners of the building and an additional two that were roving around the perimeter with German Shepherd attack dogs. It was clear that this was a 24/7 operation. So, it looked like six guards and two dogs, not eight guards.

The day pictures were noticeably clear. The night photos were difficult to see because the place was completely dark. There was no light whatsoever. One photo showed a bit of light, but it was the reflection from one of the guards who had lit a cigarette. They could not tell about the electronic security, but they were both sure it was there. It did appear that the first scientist that arrived in the morning went into the warehouse alone which indicated to them that he probably disarmed the system for the others to enter.

Access to the building was by a ramp that led up to the building level from the small dock. The photos taken during the day made it clear that the scientists were transported by an electric motorboat. The photos indicated that the scientists were taken to work and home in two groups. The early photos indicated that the first group was made up of six people and the boat driver and the second group was three and the boat driver.

Ashley noted one thing and said to Roscoe, "Do you see anything different between the early photos and the current ones?"

"No, what am I missing Ash?"

"The early photos have six scientists, the latter ones, taken just recently show five scientists."

"Great catch Ash looks like they dropped one scientist. I wonder why?"

They then turned their attention to the photos of the barge. It was long, narrow and built remarkably close to the water. In fact, you could easily step off it and into the electric transportation boat. Roscoe said, "Ashley, the way this barge is built will help us out. It should be easy to access with no ladders or walkways to climb."

The photos were clear. The barge, like the warehouse, had armed guards stationed at each corner. Interestingly, it had a large surface area on top of it with a 6-foot-high wall around it. Anything or anyone out on the top deck could not be seen from the shore or anywhere else except from the air.

Ashley started to laugh as she looked at one of the barge photos. "Hey boss, you're going to want to check this photo out in detail." She handed it to him smiling the entire time. The photo was taken directly down from the satellite. It gave an incredibly detailed view of the top of the barge and of the enclosed area. There, lounging in the sun, were two topless women.

"We'll all be damned; maybe this assignment won't be so tough after all?"

He smiled as he handed the photo back to her.

While there was no floor layout of the warehouse structure there was a floor layout drawing of the structure of the barge. It showed that there was a large sleeping quarters on the aft end of the barge. This, they presumed was where the women slept. There was a kitchen and eating area next to the large sleeping quarter area.

At the front end of the barge there were two additional sleeping quarters. One was larger than the other. They assumed that the five or six Korean scientists were housed in the larger room and the three Chinese scientists were housed in the smaller room. They also noticed that there was a narrow hall that led from the eating area straight up the center of the barge.

It had several small single rooms built off it. They assumed this is where the women worked and serviced the men.

After a couple of hours of reviewing the photos and other enclosed documents Roscoe began to form a plan in his head. It was a very high-level plan at this point, but it was a plan, nevertheless.

"Ashley, I think I'm getting a sense of what we're going to need to do to pull this thing off. Let me give you my thoughts at a very high level and see what you think."

"I'm all ears, boss."

"Let's start with the submarine. We heard the Admiral say to Jason that the Yellow Sea is only 500 feet deep at its deepest. We all heard Jason say that the body of water is constantly being monitored by both the Chinese and the Koreans both North and South. So that means to me that Jason can't afford to bring the Louisville in any closer than 200 feet in depth and it must be done when it's pitch dark."

"For us that means a night operation which begins at 200 feet and will require scuba gear. We know our vehicle maxes out with 10 people which means we will need to be smart about how we staff our mission. It also means that when we set the mini sub down on the bottom in that bay all of us will have a job to do. This means we won't have the luxury of having someone remain on board to wait for everyone to return."

"Because we will bring back three additional passengers that means our operations team can only be made up of seven which includes the driver and the navigator."

"When we leave the mini sub on the bottom, we will have to wear our LAR Draeger rebreathing front packs so that means the scuba gear will need to be stored in a vehicle for the use on our return."

"I'm thinking that we will have two teams of three and one one-man team who will work on his own. One team will hit the warehouse and the other the barge. The floater man team will set the explosives on the bottom of the barge."

"We will need to refine this a bit, but my thoughts are that I want experienced fighters on the team that goes after the warehouse.

That would include me, Gunny Sanchez and Sam Pierce. Our second team, which you will lead, will include Charlie Chan, who speaks both Chinese and Korean, and our Indian chief Al Fineman. Al is a one-man wrecking crew and he is an expert with a knife. I do not think the barge guards will be much of a challenge for him. You and Charlie will be charged with bringing the Chinese scientists back and dealing with the others on the barge."

"My thought is we will first kill the guards on the barge, lock the Korean scientists in their room and bring the Chinese dudes back to the vehicle. We will lock the door to the woman's room until the last minute and then unlock it so they can escape using the electric boat."

"If they're smart, they will make a run for it and get off the thing before it blows up."

"That leaves us with our one-man team three. Our rover will be the guy charged with placing the limpet mines and timers on the bottom of the barge. The perfect choice for this task is Ray Odemier. Odie is the best we have to set up the limpet mines and timers."

"So, our story has a happy ending today. Team one blows up the warehouse and destroys the virus then swims back to relax in the vehicle, while team two brings the three Chinese dudes back to the mini sub to join the others on the board. Then the rover sets the charges and returns to the vehicle.

We say, "all aboard" and head off to meet the submarine. We do all of this in the pitch dark of night."

"So, what you think Ashley?"

"I always liked happy endings."

Roscoe then said, "I now realize that this operation could not have been completed with our old sled. The new mini will pay for itself if we can pull this off."

They packed up their materials and agreed to meet at 6:30 at Roy's for dinner. They both knew there was a lot to do to detail out the plan, but Ashley knew that what Roscoe had in mind would work and the players he had selected for the mission were the right ones. They met for dinner at Roy's.

They were both in uniform but that did not make them stand out at all. In fact, there were probably seven or eight others in the restaurant in uniform as well.

Ashley ordered the Maui wowie salad to start. It came with shrimp, feta cheese, avocado and caper lime vinaigrette. She ordered the seared sea scallops for her entrée. They came on a potato purée with a honey apple glaze.

Roscoe ordered the ebi roll which was a shrimp tempura, coconut cream cheese and avocado appetizer. He followed it with the teppanyaki shrimp which came with fried rice and baby bok choy.

They said good night and would meet the following Monday morning to begin to detail out the plan. They both knew that they could not say anything to anyone about their meeting or the upcoming operation. It was a given. They were both up early and headed to the airport separately. Ashley was flying Hawaiian air and Roscoe was on United.

Ashley arrived at Honolulu International on time at about 11 AM Hawaiian time. She grabbed a cab to her apartment and was in and changed by noon.

Ryan would be there at 6 PM so she needed to make a run to Safeway to get something for dinner. She decided on fresh salmon fillets.

They were on special and she purchased two half pound tail fillets. She would dress them with real butter and lemon. She decided a butter lettuce salad with mandarin oranges and sliced almonds would work well with the salmon. She selected two bottles of Duckhorn Sauvignon Blanc to go with it.

At 6 PM there was a knock on the door and the evening went off as planned. Ashley knew Ryan would be very curious to know what she has been up to so she just told him with his first question that it was about business and she could not talk about it. Her later actions made him stop thinking about it completely

CHAPTER 38
THE PLAN BEGINS TO TAKE SHAPE

Sunday morning, they slept in. It was 9 AM and Ashley was awake. Her mind was a mixture of all kinds of thoughts about all kinds of things. Ryan was the main thing on her mind. They had had a great evening together but for the first time she felt that she was not being totally honest with him. She knew she had done the right thing by telling him that it was business and she could not discuss it, but she did not like doing it.

She was also going over in her mind the broad outline that Roscoe had discussed with her. On Monday they would meet to begin working out the details. There was no question that what they had been tasked to do was extremely dangerous and who knows how it would all come out.

Ryan stirred a bit and put his arm around her. She put her head on his shoulder and said "Good morning, sunshine. How did you sleep?"

"Like a rock. Did I tell you how much I missed you?"

"About 1000 times. I'm back however, so the future is ours to have, speaking of that, it's time to get up, shower and find something creative to do about breakfast."

There was nothing in the house to eat so after their shower they put on their beach clothes and headed down the path in search of a food truck. The first one they came to was Elena's Restaurant food truck. It was established and has been operating in Honolulu since the mid-70s. The truck specialized in Filipino food, which was a food they rarely had tried. It was after 11 AM so they ordered one order of pork adobo and one order of lumpia and two Diet Cokes to wash it down with. They found a bench along the beach walkway and sat down to a mini no hassle lunch. The food was delicious and they both vowed to come back to it again in the future.

They spent the day at the beach and then headed home for a light dinner. Dinner was as easy as it gets. Ashley just took a large frozen California Pizza Company barbecued chicken pizza out of the freezer and that was it.

She had Ryan open a bottle of four graces Pinot Noir and they were all set. Both needed to be to work early on Monday morning, so it was early to bed, a bit of a roll in the hay and then to sleep. They were up at 6 AM and back on the base at 7:30 AM.

Roscoe had Gunny Sanchez working the men out during the morning and then he arranged for them to have more small arms practice in the afternoon. That gave he and Ashley the entire day to work on the details of their plan.

They met at 0900 in the small conference room in the SEAL Team building. They began with a fresh new look at all the photos.

"Ash, did you think about the plan we discussed?"

"Yes, I thought a lot about it. It will be dangerous, and it will require perfect timing on the part of all of us that are involved. The one thing that concerns me seems to be trivial when you look at the overall problem."

"What is that, Ash?"

"Let's assume that the plan goes as scheduled. We now have three additional people on board and were going to load them in from the surface which is no problem. The problem seems to come when we need to get them out from our vehicle to the submarine at a depth of 200 feet. I am going to assume that none of them have ever even snorkeled let alone had to breathe through a scuba lung at a depth of 200 feet. That coupled with the fact that they are going to be scared to death makes the transfer even more difficult. It is just something I do not want us to underestimate."

"Your point is well taken, and it will not be underestimated. We will have a solution before we begin this mission. I spent last night reviewing the yellow Sea topographical maps and depth chart."

"From what I can tell the closest that Jason will be able to get us to the channel, while maintaining a depth of 200 feet, is about 5 miles. At our maximum speed of 8 knots that means were going to need to allow for about a half an hour of transport time to and from the point of attack.

So, if we were to begin our operation with a submarine departure at 0200, our actual operation would not begin until somewhere between 0230 a.m. and 0300 a.m."

"If we assume that the mission is going to have to be completed in one hour or less then we would need to be back in the mini sub and headed home by 4 AM. That would put us back on board by 0430 and Jason would be able to clear the area by

0500. Even if it all goes as planned it will still be a tight schedule with little room for screw ups."

"So, for planning purposes, I would like to use this as our timeline. Of course, it will be left up to Jason to confirm, but based on what I can see, this will allow us to complete all aspects of the mission in the dark of night."

They worked the rest of the morning on the details of where best the submarine might let them off and the timing needed to get the mini sub in place for the mission to proceed. At noon, they broke for lunch and walked over to the officer's club together. Neither of them mentioned anything about the mission until they were back in the conference room after lunch.

"Ashley, I would like to spend this afternoon talking about the weapons I think our team is going to need in order to pull this thing off. As we discussed earlier, I see this going down with three teams. Let 's call them team 1,2 and 3. Team 1 will be made up of me, Gunny Sanchez and Sam Pierce. The job of team 1 will be to destroy the research facility and the virus. Our goal will be to leave the place with nothing left alive including both humans and virus. This team, I feel, must be fully armed. I will want them to have fighting knives, Sig Sauer P226's and M4 A51 Assault Rifles. This group will also have to carry with them whatever's SEAL headquarters comes up with to destroy the virus. All weapons should be silenced."

"Team 2, which you will lead, is going to need their hands free. You will have the task of bringing the three scientists on board our mini submarine and they probably are not going to want to come. My thought is you; Charlie and Al will be armed with your knives and your Sig Sauer pistols.

The pistols will be silenced as well. Team 3 is one guy, Odie. He will carry only his knife and the four mines needed to blow up the barge. My thought is each mine will have a timer that will be set to go off 45 minutes from the moment it is set."

"The way I see it team 1 and team 2 will leave the mini sub at the same time. Odie will follow a few minutes later. That will give us all a chance to do our thing and head back before the bombs are set to go off. Unfortunately, this mission is going to have to be completed in complete silence so we will not have any radio contact with each other. When our respective missions are accomplished, we head back to the mini."

"With luck I will be the first one back so I can bring the vehicle up to the surface. When that happens, you should be in position to board the scientists. We will all wear our re-breathing devices. Odie's will be rigged to hold the mines he must carry. My guess is each mine will weigh about 5 pounds."

They spent the next two hours going over details and finally Roscoe said "well Ash, it is getting late and I am tired. I have scheduled a meeting with Jason for us tomorrow at 1400. Let us plan to meet here again tomorrow morning at 0900 and go over the plan again."

"Roscoe, when do you think we will be able to tell friends and family that were going to be shipping out in mid-November? That is exactly 3 weeks away?"

"My thought is we leave that decision to Jason and ask him what he thinks. We can discuss it with him tomorrow."

"Okay see you in the morning."

Ashley was tired too. She and Ryan had agreed that they would not meet again until Thursday night, so she had the evening to herself. She was looking forward to the quiet. She loved being with Ryan but now, with this operation hanging over her head, it would be more difficult being together because she could not say a word about it.

She asked her Uber driver to let her out at the Ala Moana Shopping Center. She wanted to pick up Thai food at the S&S Thai kitchen. She knew right where the restaurant was and ordered as soon as she walked in the door.

She ordered one order of spring rolls, one order of green curry with chicken and one order of spicy beef onion. She added brown rice to the order and thought she would be set for tonight and tomorrow night. She loved Thai food and the S&S kitchen was one of her favorites.

With her order in hand she walked the two blocks home. She changed, poured a glass of Dry Creek Fume Blanc and sat down on her patio looking at the yachts sway back and forth.

It was a beautiful evening and she was happy and content. She had purchased a local paper at the store and spent the next hour reading it and catching up on what was going on in the world. Almost every article was related in some way to the Coronavirus. It was not yet ready to take over Hawaii, but it was clearly moving their way. She wondered if they would be gone by the time it became serious threat to the Hawaiian way of life.

She went to bed early and was up early as well. She showered and dressed in her uniform and headed for the base. She grabbed a bite to eat in the wardroom and then at 0845 she left the submarine and headed for the conference room to meet with Roscoe. When she arrived, he was already there and busy going over the maps again. He had also spread out the photos.

"Hey boss, you got a head start on me."

"Good morning, Ashley."

"The truth is I have been thinking about this mission and the more I think about it the more I want to make sure that our plans are really well thought out. Today, I noticed that there are two electric boats tied up to the barge. If you find this to be the case when you board the barge it will work to our advantage. We will reserve one boat for you to use to bring the Chinese scientists back to the mini and we will leave the other boat for the ladies to take from the barge before it blows up."

"My thought is your team will lock both the Korean scientists and the ladies in their respective rooms while you and Charlie get the Chinese scientists off the barge and into the electric boat. Once that is done, we will have Al unlock the ladies' room and jump overboard to swim home."

They spent the rest of the morning going over the plan again in detail. They had lunch at the Officers' Club and then headed over to the submarine to meet with Captain Miles at 1400.

They met with the Captain at 1400. It was just the three of them in the wardroom. Roscoe had brought all the maps and the photos with him as he wanted to detail the plan for Captain Miles.

"Well, Roscoe this is your show. What have you got?"

Roscoe took the Captain through the entire plan. He did not leave out anything. They were all in agreement as to how far into the Yellow Sea the submarine could go before it let the team out. Captain Miles was not surprised that Roscoe had a very well thought out plan. He knew after the briefing that the plan was now ready to be communicated to Admiral Omark.

They spent a full three hours going through the plan and when they were done, they all felt that the plan could work but it would be extremely dangerous for the entire SEAL team participating.

They discussed the communication plan and Captain Miles decided to inform the sailors about the deployment the next day.

He would tell them that their deployment had been moved up and therefore they would be departing for the Far East on November 15 which was a little more than two weeks away. By leaving the communication to the Captain there was no emphasis on the SEAL team. They were simply attached to the ship and would follow the orders of Captain Miles.

The next morning Roscoe phoned Admiral Omark and made arrangements for he and Ashley to meet with him the following Monday morning. They would travel separately again and make their own arrangements.

Wednesday the sailors and the SEAL Team members learned that their deployment date had been moved forward. There were lots of request for leave before departure and Ashley spent the day trying to accommodate all requests.

She was beat when she arrived home Wednesday. She changed, had a brief dinner and then began to think about the next few days with Ryan. She called the airlines and decided to fly to San Diego on Sunday with a return flight scheduled on Tuesday. At 930 she was sound asleep

CHAPTER 39
DETAILS, DETAILS, DETAILS

On Thursday morning Roscoe got a call from Captain Miles. The Captain wanted to see him that afternoon to talk further about the plan. It was clear from the conversation that Captain Miles had spent a lot of time studying the Yellow Sea typography maps and that he had some concerns.

Roscoe was not sure what he might be concerned about but whatever it was, he was glad to have the opportunity to discuss it with him before he met with Admiral Omark on the following Monday.

At 1400 Roscoe entered the wardroom. Captain Miles was seated and had the topographical maps laid out in front of him.

"Hey Roscoe, thanks for coming. I've spent a bunch of time going over our plan and I wanted to let you know a couple of things I've learned so you may pass some additional information on to the Admiral on Monday"

"First, my number one concern has been detection. I do not want anyone to know we are there and if someone figures it out it could screw up our whole operation."

"I've been thinking about some of the emerging non-acoustic detection technologies that have the potential to expose the location of ballistic missile submarines. I understand due to advances in stealth submarine technology including ultra-quiet diesel and nuclear engines, sound dampening mounts and stealth paint that most active and passive acoustic methods are incapable of detecting the presence of vessels like ours. However, advances in non-acoustic detection tools have the potential to reveal the location of SSBN's"

"I spent the last 14 hours learning as much as I can about non-acoustic submarine detection technologies. These are technologies that do not rely on the collection of sound waves emitted or reflected by a submerged vehicle."

"Significant improvements have taken place with light-based imaging and magnetic anomaly detection."

"This is modern light-based imaging that relies on light detection and ranging technology. It is referred to as LIDAR technology. LIDAR works by admitting laser pulses and measuring the return time and strength of the reflected light. When deployed from space, aeronautic or naval platforms, LIDAR can track a submarine's distance to the ocean surface or in some circumstances it can directly image a vehicle. LIDAR is presently limited to sensing depths up to 200 meters."

"To be clear, I'm not at all worried that the North Koreans have this technology or even if they were experimenting with it that they would be able to use it over the Yellow Sea. The Chinese on the other hand are different matter. They are trying to develop the technology and refine it just like we are. What I have learned is, like us, they are not there yet. So, I believe that our plan to keep our submarine at 200 feet should work well, particularly since it will be at night."

"Captain, that's good information to know and I will definitely pass it on to Admiral Omark. Our plan will be to leave you in the dark at 200 feet and return to you in the dark at 200 feet and they get the hell out of there."

"Roscoe, don't forget to ask the Admiral what we are to do with these Chinese scientists once we leave the Yellow Sea? I always feel better when I know where I'm going and that's still a mystery part of this puzzle."

"Will do, sir."

With that said, Roscoe left the office feeling a little less worried than he did when he went in.

Ashley spent the afternoon making her hotel reservations and thinking about Friday and Saturday night dinners. It was Thursday at 1600. Ashley was done for the day and headed home via Safeway. She had thought through dinners for tonight and Friday night.

She left Saturday night open she did not want a bunch of food left in the house while she was gone. Tonight's dinner was simple and All-American. She would have meatloaf and broccoli with apple pie for dessert.

Safeway had a pre-made meatloaf mixture which she had had before. It was very tasty and easy to cook. She just needed to put it in a small disposable tinfoil pan and cook it in the oven at 375 for 50 minutes. She went to the bakery and grabbed a whole apple pie and then went to the freezer section and grabbed a pint of vanilla ice cream.

Friday night's dinner would be a little more complex, but it would keep Ryan busy.

She decided on Southwestern flank steak, Mexican corn cups and a pinenut and butter leaf lettuce salad. She would have the rest of the pie for dessert. She grabbed three bottles of four graces Oregon Pinot Noir and three bottles of Coelho Renovacao Oregon Pinot Gris and put them in her wine carrier.

When she had her shopping done, she headed home. She was home at 5 PM. She had one hour before Ryan would be there. She put the white wine in the refrigerator and put the meatloaf in the small tin pan she had purchased. Then she hit the shower and put on her evening clothes which consisted of noticeably short shorts, a white almost see-through dry fit top and sandals. She was so brown that the outfit stood out like no other against her skin. As usual she did not wear makeup and did not need it. Makeup did not work for her because it always came off as she was in the water so much of the time. She went to work making the filling for the Mexican corn cups and put them in the refrigerator for tomorrow night's dinner.

Ryan was on time and in uniform. She opened the door and he almost fell over "Ashley, you look amazing."

She gave him a long kiss and a big hug and said, "Not really, you just haven't seen me in four days."

"It seems like a year to me. Let me grab a quick shower and change. I'll be back in a few minutes."

She had a glass of Pinot Gris waiting for him when he returned. They touched glasses and said cheers and took their first taste. "This is really good, is it a new one?

"It is Coelho Renovacao from the Willamette Valley in Oregon. It is known for its pure flavors of pear, white nectarine and melon. It was a wine enthusiast editor's choice. I should also add that it is more expensive than I am used to paying for Pinot Gris. Each bottle was just under 20 bucks."

"Well this is really good. Thanks for bringing the new taste treat home. How was your day?" "Well it was pretty boring actually. Captain Miles announced that he had received orders to head out on deployment two or three weeks before we were scheduled to go. So that means we leave in two weeks on November 15. I spent the entire day trying to adjust schedules so the guys could get time off before we leave this island."

"That is not welcome news to me. Two weeks will go by fast and then what am I going to do without you?"

"I don't think you'll have any trouble staying busy. Somehow you got by without me for a few years, so my suggestion is to just fall back into your pre-Ashley routine."

"To be honest, I'm going to miss you and I just don't want to think about it now. I also have to go back to the mainland on business on Sunday morning and I won't be back until Tuesday night."

"Let me guess, you can't talk about it."

"You got that right, so let's focus on tonight and tomorrow night."

"Okay. What's for dinner and how can I help?"

"Tonight, were having an All-American dinner. Our dinner will be meatloaf, broccoli and apple pie for dessert. You don't have to do anything but drink and look at me."

"Now that's the best instruction you've ever given me."

The meatloaf came out perfectly. The broccoli was simple. She just boiled it for three minutes and served it with a bit of salt-and-pepper sprinkled on it. She put a bottle of Ketchup up on the table to go with the meatloaf and dinner was served with a bottle of Four Graces Pinot Noir. After dinner, they cleaned up and decided to take a walk down the path to Waikiki Beach.

Once there, they picked up the Boardwalk path and continued down past all the big hotels. It was dusk and all the lights were going on. It was a beautiful evening and they held hands most of the walk. Neither of them talked much they just enjoyed the view and each other's company.

They were home and in bed at 930. They rolled around and giggled for a while and then fell sound asleep. They were up early and on the base at 730 in the morning. Ashley met with Roscoe at 0900 to go through the plans once more and to make out the formal equipment list that they planned to give to the Admiral on Monday.

The day went by quickly and Ashley and Roscoe agreed to meet for dinner at Roy's on Sunday night in San Diego.

Ashley left the base in 1700 and headed home. Ryan would be over at 6 PM and she wanted to look good for him. She left dinner up to him on Saturday night by saying, "I don't care where we go or what kind of food we have. I just need to be home and in bed by 9 PM."

Friday's dinner was Southwestern flank steak. Ashley put Ryan in charge. She told him he needed to pound the flank steak and then apply the Southwestern spice mixture that she had made up. It included coriander, cumin, salt and pepper and olive oil. Then she told him to finally chop cilantro and mix it with the spice mixture and when that was done to spread the mixture all over the flank steak. He did what he was told. Ashley told him to barbecue it for seven minutes on each side and then slice it very thin on the diagonal.

In the meantime, Ashley made a salad of toasted pine nuts and romaine lettuce.

The dressing was made with Dijon mustard, red wine vinegar garlic and salt-and-pepper the salad was then topped with parmesan cheese.

She had premade the corn cups and would serve them with salsa. They went perfectly with the meal. It was a great evening. They ended up with a glass of Four Graces Pinot Noir watching the boats in the yacht harbor sway back and forth.

Saturday was spent at the beach. They were back early so Ashley could pack a few things. Ryan had reservations for dinner in Waikiki at Dukes on the beach. They arrived for dinner at 6 PM and were seated with a great view out to the ocean. They split a caramelized beet salad which was made with arugula, goat cheese and macadamia nuts. They each ordered their own entrée. Ryan went with the baby back ribs and Ashley had the coconut shrimp. They ended the meal by splitting a slice of kimo's original hula pie.

They walked home as the sunset feeling a bit like two beached whales.

Ashley took her time getting ready for bed. She needed to go to sleep early in order to make her early flight, so she started getting ready for bed at 830. When she came out of the bathroom Ryan went nuts. She made sure he would not forget her by wearing a sexy black lace thong panty with nothing else on. It was a night to remember. She was up early and before she knew it, she was on an airplane and headed for San Diego.

Her flight arrived on time in San Diego. It was 3 PM West Coast time. She had three hours before she would meet Roscoe for dinner. She decided to call her Mom and let her know that they would be leaving for their deployment early. She got updated on the Coronavirus and as she suspected the situation was getting worse not better. Her Mom explained that the center of concern had shifted from Washington to New York and gradually everything was closing down.

Sarah told her that her Dad and Brother were both now working from home and that it looked like they would be doing so for some time.

She told her about the senior grocery store hours which was all new to Ashley. They talked for a good hour. The conversation covered everything including Ryan.

"Ashley, when you get back, my hope is that this virus thing will be over and will get to see your new digs in Hawaii and meet this guy who's captured your attention. It is something I will really look forward to."

"I'm excited for that to happen as well, Mom."

They ended the conversation. Ashley put her swimsuit on went down to the pool. She swam 30 laps with ease and then went up to her room, showered and dressed in her uniform for dinner.

As usual, Roscoe was right on time. He had asked for a table that provided them with privacy and they spent most of the dinner talking about how they would handle their discussion with Admiral Omark the next morning.

It was another great dinner at Roy's. Roscoe ordered the rainbow poky which was Ahi Tuna in a sesame vinaigrette. It was served with avocado salsa and crispy chips. For his entrée he had the misoyaki butterfish which was a black cod in spicy Asian sauce.

Ashley had a cup of the lobster bisque and the Hibachi grilled salmon. They took their time with dinner and split a bottle of Cakebread Sauvignon Blanc. Neither of them wanted any dessert so they left the table and went up to their rooms. They met at 8:30 the following morning and headed directly to the base and Admiral Omarks office.

CHAPTER 40
THE BRIEFING

Roscoe and Ashley arrived at Admiral Omark's office at 0855. They were greeted by Ms. Abelson, the Admiral's assistant. "Good morning, Commander and to you as well, Captain. The Admiral is expecting you. I will let him know that you are here."

"Thank you, Ms. Abelson," Roscoe said.

The door open to the Admiral's office and he came right out and shook both of their hands. "Good to see you both. Let's go into my conference room, I'm anxious to hear what you have planned."

They followed him in and accepted coffee from Ms. Abelson. "Well Roscoe, this is your show. Tell me what you have planned."

"Yes sir."

Roscoe opened his briefcase and took out the Yellow Sea topographical map as well as the photos of the warehouse and the barge.

"Let me begin by saying, Captain Miles sends his best to you and wants you to know that he agrees with the plans we plan to present to you today. He has spent a lot of time studying the Yellow Sea and is now convinced that he can get us in and out of the Yellow Sea without fear of detection."

"That is good to know and was one of the first questions I had on my mind."

"Our plan is to leave Hawaii and transit directly to the Yellow Sea. We will go unaccompanied and only a very few people will know where we are. The plan is to follow the path outlined on the map in front of you. You will see that the destination is a point in the Yellow Sea that is about 5 miles from the beginning of the channel that leads into Haeju Harbor. This is the point where Captain Miles will let us out. The water depth is 200 feet which means our SEAL team can work with scuba gear."

"We have developed a team of SEALs that have the specific skills to handle the job at hand."

"Ashley and I have been through our personnel a number of times and both of us believe we have the right people for this mission. At this point, however, no one knows anything other than Captain Miles. Our new transport vehicle can hold up to 10 people with full gear, but we now know that when it is full it is a tight squeeze for everyone inside."

"As you are aware, we plan to bring the three Chinese scientists out with us, so we are limited to an operations team of seven SEALs for this mission."

"At about 8 knots we believe our mini sub can make it to and up the channel in about half an hour. Once we have made it through the channel, we plan to park the mini sub on the bottom in about 25 feet of water. Our plan is to begin our mission leaving the submarine at 0200 in total darkness. If the plan goes as planned, we will have one hour to complete our mission and then another half an hour to transit back to the submarine.

The plan calls for us to be back on board by 0400 and heading back out to sea. So, this is a mission that will need to start and finish in total darkness."

"We have divided our SEAL group into three teams. Team 1, I will lead. Team 1 will be made up of three of us. Team 1's focus is to attack the warehouse and destroy the virus that is being worked on. Team 2, Ashley will lead. Team 2 will also have three SEALs; Team 2 will focus on getting the three Chinese scientists out and safely back on board the mini submarine. Last, we have Team 3. Team 3 will be made up of a single SEAL whose job it will be to blow the barge up and sink it."

I would like to discuss at this point, each team plan in detail. Team 1 will be made up of me, my Gunny Sergeant Juan Sanchez and one of our men whose name is Sam Pierce.

I believe you know Juan, but I do not believe you know Sam. Sam is a first-class petty officer who is very experienced SEAL. He has been on a number of missions, is an excellent swimmer, an excellent marksman and one tough fighter. We know from our satellite reconnaissance that the old warehouse is surrounded by armed guards in each corner and that there are two guards constantly moving around the building with dogs.

Our plan will be for Juan to take all of the guards out on one side of the building and for Sam to take all of them out on the other side of the building."

"In the meantime, my job will be to enter the warehouse and destroy the virus. We do not intend to leave anything or anyone alive in or around that facility."

"Team 2 will be made up of three SEALs. Ashley will lead the team. She will be assisted by Charlie Chan and Albert Fineman. Charlie is fluent in both Chinese and Korean and, as you know, Ashley is fluent in Chinese. Al is an American Indian who is pound for pound one of the toughest guys I have ever met. It will be Al's job to take out the guards that are stationed at either end of the barge while Charlie and Ashley deal with the scientists on board, the ones we want to bring back with us and the girls who are also on board."

"Our plan is simple. The Chinese scientists are housed together in one room and the Korean scientists are in another. The ladies are all housed in a large room at the end of the barge. Our plan will be to lock the Korean scientists in their room and the ladies in theirs as well.

Once that is done, we will grab the Chinese scientists and move them off the barge using one of the electric boats that is tied up to the barge. Ashley and Charlie will then bring them to the vehicle for loading. My plan is to be back in time to bring the mini sub up to the surface which will allow Ashley to load the Chinese scientists without them getting in the water."

"We know there are two electric motorboats attached to the barge. As I indicated, we plan to use one of the boats to transport the Chinese scientists back to the vehicle. The other we will leave for the ladies to help them with their escape."

The last one to leave the barge will be Al. Before he goes, he will unlock the door to the lady's room and tell them they have 10 minutes to get off the barge. Al will then dive into the bay and swim back to the vehicle."

"Team 3 is made up of one guy. His name is Raymond Odemier. Odie is a SEAL with nerves of steel. Nothing rattles him. Both Ashley and I have watched him work during our underwater demolition exercises."

"He is the best we have. Odie's job will be to swim from the vehicle to the barge. He will then place two Limpet Mines on the aft end of the barge and two Limpet Mines on the front of the barge. The timers will be set for 45 minutes. This should give us all time enough to be back on board our mini sub and heading to the submarine before the barge blows up."

"It should also give the women a chance to escape."

"Our plan is to leave the Korean scientists locked in their rooms. They will go down with the ship. We do not intend to leave any man alive on this mission."

"We will use our re-breathing gear to avoid bubbles of any kind and we plan to have all of our weapons silenced as you will see from the weapons list, we prepared for you.

As you will note, it is specific and contains everything we think at this point we will need. You will need to let me know how I am to destroy the virus and what tools or weapons I will need to have with me in order to accomplish that task. You had indicated that we had people working on this so that is an important need to have before this moves forward."

"Roscoe that is a very well-designed strategy. It is easy to see, however, that this is not going to be easy. The restricted manpower is genuinely concerning, but I see no other way around. We must use the vehicle and it has its manpower limits."

"Let me address your concern first. Our scientists believe that the virus will be contained in a lead vault inside the warehouse facility."

"To enter you will need access to the inside of the building. To achieve this, they have designed a simple hot charge which you will place on the door lock. It will cause a silent mini explosion when you detonate it and it will render the door lock unusable and open. I am told that it is guaranteed to blow any lock they have designed. Once inside you will need to locate the lead vault. To enter it you will use a second door explosive. Once that door is open and you enter, you should see several rows of experiment trays. They all contain the virus in some form or another. You are not to touch or go near any of the trays."

You will be provided with a newly developed mini firebomb. You are to place the mini firebomb in the middle of the virus room and set the timer for 10 minutes and get the hell out of there. You must close the door to the lead vault and prop something against it, so it does not open. The explosion is going to create a heat wave inside the vault that nothing can survive. It should not light the building on fire but rather kill everything inside the vault. You will use a second mini firebomb in the center of the research facility. It will destroy anything that may be alive at the workstations. Our goal will be for you to conduct the operation and leave the building standing like you found it, only it will be a ghost town with a dead virus."

"The boys have also given thought to the Limpet Mines that Odie must place. They each weigh 4 pounds and have timers that are easy to set. They are designed to blow significant holes in the bottom of the barge but with little if any noticeable noise. The idea will again be for the barge to go down to the bottom silently. We want you and your SEAL team in and out with as little noise as possible. Our goal will be for the Koreans to wake up to a real surprise." Our research guys are also working on the internal alarm system. They plan to have something for you to deal with that as well.

"I understand Admiral."

"Roscoe, there is one other bit of advice I have for you and your team. This is a case where you could encounter hand-to-hand combat. I would like you to avoid that if possible. I want your team to use their silenced Sig P226's. There is absolutely no time in this plan for screwing around in a hand-to-hand combat situation. I want you and your team to shoot and not ask questions. Is that clear?"

"Yes sir. We both understand and will avoid that kind of combat."

"Now, I have a couple of questions for you. I understand that the three Chinese scientists will be brought to the vehicle by electric motorboat and loaded into the vehicle from the surface. How do you plan to get them from the vehicle at 200 feet in depth into the submarine?"

"Well Admiral, that is the first question Ashley asked me when we began the planning for this mission. We know the Chinese scientists are going to be very afraid. In fact, we think we will need to handcuff them just to make sure they do not do something stupid while we are trying to load them into our vehicle."

"Our plan is to take three extra wetsuits with us and three extra scuba tanks. Ashley and Charlie will play a critical role here and will need to use their language skills. They will use the time during our transit back to explain exactly what the scientists will need to do regarding breathing."

"My plan is to get the mini sub as close to the In and out hatch as possible. I will also ask a couple of our seal team members who are left on the submarine to come out and help us load them."

"Our plan is to have Charlie exit the mini sub first and enter the submarine through the in and out hatch. Once he is in, Ashley will bring the first scientist out of the mini and get him into the in and out hatch. She will hold on to him the entire time while she is monitoring his breathing. The in and out hatch will easily hold two people at a time, so Ashley will stay with a guy until he is safely inside the submarine. Once she has him in the sub, Charlie will take over and reassure the scientist that all is well. When she has the first one safely on board, she will then come back for the second and finally the third.

Once that is accomplished, we will move the mini to position it on its mountings on the Louisville. After that, all of us will enter the submarine.

"That sounds like a plan. Ashley, it is going to take a lot of convincing to get these guys calm enough to make the transfer. What do you think?"

"I think we can do it. Charlie is very fluent as well and we think that having a woman take them one at a time will be somewhat reassuring. You know, Admiral, there is that macho man thing that says if a woman can do it then so can I attitude which lots of men have. In this case it just might help us out."

"I guess you're right, Ash, but in this case what they don't know is they are not dealing with a typical woman. If you know what I mean." They all laughed

"Roscoe, I've been advised that all the weapons on your list, along with the explosive devices, are being shipped directly to the Louisville. Captain Miles will be advised when they arrive. It will be up to you and Ashley to go through the stockpile once it is there and make sure you have everything you need. I only want to have to do this operation once."

"I just thought of one other thing. I will ask our technical guys how you can lock these folks in the rooms from the outside without a key. It seems to me we need something that will be easy to apply and yet strong enough that it can't be broken from the inside."

"Thanks Admiral, that is a detail I hadn't thought about. A device like that would be extremely helpful to Ashley and her team."

"Now Roscoe, talk to me about communication. When are you going to let your team know what the mission is and what the plan is? How do you plan to communicate it to them? I don't know a lot, but I know SEALs and I don't want a few macho guys feeling bad because they were not selected to possibly kill themselves."

"Ashley and I have been through that. In fact, that is why we were so careful to select the team one by one. All our guys know who is good at what and no one is going to question why we selected who we did once they understand what the task is at hand.

I think that the plan and the skill sets of the individual selected will be enough to smooth any egos that might be jacked out of shape. We do not plan to tell anyone about the mission until we are underway and then we will explain it to the SEAL Team only. Captain Miles does not see why his crew needs to know anything other than they are letting a few of our team off in the middle of the Yellow Sea to conduct a training exercise. Our guys will be told that no one is to know about this mission."

"Well, I'm extremely impressed. This is one complicated mission and is not without its challenges. I must tell you that there is a part of me that is envious. This mission has national and international significance and it is one that every SEAL would want to be a part of. I don't have to tell you that both of you will be risking your lives and the lives of your team but the cause is worth it and I believe that you are both prepared to handle the challenges presented."

"Roscoe, I will want you to let me know the result of the mission as soon as you are back on the submarine. Captain Miles will be able to securely contact me and I will advise him that your communication is of vital importance. With that, I wish both of you the best of luck and wish you Godspeed as you take this challenge on. Thanks very much for the briefing."

"Roscoe and Ashley stood and shook the Admiral's hand and then left the conference room. They both said goodbye to

Marcia Abelson. Once outside, Roscoe looked at Ash and said, "What did you think?"

"I think it went well and that we have our hands full."

"Me too. We are both flying out tomorrow morning. I know we both have early flights on different airlines. I was thinking it might be fun to have an early dinner in San Diego's old town. I know great Mexican restaurant that is called Chiquita's Mexican restaurant. Would you be up to trying it?"

"Sure, we both have had our fill of Roy's and the change to Mexican would be fun, especially here in San Diego."

"Okay then. I will make a reservation for 5 PM and meet you in the hotel lobby at 4:30. I've got some people to see this afternoon, so I'll leave you for now and see you later."

They met at 4:30 and caught a cab to Chiquita's. Roscoe ordered New Mexico enchiladas and Ashley had a shrimp dish called camarones chiquita's. They both had a margarita and ships with salsa before dinner.

During dinner Roscoe asked Ashley if she remembered the question, he had asked her during her time at the YARD? The question was, "Do you think you can kill another person if you have to?"

Her answer then was "If it has to be done, I can do it." She answered the question just the same at dinner as she had at the YARD. She had no doubt about how she would act on this mission and what had to be done and why. They finished early and were back to the hotel by 7 PM.

Ashley was up early and caught her flight to Honolulu at 7 AM. She was home in her apartment by noon. She called Ryan and let him know she was home and hoped he would be able to come over for dinner and evening. She left a message and started to think about what to do for dinner.

She wanted to be simple and she was still full from the Mexican restaurant. She decided that a nice seafood salad would work with sesame crackers. Once she was changed and in her evening island apparel, she headed out the door for Safeway seafood department. She stopped by Mr. Piedmont's apartment on the way to let him know what her schedule would be.

She decided not to sublease her apartment for this deployment because she had no idea how long she would be gone.

Mr. Piedmont opened the door with a big smile on his face. "Ashley, it's great to see you, how have you been?"

"I've been good Mr. Piedmont, thanks for asking. I stopped by to tell you that in two weeks we are going to head out to the South China Sea but I don't know how long we will be gone so I decided to continue to pay you the rent while I'm gone and not try to sublease the apartment. So, if it is okay with you, I would just ask that the cleaning folks come by each week to give it a once over. As soon as I have any idea what my schedule will be, I'll let you know."

"No problem Ash, we will watch over it for you. Have a safe trip."

"Thanks, Mr. Piedmont."

Ashley was in and out of Safeway quickly. She bought a head of iceberg lettuce and some thousand island dressing. She also bought a quarter pound of crabmeat, a quarter pound of fancy cooked shrimp and a small package of smoked salmon. She headed to the vegetable section and grabbed a red and yellow bell pepper, a cucumber and a package of sesame crackers. She had a couple of bottles of Dry Creek Sauvignon Blanc in the refrigerator, so she was all set.

She got back and did some prep work for her salad and put it all in the refrigerator. It would go together quickly and should be very tasty. It was another beautiful day in Hawaii. Ashley had grown up in Oregon. When you grow up in Oregon that is all you know weather-wise. It rains often and is overcast and drizzly. When it is beautiful it is just that but the rest of the time it can be depressing but not if you grow up in it. She often remembered what the most common question that Oregonians ask each other weekly and that is, "Do you think it's going to rain on the weekend?"

Ashley was getting so spoiled with the Hawaiian whether she often wondered if she could ever go back to the overcast and gray days of the Willamette Valley.

Ryan was on time as usual and greeted her with what was now becoming normal, a giant hug and kiss. He was in the shower and changed in no time and out hunting for his glass of wine.

She had a glass ready for him and she joined him on the deck in what was becoming their favorite place. "Cheers Ash, nice to have you back and guess what? I am not going to ask you where you went or what you did. How's that?"

"Thanks" is all she said, and they clicked their glasses. "Cheers."

"How was your day, Ryan?"

"To tell the truth Ash, this being stranded on the ground without you gets really old, really quick. It is great when I am flying but when we are grounded it is a real drag without you to look forward to. I feel a bit lost."

"I think you just paid me a real compliment."

"You're right about that. I can't sing but there is an old song that I remember that says something about being stuck on you. And, frankly, I'm stuck." They both laughed.

The dinner was easy and great. The seafood was cold, and the dressing was light. The crackers went well with it and the wine fit perfectly. It was another great evening which ended with a long, slow lovemaking session followed by a deep sleep.

CHAPTER 41
WESTPAC PLANNING

It was Monday morning. Ryan and Ashley had taken an Uber car to the base and they were both on their respective ships by 0730. Scotty was in the state room when Ryan arrived on board. "Hey pal; I assume you had a good weekend?"

"It wasn't good, it was great. I do not know what it is like to fall head over heels for someone but if things continue to progress like they have been, I am bound to be headed down that road. Scotty, I have just never met or been around anyone like Ashley. She can do anything, and everything she does, she does well."

"I envy you. Like we say in Texas, I'd like to have one decent date but so far the wells I've tried are just plain dry."

"Have you had breakfast?"

"No, let's go for it." They left their state room and headed for the wardroom. Over breakfast most of the talk was about the Coronavirus and its impact on the world so far. There was also some talk about its impact on the Navy. The last thing people wanted to happen was to be stuck on a ship with no elbowroom packed in like sardines while the virus silently moved around attacking people one by one.

"Hey Ryan, I got the first confirmation yesterday about our deployment. And now it looks like we will be departing here on December 1st. So much for Christmas in Hawaii. How does the song go Melee Kalikimaka or something like that?" "Christmas looks like it's going to be about you and me and with no tree or packages. You know when I was a kid, Christmas was everything and it stayed that way in my family for as long as I can remember. When I was at the Naval Academy, I always planned to be home for Christmas but now that we are working that is not something that we can easily control any longer."

"I did get some good news this weekend though. My request to fly the super hornet has come through and I am scheduled to take one out from land on Wednesday. I'm really looking forward to it."

"You will do well, and you will love it. It is a really nice aircraft and you won't believe the power."

Ryan spent the rest of the day with his Super Hornet and the crew. He enjoyed being around the guys and found each time he was with them he learned a little bit more about the airplane. The crew really liked and respected him, and they were all super proud of how he handled the aircraft when he guided the F-18 Hornet in without instruments for a landing. He knew that the crew had never seen that done before and to bring the Super Hornet in with only 3 feet to spare between it and the deck was something they would all remember. He did notice one thing that was different. Behind his name, which was painted on the side of the plane, there was now a second name and it was Reggie's. "Looks like Reggie doesn't want to change horses" he thought.

Ryan never mentioned the Super Hornet drive by to his landing crew. It just was not his nature to ever boast or talk about his achievements.

THE HAEJU VIRUS

He thought it was a bit odd that he paid no attention to the things he accomplished but he was always there to make sure that everyone knew what Ashley had done. He was just one of those guys who wanted to treat people like you would like others to treat you. He always made sure that he showed respect to everyone and made sure he recognized their own unique abilities.

Just before dinner he got a call from Reggie which confirmed their departure on December 1st. Reggie told him they would be gone for a little over six months returning to Hawaii on June 1st. He also told Ryan that he would be his personal chauffeur for the entire six months. He explained that this tour was designed to be somewhat of a goodwill tour for the carrier with stops along the way at Midway Island, Guam, Subic Bay, Hong Kong, Taiwan and a couple of ports in Japan.

At this point the world was not at war so Reggie did not expect to encounter any military airpower action during the trip.

Reggie then dropped a bit of a bomb on Ryan. He told him that he expected this would be the USS Yorktown's last deployment. He was not sure yet, but he thought that when they returned, the Yorktown would be decommissioned, and all the officers and men would be transferred to other naval assignments.

He reminded Ryan that he was about to start his third tour overseas. Because of that, he would be up for reassignment when they returned. He suggested that Ryan start thinking about his future now. He told him that by doing so it would allow him to put his request in while they were gone and hopefully have an answer by the time they returned. Reggie learned a long time ago not to trust the detailers and that in the Navy it is important to make your own luck and you did that by lots of advanced planning.

So, in that brief conversation Reggie managed to make Ryan's head spin. What would be next for him? For he and Ashley? And for both of their careers? His thoughts moved quickly to Thursday night. He knew he needed to tell Ashley about the conversation and that he would value her opinion, but he just did not know what to expect. It was a given that their discussion Thursday would be an interesting one.

He spent the next couple of hours thinking about what he might want to do. He knew that at some point he wanted to apply to fly with the Blue Angels. That would be the height of his air career, but he also knew if you wanted to stay in the Navy and reach the highest level, that additional education would be necessary. He needed to talk to someone about his career and what his next best step might be. After four years and three deployments he knew that a shore duty assignment was probably the next step. Graduate school seemed to be the one alternative that he should consider and that meant the Naval Postgraduate School in Monterey, California. He decided he would talk to Reggie about it and get his point of view.

Ashley spent all day Monday and Tuesday with Roscoe. They went over the plans time and time again and paid particular attention to the timing. Timing was critical. There was not a lot of time to accomplish what they needed to do on their mission, so they put the timeframe up against every possible scenario they could think up.

They worked late both nights and Ashley just stayed aboard the submarine. She did not go home until Wednesday night.

On Wednesday, the equipment they discussed with Admiral Omark arrived and was brought aboard the submarine. They did a complete inventory of everything and went over their list twice before they were satisfied, that they had everything. Roscoe was fascinated with the incendiary devices he was given the blow the doors open with. They were very small and were designed to just stick on the lock. He had one button to push and 10 seconds after that it went off. Slick he thought. The firebombs that he was to use in the vault and in the center of the facility room were just as small but a lot more powerful. He had 30 seconds from the time he set them off. After that he knew they would blow the contents of the vault to hell as well as anything left alive in the room itself. So his plan would be to set the vault off first and then throw the other one in the room before he departed. He would be the last in the water to leave the dock.

The door locks that Ashley would need were equally slick. They stuck on the doors with no need to fasten them.

They were solid and could only be broken if cut from the outside with a knife. She reminded herself to make sure Al knew about that so he would be able to release the ladies once the barge was clear of the Chinese scientists.

When Ashley got home, she was beat. There was a voicemail on her phone from Ryan saying he was really looking forward to seeing her and would be there at 6 PM she was happy to hear his voice and the timing was good. She would be off the base at 1600 with two hours to get her act together before his arrival.

She poured a glass of wine and grabbed her notepad and went out to the deck. It was another made for tourist day in Hawaii. There was a light breeze blowing and it cooled things down a bit as she looked out at the boats.

"What to do for dinner she thought." She had Thursday, Friday, Saturday and Sunday to think about. She crossed out Sunday and wrote out to dinner. She thought about the other three nights and decided to do three things she knew he would like, and he could participate in the making the dinner. Thursday would be easy she would do filet mignon barbecued shish kebabs with barbecued pineapple. Friday would be fish tacos made with mahi-mahi and Saturday would be shrimp fettuccine. She made out a grocery list and put it next to her uniform and wallet. She would make the Safeway run on the way home tomorrow evening.

She was not very hungry, so she snacked on left over smoked salmon while she contemplated the next few days. She would leave the dinner up to him on Sunday. She also realized this would be the second to last time she would be with him until she and he returned from overseas. She was bound and determined to make the evenings memorable enough that he would not forget her. In fact, her goal was to give him fantasies that he would dream about for the next six months.

Thursday was another inventory day with special attention paid to the weapons they would need and the silencers that were mounted on each. Everything had to work perfectly if they were going to pull this off. Any screwup, of any kind, could easily mean death for one or more members of the team. Neither she nor Roscoe was going to let that happen on their watch.

She left the base at 1600 and grabbed her Uber car for home. She had her normal driver so he knew almost instinctively that she would want to shop at Safeway. She made the request as soon as she got in the car, but she added that she would like the driver to wait for her. She knew that with the wine she was just going to have too much to carry to walk home. She knew the store well by now, so it did not take her long to get all the things she needed into her shopping cart. She picked three bottles of red wine and three bottles of white wine. She had wine at home but wanted to make sure they would not run out until Sunday night.

The driver dropped her off at home and helped her carry the bags up to her apartment. She thanked him and gave him an extra $10 tip.

She changed out of her uniform and jumped into the shower. She stayed in it longer than normal and just let the hot water run all over her body.

She could tell that all this planning and the thinking that had gone into it was taking its toll on her.

Once she was out of the shower she put on her short white shorts and a white tank top and headed for the kitchen. She pulled out a number of small bowls and started to fill each with items that would go on the kebabs. First, she cut the filet mignon into squares that were about 1" x 1" thick. Then she forked the new potatoes and put them in the microwave for about four minutes. When they were out, they went into their own bowl. Then she cut the tails off the mushrooms and made sure they were all clean and in put them in their own bowl. Next she sliced the red onion into cubes that would easily fit on the skewers and put the chunks into their own bowl and last she sliced the zucchini and the red and yellow bell peppers into pieces that would fit on the skewers.

Once that was done, she poured herself a glass of Duckhorn Sauvignon Blanc and sat in her chair and the deck. It was 5:45 PM.

CHAPTER 42
THE DISCUSSION

At exactly 6 o'clock there was a familiar knock on her door. Ashley opened it and immediately jumped into Ryan's arms. "Boy, have I missed you," she said.

Ryan gave her a long kiss and said, "me too."

"Ash, have I got time to shower? I feel pretty pitted out. I spent the day with my plane and the guys who take care of it for me in the hangar. The hangar was hot and humid I am not sure how they deal with it every day."

"No problem, I have my wine on the deck and will just sip along until you can join me."

"Sounds like a good plan to me. I will be out in just a few minutes."

Ryan was out very shortly and dressed in his normal shorts and underarmor dry fit T-shirt. Ashley poured him a glass of wine and had it waiting for him on the deck table.

"So how was your day."

"To tell the truth it was a bit of an eye-opener and will provide us with a few things to talk about as we move through the evening."

"That sounds pretty ominous to me. I am not used to the serious tone that brought that sentence out."

"I guess it is a topic I would like to avoid for a while but, unfortunately, given our schedule it is one that needs to be discussed. Reggie called me today and confirmed that we will leave for deployment on December 1. So, I will leave about two weeks after you leave. He also told me that we would return on or about June 1 so we will be out a little over six months."

"Then he kind of dropped a bomb on me. He told me that he was sure that our carrier would be decommissioned when we return and that all the crew will be reassigned. He then told me that I should start thinking about what I would like for my next assignment as this will be my third deployment and I will be up for reassignment on return."

"Okay, now I get the picture. We need to discuss us and your pending possible reassignment. Am I right?"

"Yes, to be honest, I have totally fallen head over heels for you. I am not sure what it feels like to be in love, but I can tell you that I have never ever had feelings for someone like I do for you. The thought of not being with you is just something I do not want to think about but I know the Navy and I know the Navy detailers. They will not wait to reassign me when I get back, so I need to think through what I want them to look into and stay ahead of them so to speak."

"Well Ryan, I want you to know something. My feelings for you are just as strong if not stronger than what you just described. We went through this once and we both knew at the time that a relationship then was not smart given the career paths we have chosen. Now we are where we are, and we know a lot more about each other than we did. I am not going to sit by and let the wind blow you wherever it wants. I am going to butt in and participate in that discussion. You are part of my future and I intend to make sure that happens. So, what I am saying is I want to be part of your decision-making and I know together we will make the right decision for you and for us. So, what do you say to that?"

Ryan just lifted his glass and said, "Cheers to the greatest woman on the planet earth."

Then he gave her an awfully long and slow kiss. "What is for dinner and how can I help?"

"Tonight, were having filet mignon shish kebabs. The skewers are on the counter and there is a bowl of each item that is to go on them you need to thread four of them for us."

"Start by putting two pieces of meat on the bottom then add the other items. When you finish you should have four identical skewers. Make sure that you use all the items in the bowls and then repeat until the skewers full. Once that is done, you can barbecue them. They will take about 13 minutes and you should coat them frequently with Maggie Gins stir fry sauce."

"I have red wine to go with the kebabs. It is a Frank family Pinot Noir. I ventured away from my Oregon Pinots and thought I would try something different. After dinner, I would like to hear what you been thinking about regarding yourself and that will begin a discussion that will probably go on for the next four days. Oh, one other thing. I left Sunday dinner open. It is up to you to decide and make the reservations."

"No problem. I now have my marching orders and I will go to work."

Dinner was great, the meat was tender, and the Maggie Gin's marinade made everything on the skewer taste perfect. After dinner they sat on the deck and Ashley said, "okay, what have you been thinking about?"

"Well I decided two things earlier in the day. The first was I would tell you and the second was I would sit with Reggie and ask him for advice. So, my plan is to run things by you for the next four days and then meet with him next week. My goal will be to have a plan in place that we both agree makes the most sense before you leave a week from Monday."

"That sounds good to me. What have you been thinking about?"

"Well, have never told this to anyone before but one of my long-term goals has always been to fly with the Navy's Blue Angel Demonstration Squadron. They are the best pilots the Navy produces, and I want to be one of them. I will tell you more about that goal later, but I also know that I want to make the Navy a career and go up as high as I can before I must retire at age 62. To achieve that goal, I am going to need to increase my education with a Master's degree and perhaps even a PhD."

"Given the fact that I have been at sea and flying for the past three years, I am due to go ashore, and thus, this might be the best time to get the education issue out of the way. The Navy's postgraduate school is in Monterey, California."

"Of course, the other option might be to look into shore duty assignment here in Honolulu, but I am not sure that, given my long-term goals, that would be the best choice."

"Wow, you have given this thing some real thought. I do not know anything about the Blue Angels other than it is one skilled flying team. I have never thought about the extra education idea, but I am sure it will be important if you continue to move up the ladder. Tell me a little bit about the Blue Angels."

"I can tell you what I know but that is not a whole lot. The Blue Angels have been around for a long time."

"They were formed in 1946 right after World War II. They are the second oldest flying aerobatic team in the world. The French have us beat as their group was formed in 1931."

"The Blue Angels typically fly more than 70 shows per year and the shows are performed all over. Their season runs from March until November. Weather is always an issue, so they have the winter months off to train. So, the first disadvantage is you move around a lot. In the winter they train out of California and in the summer their home is in Florida. They are back in full form now but for a short time after 2013 they stopped performing because of budget."

"The team is made up of 6 pilots that fly F-18 Super Hornets. Just like the one I have been flying. They fly both solo and in formation and run from faster speeds of about 750 mph to their slow speed of about 120 mph. Most of the formation flying is done in a diamond formation which is usually a tight formation and at speeds of about 400 miles per hour. When formation flying, they perform maneuvers such as formation loops, barrel rolls, and transitions from one formation to another."

"When they fly solo, they perform high-speed passes, slow passes, fast rolls, slow rolls and very tight turns."

"All team members, both officer and enlisted, pilots and staff officers, come from the ranks of the regular Navy or the Marine Corps. Pilots serve 2 to 3 years and position assignments are made according to team needs, pilot experience levels and career considerations. The officer selection process requires pilots and support officers to apply formally via their chain of command with a personal statement, letters of recommendation and flight records. Pilots must have at least 1250 tactical jet hours and they must be carrier qualified. So, I meet at least the last two criteria."

"This sounds like it is as special as the SEAL Triton is."

"Yes, if you are selected to be a member of the team you are a Blue Angel for life and there is a special designation crest that you wear for life like the Triton."

"So that is about all I can tell you. It is a long-term goal, but it is such a narrow pyramid that I have never discussed it with anyone."

"That sounds like it would be an incredible honor to be selected. In fact, it is probably a big honor just to be considered. Are your chances to be selected improved if you are actively flying now? I guess I am asking if you select the school alternative would that hurt you in your effort to attain your goal?"

"I have no idea, but it is a question I will have for Reggie. So, enough talk about me tonight. I would like to have another glass of wine and do what I love to do which is to sit here and look at you."

"You know, sometimes you say just the right things at the right time."

They went to bed at 10 PM which was late for both of them. They had to work on Friday but neither of them was thinking about that. They made love very slowly and both came at the same time. They were fast asleep in no time.

They were on the base at 730 in the morning and they both headed for their respective ships. There was a note waiting for Ashley when she arrived at her stateroom. It said, please call Roscoe.

"Hey boss, it is Ash."

"Hi Ash, thanks for calling. Today I want to take our mission weapons out to the range and make sure that every one of them works perfectly. It will be just the two of us as I do not want anyone else to know. The other thing I wanted you to know is I spoke with Chief Johnson yesterday and told him our mission had been moved up. He understood but wants to move his wedding up to next Wednesday so the guys can all attend before we leave, and he is really looking forward to your standing up as his best man."

"Well that will be something to look forward to. It will be a change that I will welcome. Did he say what his plan will be?"

"Yes, it is designed around us. His potential wife must be a saint. He wants the wedding to be at four, followed by a dinner with drinks.

The only dance will be his with his new wife. He wants everyone to be in their dress uniforms. That will be his last official Navy event. He will retire the next day."

"Well that will be fun for all of us. What time do you want to go to the range?"

"Let us go at 1000. Then we can go to lunch together at the officer's club. Oh, I said it would just be the two of us, but I have asked Chief Johnson to join us as well. He is an expert with weapons and will be a good observer to have along. He does not know anything about our mission."

They walked over to the range together. Chief Johnson had arranged to have all the weapons they ordered sent to the range and he was waiting for them when they arrived. They did not need to explain anything to him. He knew they were about to go on a mission and based on the weapons they were taking he knew that it was not an easy one. They checked out every Sig handgun first and made sure the silencers were all working.

They then moved to the automatic weapons. They paid a lot of attention to how they fired with the silencers in place. When they were finished, they asked the Chief to make sure the weapons were all cleaned and then returned to the ship. He was happy to do it and did it well.

They left for lunch after a brief discussion about the wedding. The Chief told them that his wife to be, was planning the entire thing and it would be in a small chapel on the way to Diamond Head. Every member of the team was invited, and he wanted them all-in full-dress uniforms. He asked that Ashley arrive one hour before the wedding so she could be briefed on her role, the ring etc. She told him she would be there with rings on her fingers and bells on her toes. He just laughed. She had a good light lunch with Roscoe, did some paperwork in the afternoon and then left the base at 1600. She was home, showered and changed in time to get the fish tacos together. She shredded some cabbage, created a sauce with sour cream, mayonnaise, lime juice, garlic powder and sriracha sauce. Then she chopped up some cilantro and tomato and put a dish out with Cotija Mexican cheese in it. The sauce was spicy but would go great with the mahi-mahi. She took the fish out and lightly brushed it with all of oil, salt, and pepper and put it back in the refrigerator. Ryan would be there at 6 PM so she had a half an hour to spare before his arrival.

He was on time as usual and on the deck in no time. He asked about the dinner and she told him what they were having. His job was to cook the fish and warm the tortillas. She told him only three minutes aside on the mahi-mahi. He did what he was told, and dinner was perfect. She went back to her Oregon Pinot Gris stash and opened another bottle of Coelho Renovacao. She knew he loved it the first time and it worked just as well the second time.

After dinner, she wanted to know more about the Naval Postgraduate School in Monterey.

"I probably know less about the PG school that I did about the Blue Angels. The Naval Postgraduate School is a public graduate school operated by the Navy and located in Monterey, California."

"It grants Master's degrees, doctoral degrees and certificates. It has been around for a long time as it was founded in 1909. I know it moved to Monterey in 1951 and that it has over 40 programs of study. The Masters and PhD programs are in management, national security affairs, electrical and computer engineering, mechanical and astrological engineering, space systems oceanography and a number of others."

"If you went back to graduate school what would interest you?"

"I think I would want my study to be generally applicable to managing, therefore, I would probably want to stay in the school of management. All the engineering programs are technical, and they really do not interest me. I want to someday manage a bunch of Navy pilots and I do not want to try to do it without a defined set of management skills."

"The campus is beautiful and located in Monterey right next to Carmel and Pacific Grove. I do not know if you have spent any time on the Monterey Peninsula, but I can tell you it is one of the most scenic places in the world."

"I have never been there, but I have watched the golf tournament from Pebble Beach, so I have a pretty good idea what you are talking about."

"Well that ends another night of discussion. I am ready for final glass of wine and then I plan to try to keep you awake with some physical activity if you do not mind." She did not mind, and they were sound asleep by 10 PM.

CHAPTER 43
THE FINAL WEEK

It was early on Saturday morning. Roscoe had been up for two hours when the phone rang at 0700. "Good morning, this is Lieutenant Commander Cook speaking, how may I help you?"

"Roscoe, it is Ralph Omark."

"Good morning Admiral, what may I do for you?"

"Well I wanted to check with you to see how your mission planning is going and to let you know I have sent you today by special messenger one last toy our folks have come up with that may assist you during your mission. I am sending a handheld EMP device that will screw up any electrical system within a quarter of a mile of where it is triggered. It is a transient electromagnetic disturbance device that will not hurt people, but it will cut the power off everything within a quarter mile of its activation position. This means, when you set it off, the power to everything within a quarter of a mile surrounding you will go off. That means no lights, no camera, etc. I think it may help you out. This should take care of any internal security system they have in operation as well."

"Yes sir, that is really good news. It will really come in handy when we attack the warehouse. We have double checked everything and are ready to go. Ashley and I will personally pack the vehicle with the things we will need this week to ensure we do not leave anything behind. We have a detailed checklist that we have been through many times and will follow it to the letter. We have already tested all the weapons and they are all ready to go. We plan to brief Captain Miles this week and then once we are underway, we will bring our team together and go over the plan."

"Good Roscoe. Do not forget to make sure I know how it went. I need to be the first to know."

"I understand completely, sir and I have already discussed the communication issue with Captain Miles. He is on board and will get word to you as soon as we are back with our report."

"Okay Roscoe. Best of luck. I look forward to hearing some good news from you when this thing is over."

"Thank you, sir."

Roscoe hung up and thought about the EMP device. It would really come in handy he thought.

Ashley rolled over in bed. It was Saturday morning and just a bit after 730. She snuggled under Ryan's arm and just laid there with her eyes wide open staring at the ceiling. This would be the beginning of her last week with Ryan. She had today and tomorrow and then the following Thursday, Friday and Saturday. She would stay on board the submarine on Sunday night as they would be leaving first thing in the morning. She and Ryan had two good nights of discussion and they had talked through both alternatives. A lot would hinge on Ryan's discussion with Reggie. Ashley knew that Reggie really valued Ryan and that he would know what the best path for Ryan would be. She also knew she was not going to let this guy go and that the path he chose would clearly have an impact on her. It was all unclear at this point but the one thing that was clear was their relationship. It was real and it would last.

Her next thought was what to do today? It took her no time to decide; "We are going to the beach and soak up the sun." Tonight's dinner was already planned and together they were going to make shrimp fettuccine. Tomorrow would be another day spent totally together with dinner out as a special treat. She had no idea what Ryan had planned but she knew it would be fun and special.

Ryan finally started to wake up and it was clear to Ashley that he was ready but not ready to get up. She just giggled and said, "good morning, sunshine. Do I sense you are not ready to get up yet?

He rolled into her and said, "Now what gave you that idea?" Ashley just giggled and went to work. They were in the shower together by 8 AM. Over breakfast and coffee, Ashley asked Ryan what he had planned for dinner on Sunday evening.

"I made a reservation at 6 PM for us at La Mer. It is a fine dining restaurant in the Halekulani Hotel. I am told that it was voted the best French restaurant in Honolulu. The views of the ocean are supposed to be super, so I am looking forward to a very relaxed evening together. We will need to dress up a bit so we may even want to go in uniform which will work as the proper attire."

"Wow, a dinner together in uniform. That will be quite a change from our normal shorts and sandals don't you think?"

"You got that right, my dear."

"Okay let us clean up these dishes and head for the beach." They packed their beach bag and took two lightweight beach chairs and headed out the door and down the path to their favorite spot. While they were sitting on the beach Ashley told Ryan about the wedding that would be held on Wednesday and her role as best man. He had forgotten all about it until she mentioned it.

"That sounds like a very fun evening for you and your entire team."

"Yes, Chief Johnson has been a mainstay for me and for most of the guys. He will be missed. Gunny Sanchez, however, has fit in like a glove and life will go on. I am anxious to meet the bride to be, I am told she is one great person. From my perspective she must be, to be willing and flexible enough to have her wedding fit in around our crazy SEAL schedule."

They had a great day at the beach. At dinner they talked through the possibility of Ryan requesting shore duty at Pearl Harbor. They both ruled it out. It would be the wrong move for his career, and he had made it clear that he wanted to spend his career in the Navy with a goal to attain the highest rank he could.

They had a lazy day on Sunday. They read the paper from cover to cover. Then they went for a walk over to the Ala Moana Center and looked at a lot of shops. They were back in time to clean up, put on their uniforms on and head to La Mer for dinner.

The restaurant was everything Ryan had hoped for. They were given a great table and lots of folks looked at them. They were not only a striking couple but one of them had on fighter wings and the other a Navy Seal Triton.

Their table had a great view and the service was unbelievable. They decided to begin with a bottle of dry Rose from Provence. Ryan knew nothing about French wines, and he was not about to bluff his way through the list. He just told the waiter he wanted to start with a dry rose from Provence and then have a light burgundy with the main course. The waiter suggested a Rose by Cotes De Provence. It was light, cold and good. For the red he suggested a Bordeaux blend red wine by Chateau Malmaison. It was light and smooth. The Rose ran about $20 and the red wine about $50.

After the finished their first glass of Rose, they looked at the menu and decided. Ashley started with the cured mackerel salad with coconut and anchovy sauce and Ryan ordered the beef tartar which was placed on a bed of hearts of palm with a watercress puréed. For her entrée Ashley ordered Opakapaka which was placed on a bed of squid ink ravioli filled with zucchini and basil. Ryan had the duck filet with a pepper sauce. Both were excellent. The wine was superb, and they left the restaurant saying they would be back. This was one place that was going to stay on their list. They walked home in the dark and it was just a perfect night.

They were up early and on the base by 730. Ashley had a note in a room to call Roscoe when she was in and she did so. "Hey Ash, thanks for the call. Today I have asked Chief and Gunny to work the guys out in the water. I want them out of here because I want the two of us to pack the vehicle. The more we do while we are out of the water, the easier this is going to be.

I also want to tell you about a call I got from Admiral Omark yesterday morning. He has a new toy for us that should really come in handy. Let's meet at the equipment locker at **0900**. Bring your checklist so we can double check everything together."

Ryan called Reggie at **0800** and asked him if he could meet with him later in the day.

Reggie was happy to meet with him and they agreed they would meet in the Wardroom at **1400**. Ryan told him it was about his career decision and he wanted some advice which Reggie said he would be happy to provide.

At **0900** Ashley and Roscoe began going over the equipment they would need for the mission. They wanted to put as much of it in the vehicle before they left on the mission, so nothing was left to chance. This avoided the need to depend on each member of the team to bring what they thought they would need. First, they checked out the seven Sig silenced hand pistols with holsters. Next it was the three silenced automatic rifles and last the three extra wetsuits and three extra single tanks. They proceeded down the list and double checked every item. The last things they put in were the four mines that Odie would need to sink the barge. They also made sure they had an ample supply of ammunition.

Each member of the team would wear a combat knife which they would bring themselves. They loaded the night goggles. They were an absolute necessity. They also loaded the rebreathing front packs for all members. Once that was done, Ashley thought of one more thing that might be helpful. She left Roscoe and went to the ship's pharmacy. There she asked for three valiums. She returned and packed them and told Roscoe that might come in handy for use with the three Chinese guys.

Roscoe told her they would brief Captain Miles on the entire plan in the morning at 0730 so she decided to stay on the ship overnight so she would be ready to go first thing.

At exactly 0725 they met with Captain Miles in the wardroom. They took him through the plan in total detail. It took two full hours. Captain Miles also gave them some information that was important to the mission regarding the Yellow Sea.

The first thing he told them is that the average depth of the Yellow Sea is only 144 feet but as you move from north to south it gets deeper. He showed them on the map where he intended to let the SEALs off. The water depth at that point would be a full 200 feet. He also told them that The Yellow Sea has that name for a reason.

Captain Miles told him that there is a large silt build up on the bottom of the Yellow Sea which is the result of the river flows coming into it. Visibility is awfully bad. The water temperature at times, can be as cold as the air temperature. Captain miles told them that in the winter in the North the average temperature can be 20° with strong northerly monsoons. He indicated however the farther south you move the air temperature warms as does the water temperature. Between June and October, the weather is very mild, probably, on average in the 60° range. He indicated they would arrive just as the colder temperatures are beginning. So, the water temperature could be 50°. He also said that they must be very mindful of the mud flats that hug the coast. If they center the mini down the center of the channel, they will be fine but if they veer off, they could find themselves stuck in the mud with no way to get out of it. This was not a pretty thought for any of them.

Captain Miles told him there would be little sea life. He told them that the yellow Sea is considered among the most degraded marine areas on earth. Most of the sea life had died off due to the quality of the water. The only thing that has survived are spotted seals and, occasionally, a great white shark that comes into the shallow water looking for a seal dinner.

With that comment Ashley laughed. If I may say so, I have had my fill of sharks this year.

"I am happy to know that these great whites are looking for a normal seal dinner not an abnormal SEAL dinner." Both Roscoe and Captain Miles laughed.

They finished their briefing by noon and the three of them had lunch together. Ashley left after lunch and picked up her Dress Blue/White Marine Uniform from the cleaners. Tomorrow is the wedding and she intended to look good as the Chief's best man.

She headed for her apartment. She told Roscoe unless he needed her for something, she would take the day off so she could be at the Chapel on Diamond Head by 3 PM. He was fine with it, so she had the evening and the next morning to herself.

Ryan met with Reggie at 1400 as planned. "Hey Ryan, it was good to get your call, sounds like you have been thinking about the possible next assignment. Am I right?"

"Yes sir, you hit the nail on the head. I have been thinking a lot about it and I would appreciate your thoughts on my career. I want to make the Navy my career and I want to achieve the highest level I can before I am forced to retire at 62."

"I love to fly. My dream job is to be a member of the Blue Angel Demonstration Team. On the other hand, I know that education is extremely important as you move up the command ladder and I do not want to pass up an opportunity to get the additional education if the opportunity is available. I would like your thoughts on my best career path."

"Ryan, you are one hell of a pilot and no matter which way you go you are going to get two extraordinarily strong Blue Angel recommendations. One will come for me and the other from Captain John Jacobs.

He saw you lead that F 18 Hornet in for a night landing and he told me the next morning that it was one of the best pieces of flying he had ever seen. He also said that if you ever needed a recommendation for the Blue Angels, he would provide one and he was a Blue Angel, so his recommendation really counts."

"In any event, back to you and your career path. You have been flying for over three years and after this deployment you will have had three deployments. It is time for you to take a break and stay ashore. If you are committed to a Navy career, I would recommend that you take this opportunity to get your Master's degree and if you can squeeze it in, in the time allotted, go for your PhD as well.

Education means a lot as you get higher in rank and the management of people becomes the key. Learning to manage is a skill and one that will only pay off as you move up the Navy's political ladder. So, my recommendation would be to put in for the PG school in Monterey and follow that assignment with the Blue Angel request. If you decide to go that route just tell me and we will make sure that the recommendations for the Blue Angels are filed with the right people."

"Well, thank you sir. I appreciate your confidence in me, and I plan to follow your recommendation. I look forward to flying you around for the next six months. Thanks again for your time and support."

"No problem Ryan, anytime."

CHAPTER 44
THE WEDDING

Ashley was up at her normal time. She put on her shorts and sandals and headed to the beach path. She grabbed a paper from the newsstand and headed back. Then she made a cup of coffee and took the next half an hour to read the paper. The Coronavirus was in the news on every page. It hit New York in a major way and Governor Como seemed to be taking charge and communicating everything to the public daily. She guessed that shipping out on Monday would come just at the right time. She just hoped the thing was passed by the time they returned. She and Roscoe had been so focused on their upcoming mission that she had not even bothered to ask what or where they were going once the mission was completed. The more she thought about it the less she cared. The mission was the only thing that she cared about and what happened after that would just happen.

When she was finished with the paper she went into her bedroom and laid out her Marine Corps Officer Dress Blue and White Uniform.

The Blue and White Uniform replaced the All-White Dress Marine Officer uniform in 2000. Her pants were white, and her shoes were black. The coat was blue with gold buttons. There were metals worn instead of ribbons and she had three of them. One was her active service metal. The other two metals were those that were given to her team when they rescued the Chinese freighter sailors as their ship was about to sink in the typhoon. She wore her gold Triton pin above the metals. Her belt was white, and she wore her authorized sword. Chief Johnson had specifically asked Roscoe that the team please wear their swords as he wanted them to form a sword line under which he and his bride would walk when the ceremony concluded.

Everything looked good to her. The wedding was set for 4 o'clock. She would be there early.

The Chief had said 3:00 but she would be there at 2:30 because she wanted to meet the bride and that would be the only time, she would have the opportunity to do it.

The wedding was to be held at the Anela Garden Chapel. It was only 15 minutes by car from her apartment and was on the way to Diamond Head. She had never been in it, but she had driven by it on a couple of occasions. She knew it was an extremely popular place in Honolulu for small weddings. She had purchased a silver bowl as a wedding gift and had ordered for the bride, Sarah Miles, a white flower lei which she planned to give her when they met. She called and ordered an Uber to pick her up at 2:15. She told the driver she needed to stop at the flower shop and then she told him to take her to 3050 Montserrat Avenue. "Oh, you are going to the wedding chapel. As beautiful as you look may I ask if you are the bride-to-be?"

"You can ask, and I am glad you did, but I am not the bride-to-be I am the best man."

The Uber driver was puzzled but decided not to bring the subject up again. He just thought to himself, how can a woman be a best man? Oh well the times they are a changing in thought.

He dropped her off at the curb in front of the chapel. She grabbed her gift and the lei and headed in to find the bride or the groom.

She opened the door to the chapel and was amazed how beautiful it was. It was small but it had an extremely high arched ceiling. There were seats on both sides of the isle that led to the front of the chapel. She did not know how many it would hold but it looked like it could easily handle 100 people and that was the number that the chief had told her were invited. There was no one around so she walked down a small hall where she could hear women's voices. She arrived at the room and realized that it was a room designed for the bride and her bridesmaids to dress, do their makeup and prepare for the wedding. She knocked on the door and the door was answered by an attractive petite woman in her early 50s. "You must be Ashley, the woman I have heard so much about. Am I right?"

"Yes Ma'am, I am Ashley Jamison."

"Well Ash, I am Sarah Miles and is a pleasure to meet you. Please come in and meet the girls." Ashley was then introduced to three very pretty women all in their 50s. "Ladies, this is Ashley Morgan Jamison. She may not look like it to you, but she is a for real superhero and my husband to be thinks the world of her. She is here to stand in for Mark and be the Chief's Best Man."

"Ashley these three attractive chicks are my bridesmaids. This is Mini More, Amber Parker and Chloe Mi."

The ladies each stepped forward to shake hands with Ashley. "Ashley, are you the woman we all read about that kicked the crap out of those creeps at the Ala Mona Center?" Chloe asked.

"Yes, I am the one. They were all creeps and I am happy to say they will not be walking around on the streets of Honolulu for some time. Oh Sarah, before I forget I have a small gift for you and the Chief where would you like me to put it?"

"Just put it on the table Ash, thanks for thinking of us."

"I also had this made for you and I thought you might want to wear it after the ceremony is over." Ashley pulled the handmade lei out of the box and gave it to Sarah.

"Wow, this is beautiful. It will go perfectly with my dress. In fact, I think I will wear it down the aisle." Everyone clapped and said, "Nice job Ash."

"Sarah, do you know where I can find the Chief. He wanted to tell me what I am supposed to do so I don't mess this event up."

They all laughed, and Sarah told Ashley that she could find the Chief at the other end of the chapel. There was a room where guys could change, and he was in it.

She also told Ashley that the Chief was alone because she was his best man.

"Thanks, I will go find him now. Nice to meet all of you ladies."

Ashley headed to the other end of the chapel. There she found Chief Johnson. He was dressed in his Dress White Navy Uniform and he had so many medals on his left side she could not imagine how he could stand up. His gold Triton was pinned above all of them and it stood out.

Ashley knocked as she entered. "Hey Ash, it is great to have you here with me."

"Chief I have never seen you in Dress Whites before. If I had that many medals to pin on, I would not be able to stand up."

"Don't get to put this monkey suit on very often. It does represent 27 years as a SEAL so I guess I should be a little sad that this is the last time I will put this thing on. To be honest I am ready for retirement and excited about the next stage of my life. I cannot wait for you to meet Sarah."

"I just left her and the ladies that are standing up with her. She is a doll and so are the women who will stand with her."

"Oh great. I am glad you met. I am on strict orders not to go anywhere close to that dressing room."

"So here is what we have planned. The ceremony is short, sweet and to the point. I told the Minister it could be no longer than 15 minutes and we did not want it to be religious. He agreed, so this whole thing should not take long. Once everyone is seated at about 10 minutes to 4:00 the music will begin. It will be one guy playing an Organ. At 4 PM exactly, the minister will come out and stand facing the folks. He will say a few words of welcome and then will signal to the organ player to begin a new song. That song will be "cannot help falling in love" by Haley Reinhart. That will be your queue. You will be the first one to walk down the aisle and will do so when the music changes.

You will have this ring with you." The Chief then pulled a ring out of a box in his pocket and gave it to Ashley.

"Chief, may I look at it?"

"Sure, look all you want but please do not lose it." He said it was a huge smile on his face.

"It is beautiful, and it is huge. How many carats is this diamond?"

"Three."

"Well you did well sir."

"Okay back to the wedding. Once you are down the aisle you will take a position to the right of the front of the chapel. I will then follow you down and take a position standing next to you. Once we are set, Sarah's pals will begin. I think Mimi will go first, then Amber and last Chloe. They will line up on the left side as we face the chapel front. The music will then change to "Here comes the bride" and Sarah will make her entrance and head down the aisle. When she is there, I will join her facing the minister."

"I have asked Roscoe to have all the guys wear their swords and position a man on the end of each aisle. When the minister says, "I now pronounce you man and wife," all the guys will stand and on Roscoe's signal they will raise their swords in what is known as the Sabre Arch. It is a tradition often performed at military weddings. The music will then change to "perfect" by Ed Sheeran.

Once that happens, Sarah and I will walk back down the aisle together under the Sabre Arch. Each of the women will then follow individually. You will be the last to walk under the arch. Once you are through Roscoe will give the signal and the Sabre Arch will disappear. Once that is done the guests will begin to leave by aisle from front to back."

"We will then proceed to glasses of champagne and a dinner served outside under the trees. It should all be over and done with by 7 PM. In any event that is the plan."

"Sounds like a great plan to me Chief."

"I would like to go to the chapel with you to make sure I know where you want me to stand if that is okay."

"Sure, let us go now before anyone is around."

They did. The chief showed Ashley where she was to stand and where the others would be. At 3:30 the guests began to arrive. Roscoe had his guys there and he positioned them along the aisle in each row.

Ashley was not sure, but she thought there were about 100 people in attendance. The guys in uniform were all SEAL's but they were different dress uniforms based on whether they were Navy or Marines. Roscoe was in Navy Dress Whites just like the Chief and Gunny Sanchez was in his Marine Blue and White Uniform. Roscoe and the Gunny had so many medals on they actually gave the Chief a run for his money.

At exactly 10 minutes to 4:00 the organ began to play, and Ashley and the Chief took their positions at the back of the chapel. At exactly 4 PM the minister appeared and took his position in front of the chapel.

"Good day ladies and gentlemen. Today I have the privilege of joining two great people in marriage. Each of you know one of them well, some of you may have met both of them but you do not know them well as a couple. After today you will all have the privilege of knowing them both well as a couple. I can tell you there is an old Jack Johnson song that says, "they are better together" and I can tell you that will be the case with Sarah and the Chief."

With that said, the minister nodded his head and the music changed. Ashley was on queue and began her slow walk down the aisle. She took her position at the front of the chapel and was followed by a smiling Chief.

Once Ashley and the Chief had taken their positions Mini, Amber and Chloe walked individually and slowly down the aisle. They were all dressed in low-cut mild yellow dresses that fit each of them perfectly. They were three good-looking women. When Chloe was in place the music changed again and "Here comes the bride" began to play

Sarah was stunning in a white dress that was cut just like her bridesmaids. The only difference was hers was white. She wore the handmade lei that Ashley had brought her and it went perfect with the dress. She looked super and everyone noticed it

The ceremony went as planned and when it was over Roscoe gave the signal and the men on each side of the aisle stood and faced each other. On Roscoe's command they drew their swords and made the Sabre Arch. The Chief and his new bride were first under the arch. They were followed by Chloe, Amber and Mini. Ashley was the last to walk under the arch. When she had finished her walk down the aisle, Roscoe gave the command and the swords were placed back in their sheaths and the arch disappeared. It was very impressive to all of those that had not seen done before.

The champagne began to flow, and the dinner was super. There were a few toasts and a lot of laughter. The Chief and his bride made the rounds and met everyone at every table. By 7 PM the party was ending, and folks were starting to leave. Sarah and the Chief were the first to go. Ashley had not asked if or where they were going on their honeymoon. She just hoped that the Coronavirus was not going to screw it up. She was tired so she called and Uber and was home by 8 PM.

It had been a great day and an even greater wedding. She poured herself a glass of Duckhorn Fume Blanc and sat on her deck thinking about tomorrow. That would begin the last few days she would have with Ryan. She was looking forward to hearing how is talk with Reggie went and what path he thought would be best for his career.

CHAPTER 45
GOODBYE FOR NOW

On Thursday morning everyone seemed tired but in a good mood. The Chief's wedding was a positive for everyone and everyone seemed to have a great time. Roscoe had made a nice talk about the Chief and his career and he made sure that everyone in attendance knew that the Chief was a retiring hero in the eyes of all his and her SEAL brothers. It touched everyone including the Chief who had a tear in his eye.

Ashley spent the entire morning with Roscoe thinking and planning. Both were now feeling like they had a plan that would work along with the team and tools to pull it off. They were still concerned about the heavy silt and mud they could encounter but they felt if they stayed in the middle of the channel in the middle of the night that things should go as planned. They also knew now better than ever that without the new mini sub their plan would simply not have had a chance to work.

Gunny Sanchez knew something was up, but he also knew he would be told when it was appropriate, so he kept his mouth shut. Most of the others just thought it was business as usual and another deployment that would be filled up with training exercises. Ashley left the base at 1600 and grabbed an Uber home. She was too tired to think about dinner, so she ordered sushi to be delivered from Hironouchi which was a Japanese sushi restaurant inside the Haus Supper Cub in the Ala Moana Shopping Center. She ordered four things which he thought would fill both she and Ryan. She ordered:

- Sesame shrimp toast
- mozzarella spring rolls
- crispy bao buns
- two orders of nori salt calamari
- brown rice along with chopsticks

They said her order would be delivered by 7 PM. When that was done, she changed out of her uniform and took a long hot shower.

She felt very tired, but she knew it was all mental from the work she had been doing with Roscoe. She planned to work Friday but would take Saturday and Sunday morning off. She would stay on the submarine on Sunday night as they were getting underway first thing on Monday morning. At 6 PM Ryan knocked on the door and they went through their welcome ritual; however, they seemed to hold onto each other longer than normal.

"Hi sailor, how was your week?"

"It was good. I did have a chance to speak with Reggie and he was extremely helpful. I want to tell you all about it and hear about the Chief's wedding. I will grab a shower and change and be right with you."

Ashley opened a bottle of Cakebread Sauvignon Blanc and poured two glasses and took a seat on the deck. The sun was still out, and it was about 85°. The deck had shade, so the temperature was perfect.

Ryan was back in no time and took the other chair on the deck. He lifted his glass of wine to Ashley and said, "to the most wonderful woman in the world."

"I do not think that statement is true, but I do not want to debate it tonight. I missed you and I am really looking forward to next three days together."

"Are you still going back to the submarine on Sunday?"

"Yes. I am going back around noon. We get underway first thing on Monday and Roscoe wants to double check all of our gear on Sunday afternoon."

"I am anxious to hear about your discussion with Reggie. Tell me how it went."

"I explained to him that I have made the decision to make the Navy my career and I want to achieve the highest level I can during the process. I told him that my dream job would be to fly with the Blue Angels Demonstration Team, but I am also aware that as you move up the ladder that education and management skills are particularly important. To my surprise, Reggie told me that he had already made up his mind to discuss the Blue Angel option with me.

"He told me that he had recently discussed it with Captain John Jacobs who is the Flight Commander on the carrier and Reggie's supervisor. I think I told you this, in one of our recent night training sessions, one of our guys lost control of the landing electronics in his plane, so it made a night landing on the carrier almost impossible. To solve the problem Reggie had me lead the pilot in for a landing on the carrier. It meant I had to fly onto the carrier like I was going to land with no landing gear down, just skim the top of the carrier so the guy could follow me with his landing gear down."

"To do it, I flew the length of the carrier about 3 feet off the surface and then pulled the stick up once I was past the end of the carrier. To make a long story short, it all went as planned and we got the guy down safely. Apparently, Captain Jacobs watched the entire thing and told Reggie that he was most impressed and that he would be willing write a recommendation on my behalf to the Blue Angles. It does not hurt that Captain Jacobs was a Blue Angel himself."

"Does that mean that Reggie thought the Blue Angel option was the right next step?"

"No, not at all, he actually thinks that it should be my next active flying step but since I will have three tours under my belt when we return, I am due to spend some time on land. He thinks that I should take the time to advance my education at the Naval Postgraduate School in Monterey. Then, once I have done that, to apply to fly with the Blue Angels Demonstration Team.

"So, I have spent the last couple of days researching what it would mean to go to the Naval Postgraduate School."

"Now you have my attention. What does it mean if you are accepted?"

"Well I do not know a lot at this point, but I do know that they offer an MBA in the graduate school of defense management. The MBA program is 18 months and is specifically designed to provide a defense focused graduate level of education in business."

"The objectives of the program are to prepare officers for management positions in the Department of Defense or in the Navy overall.

The program is focused on developing the participants skill and knowledge which will help them to develop broad critical thinking and analytical abilities."

"Does that mean you would stay in Monterey for the entire 18 months?"

"Yes, I think so. I still have a lot to learn about the program, but I do know Monterey and the Monterey Peninsula is a really a great spot to be located. If I know that I'm going to be there in one spot for a long period of time it would make it a lot easier for us to design a strategy that works for our relationship."

"I agree. I am hungry and if I am right, we are about to get a knock on the door for dinner."

"We aren't cooking here tonight?"

"Nope, I ordered takeout from Hironouchi in the Ala Moana Center. It is supposed to be delivered at 7 PM which is right about now."

Within five minutes there was a knock on the door. Ryan opened it and accepted the two bags from the deliveryman. Ashley had prepaid so they were ready to sit down to dinner.

"What surprise did you order for us?" Ryan asked as he began to open the bags.

"I ordered four things. You should find some shrimp toast, spring rolls, bao buns and calamari along with brown rice and chopsticks."

"It is all here, and it smells great."

During dinner they continued talking about Ryan's options, but Ashley also took him through the wedding and the sword ceremony. She also told him about the chapel and how it worked perfectly for the size of the group. After dinner they talked about the next three days and what to do to fill them.

"Ash, would you mind if we called Sam and Esther Owens and see what their catamaran schedule is like. I think it would be fun to spend another day together on their boat.

I really enjoyed our day with them and the snorkeling with you. I do not want to go if they have a bunch of people booked but who knows we just might luck out again. We have to work tomorrow, so Saturday, will be our last full day together and if we enjoy it as much as we did the last time it will create a lasting memory."

"I think that is a great idea. Let me call them right now before it gets too late."

"Hello, this is Esther Owens and Lagoon Catamaran, how can I help you?"

"Esther, it is Ashley Jamison. You and Sam hosted my pal Ryan and me a few months ago and we wanted to know if you have any availability on Saturday?"

"Hi Ash, it is great to talk to you. Of course, I remember you and that handsome friend of yours. How could I forget you guys, you could be on the cover of some sort of fitness magazine or one that features perfect couples."

"Thanks Esther, that is really nice thing to hear."

"We are going out on Saturday morning. Right now, we have one other couple booked. If you would like to join us, we obviously have the space. We will be leaving at 10 AM and will return about 3 PM. It is a snorkel trip back to the same Cove you and Ryan explored."

"Please book us Esther. We are really looking forward to seeing you guys again."

"Ryan, they have one other couple booked for Saturday and they are taking the same trip we took. I booked us in, the yacht leaves at 10 AM so we will need to be out of here at 9:15."

"No problem, Ash, that sounds great."

The rest of the evening they spent sitting on the deck watching the boat sway back and forth in the harbor. They were in bed and in each other's arms at 9 PM and when they were finally done fooling around, they were asleep by 10 PM. They were both up early and back on their respective ships by 8 AM.

Captain Miles and his crew were busy all day preparing the submarine for deployment, it seemed like every department was busy.

Ashley left the sub and spent the day in the SEAL office on base. The guys were coming back off leave and she had paperwork to do. She left the base at 1600 and headed for home. She decided that dinner would again be takeout as she did not want to leave anything in the refrigerator while she was gone. She thought about dinner and decided to call Taco'ako. The motto of Taco'ako was "For the love of fresh tacos."

Ashley ordered three grilled octopus tacos with salsa roja, cucumber, cilantro and pico de gallo. She also ordered one order of Frijoles which were refried pinto beans with vegetarian black beans. The order was for 7 PM.

Ryan arrived at 6 PM. The wine was poured, and the dinner arrived on time. Ashley told him she did not shop because she wanted an empty refrigerator come Sunday morning. She knew that there would be a great deal of food to eat on the yacht, so she was not worried about starving to death on Saturday.

They made love slowly on Friday night. Their time together was ending and neither one of them was looking forward to saying goodbye.

Saturday was perfect. The boat, the food and Esther and Sam were great. The other couple that had joined them were on their honeymoon and thus they were totally in a world of their own. Ashley and Ryan hardly saw them. The diving was super, and Ryan and Ashley were back in the apartment by 4:30 PM.

Dinner was made up of Cakebread Pinot Noir and cheese that was in the refrigerator. They took their time in bed and knew the night needed to be special and it was. They went out for breakfast and then they came back and packed their things.

Before they left the apartment and headed for the base, Ryan came up behind Ashley and tapped her on the shoulder. She turned around and he said, "I did not want this time to end without telling you something important."

"What is that?" She said.

"I wanted you to know that I love you. I just needed for you to know that before we part."

A tear formed in Ashley's eye and she said, "I love you too, so very much."

They kissed and that was the goodbye that would last both for at least six months.

The Uber driver picked them up and they were back on the base at noon. Ashley and Ryan gave each other one last hug and a reminder to please write and they were off on their separate ways. Both were sad but at the same time both were incredibly happy. Their relationship had flourished and was getting stronger with each passing day. Neither knew what the future would hold both knew it was going to be together.

Ashley spent the afternoon with Roscoe. They checked their list more than once and by 8 PM Ashley was in bed and sound asleep

CHAPTER 46
UNDERWAY

At exactly 0800 on Monday morning the USS Louisville SSN 724 was underway and headed to the Yellow Sea. Within an hour the submarine had reached its cruising depth of 500 feet and cruising speed of 30 knots. Captain Miles called Roscoe and asked him to meet in the small conference room off the Wardroom. The Captain was in the room when Roscoe arrived. "Good morning Roscoe. Would you like a cup of coffee?"

"Yes, sir that would be great."

"We are underway and headed to the Yellow Sea. We have about 2500 miles to go before we arrive at our destination. We will be moving at about 30 knots which means we will travel about 800 miles per 24-hour period. At that rate we will be at our destination in about three days. My thought is, if we stay on schedule, we should be ready to launch the operation over the weekend. From what we know their supply ship arrives every Tuesday, so my suggestion is we hit them at about 2 AM Sunday morning. What do you think?"

"Sounds good to me, sir. That will give me one full day prior to the launch of our operation to make sure we have everything covered. The last thing I want to do in this operation is to rush. Everything will come in due time and I want it to go smoothly."

"Sounds like a plan to me. I will let you know when we reach our destination, we can assess how things look then. If my calculations are correct, we will have you in a position that is about 5 miles from the center of Haeju Harbor. When are you going to meet with your team?"

"I have called a meeting for 1400 this afternoon. I am going to tell the entire SEAL team what is going on and what their respective roles are going to be. I am also going to tell them they are not to discuss the operation with anyone."

"Good, I do not intend to tell the submarine screw anything other than that we will be stopping in the Yellow Sea for a SEAL Team operation."

"Sounds good to me sir. Thanks for the coffee." Roscoe left the conference room and went to his stateroom. After lunch he met with the SEAL Team.

1400 LARGE CONFERENCE ROOM
USS LOUISVILLE

"Good afternoon everyone. I asked you to meet today because I have a message, I want you to hear. It is also a message that is not to be passed on to anyone. The only people that you may discuss this meeting with are those in this room. Is that clear to everyone?"

"Yes sir," was the statement made in unison.

"I have just met with Captain Miles. He has been directed to deliver our team to our next mission site. We are headed for the Yellow Sea which is a body of the water that separates China from Korea."

"For the past month, Ashley and I have been working on a plan that I am going to outline for you today. The operation we are about to take on is at minimum extremely dangerous and, unfortunately because of equipment constraints, will only involve a small number of our team."

"Our intelligence sources have informed SEAL command that the North Koreans, under the direction of Kim Jong-un, have established and are operating a virus research lab in the port town of Haeju.

We have been told that the virus underdevelopment is designed to kill humans instantly when infected with it. We have also been informed that over two years ago, the Koreans kidnapped three virus research scientists from China. They have been using these three scientists to spearhead the current virus project."

"Our mission is simple to state but difficult to pull off. We have been asked to destroy the virus and the virus operation and bring the three Chinese scientists back to China."

"I should also tell you that China knows nothing about this nor do they have any information that it was the Koreans who kidnapped their scientists. They just know that the scientists disappeared, but they have been so focused on the Coronavirus that they have been unable to devote the resources needed to find out what happened to them. Our plan will require that we return the three scientists to the Chinese government but not before they are interrogated extensively. In fact, there is an interrogation team now on board the Louisville."

"Here is what our plan requires. Let me begin with the submarine. The Captain has informed us that the yellow Sea is a very shallow sea. Its maximum depth is about 500 feet and the average is about 150 feet. The Captain plans to deliver us to a spot in the yellow Sea where the depth is 200 feet. This spot is about five miles from the entrance to Haeju Harbor. The Captain plans to hold the submarine in this spot until we return. His crew does not know anything about this mission. They will be told that the SEAL Team will conduct a training operation and that is the reason for the stop."

"As you are all painfully aware our mini sub only holds 10. When we are at maximum we are packed in like sardines. For planning purposes, it also means we will be bringing back three people that will not be with us on the way out. That means we will undertake this action with a SEAL Team made up of seven of us."

"I will lead the first team of three. We will call this team 1. The goal of team 1 will be to destroy the virus and everyone that is trying to protect it. Team 1 will include Gunny Sanchez and Sam Pierce. The three of us were selected for this team as we have the most experience when it comes to killing. Sam, as you all know, has the experience and is an exceptionally good marksman."

"Team 2 will be led by Ashley. Team 2 will be made up of three SEALs as well. Charlie Chan and Al Fineman will be the two SEALs to assist Ashley on Team 2. As you know, Ashley and Charlie both speak fluent Chinese. Charlie can also speak Korean. The Chinese language is an absolute necessity if we are to get these Chinese scientists back alive."

"We also expect that this team will encounter resistance, but it will probably come in the form of hand-to-hand combat in close quarters. I think, given that description, you can understand why we added Al to the team."

"Last, we have Team 3. Team 3 is going to be made up of one man, Ray Odemier. Odie has an underwater demolition role to play and he will be on his own to pull it off. I do not have to tell any of you why he was selected for the UDT mine placement role."

"Now, before I give you details of what we must face, I want to talk to all of you about you. You are all trained as fighters and I know all of you would want to be a part of this operation. Unfortunately, we must work with what we have and that is limited by the size of our mini sub. I do not want any hurt egos so if that could be you, get over it. Some of you will play a role in helping us on our return mission as we are going to have to get the Chinese scientists from the mini to the Louisville at 200 feet. As you can imagine they are going to be scared to death."

"Now I want to detail out to you what needs to be done. I am going to give this all to you in detail because I want you to think it through and let me or Ashley know if we missed anything or you can think of something we have not thought of. So please listen carefully."

"Our plan is to leave the Louisville at a little before 0200 on Sunday morning. We will board the mini sub and head for the channel to the harbor. It is about five miles so it should take us about a half an hour. We have been advised that there is a lot of silt and mud along the shore and that it will be critical that we stay in the channel. Ashley is going to navigate us through this, and I am going to drive. We have packed the mini with all the weapons we need, and all the weapons have been silenced and tested.

We also will be taking four mines with us that Odie will use." "Our rebreathing equipment has all been tested and is stored in the mini sub and we have also included three wetsuits and three extra tanks for the scientists."

"The channel that takes us into the harbor is narrow and shallow. We anticipate that in the center of the harbor the water will be about 25 feet in depth and that is where we plan to put the mini on the bottom. Using our rebreathing gear, we will then leave the vehicle. The actual lab and virus research is being done in an old warehouse next to the water. Team 1 will take down those guarding the warehouse, enter it, and destroy the virus. Once that is accomplished Team 1 will return to the vehicle and board."

"Team 2 will head for a barge that is anchored in the harbor. That barge contains five or six Korean scientists and the three Chinese scientists. This is where they live, eat and are entertained. Yes, I said entertained. The Koreans also included for the enjoyment of the scientists six or eight ladies of the night. Our plan is to kill those guarding the barge, lock the Korean scientists in their room, take the Chinese guys off the barge and put them in the mini sub. The ladies will be locked in their rooms but the last SEAL off the barge will unlock their room so they may escape. The Korean scientists are going to go down with the barge. There are two electric motorboats attached to the barge. Ashley and Charlie will use one to get the scientists to the mini. My plan is to surface the mini and load the scientists in on top of the water then put it back down for Al and Odie to return."

"That brings me to Team 3 and Odie. Odie will carry with him four underwater mines. He will set two of them on the bow of the barge and two on the Stern. The timers will be set for 45 minutes so Ashley and her team need to get their work done and get out of there. We anticipate that Al will be the last off the barge. He will open the lady's door and swim back to the mini sub. Charlie will teach him how to tell the women in Korean to get the hell off the barge. All of Team 2 and Odie will have watches that are synchronized to make sure everyone knows how much time is left before the barge begins to sink. The total operation time from start to finish must be completed in one hour from the time we enter the harbor. If we hold to that timeframe, we will be back in the Louisville by 4 AM and underway."

"I mentioned that all of our weapons are silenced. We do not intend to make any noise. We intend to get in, get out and have the Koreans wake up in the morning only to find that their barge is missing, and their virus and research facility has been destroyed. Even the mines that Odie will set have been designed to make minimal noise. We do not intend to leave anyone alive except for the ladies who are harmless. Everyone that we encounter will be killed."

"Do any of you have any questions?" There were no question so Roscoe said, "Ashley and I will appreciate your thinking about the mission if you can think of anything we need to know, for God sakes, tell us. Thanks for your attention, you are dismissed."

Ashley and Roscoe stayed behind until all the team had left. "What did you think Ash?"

"I thought that your explanation was right on and I only saw heads nodding in approval as you mentioned the names of the team. To be honest, I do not think any of our guys are going to question the decisions we made regarding the team. In fact, I am sure even though we have a bunch of tough guys that some of them are really happy that they were not part of the magnificent seven."

The reference to the magnificent seven made Roscoe laugh.

"Yeah, I thought the same thing. You know Ash, this is not going to be an easy mission."

"Yes, but were ready for it, let's get it done."

It would take a full 3 ½ days for the submarine to transit to the drop zone in the Yellow Sea. Captain Miles told Roscoe that he anticipated they would arrive late on Friday night at about 9 PM. During transit, Captain Miles asked Roscoe again if he would be ready to go early Sunday morning. Roscoe said they were all set to go.

Roscoe called Ashley and told her he wanted the SEAL Team of seven members to be in the small conference room at 9 AM the next morning.

At 0900 the seven SEAL Team members selected were assembled in the conference room. Roscoe thanked them for coming and then took the team through the entire operation again. He did it step-by-step. He wanted no screw ups and he wanted everyone on board at all times.

Ashley was amazed at how Roscoe managed the entire process. He was detailed, firm and respectful of those participating and those who were not. It was a clear example of how leadership should really work.

She left the meeting with an incredibly positive feeling. Today was one of just checking details and all went well.

During the transit to the Yellow Sea, Ashley spent her time reading and writing. Her writing was in the form of a letter to Ryan. She had no idea if, or when, he would ever receive it, but she decided to write it and send it whenever she could.

The letter was short and sweet. It said, "Ryan, I miss you more than I could ever express, and I love you more with each day that has passes. Take care. Love Ashley."

CHAPTER 47
THE CALM BEFORE THE STORM

It was Friday morning about 10 AM. Roscoe was reading in his Stateroom when his phone rang. "Roscoe, it is Captain Miles."

"Good morning Captain. How can I help you?"

"I just wanted you to know that based on our current calculations we should arrive at our target location at about 2000 tonight. Are you still a go for 0200 Sunday morning?"

"Yes sir, our teams are ready, and our plan is set. We will be assembled in the in and out room at 0145 on Sunday morning."

"Good. I will let you know when we have arrived and then will give you the specifics of how far to the Haeju Bay, the water temperature, currents and other items like that."

"Thanks Captain, that will be most appreciated."

Roscoe picked up his phone and called Ashley. "Hi, this is Ash."

"Ash, it is Roscoe. I just got a call from Captain Miles. He believes he will have us to the drop off site about 2000 tonight. Have you finished with your team meetings?"

"Yes, I met with all members of the team two or three times and with Odie on two occasions. We have all gone through the floor plans of the barge and Odie is extremely comfortable where he must place the mines. We will all set our timers for one hour which we will begin when we leave the mini. I have noticed one thing from the satellite photos that I had not noticed before. On some nights there are three guards on the barge and on others there are four. There does not seem to be any pattern so were going to plan on four. Our plan will be to take the guards out first and during the process lock all the folks in their quarters. Al and I will focus on the guards while Charlie locks the folks in their rooms."

"When we have disposed of the guards, we will unlock the Chinese scientist's room and get them into the electric boat. Once that is done, Al will unlock the lady's room and dive overboard. Charlie has taught him what to say to the ladies in Korean."

"Odie will set the charges to go off exactly one hour from the time we leave the minisub so we should all be back on board before they detonate. That should give the ladies between 15 and 30 minutes to get off the thing before it begins to sink. Obviously, my hope is you will beat us back to the mini sub and bring it to the surface before we return. That will be a big help when it comes to transferring the scientist from the electric boat to the mini."

"Sounds like a good plan to me, Ash. I will let you know when we are on site. The Captain said once he has us there, he will fill us in on the details including the actual distance to the harbor, water temperature, and any additional information he thinks will be beneficial. I will call you when I hear. Talk to you later."

At about 2100 Roscoe got a call from the captain. "Roscoe we are on site and in 200 feet of water. The water temperature is 50 degrees and based on my calculation we are about 5.2 miles from the center of Haeju Harbor. From what we can tell the water is not clear. There is extremely high silt content so you will have limited visibility and will be navigating in the dark most of the way."

"Thanks Captain. I have a briefing schedule with my team tomorrow and we will be set to go following that. I will talk to you soon."

Roscoe called Ashley and told her the facts that it been given to him by the Captain. "Ash, I want one last meeting with the launch team, and I would like to have you also invite Ron and Mattie Forkman. I would like to have those two guys be our reception crew on our return. They work so well together they may be extremely helpful in getting the scientists into the submarine."

"No problem, I will have them there.

At 1000 the next morning the seven SEAL Team members and the Forkman brothers all met in the conference room.

Roscoe took the group through the entire operation in detail over the next two hours. He told them he would meet them all at 0145 in the in and out room and they should come dressed for the occasion which made them all smile. He explained to the Forman brothers what the timeline was and that he wanted them outside the sub and ready to assist the team when they returned at 0400. There would be no contact between the team members. It would be a complete radio silence mission. Team members would be allowed to speak in the minisub but once they were out, they were to be in silence mode.

After the meeting Ashley returned to her stateroom. She was anxious for the mission to begin but was surprised that she did not feel any nervousness or concern. She planned to be in bed at 2000 and would be up and dressed and ready to go by 0130. She had been through the navigation charts so many times that she almost had them totally memorized so she was not at all concerned with getting the mini to the teams launch point.

She went to bed as planned at 2000 and was surprised to have no problems going to sleep. She awoke at one in the morning and began the process of getting her gear on. At 0130 she headed for the in and out room. Roscoe was there when she arrived, and the others were all assembled shortly thereafter. At exactly 0145 the team began to exit the submarine. When everyone was out, they begin the process of moving the minisub into loading position. Ashley and Roscoe were first to board while the others began the process of unlatching the vehicle from the Louisville. The Captain was right. The water was full of silt and visibility was terrible. Roscoe moved the mini away from the submarine and the other five members of the team loaded. Ashley gave the coordinates to Roscoe and the minisub slowly moved towards its destination. There was not much talk among the team members. They all knew what they had to do, and they were very aware of the danger they faced but not one of them was fazed by it.

They were Navy SEALs and built tough to last.

The water was just as described, full of silt. The visibility was poor but once they were in the harbor, they would have no problem finding the warehouse or the barge.

They had no idea what the outside weather was, but it was November and thus they expected the temperature to be about 50 degrees with a high probability of rain. Ashley was hoping that it was raining as it would provide an extra amount of cover that clear weather did not provide.

Roscoe brought the minisub up as they moved toward the channel. As he expected the rise from 200 feet was gradual but steady over the five miles they had to transit. During the transit, the men stored their scuba tanks and then put on their rebreathing gear. They also loaded the weapons that each would take. Everyone made sure that their night goggles were attached and then they double checked everything.

Odie attached all four mines to his rebreathing vest. It added an extra 20 pounds to his gear load, but it was no big deal. He checked the timers on each and they were all set to be activated.

Charlie made sure he had the attachable locks and double checked his sig and knife. Al did the same.

The small submarine made progress at about eight knots which was what Roscoe had figured would be their speed. As the mini got closer to the harbor entrance the water became shallow very quickly. Ashley kept her eye on her navigation charts. She did not want to make a mistake and run into a pile of mud. Roscoe slowed the mini as it started to enter the harbor. He watched the depth gauge and eventually arrived at the 25-foot depth as planned. He gently set the mini down on the bottom and shut it down.

He and Ashley then put their gear on and double checked everything. Roscoe made sure that he had the two lock exploding bombs that he would carry with him. One would be used on front door and the other he would use on the vault door. He also had the heat bombs that he would use in the vault and in the middle of the research lab.

Gunny Sanchez and Sam Pierce checked their weapons and they checked Roscoe's as well. They were all carrying their sigs, knives and automatic rifles. "Okay everyone. I want you to all check each other. I want you all to ask yourself, "Do you have what you are supposed to have to pull this mission off?"

If the answer to that question is yes, then we are ready to get the show underway. I want you all to remember. Do not wait if you have an opportunity to shoot. We want the opposition down as quickly as possible. No need to ask or wait for a better shot. Take it when you have the opportunity."

The time was 0230 so they were on schedule.

Roscoe, Gunny and Sam left the mini first. They had a bit of a swim to get to their target. They were followed by Ashley, Charlie and Al. Odie was the last out of the mini. They had all set their watches to make sure they knew how much time they had. They would have exactly one hour to get their task done and get back to the mini. That meant they needed to be back by 0330. Both Team 1 and Team 2 along with Odie stayed down on the bottom swimming as they used their compasses to guide them to their target.

Roscoe and Team 1 found that the water level continued to decrease in depth as they neared the warehouse while Ashley and her team could stay down at the 25-foot level until they were directly below the barge.

Ashley and Charlie would ditch their fins when they boarded the barge. Al would keep his on the back of the barge and grab them when he left to return. Odie would just swim back once he had the mines in place.

Roscoe and Team 1 made good progress. It took them less than 15 minutes to swim to their entry point where the shallow water faced the warehouse. Ashley and her team were under the barge in 10 minutes. The operation was about to start.

Team 1 approached the warehouse. Roscoe motioned for Gunny to take the right and for Sam to take the left. The entrance was right in the middle, so Roscoe positioned himself to go straight at the front door.

CHAPTER 48
OPERATION UNDERWAY

TEAM ONE PROGRESS

The water was only five feet deep when Gunny lifted his head out of it. He could easily stand on the bottom. He was about 15 yards from the dock that the warehouse stood on. It was raining but with his night goggles on he could see clear as if it were broad daylight. Neither Sam nor Roscoe had come to the surface yet. The first thing Gunny noticed was a flashlight beam that was aimed at the water. It was held by one of the Guards and he had a dog with him.

Gunny took out his automatic rifle and put it on single shot. His first shot took the dog out and when the guard looked to see what happened he dropped the light in the water when he was hit with the second shot. Neither of them moved. Gunny moved slowly in the water to the dock where they were both lying. He hopped out of the water and slid both the guard and the dog into the water. When he looked back, he could see both Sam and Roscoe moving toward the dock.

Sam's gun flashed and he only needed one shot to take out the first guard at the corner of his side of the building. Gunny moved down the side of the building and just as he was about to near the corner a guard came around the corner. Gunny's Sig was out and when he pulled the trigger the bullet went directly between the guys eyes. He fell to the floor immediately.

Roscoe was up on the dock and at the front door. He pulled out the handheld EMP power device and triggered it. Everything went dark. He applied the explosive device to the lock and pushed the button. A slight flame appeared and then the door swung open. The second guard dog must have heard the guard fall as he began to bark, and Gunny could hear someone running with the dog toward the guard that had fallen. The dog came around the corner of the building first. It was clear that he had picked up Gunny's scent. Gunny did not hesitate. He shot the dog before it made it around the corner and with the guard following holding on to the leash. He went down as soon as he reached the corner.

Roscoe was inside in no time and just like he had been advised, there was a large lead vault in one corner of the room. He used the second explosive device to destroy the lock on the vault. It worked just as well as the first one did on the front door. The door to the vault opened just as a guard came through the open front door. Roscoe saw him first with his night goggles on. He pulled out his Sig and put a bullet directly into the guard's heart. The guard went down immediately. He didn't even know what hit him. Roscoe just left him where he fell and went to work placing the explosive in the vault. He could see the virus trays but made sure he didn't go near any of them. He set the timer for five minutes and then placed the charge in the middle of the vault. It was designed to destroy the contents of the vault which would include the virus. Just as he was about to close the door to the vault, he heard another shot from Sam's side of the building. After that there was nothing but silence. Roscoe closed the vault door and pulled a cabinet in front of it so it would stay shut. Gunny came around the corner on his side of the building just as Sam emerged from his side.

Roscoe set the second explosive charge in the middle of the lab and closed the door. He met Sam and Gunny outside and the three of them slid silently into the water.

They took their night goggles off and began the swim back to the mini sub. Two minutes later they could see two bright flashes of light from the inside of the lab. The bombs had done their thing.

TEAM TWO AND THREE PROGRESS

Ashley and Charlie moved to the bow of the barge. Al went to the stern. It was totally dark everywhere, so Ashley knew that Roscoe had used the handheld EMP and it had worked. Ash and Charlie broke the surface of the water very quietly but stayed like glue to the side of the barge. They both then put their night goggles on. Ashley peeked up first and could see a guard was stationed on the front corner of the barge where she and Charlie were going to board. She drew her Sig and in one quick turn but a bullet through his head. He fell silently into the water. Al did the same as he pulled himself up on the stern of the ship. Al left his fins on the corner with this mask and began his search for guards.

Ash heard the pop first and she figured that Al had come across his first guard and dealt with him.

Ash and Charlie moved down the side of the barge. Ash began to apply the lock tape to the Korean scientist's room while Charlie moved farther down to do the same to the door to the ladies' room. Something caught Ashley's eye and she looked down the side of the barge to where Charlie was applying the tape lock.

With her night goggles on she could see a guard approaching Charlie from behind with a knife drawn. Ash took her Sig and didn't think twice as she aimed and fired. She hit the guard directly between the eyes and in doing so missed Charlies head by about six inches. The guard went down immediately and fell over the side of the barge into the water.

Ashley then heard another pop from somewhere on the aft end of the barge. Al was at it again. Then there were no sounds to be heard.

Ash and Charlie then approached the door to the Chinese scientist's room. The door was unlocked so they entered the room. With their night goggles on they could easily see that the three scientists were each asleep in their own bed. Charlie took out his hand cuffs just as Ashley said once to all of them in Chinese, "**Gentlemen, get up and out of bed. Put your feet on the floor and your hands out in front of you. Now**".

Ashley's voice was so strong, it even scared Charlie. The three scientists were groggy, but they did what they were told. Charlie put the hand cuffs on each of them and then explained to them in Chinese that they were going to take a little boat ride in the rain.

Charlie lined them up and told them they were to follow Ashley. The barge was completely quiet, so Ash knew that Al had completed his task and was soon to cut the lock on the ladies' room and get back in the water.

Ashley led the way to the electric boat and told the men to get in it. The first two did as they were told but the last one decided to try to escape and swung his arms at Ashley. That was a huge mistake. Ashley kicked him in the crotch so hard he threw up. He just fell into the boat.

Ash looked at him and said in Chinese "**You ever try that again young man and you will instantly become fish food. Do you understand?**

The man just groaned as he lay on the bottom of the boat. Once they had seen it happen the other two did not even think about an escape.

Ash started the electric motor and had the group moving toward the mini sub. Meantime Odie had completed his work and was back at the sub.

The mini was sitting on the bottom just like they left it when Roscoe and Team 1 arrived. They boarded the sub and Roscoe brought it up to the surface. It was on the surface when Ash and Charlie pulled up next to it with the three scientists. Charlie boarded the mini first so he could help guide the scientists as they entered. It was a slow process, but they managed to get each of the scientists loaded into the mini sub one by one. Once that was complete, Roscoe took it back down to the bottom where Ashley entered it. Odie was not far behind and boarded next.

Al was the last to leave the barge but before he did, he cut the tape to the ladies door and yelled at them in Korean the five words Charlie had taught him to say, "**Get off of this barge now!**"

With that done, he put on his mask and fins and headed back to the mini. He was the last to arrive and boarded with no problem.

They were all on board and about to head back to the Louisville when they heard the first of four pops. Odie's magic had worked. When they were underway, Roscoe said to Ash, "What happened to that scientist. He looks ill and keeps holding his crotch or stomach?"

Ash then said, "He made a mistake and sometimes shit just happens."

Roscoe just smiled. When they were on their way back Charlie said to Ash, "Hey Ash, nice shot. I'm sure you missed me by at least three inches." He was smiling as he said it.

"Thanks Charlie, sorry to come that close but time didn't allow me to ask the gentleman to please move away from you." They both laughed.

Roscoe turned to Ash and said, "I will want to hear about this story when we have time. It sounds like a good bedtime story."

"Hey Al," Ashley said. "How did it go with the women?"

"I have no idea, I cut the tape on the door and yelled in Korean for them to get off the barge now and then I dove in. No one even saw me. I hope they were smart enough to do it or they are all about to have to swim to shore."

On the way back Charlie explained to the three scientists that the team was made up of Americans who were going to take them back to China. He also explained that they would have to get wet and breath through an aqua lung to make the final transfer, but they would have a buddy helping them each step of the way. They all seemed to understand and one of them had used scuba gear before. He would be the easiest of the three when it came time to enter the Louisville. Ash gave the coordinates to Roscoe and the mini sub moved along at a solid eight knots.

They were on schedule and it was about 0350 when they arrived back at the submarine. The Forkman brothers were outside of the Louisville waiting for them when they arrived. Roscoe brought the mini sub in as close as he could to the in and out hatch. Once he was in position, they were ready to begin the transfer.

Charlie was out of the mini sub first and he entered the Louisville in and out hatch so he could be in the sub when each scientist was brought in. Ash brought the first one out and reminded him in Chinese to keep breathing slowly. The Forkman brothers helped her get him in and then waited for her to return. Ash brought each scientist in one by one and Charlie took over from her once they had them inside the Louisville.

Once they had the three on board, Roscoe brought the mini around and the team latched it back on the Louisville. The team was all on board the submarine and Captain Miles had it headed back out to sea. The time was 0430.

Charlie and Ashley got the wet suits off the scientists and got them dry and into warm clothes. Ash explained to them that they were on an American Submarine and that they would be returning them to their homes shortly. She offered them breakfast, but they were still too scared to eat. The Captain had arranged for them to be together in their own room but that the room would always be under guard while they were in it.

The interrogation would begin later that morning. Captain Miles had been ordered to take the men to Subic Bay where a Chinese delegation would meet them.

As dawn brought daylight to the town of Haeju it was clear that something had shut off all the power. No lights or power of any sort would go on.

General Ho had woken up early. He was surprised as everyone to find that he had no power in his rented home. He couldn't even make coffee. He went to the window and looked out to the bay. Something was different but he couldn't place it at first. Then it dawned on him as he looked out to the bay.

The barge was gone. It had just disappeared. Impossible he thought. A huge barge with armed men guarding it cannot just disappear.

His eyes went immediately to the warehouse, but it looked fine from what he could see from his window. He immediately dressed and headed down to the warehouse. Everything was totally quiet and there were no guards or guard dogs anywhere to be seen.

He arrived at the front door of the warehouse and was surprised to find it wide open. He could smell the scent of something that had burned but he could not tell what or where it was coming from.

He looked down and saw the body of the dead guard who lay across the floor. His eyes immediately went to the vault and the door was ajar.

Oh no he thought. The virus had been attacked by something. He stepped over the guard and went to the vault. The smell coming out of it told him that all had been destroyed. Oh my god he thought. I must tell the Supreme Leader immediately.

On his way back up to his rented home General Ho ran into one of the women that he knew had been on the barge. She looked terrible and was soaking wet. He approached her and said, "What happened to the barge?" She just looked at him with dead eyes and said "It sank. I do not know how, it just sank. We didn't see or hear anything until someone yelled in Korean to us to get out of our room and off the barge. We went out the door and could see that the barge was sinking. Some of the girls made it onto the electrical boat, but others like me had to swim. I do not know who made it or not. That is all I know General."

The General was beside himself.

CHAPTER 49
THE AFTERMATH

Roscoe and his team were all back on board and in no time Captain Miles had the Louisville moving out to deep water at 30 knots. Charlie worked with the ships staff to get the three Chinese scientists into a room where they could begin to rest. Ashley and the other members of the team went to their respective rooms to sleep.

Roscoe was asked to meet with Captain Miles in the wardroom for a debriefing. He took a quick shower and changed into clean clothes and headed to the wardroom. Captain Miles was already there and had a hot cup of coffee waiting for him.

"Good Morning, Roscoe. I bet you have had one heck of a morning?"

"Good Morning, sir. Yes, I think one could say that might even be an understatement."

"I'm going to want to hear all of the details of the operation but I know that you must be tired so I will hold off on the details until later. We do need to get the word to Admiral Omark at SEAL Command now, however, as I know he is probably waiting for some word from us already."

"Yes Sir. I am sure you are right. Here are the key points that I know he will want to know. If you agree we can get this off right away and it will be followed by a detailed report. He is going to have to tell us what to do with these scientists and when."

"I have already heard from the Navy again this morning. They prefaced their message by saying if you are successful in your mission then we would like you to take the Chinese scientists to Subic Bay in the Philippines."

Their message went on to say, "Once we have confirmed the success of the mission the US Government will handle all communications with the Chinese Government."

"OK, I think we should be brief and to the point. Here are the important bullet points that the Admiral will want to know:

- Mission successful. No SEAL causalities
- Virus and Lab destroyed
- Three Chinese scientists rescued and currently on board the Louisville
- Six armed guards and two guard dogs killed at the Virus Lab
- Four armed guards killed on the barge
- Barge sunk with five or six Korean scientists on board. Presumed drowned
- Six or eight ladies of the night released prior to the barge sinking. Presume they made it to shore.
- Operation completed according to plan. Power was cut and operation was completed in the dark and with complete silence. No one saw any of the SEAL team members at any time.
- Impossible for North Korea to know who pulled this off
- Mini Sub worked well. It would have been impossible without it.
- Details to follow

"I think that should do it."

"Thanks Roscoe, one hell of a job. I wrote the points down and will get a secure message off to the Admiral right away. I don't think he will be surprised but I do think he is going to be one happy man. You can now get some sleep. We will spend time later going over the details and I will want to read your final report when it is ready to go. Have a nice night's sleep."

"Thank you, Sir. I plan to take you up on your offer."

KUMSUSAN PALACE OF THE SUN PYONGYANG, NORTH KOREA

The intercom buzzed in his office and Kim Jong-un picked it up immediately. "Yes, Chloe, what is it?"

"Sir, I have General Ho on the line, and he said that it is urgent that he talk to you."

"Are you sure he said urgent?"

"Yes Sir."

"Then put him on."

"Good Morning, General. What is it that is so urgent?"

"Good Morning Supreme Leader. I have terrible news to report.

Our virus operation has been destroyed. Somehow overnight someone entered our facility and destroyed the virus and all the virus operation. All of our armed guards are dead and the barge, that housed our scientists, has disappeared."

"What do you mean disappeared, that is impossible."

"No sir, it appears to have been sunk in the middle of Haeju Harbor. I will confirm this later when I can get divers out to inspect it."

"Wasn't it manned with armed guards as well?"

"Yes Sir. There is no trace of either the guards or the scientists.

"What about the Chinese scientists?"

"I don't know, they have disappeared as well. I will get full details to you but at this time communication is very difficult. All the power in Haeju is out. Nothing will work."

"Ho, this is a major disaster and a potential major problem, and you let it happen on your watch. I want details and I want them fast" With that he hung the phone up. He was furious.

"This is totally unacceptable. Someone will pay a high price for this." He thought.

General Ho spent the day trying to figure out what happened and who did it. The attack had to have come from the sea in the middle of the night.

Late in the day his divers confirmed that the barge had been sunk in the harbor and the divers had found the bodies of five Korean scientists. They also found four guards all of them were dead by single gun shots. There was no trace of the Chinese scientists. By the end of the day, power had been restored but no one could yet figure out how it went out.

The General was also able to locate three of the women that were on the barge. They did not know where the others were or if they made it off the barge alive. None of them saw anything. They only heard a voice tell them in Korean to get off the barge.

The General was beside himself. He put his report together and made an appointment with the Supreme Leader to brief him the next day. He met the next morning with the Supreme Leader and gave him all the details he could. He also told him that he had been unable to locate the three Chinese scientists. It was clear the Supreme Leader was as mad as he had ever seen him, and he could not wait to get out of his office. When Chloe finally came in to say the Supreme Leader's next appointment had arrived, he walked out of the office with Chloe. As the General left the building, three security police officers were waiting for him and took him into custody. He was never seen or heard from again.

SEAL TEAM HEADQUARTERS
SAN DIEGO, CALIFORNIA

The admiral was in his office and it was 0700. Marcia knocked on the door and said that she had a secure message for him that had just arrived. She did not open it but just handed it to him and left the office. He opened it and read the 10 bullet points.

Then he said to himself, "I knew they could do it and they did. This is a major accomplishment." He buzzed Marcia and asked that she put in a priority call of great importance to Admiral Peter James, Chief of Naval Operations in Washington D.C.

"Sir, I have a priority call for you from Admiral Omark at SEAL Team Command in San Diego."

"Thanks Justin, please put it through on my private and confidential line."

"Ralph how are you and what brings you to make a priority call to me this morning?"

"Good Morning Pete. I have just received notification from SEAL Delivery Team 1. They have completed their operation in Haeju, North Korea. These are the ten bullet points I received from them just now. Here they are:

- Mission successful. No SEAL causalities
- Virus and Lab destroyed
- Three Chinese Scientists rescued and are now aboard the USS Louisville
- Six armed guards and two guard dogs killed at the virus lab
- Four armed guards killed on the barge
- Six ladies of the night released assume they made it to shore
- Operation went according to plan, completed in total darkness
- No one saw or spoke with a SEAL Team member impossible for anyone to know who did this.
- New mini worked well. Could not have done it without it.
- Details to follow

"Ralph, now I understand why your call was a priority. Please tell your SEAL Team congratulations. The President of the United States is going to want to hear this right now. It will be good to give him something to think about besides Coronavirus. I will look forward to reading the detailed report. Have a good rest of the day. I will be back to you with what we are to do next."

The Admiral hung up and buzzed Marcia. "Marcia, please send a note back to Captain Miles and Roscoe Cook on the USS Louisville. All I want you to say is well done and thank you. Detailed orders to follow. Sign it from me."

"Yes Sir. I will send it out right away."

It was a little after noon when Ashley woke up. She took a shower and put on a clean uniform and headed for the Wardroom. She was hungry and needed some lunch. She was surprised to find Roscoe and Captain Miles having lunch as well. Both greeted her with big smiles. Roscoe looked at her and said "Nice job last night Ash. Your team did well"

"Thanks Boss."

"I am curious to know about two things. Why was one of the Chinese Scientists so bent over and in pain when we put him in the mini sub? And what did Charlie mean when he said your shot missed him by perhaps a couple of inches?"

"Oh, there are simple answers to both of your questions. The scientist thought he could get away from me by trying to hit me over the head with his hands cuffed. I kicked him in the groin and that solved the problem. I also told him in Chinese that if he ever tried anything like that again he was going to become fish food. He and his buddies got the point. After that he and his buddies were cooperative. The answer to your second question is also simple. When Charlie was in the process of taping the door to the ladies' room shut, a guard came up behind him with a knife. I saw him and put a bullet through his head before he could begin to use the knife. He fell overboard. It just so happens the guard was directly behind Charlie, so I did not have much to work with. That is why the shot was close to him."

"Well that explains it." Both Roscoe and the Captain started to laugh. The Captain then said, "A little humor at a time like this is most welcome Ash. Congratulations."

The steward arrived and Ash ordered a turkey sandwich and a diet coke.

Roscoe then said, "Ash, I have to put our preliminary report together for SEAL Team Command. I'm going to start it after lunch, when you're finished will you sit down with me and make sure I don't miss anything?"

"Yes Sir. By the way Captain, thanks for the heads up on those mud flats. The silt was heavy as you said it would be and knowing about it in advance helped us avoid some real potential trouble."

"No problem, Ash, I'm just here to support the team." He said with a smile on his face. They all laughed, and Ash finished her lunch.

After lunch Ash worked with Roscoe on the preliminary operation report. They did it from start to finish and explained each step of the operation. They were very specific which meant they mentioned the names of each SEAL Team member that had participated and what they were responsible for. They also provided a critique of the weapons they had used and how they had performed. This was the first of two reports they would provide. The second would be the final and would include all relevant details.

Roscoe was very pleased with the door lock explosives and the explosives that were designed to destroy the virus and the virus equipment without causing a huge fire. It took them most of the afternoon but by the time dinner was served they were finished with the preliminary report. They provided a copy of the report to Captain Miles for his after-dinner reading. Early the next morning the Captain rang Roscoe and told him that the report was outstanding, and he was ready to send it on to Admiral Omark.

CHAPTER 50
THE TELEPHONE CALL

The interview team had been working with the three Chinese scientists for two days. They now had a clear picture of how the men were kidnapped and how they were forced to work on the virus which they referred to as **V**.

They explained in detail how the virus developed was designed to kill humans instantly, but they also indicated they had not yet perfected how to specifically target it. They believed that they were getting close to a solution but that it was probably six months away.

They explained that they were each taken separately from different areas of China and they did not know each other until they were brought to the Virus research center. They explained that they were all reluctant to help but they were forced to work, or they would be killed by the Korean General. His name was Fong Ho, but he made sure everyone addressed him as General.

They explained in detail what it took to develop **V** and the chemical elements that made it up. They also confirmed that there were six Korean scientists that worked with them but that one of them was killed when he tried to leave the barge one night.

As to the ladies of the night, they were used purely for sex. They were good at what they were asked to do. The General made it clear that the ladies would continue to please the scientists if they did what they were asked to do.

During the inquiry, the one scientist who attempted to flee was very apologetic and sorry. He indicated he was scared and feared for his life. When he learned that it was a woman who took him down, he could hardly believe it. Ash did not see him again nor did he ever have the opportunity to see her.

THE WHITE HOUSE
WASHINGTON D.C.

The President of the United States smiled through the entire briefing session

Not only did he have the three Chinese scientists under his control, but he knew that no one knew he had taken them including the Chinese Paramount Leader, Xi Jinping. He could not wait to call him directly and say, "Oh, by the way, we want to return your three scientists to you. These are the three that were kidnapped and taken from your country and put to bad use by your North Korean friend Kim Jong-un."

This was going to be the ultimate "got you" and he could not wait to say it. As to Kim Jong-un he was sure that he was not going to like it when he received a personal call from the Paramount Leader.

The President waited until he was told that the USS Louisville had made port in Subic Bay. Once he had that confirmed he made the call to the Chinese leader.

"Good Morning, the office of the General Secretary of the Communist Party of China. How may I help you?"

"Good Morning, I have a call for the Paramount Leader from the President of the United States."

"Please hold the line for the Paramount Leader."

"Good Morning Mr. President. To what do I owe the pleasure of your call."

"Good Morning Xi, I hope you are in good health given the problems with this Coronavirus?"

"Yes, thank you."

"I called this morning to advise you of a situation."

"Go ahead I am listening."

"Well, as you may recall almost three years ago three of your top Scientists disappeared from your country."

"Yes, I am well aware of that fact."

"Well I wanted you to know that we now have the three scientists and have taken them to Subic bay in the Philippines so they may be returned to your country."

The Paramount Leader was totally silent. "So", the President continued. "As it turns out, your friend Kim Jong-un kidnapped them, took them from your country to North Korea. Once there he put them to work building a virus that was designed to kill on contact. The virus and the virus development facilities have now been destroyed and we are happy to return your people to you."

"Mr. President are you sure of the facts that you just passed on to me?"

"I am very sure my friend and I'm sure that your scientists will confirm everything I have said to you. We will hold them for you in Subic Bay until you can arrange to pick them up."

"We will be there to pick them up tomorrow morning. Thank you, Mr. President, and have a good day."

The President hung up. He had a huge smile on his face.

SUBIC BAY
THE PHILLIPINES
ON BOARD THE USS LOUISVILLE.

By the time the submarine made it to Subic Bay the crew understood the SEAL Team had conducted a major operation in the waters off North Korea. No one confirmed or denied that an operation had occurred, and it was clear no one was going to talk about it until they were cleared to do so.

The interrogation team had taken the three scientists off the ship and housed them overnight on the Naval Base. The team had extracted everything they wanted to know from the three and they planned to fly back to Washington DC from Subic Bay as soon as the Chinese Government picked up their scientists.

The transfer was made the next morning.

Captain Miles received orders that he was to remain in the Pacific with stops along the coast for goodwill purposes. Stops would include Singapore in Malaysia, Bangkok in Thailand,

Hanoi in Viet Nam, Hong Kong and Shanghai in China and Seoul in South Korea. The last port of call would be Tokyo Japan. It was a three-month tour with a return to Pearl Harbor scheduled for April lst.

The transit between Ports of Call would include both SEAL training and Submarine exercises.

The Louisville was scheduled to get underway in two days. Mail was delivered just prior to their departure and there was one letter for Ashley. It was post marked Pearl Harbor Hawaii and it was a very brief note from Ryan. All it said was "Ash, I love you and miss you already." It was postmarked the day they left Pearl Harbor. She smiled and put it in her desk drawer. It would be the first of many letters she would receive on this deployment.

Before the Louisville got underway, Captain Miles made an announcement to the crew. "Good Morning everyone, this is the Captain speaking. As the rumor mill has informed you our SEAL team completed an Operation off the North Korean coast a little more than a week ago. I am not at liberty to discuss the operation, but I can tell you it was successful and that I am proud of all of you for your attention to duty during that period. It was a complicated operation and was performed well."

"This morning, I was informed that we will remain in Southeast Asia for the next three months. We have been assigned to conduct a goodwill tour which means we will make several ports of call. We will represent our country in each location we stop. In that regard you are all expected to represent yourself, your Navy and your Country in the most professional way possible."

"We will be stopping in Singapore Malaysia, Bangkok Thailand, Hanoi Vietnam, Hong Kong and Shanghai China, Seoul South Korea and last Tokyo Japan. We expect to be back to Pearl Harbor on April lst."

The buzz was everywhere on the ship. Everyone was excited by the news including Ashley who had never been to any of these ports in her life.

Three days had passed since the scientists were picked up by the Chinese Government and returned to China. They had all been extensively debriefed on their stay with the North Koreans. Special care was taken to make sure that their stay with the Americans on the Sub was pleasant and without anything to complain about.

OFFICE OF THE GENERAL SECRETARY OF THE COMMUNIST PARTY OF CHINA

The Chinese Government picked up the three Scientists in Subic bay and immediately began a debrief with them. They wanted all the details regarding both the Koreans and the Americans. When they were finished, they drafted a detailed report and prepared a briefing for the Paramount Leader.

When the briefing was completed the detailed report was given to the Paramount Leader. He read it completely twice before he picked up the phone.

PYONGYANG NORTH KOREA
KUMSUSAN PALACE OF THE SUN

Kim Jong-un sat in his office at the Kumsusan Palace of the Sun. His secretary buzzed him. "Yes Chloe, what is it?"

"Supreme Leader, you have a call from the Paramount Leader of China Xi Jinping."

All Kim could think about was what was about to come. He knew that this would not be a pleasant call. His hands started to shake as he picked up the phone. "Good Morning, Paramount Leader."

"This is not a good day for me nor is it a good day for you, Jong-un. I have now heard in detail the events that surrounded three of our top scientists who were kidnapped by you and your thugs."

"Paramount Leader, I can explain. This was all the doing of a rouge General who is no longer on this earth."

"Bull Shit and you know it. I only have one thing to say to you Jong-un. You have made a very grave mistake for you and your people. There is an old saying that applies directly to your stupidity. Never bite the hand that feeds you.

You sir have not only taken a bite, but you have broken the skin and left a scar. You will feel the pressure as your economy begins to collapse. Do not look for assistance from China for a period of two years. After that we may reconsider if you are alive at that time."

With that the Paramount Leader hung up the phone. Every bone in Kim Jong-un's body was shaking. He took a few deep breaths, but his heart was pounding hard and he did not feel at all well.

The Paramount Leader then directed his economic and military staff to immediately cut off all relations with North Korea. He said, "No exceptions on any goods or services. Put this order in effect for the next two years."

Captain Miles set course for Singapore. He figured it would take two days. Once there they would stay in port for an entire week.

Roscoe called Ash and said, "We are going to make our first stop in Singapore in a couple of days. Captain Miles has told me we will be in port for one week so the team will have plenty of time to see the place. Would you please coordinate with Gunny, so we always have a minimal presence on the Louisville? I do not want to have everyone gone at once. We also need to complete our final report by going through the preliminary report in detail. We need to make any changes and any details we may have forgotten so we can put this to bed and send a final report to Admiral Omark. I would like to have this final report ready to go when we arrive in Singapore in two days."

"No problem boss, I will discuss it again with the guys and will get going on my review today. I will try to have a copy with any changes or additions ready for you tomorrow."

Ashley called Odie and explained to him that she and Roscoe were now preparing the final report for Admiral Omark. She asked him to once again give her the exact details of how he planted the mines. She then set up a meeting with Gunny Sanchez to develop the leave schedule. Once the leave schedule was set, she went to work on the operation report. By late that evening she had a good draft and had incorporated Odie's report within the body of hers.

As to the leave schedule, she gave herself three full days off in Singapore. She had heard about the country, its cleanliness and its very strict laws. She was anxious to see it on her own, but she knew that if she were to see what she should see in three days she would need a guide.

The next morning, she went through her operation draft one more time and then gave a copy to Roscoe.

She then got on the internet and found a young woman who provided guide services on an individual basis in Singapore. She confirmed an appointment with her and booked her for the three days she planned to be off. Her guide would meet her the first two days at the ship beginning at 9 AM and they would tour each day until 4 PM. The third day the guide suggested that she pick her up at 4PM and return her to the ship at 11 PM. That would allow Ashley to see Singapore by night. The charge was $100.00 per day plus lunch. Ashley thought that was a good deal and accepted.

Roscoe spent the entire second day going through the final report. When it was complete, he read it and asked that Ashley do the same.

When she was finished, he made a few minor corrections and provided a copy to Captain Miles. Captain Miles was not only fascinated with the details included in the final report, but he was once again in awe of what the SEAL Team had accomplished.

He congratulated Roscoe once again and said he would make sure the report was sent off to Admiral Omark as soon as they arrived in Singapore.

CHAPTER 51
WHAT A REPORT

Marcia buzzed Admiral Omak and said, "Sir, a confidential report has arrived from Captain Miles. Would you like me to bring it in?"

"Yes please, Marcia. Thank you."

The report was larger than he anticipated as it spelled out the SEAL Team Operation in North Korea in significant detail. Roscoe had done a very thorough job and it read like an action novel. Admiral Omark read the report twice before he put it aside.

His plan was to send the final report to Admiral Peter James, Chief of Naval Operations. He would send the report personal and confidential with award recommendations for Captain Miles and his entire submarine crew and for Roscoe and his SEAL Team.

He thought long and hard about the award recommendations and he came up with the following:

Captain Miles and the members of his crew- The Navy achievement medal.

Captain Miles individually- The Navy Distinguished Service Medal and the Navy Expeditionary Medal.

Lieutenant Commander Roscoe Cook – Navy Cross for Extraordinary Heroism and the Navy Silver Star for gallantry in action.

Captain Ashley Morgan Jamison – Navy Cross for Extraordinary Heroism and the Navy Silver Star for gallantry in action.

Gunny Sergeant Juan Sanchez, Petty Officer Charles Chan, Petty Officer Albert Fineman, Petty Officer Raymond Odemier, Petty Officer Samuel Franklin Pierce-The Bronze Star for meritorious Service in a war zone.

All members of the SEAL Team – The Navy achievement medal and the Navy Expeditionary Medal.

When he had completed his recommendations, he enclosed them with the detailed operation report and had Marcia send it personal and confidential for addressee only. It was addressed to Admiral James, Chief of Naval Operations. He did not know if his recommendations would be accepted but he felt that every one of them was earned. The SEAL Team had performed beyond expectations.

It took three days of transit for the Louisville to get to Singapore. They did not conduct any training during the transit, so it was a very relaxed couple of days at sea. Ashley wrote Ryan a long letter but did not mention anything about the SEAL operation. She also wrote a letter to her Mom and Dad and to her Brother.

It was a perfect time to do it. She explained to all of them that for the next three months her team would play the role of United States Ambassadors visiting several cities and countries in Southeast Asia.

Captain Miles brought the submarine into the pier in Singapore harbor. It was a Thursday morning so they would be tied up for the next seven days before they departed for Bangkok.

Ashley was off on Sunday Monday and Tuesday. It was on Sunday morning that her guide showed up on the pier at 9 AM sharp. Ashley saw her coming and met her on the pier, Ashley was dressed in her civilian clothes. Her guides name was Emma Tam and she was 25 years old which meant they were not far apart in age. This turned out to be a blessing as they had so many things in common.

Emma explained to Ashley that Singapore was one of the most popular destinations in Southeast Asia. That, while it was small, it was a breath of fresh air to all who visited it. It had a great transportation system, clean air and water and a very pleasant environment. She told Ash that she had arranged a schedule that would allow her to see the major things that were important by day light but that on the last day they would see and experience Singapore at night. She said that she was sure that would provide a lasting memory for Ash.

Her days off went by fast. Emma managed to take her to the Gardens by the Bay and the Botanical Gardens. They visited Merlion Park and Little India and spent one day visiting three temples.

Her evening on the town was what she enjoyed the most. They went to Sentosa and visited a bunch of roof top bars. They were all full of neon lighting and loud music. People were mixing, drinking, dancing and having a lot of fun. Everyone seemed happy. The weather was spectacular and the memory she would take away from Singapore was all about that night. Just like Emma said she would.

The deployment continued. The SEAL Team conducted a variety of exercises using the mini sub while in transit to Bangkok. The visits to Bangkok and Hanoi were both interesting and hot. The temperatures in both places were near 100 degrees with extremely high humidity.

She had experienced humidity while going to the Naval Academy but nothing like what she experienced while visiting Thailand and Vietnam.

Ashley contacted her dear fiend Ming Lee and planned for Ming to meet her when the submarine pulled into Shanghai harbor.

Ming was her language tutor and guide while she spent one summer over a six-week period studying Chinese at Peking University in Beijing. It was a total emersion course into Chinese Language and Culture. Ming was not only a mentor and tutor, but she became a good friend and even spent one Christmas with Ashley and her family in Portland, Oregon.

Ming caught a flight from Beijing to Shanghai and booked a hotel room for the two of them for three nights at the Langham Shanghai Xintiandi Hotel on the Bund in Shanghai. The plan was to spend three full days and nights together. When the submarine docked in Shanghai Harbor, Ming was waiting on the pier.

Ashley was so excited to see Ming that she almost jumped off the ship onto the pier. They hugged like one would expect sisters to do

Ming told her she had booked three nights at the Shanghai Xintiandi Hotel. She explained that it was a five-star luxury hotel in the heart of Shanghai. It was close to Shanghai Times

Square and it has an incredibly beautiful spa and indoor pool. Ashley left the ship that day and spent three incredible days in Shanghai. They burnt the candle at both ends and shopped until they dropped. The days went by so fast she could not believe it.

The two of them were like sisters and did not stop talking, laughing and having a great time for three full days. There was only one time when the conversation was a bit awkward for Ash. Because Ming was totally fluent in English and Chinese it was natural that she would eventually end up working for the government of China, which she did. She was a trade analyst in the department of foreign trade. One night, after a lot of wine she asked Ash if she knew anything about an issue with North Korea. Ash just played dumb and said, "No why."

"I was just curious. Rumor has it that something went on a couple of months ago that involved the US and North Korea.

I don't know any details, but the rumor has it that the US was involved in returning three key scientists to China. Apparently, these scientists were kidnapped by the North Korean Government two or three years ago.

I have no idea if the rumors have any truth to them, but I do know that we have now cut off all trade with North Korea. I also know that if we continue to hold back support for them that it will not take long for the North Korean economy to totally tank. I just thought it was odd that you would be here with your SEAL Team not long after what ever happened happened. Oh, never mind, we have better things to talk about."

They were both sad when they had to part. They were like sisters and visits like they had just experienced were few and far between.

The first thing Ashley did when she got back on the ship was to get hold of Roscoe and tell him what she had heard.

"Hey Boss"

"Hi Ash. How was your three days off with your pal?"

"It was super and that hotel that Ming booked for us was the nicest hotel I have ever been in. The spa, pool, bars and restaurants were all first class. The reason I called is my friend Ming works for the Chinese Government in the Foreign Trade Department. One night she asked me if I knew anything about the US returning some scientists to China. She said there was a rumor circulating that North Korea had kidnapped these scientists and that somehow the US got them and brought them home. I just played dumb and said I didn't know anything about it."

She then told me something that was not a rumor. She said China has now cut off all trade with North Korea and if it continues it will surely tank the North Korean economy."

"Now that is really interesting. In fact, that is so interesting I think I will pass it on to Captain Miles and Admiral Omark. Thanks for the info Ash."

"I thought you might want to pass that on. I'm sure the US Government would be extremely interested to know it, if they don't know already."

Roscoe saw Captain Miles at lunch and passed the information on to him. It was clear he was extremely interested and eager to get it to Admiral Omark.

After lunch he went up to his stateroom to send a message to the Admiral. It simply said, "We are in Shanghai. Rumor has it that China has now cut off all trade with North Korea. Thought you would like to know."

Admiral Omark got the message and called his boss in Washington D.C. The message was relayed and those in Washington were delighted with the news.

CHAPTER 52
UNEXPECTED RECOGNITION

The United States National Intelligence Agency was finally able to confirm the rumor that was passed on to them by the Chief of Naval Operations. China had taken direct action against Kim Jung-un and North Korea. The extent of the action could not be determined but it was clear that trade between the two countries had abruptly stopped. The President of the United States was thrilled when he heard the confirming news. "Leave it to the Navy to once again set the stage for our victory?" He thought. The intelligence survey also confirmed a fact that was now becoming apparent. Kim Jong-un had not been seen in public for the past four weeks.

The USS Louisville left Shanghai and headed to Seoul, South Korea. The Coronavirus had taken a direct path through the country, but a great deal of time had passed since its outbreak and the country was now getting back on its feet and moving forward. The President of South Korea had been informed about the ship and its role in the North Korean Virus saga so he arranged a welcome party for the sub as it pulled into its pier. The President had ordered his most Senior Staff Members to greet the ship on arrival and to send his personal greetings to Captain Miles.

Captain Miles had never had such a reception in his entire naval career and at first, he was baffled by it. He soon recognized why they were being treated so well and it became clear that it was a result of the SEAL mission.

The Presidents Senior Staff Members welcomed the Captain and his crew and gave Captain Miles a few gifts from the President.

They also provided the Captain with passes for all the crew that allowed them to enter the many nightclubs in town at no cost and no charge for the first three drinks. The crews, both sub and SEAL Team members were thrilled.

There were many invitations sent to Captain Miles, but one was incredibly special.

It was a formal invitation to the Captain, his Executive Officer, James Michelson, Lieutenant Commander Roscoe Cook and his AIOC Captain Ashley Jamison to join him for a private lunch at the Blue House which was the center of the South Korean Government.

They all accepted the invitation and joined the President at the appointed time. They were all in dress uniform. They were escorted into a private dining room in the Blue House. The President was waiting for them on arrival and introduced himself to each of them.

"Good Afternoon. Thank you for joining me for lunch this afternoon. Our lunch, and this meeting is confidential and thus I would appreciate it if you would keep the content of the meeting confined to those in this room. Before we have lunch, I want you to know that I have been thoroughly briefed on the actions that you recently undertook regarding our friends to the North. The success of your mission can not be underestimated in its importance. You, my friends, have saved the entire world from what could have been a major problem."

If there is one thing I have learned about Kim Jong-un, it is, he would have not hesitated to use the V Virus as a weapon had it become part of his arsenal. To recognize your accomplishment, I want to personally award each of you with the Order of National Security Merit Medal of Korea. This medal can only be awarded by the President of South Korea and it is in recognition of outstanding meritorious service in the interest of our National Security. I have checked with your Secretary of the Navy and you will be allowed to display this medal and its ribbon on your Naval Uniforms. Please accept my congratulations."

Once the President had finished, he proceeded to pin a medal on each of the officers. When this was done, they were served one of the most lavish Korean lunches any of them had ever had.

When Captain Miles finally moved the Louisville out to sea, he was exhausted from all the attention he and the crew had received.

He was incredibly happy that they had been treated so well but he was also happy to be back at sea. He set the course for Tokyo, Japan which was their last stop on the deployment tour.

Ashley was familiar with Tokyo because that was the city in which she won her Olympic medals. She was tired but decided to take a tour of the city by herself on the on and off bus. It was called the "So you only have one day to see Tokyo," bus tour.

It was designed to provide customers with a lot to see in a limited amount of time. The tour was 10 hours because it also included a lunch. The lunch was featured as a "Sumo Style Lunch" which Ashley thought would be interesting.

She was picked up at a local hotel close to the pier and the tour began. She saw the Imperial Palace, the Meiji Shrine and the Asakusa Temple. The tour also included a boat cruise of the bay and the Sumo Style Lunch. The tour ended with a visit to the Tokyo Sky Tree observation deck and the Cocoon Tower.

The Sumo Style Lunch was the memory of the day. It was a Chako Hot Pot, high calorie dense meal that included fish, vegetables, meat and tofu served with rice and cold beer.

When the day was over, she was tired and full. She headed for her stateroom and slept for 12 hours. She did not go back into town, but Tokyo held many great memories for her.

Captain Miles had the submarine underway on March 26th heading for Pearl Harbor. The crew of the ship and the entire SEAL Team were anxious to get home. There were no training exercises conducted on the way back. Everyone was tired and ready to be home.

For those who have never been deployed there is something that comes over you about three days before arrival and it means you simply do not sleep in anticipation of the homecoming.

Ash was no different even though she had no one waiting for her at the pier on arrival. She missed her apartment and her deck, and she missed Ryan more than she could possibly imagine. She would be home one full month before he was due home.

Captain Miles brought the submarine home at 10 AM on the morning of April lst. The pier was lined with family members waiting to meet their loved ones.

Ashley was on deck and watched all the great reunions as they happened for both the sailors on the submarine and the members of her SEAL Team.

Prior to arrival Captain Miles made an announcement that all crew members were to be back on board for a meeting three days after arrival. It was a required meeting that would be conducted at 0900. He also told them that those who were on leave would be free to leave again at noon. Roscoe was advised that he needed to have all his SEAL Team present for the morning meeting and that the members of his SEAL Team were to reassemble at 1330 in the SEAL Team headquarters that afternoon.

Ash watched as the reunions took place one by one. It was a very moving and meaningful moment for her. Families were so important and only those in the military could experience the reunion feeling that one has when meeting loved ones after a deployment.

Ashley stayed on the ship until after lunch and then called Mr. Piedmont. "Hi Mr. Piedmont, Its Ashley."

"Hey Ash, great to hear your voice."

"I just wanted to let you know I'm home and headed for my apartment."

"Great, we have looked after it for you and I'm sure you will find it exactly the way you left it."

"Thanks so much, Mr. Piedmont."

Ash had arranged with Roscoe to be off for a couple of days. She would be back on the ship in time for Captain Miles meeting.

She left the ship. Got an Uber driver to take her to Safeway and drop her off. After that it was into the store. She got a few things to fill the refrigerator with and walked home. She was home with three bags of groceries. She opened the door and just smiled. The place was exactly like she left it but probably cleaner.

Dinner for her would be super simple. It was Sushi and white wine. What a way to go and it would happen on her deck looking at the boat harbor.

The message arrived at Admiral Omarks office just three days after his operational report and message were sent to the Chief of Naval Operations. His recommendations for awards had all been approved and were now ordered and would be sent out to him shortly for presentation.

The Admiral buzzed Marcia and asked her to find out where Captain Miles and his crew were and when they were expected back in Pearl Harbor. She was back to him within an hour. "Sir, they are currently in Tokyo, Japan and are due to leave on March 26th for return to Pearl Harbor. They are expected to dock in Pearl Harbor on April lst."

"Thanks Marcia, here is a message I would like you to send to Captain Miles."

"Dear Jason, you have had an extraordinary deployment and the success from your SEAL mission has not been unnoticed.

STEPHEN A ENNA

I plan to be in Pearl Harbor on April 4th, and I would like to address you and your crew as well as the SEAL Team. Please call a general assembly for April 4th at 0900. I would like all the Louisville crew members present as well as the members of the SEAL Team. Please tell Roscoe that I would like a second meeting for just the members of the SEAL Team to be held at 1330 in the SEAL conference room on the base. I appreciate your organizing this for me. Sincerely, Mark Omark."

Ashley poured a glass of Oregon Pinot Gris and took a seat on her deck. She was tired but very content. Ryan would be back in a month and after that who knew. For now, she had that to look forward to.

She opened her Sushi box and snacked on a California Roll. The wine was cold and the view to the Harbor was just as she had left it......perfect.

She spent the next day just lounging around. She didn't go to the beach but stayed home and rested. She hadn't had time to think much about the SEAL operation or the fact that during it she had blown two guys off the face of the earth and drowned five or six others.

She surprised herself a bit because she didn't feel bad about any of it.

On the morning of the 4th she was up early and on the submarine by 0730.

Roscoe had left her a note that all the SEAL Team was to meet and form up at amidships at 0830 and they were all required to be there. He also confirmed their second meeting which would occur at 1330 in the SEAL conference room on the base.

All the SEALs were assembled amidships at 0830 and Captain Miles had his entire crew on deck as well. No one had any idea what was coming except Captain Miles and he really didn't know much.

At 0900 a voice came over the submarine loudspeaker that said "Attention. Stand by for Admiral Ralph Omark, Commander of SEAL Operations." Admiral Omark then appeared from a side door and took his position facing the subs crew and SEAL team.

"Good Morning Ladies and Gentlemen. I am here today to thank you personally for your efforts on behalf of the United States Government and the United States Navy."

"The operation which you successfully conducted on your deployment was as important as any I have ever been associated with in over 30 years in the Navy. It was not only successful, but it was handled professionally with amazing bravery. For those of you who manned the Submarine, I give you my personal thanks for a job well done. For all the members of the SEAL Team I can only say that your actions make me enormously proud to wear the Triton."

"I asked you to assemble this morning for one purpose; I want you to be recognized for a job well done. All members standing on this deck will now be recognized with the Navy Achievement Medal and matching ribbon." The medals and ribbons were passed around and once everyone had them in hand the Admiral called Captain Miles and asked if he would please come forward."

When the Captain was positioned in front of him and all of his crew the Admiral said, "Sir, I would personally like to thank you and your men and in return I am proud to award you the Navy Distinguished Service Medal and the Navy Expeditionary medal." It was clear that Captain Miles did not know this was coming and he was both humbled and proud as they were presented to him by the Admiral.

When that was completed the Admiral said to all of those assembled. "Thank you. You are dismissed. Go enjoy this island."

The troops all clapped as the Admiral left the deck and headed to the wardroom with Captain Miles. Ash walked back to her stateroom with Roscoe. "Well that was a nice surprise. I did not expect it at all. Did you know he was coming out?"

"No, I didn't, and I have no idea what we are in for at 1330 but I will see you there." At 1330 the entire SEAL Team of 17 was assembled in the SEAL Team Conference Room. When the Admiral arrived, they all stood while he walked in and took a position at the front of the room.

"Good afternoon Brothers and Sister." He looked at Ash and smiled as he said Sister.

"This morning you all received the Navy achievement medal which is an indication of the importance of the mission which you just accomplished. Some of you participated in the actual operation but all of you participated in the training that went into the operation. Only a very few people will ever know how important and difficult that training was. To those who did not participate in the actual operational mission and to those of you who did, I have a second award for you. You will all receive the Navy expeditionary medal. Roscoe, will you please hand these out for me."

"Now I would like to ask Gunny Sergeant Juan Sanchez, Petty officer Charles Chan, Petty Officer Albert Fineman, Petty Officer Raymond Odemier, Petty Officer Samuel Franklin Pierce to please step forward. To each of you I am pleased to aware the Bronze Star for Meritorious Service in a war zone." He put the medal around each of their necks and shook all their hands. I cannot say how appreciative I am, personally, and the how appreciative the United states Government is overall with your bravery and operating performance. It was just outstanding."

"Now I would like Lieutenant Commander Roscoe Cook and his AIOC Captain Ashley Morgan Jamison to please step forward. Roscoe and Ash, I cannot even begin to tell you how successful your plan was designed and carried out. Your planning, organization and mission skills have been recognized at the highest level of the Naval Command."

"In appreciation of your effort I am proud to present you both with the Navy Cross for Extraordinary Heroism and the Navy Silver Star for gallantry in Action." He put the medals around the necks of Roscoe and Ashley. Neither of them said a word but both had never felt so proud. All they could say was "Thank you, sir."

Now with that having been said, the Admiral said, "One last thank you to you all. You are dismissed."

The SEAL Team did not leave. They just stood up and clapped for their bosses. It was a moment that Roscoe, Ashley and even the Admiral would never forget

CHAPTER 53

THE FINAL DAYS OF THE USS YORKTOWN CV 10

Ryan and the men and women aboard the USS Yorktown had completed five months of their deployment and everyone was thinking about returning to Pearl Harbor. The deployment had been a good one with lots of ports of call and plenty of flying time for Ryan.

The Yorktown, however, was on her final legs. She was one of the aircraft carriers built during World War 2 for the Navy. She was named after the Battle of Yorktown which occurred during the Revolutionary War and she was the fourth ship to bear the name. She was commissioned in 1943 and had gone through several conversions along the way but it was now time to take her out of service and everyone aboard knew it, but no one had yet made it official.

She had made a real name for herself and served many purposes including being the recovery ship for the Apollo 8 space mission. She was also a movie star in that she was used in the movie Tora! Tora! Tora! which recreated the Japanese attack on Pearl Harbor. As the ship headed for Pearl Harbor the formal announcement was made by the Captain. He said the Yorktown would be decommissioned shortly after arrival and then she was scheduled to become a museum ship and a National Historic Landmark.

Ryan had flown Reggie during the entire deployment and each mission he was assigned to went off without a hitch. He was an excellent pilot and it was obvious to both his peers and his superiors.

During the deployment he had stayed in touch with Ash by letter, but he had no idea what her deployment entailed. He only knew about the ports she had stopped at. He missed her a great deal and was now counting the days until they arrived back in Pearl Harbor.

During his deployment he made the final decision to apply to graduate school. He had read a great deal about the Naval Post Graduate School and the location could not have been better for him.

If Ash was stationed in Hawaii it was an easy hop to San Francisco for her and just as easy a hop to Honolulu for him. He had not heard back from his detailer, but he expected to hear soon.

Reggie told him during deployment that he had put the two letters of recommendation together and made sure that they were sent to both Ryan's detailer and the Navy's Blue Angel Command Center.

Reggie told him to advise the detailer before he began his last term that he would want to begin the application process for the Blue Angels.

It was the end of May and the Yorktown was due to tie up at Pearl Harbor on June lst. There were three days to go before they arrived, and the crew was getting anxious. Not only were they excited to get home, but they all knew that they would soon be receiving transfer orders, but no one knew where to.

Ashley had been home for the month, and she had used the time to rest and recover. She was tan and fit and had been swimming every day. Roscoe had given a lot of the paperwork to her, so a big chunk of every day was dealing with fitness reports, transfers in and out and other military requirements.

She never really got bored, but she needed to be in the water to stay happy. She focused on a self-imposed goal which was to swim at least a half of a mile every day. She did this between SEAL Team training exercises.

She talked to her Mom every other week, but she did not tell her anything about the mission they had conducted or the medals she had been awarded. Roscoe had advised her to play down or even not mention the mission they had conducted. He also reminded her that when she was in uniform with the ribbons displayed most people would not know what they represented. Military people would know, and they would know that to earn the ones she had on involved two things: great danger and a successful operation. No one else would have much of an idea and that was fine with her.

She did talk to Roscoe about Ryan. She knew he would want to know what the secret mission was all about and she also knew the minute he saw her in uniform with two of the Navy's highest medals on that he would ask.

Roscoe thought about it and advised her that when he asked, she should be honest and tell him what the mission was about and what it accomplished. He also advised her to tell him it was confidential, and she was only telling him because of their relationship and the fact that they were both military officers. She felt much better after that conversation with Roscoe.

Ryan's ship was due in the day after tomorrow and Ashley knew, based on her correspondence with him that he had requested two weeks leave on arrival. She discussed this with Roscoe and was given permission to take the two weeks leave as well.

It was now down to one day before his arrival and Ashley was totally focused on meals.

All she could think about was fresh sea food. Ryan was arriving on a Friday. That night would be crab and mango salad with white wine. Saturday would be barbecued shrimp and pineapple and Sunday would be coconut crusted Mahi Mahi. With that decided she headed off to the fish market and gathered all her groceries and a few bottles of wine and headed home. For wine she went with Oregon Pinot Gris. She picked a new one produced by Cedar + Salmon. It was a Willamette Valley Pinot Gris. She read the label. The wine carried stone fruit aromas like nectarine, peach and apricot. The winemaker had added a touch of lime oil which was supposed to add to the alluring aromas. The wine was defined as crisp on the pallet with hints of lemon rind. The finish was crisp, dry and refreshing. It sounded perfect for her fish fiesta.

She also decided that she would show up when the ship pulled in. She thought It would be fun for Ryan to have someone there to meet him. She decided to do it in civilian clothes rather than her uniform. Just thinking about it made her smile.

The morning of his arrival Ash was up early. She showered, had breakfast and got dressed. The ship was due in at 1000 and she knew exactly where it would tie up.

She decided to wear shorts but not too short of ones. She added a flowered tank top that fit her tightly and sandals that matched the tank top. She looked super. Most women would give their right arm just to be able to fit into something like the outfit she had selected but most could only dream about it.

For Ash's, swimmer body, clothes were all made to fit her perfectly. She did not put any make up on as she simply did not need it. She looked like an ad from a health and fitness magazine.

She grabbed her Uber at 9:30 and headed for the base. She was dropped off at the active duty military entrance. She showed her ID to the guards and walked into the base. She knew that both guards on duty could not take their eyes off her and all she did was smile at them. If only they knew that within the last six months, she had personally killed two men and given the order to drown five or six others.

She headed for the pier, and based on the crowd she saw forming, she would not be the only one in the reception crowd. The huge aircraft carrier was just being tied to the dock when she arrived. All the men and women were on deck in their Naval summer white uniforms and several F-18 Hornet Fighter Jets were positioned on the main deck for all to see. It was quite an impressive sight.

The Naval Band was there, and the crowd mood was more than festive. There was no way that Ash could see Ryan. There were just too many people. She found a nice place to wait in the shade and that is what she did for the next hour as the men and women began to exit the ship."

She was starting to wonder if she would ever find him when suddenly someone tapped her on the shoulder and said, "Hey Sailor, can I buy you a beer?"

She turned around and grabbed hold of him like she had never done before. "I have missed you so much big guy. I love you and am so happy to have you home."

Ryan responded by saying, "Ash you are simply the best." They kissed long and softly before he grabbed his bag and said, "shall we get out of this place?"

They headed off the base holding hands and caught an Uber car right away. Ash gave him the address and they were at the apartment in 15 minutes.

They had so much to say to each other, but their physical desire completely overtook the intellectual desire and they spent the next two hours in bed.

When they had finally had enough, they headed to the shower together and then put on their normal evening apartment dress. She was in short shorts with a bit of a transparent top with no bra and sandals. He was in shorts and an under armor dry fit shirt and sandals. Wine was poured and they took their place on the deck. It was almost like the last six months hadn't happened.

Ash was first to speak. "Did you find out anything after they announced the ship would be decommissioned?"

"No. I did apply to the Naval Post Graduate School in Monterey and I was informed that Reggie had made sure that the letters of recommendation we talked about were sent to my detailer and the Blue Angel Command. We didn't get the mail before we left the ship so my orders may be there waiting for me. I thought we might want to drop by tomorrow and see what the mail has to offer. I always wanted you to see what my plane looks like and where I live, and I thought that might be a fun outing."

"I'm all for it"

"This wine is great, and it is really cold. What is it?"

"It's a new Pinot Gris from Oregon. I have never tried it before, but I read about it and thought it would be great for your homecoming dinner which is a fresh crab and mango salad served with sesame crackers."

"Sounds perfect to me."

The evening went by so quickly they couldn't stop talking but their talk was more about them and not about their jobs or future. They were both tired by 9:30 and headed for bed. They were both asleep by 10:30. It had been a great evening. They were up early the next morning, had a light breakfast and then enjoyed their coffee on the deck. They decided to put their uniforms on and head for the base.

Ashley could tell that Ryan was anxious to know what his next assignment would be and even though he felt confident that he would get orders to PG School, it was never certain in the Navy until the orders were in your hand. Ashley put on her Marine Officer Service C uniform which meant she had on green pants with a kaki belt. She wore a short sleeve button up shirt with no tie and her green soft garrison cap. Her Triton was above her left pocket as were her ribbons.

Ryan had on his summer whites. That meant a white short sleeve shirt, white pants, white belt and shoes. His wings were over his left breast pocket and below it were two rows of ribbons. He wore his standard Naval Officer head cover.

"OK, I'm ready," Ash said.

"I just need one more minute and we're out of here" Ryan responded

He had seen Ash so many times in uniform that he really did not pay much attention to her as she put the uniform on. As they were about to go out the door, he saw them and stopped dead in his tracks. Ash, you are wearing a Navy Cross for Extraordinary Heroism and the Navy Silver Star for gallantry in Action. Those are two of the highest awards the Navy ever gives for war time action. They must be approved by both the Head of Naval Operations and the Secretary of the Navy.

I do not recognize the third one, but it does not look like a United States Navy ribbon. Something tells me that you were a busy SEAL on this deployment. Are you going to tell me what you have been up to in my absence?"

"The answer to your question is a simple one. I am going to tell you how these awards came about, and I will do so over dinner. It is a complicated story and will take time. It is not a story that can be passed on to others, but I do have permission to tell you. I simply told my boss that I would need to tell you and that I just can't hide information or make up things that are not true just to keep you in the dark. He understood and once I tell you the story you will understand as why. Now let's go and see if you have orders and how they are going to impact us."

Their uber car pulled up in front of the active duty personnel entrance.

The same two guys that were on duty when Ashley went through the gate yesterday were on duty today. They both recognized her even though she was in uniform and they both immediately saw the Triton and the Navy Cross and Silver star.

They were shocked that it was the same person that they could not take their eyes off the day before. The Triton was one thing but to have it and the two ribbons below it made it clear this was one tough and special woman.

They boarded the Aircraft Carrier. Ryan was well known, and the Officer of the Deck greeted him by name. "Josh, this is Captain Jamison. She is with me. Do you know if the mail arrived?"

"Yes Sir, it has arrived and was sorted. Your mail is on your desk in your stateroom.

"Thanks Josh. Ash follow me."

Ryan proceeded to give Ash a mini tour of the huge ship and then showed her his stateroom. His roommate Scotty was there and was delighted to finally meet Ashley. He obviously knew about the SEAL Triton, but he did not know about the ribbons that were worn below it.

"It is a pleasure to finally meet you Ash. I must have heard your name mentioned 60 times in the past couple of months."

"Thanks Scotty, it is nice to meet you as well."

Ryan went over to his desk and there was an envelope from the Bureau of Naval Personnel with his name on it.

"Looks like our surprise has arrived Ash."

"Well open it and tell us what it says."

"It says what I thought it would. I am to report to the Naval Post Graduate School in Monterey, California on September lst. Until that time, I am to remain with the ship as it prepares for decommissioning. Scotty, did you get a package as well?"

"Yes, I am heading to San Diego to join the flight crew on the USS Abraham Lincoln CVN 72. I, however, do not get to spend the summer in Hawaii. I ship out in two weeks. I'm happy about it because I will be flying the Super Hornet off her."

"That is great Scotty, I'm happy for you. Well, speaking of Super Hornets I am now going to show Ash what one looks like. Cheers Scotty. I'll see you later."

CHAPTER 54
ASHLEY MEETS REGGIE

Ryan took Ashley up to the hanger deck. It was where the planes were stored when they were not being readied for flight operations. Ash was blown away with the size of the hanger deck and the number of planes that were stored on it.

Ryan took her over to the far-left corner of the deck where there were three sailors working on a jet. "Hey Jimmy, would you and the boys come over here for a minute. I want you to meet someone."

"Sure boss."

"Ashley, I want you to meet Petty Officer lst Class Jimmy Rockmont, Petty Officer 2nd class Micky Morart and Petty Officer 3rd class Jason Rockwell. Guys this is my girlfriend Captain Ashley Morgan Jamison."

"Hey guys it is good to meet you." Ash reached out and shook each of their hands. It was clear they were all mesmerized by her. Not only was she very tall and attractive but she wore a Navy SEAL Triton Pin and below it they all recognized the Navy Cross and Silver Star.

Jimmy then said, "Captain it is great to finally meet you. Our boss has not stopped talking about you for the last six months and if half of what he has told us about you is true you must be the closest thing to God we have ever seen."

They all started to laugh and then Ash said, "Jimmy not everything people say is true"

"Ash, these three guys save my life every time I take this baby up. They have been my crew for the last three years and they are simply the best."

"So, you are now looking at my Boeing F/A 18 Super Hornet. Jimmy, you know this plane better than anyone I know. Would you give Ash an overview of her, her history and your thoughts on how she performs?"

"Sure boss, but the how she performs is probably better said by you because nobody and I do mean nobody flies her better than Lieutenant Joshua."

'Well Captain, I will try to make a long story short because I could talk about this baby for a week. Let's start with the fact that it is currently replacing the older model single and tandem seat Hornets. The Super Hornet is just a bigger, stronger fighting machine. It is a flying army in that it carries a 2 mm M61 rotary cannon and air to air and air to surface weapons. It has extra room for fuel and can double as a fuel tanker if needed."

"It was designed as a multi-role fighter and it is based on a whole bunch of earlier model fighter planes with a history too long to go into. It completed testing in about 2006 and was then put into service over a gradual period. We still have several pilots that are gradually phasing into flying it."

"The thing is super powerful and has electronic gear that can sense almost anything in the pitch dark or in the middle of a storm. Because of its added fuel capacity, it can stretch a mission out by 40% longer than the older Hornet versions."

"As I said, this is a fighting machine, it can fire missiles, drop bombs and strafe the ground at an extremely low altitude and fast speed. Our Boss proved that with a flying demonstration not long ago. He made a strafing run across our landing strip in the middle of the night during a storm and strafed the landing strip with only three feet of air between this baby and the ship's deck. I tell you, Captain, and pardon the expression, but I watched him do it and it made my shorts ride up!"

That made them all laugh. "Well enough of my talk how would you like to sit in it?"

Ryan just smiled and said, "Go ahead, try it Ash, you might like it."

Ash thought what the heck and she boarded the jet with Jimmy's help. He gave her a quick introduction to the cabin and the controls.

She could see immediately that this was more than she could handle but the feeling of power as she sat in it was almost overwhelming.

When they were done, they thanked Jimmy and his guys and headed to the Wardroom. Ryan wanted to have lunch together and then they would head back to the apartment. As it turned out Reggie was in the Wardroom about to have lunch with his flight commander Captain John Jacobs. Ryan walked in with Ash and both men stood up. "Ryan, great to see you please come join us. I believe you know Captain Jacobs."

"Yes sir, nice to see you again sir. I would like to introduce you both to my girlfriend and best friend in the world, Captain Ashley Morgan Jamison."

"Pleasure to meet you gentlemen." Ash said.

Both Senior Officers didn't have to be told anything about Ash. Her uniform said it all. First, she was wearing a Navy SEAL Triton and below it she wore three ribbons that were exceedingly rare. They both knew exactly what the ribbons represented. She wore on the top row in this order across, The Navy Cross, The Silver Star and a medal that both had only been told about but had never seen. It was the National Security Merit Medal of Korea. They both knew that it could only be awarded by the President of South Korea and that it was given in honor of meritorious service in the interest of South Korean National Security.

Reggie then said, "Ryan, we have ordered, so why don't you put your order in and we can have lunch together."

"Yes sir, I will do that."

While they were waiting for lunch to arrive Reggie said to Ashley. "Ashley, may I call you Ash?"

"Sure, everyone does including all my SEAL Team."

"Thanks, well Ash, I just want you to know, that even though I have not met you before, I feel like I know you."

"Not only has this boyfriend of yours been talking about you solid for the last six months but even before I knew you and

Ryan were seeing each other you had built up quite a Naval reputation."

"In fact, when I read the article about the three thugs that tried to mug you at the shopping center, I was impressed. Based on the article, it did not sound like any of them would every walk again. I don't think I will ever forget the headline about never attack a lady SEAL out of water."

"Yes Sir, they made an error in judgment and are probably sitting in some cold cell right now asking themselves why they decided to pick on a defenseless woman."

That made them all laugh. "Ryan did your orders arrive?"

"Yes Sir, I picked them up this morning. I will attend the Naval Post Graduate School in Monterey beginning in September. I will major in management. Until then I will stay assigned to the carrier as it begins the decommissioning process."

"Great, that sounds like the two of you will have a nice Hawaiian Summer to plan and look forward to."

'Ash, may I ask you a question," Captain Jacobs said."

"Sure, sir what is it?"

"Well I have a good friend whose name is Admiral Mark Omark. Do you know him?"

"Yes sir, I know Admiral Omark well and have both spoken and met with him recently."

"Well Mark talked to me a couple of years back about a woman that he thought was going to break the SEAL macho mold and become one. Was that person you?"

"Yes Sir, I am the first and still only woman to wear the Navy SEAL Triton."

"Well, Captain, then if half of the rumors about you I have heard over the past couple of years are true then you are better known in this man's Navy than most of us will ever be. Congratulations."

"John, you may not know this, but Ashley was making the Navy proud long before she became a SEAL. If I recall, she was a four-time NCAA swimming champion while swimming for the YARD and she won two Olympic Medals in Tokyo swimming for the US Navy."

"I'll be damn Reggie; I do remember that now. Once again Congratulations, Ash."

"Thank you, sir," Their lunch came. Over lunch they both talked to Ryan about the Blue Angels and their letters of recommendation.

Ryan was almost embarrassed by the comments that were made about him, but he did not say anything.

Ash on the other hand, was so proud she could hardly keep it inside of her. Not only was she sure that Ryan would get through graduate school with ease, but she knew that she would at some point be watching him perform as a member of the Blue Angles.

They left the base and caught an Uber to the apartment. Once they were in, they immediately changed into their evening apartment attire. They poured an iced tea for each of them and headed to the deck. "Well Ash, thanks for coming down to see my home away from home."

"Ryan it was really impressive and you my dear have captured the hearts of two senior aviators."

"It was a bit embarrassing I must say."

"No big deal. It was so nice to hear, and it should make you really proud."

"Well I'm sure you noticed that everyone you met saw that SEAL Triton you wear and below it was a row of three medals that could only impress those who knew what they mean. I can tell you with some sense of pride that everyone you met noticed them. Are you finally going to tell me where they came from?"

"I will, but first I have to tell you the rules of this confession. Rule 1, you are the only one that will hear the story. You cannot repeat it to anyone. It cannot go beyond us. Rule 2, you can ask questions, but you are better to wait until you hear the whole story because there is a lot of story to hear. Are you OK with those two rules?"

"Sure, I'm ready to hear the story."

"OK. Here goes. Before I left for deployment, I had to make a couple of trips to the Mainland. Those two trips were both to see Admiral Omark at SEAL Headquarters."

"The Admiral had been informed by the Chief of Naval Operations that the North Korean Government, under the leadership of Kim Jong-un, was in the process of developing a virus called V. This virus was designed to kill humans instantly. We were told they had completed the development of the virus, but they had not yet figured out how to target it to an individual or an entire city. They were working on how to control it, but they just weren't there yet."

"The virus research and development were being done in a lab that was specifically built for the purpose. This lab was in a Korean town called Haeju which is located on a small bay just off the Yellow Sea between China and Russia. The photos of the lab were clear. It was built inside a broken-down warehouse at the end of pier in the harbor."

"Our SEAL Team was selected to design an operation that would allow us to kill the virus and destroy the research facility. So, Roscoe and I had to develop a plan that would allow our team to enter the bay, destroy the facility and the virus itself plus destroy all of those that were involved in making it happen."

"The story has an extra complication."

"It so happens, that to help them with the virus project, the North Koreans kidnapped three of China's top scientists. They did it almost three years ago and each scientist was from a different part of the country, so they did not know each other except by reputation. So, in addition to the project goals we also had to capture the three scientists and return them to China. Obviously, China did not know who took them or what happened to them and they were so preoccupied with the Coronavirus that they didn't go after them."

"So, as you can tell this was a complex mission with a lot of moving parts and risks. Now to set the stage, I must say that Captain Miles, who is the submarine Captain, did a lot of work studying the Yellow Sea landscape. He was able to find a spot that was 200 feet deep where he could park the submarine at night while we conducted our mission. Our mission was further complicated by the fact that our mini submarine can only carry 10 at its maximum and that means we would only be able to use 7 Navy SEAL's to accomplish our task because we had to have room to bring the three scientists back with us."

"To complicate things further, the Yellow Sea is a real ugly body of water with almost no life. It is full of silt and mud and if you get to close to the mud flats you can stick your mini sub in the mud and silt and be unable to get it free. The channel that Captain Miles found would lead us to the Haeju harbor but the harbor itself is very shallow. So, once we were in the harbor, we would have to leave our mini sub parked in 25 feet of water while we conducted the mission. This means we had to leave it on the bottom. In addition, to avoid any contact with the bad guys our mission needed to be completed in total darkness. This mean that we had to leave the submarine at 0200 move our mini with our team from a depth of 200 feet to 25 feet over a five-mile course on a very narrow channel while avoiding the mud before we could even begin our operation."

"The details of the operation were worked on by Roscoe and me for almost two months. Captain Miles took the submarine with our SEAL Team to a point about five miles off the coast of Haeju Harbor. Then we began the task at hand. Our SEAL Team was split into three teams.

"Team 1 was led by Roscoe. Their goal was to destroy the virus the research facility and to kill all of those charged with guarding it. Team one was made up of three SEALs."

"I led Team 2. My team was made up of three SEALs as well. Our goal was to capture the Chinese Scientists, kill the Korean scientists and guards that were guarding them and set free some women of the night that were housed to service the men. All the staff including the women were housed on a barge in the middle of the bay."

"Team 3 was also under my command. Team 3 was made up of one man. His job was to place mines on the bottom of the barge and sink it once we had the scientists off."

"So, the mission took a lot of planning and only involved 7 of our SEAL team. We were limited by the number of people we could carry on the mini sub. We followed our plan in detail. I navigated the channel and Roscoe drove. We arrived in 25 feet of water at about 0230 in the morning. It was raining and ugly. We left the mini sub on the bottom and followed our plan."

"The plan worked. Team one killed six guards and two guard dogs. They destroyed the virus and the inside of the research facility. My teams, 2 and 3 killed four guards, drowned five or six scientists and rescued the three Chinese scientists. We also released the ladies of the night and then sunk the barge."

"The result was everything we could have hoped for. I am told that the President of the United states took great pleasure in calling the Paramount Leader of China to tell him that his friends in North Korea kidnapped his scientists and that we were returning them to him."

"I also understand that as a result, China has now cut North Korea off completely from any economic and military assistance. As such, North Korea is going to pay a major price for their actions and may economically fail next year. I have also been told that Kim Jong-un has not been seen in public in the past four months."

"The medals were awarded by the Secretary of the Navy on the recommendation of Admiral Omark. The Medal of South Korea was awarded to us by the President of South Korea on our port visit to Seoul."

"So that, my dear, is what I did on my vacation to the far east."

"Ash would you mind if I changed from iced tea to wine. I think I need a drink."

She just laughed and grabbed two glasses from the kitchen and a bottle of Duckhorn Sauvignon Blanc.

CHAPTER 55

WHO KNOWS WHAT THE FUTURE HOLDS?

They woke up early and showered together. Then they got dressed and took their positions on the deck. Each of them had a cup of hot coffee and the temperature was perfect at about 79 degrees. "Ash, that dinner of barbecued shrimp and pineapple was out of this world last night. You mentioned that we were having a trio of seafood dinners. It started with the crab and mango salad, and then it was last night's shrimp and pineapple what is the third tonight?

"Tonight, is your night to shine my dear. We are having Macadamia Nut crusted Mahi Mahi which you are going to prepare."

"I'm not sure why you think I am capable of that, but I will give it my best shot. Just so you know that I have no idea how to do what you have asked."

"Not a problem, I put the recipe on the counter for you. All the ingredients are in the kitchen. Since I know you can read, I have a lot of confidence that you can pull this off."

Ryan picked up the recipe and started to read it.

Ingredients- 2 6oz fish fillets approximately ½ inch thick. Coat with sea salt and fresh ground pepper. 2 eggs and olive oil for frying or barbequing. ¼ cup macadamia nuts crushed and ¼ cups of plain white breadcrumbs. 1 tsp orange zest, 1 tsp lime zest, 1 tsp garlic minced, 1 tsp chives, minced and 1 tsp orange zest, 1 tsp lime zest, 1 tsp garlic minced, 1 tsp chives, minced and 1 tsp basil chopped.

Directions

- Firmly press the flesh side of each filet into the crust mixture until the fish is evenly crusted.
- Season both sides of the fish with sea salt and ground pepper.
- In a bowl, beat the eggs. Dip the flesh side of each filet into the egg mixture.
- In a large pan add the olive oil and heat it on the barbecue
- Sauté the fillets, crust side down until they are golden brown, and the crust is firmly set. This should take 2 to 3 minutes.
- Remove the filets form the pan. Place on a baking sheet and bake in the oven for 3 or 4 minutes until the fish is cooked through
- Serve with papaya salsa

'Hey Ash, I think I can do this."

"Me think you can too. Oh, I saved you some time. I already made the papaya salsa and it is in the refrigerator. I also purchased a ½ pint of mashed potatoes at Safeway. I want you to heat them up and place the fish on a bed of mashed potatoes when we are ready to eat. I will make a green salad to go with the fish."

They had a light breakfast and then their conversation turned to the future. "How long does it take to get your Masters at the PG School?"

"I'm not sure but I think it takes a full year or 18 months if I try to do a double major. If I want to extend it to get a PHD then I think it could take an additional 3 years. Right now, I think I just want to get the Masters and then get back in the air flying again. One thing I have thought about though is do it in steps. Step 1 would be the Masters. Step 2 would be to fly with the Blue Angels and Step 3 would be to go back and get the PHD. After that it would be to take command of something and then get on with the rest of my career."

"You know Ryan, I like that step-based plan. I have at least two more years in Hawaii with the SEAL Team. It will probably equate to the time you will have in Monterey getting your Masters. After that I will be up for reassignment when you are flying with the Blue Angels. Those two assignments could work out if we plan them properly and then when you move to Step 3, I would probably be up for reassignment again."

"Now that I think about it, how does Director SEAL Operations, Carmel, California, sound for an assignment?" They both laughed.

"Because I know I will be here in Pearl Harbor for at least the next two years while you are in school in Monterey, we could set up an easy schedule to stay in touch. I thought of a schedule that just might work."

"What were you thinking, Ash?"

"I was thinking that if we work out a schedule it shouldn't be that hard to keep our relationship going from the distance between Pearl Harbor and The Monterey Peninsula. The distance is very workable. I was thinking that if we planned, we might be able to see each other twice per month.

I was thinking about a long weekend once on your side and another long weekend on my side. To me a long weekend would mean fly Thursday night. Spend Friday, Saturday and Sunday together and then fly home on Monday."

"That sounds like a workable plan to me Ash. I haven't started thinking about it yet as we have this summer to figure it out but I do know this, our relationship is not going to end and that is just the way it is going to be."

"Of course, the military has a way of screwing up the best made plans. I do know, however, that I have at least one more deployment in front of me before my tour ends here and, of course, I have no idea what missions may come up but if we set up a travel schedule well in advance we can probably stick to most of it. So, for now, I just want to set a plan up that we both think we can live with and then let the future be the future."

"Now, back to the present for a moment. Last night I could not believe the story you told me, and I also could not believe the level of danger that clandestine mission carried with it. You just did not seem to have any doubt about the outcome, and I could tell from the way you told it, you were not even frightened. How did you feel before during and after the thing went down?"

"To be honest, it didn't bother me at all. When we were at the yard Roscoe asked me a question before I committed to the SEAL program. That question was, "Ash, do you think you could kill another human being?" My answer to him was, yes, if it needed to be done and was justified."

"I did not hesitate when I shot and killed those two guards and I did not give a damn about drowning the scientists that were trying to design something that would kill millions. Both were justified in my book. I did not think about it then and I have not since. It was my job and I did it well. As a SEAL we have a motto and that is, "The only easy day was yesterday."

"My guess is that is true, and I will have even greater hurdles to jump in the future."

"The way I look at it. We both have been trained to kill the enemy. The only difference is I am a little closer to them then you are when it happens. The net result is however the same. The good guys win, and the bad guys lose."

"I think your right Ash. So, no more shop talk from me. I think it is time to get our suits on and take a walk down the path to Waikiki Beach."

The day was perfect. They spent the day in the water and on the sand. They stayed longer than normal and headed back down the path about 5 PM. They jumped in the shower together and then it was open the wine and watch Ryan handle the Mahi Mahi. Ashley had put two bottles of Duckhorn Fume Blanc in the refrigerator and they opened the first one while Ryan was preparing the fish for the barbecue.

When he had cooked the fish and warmed the mash potatoes it was time to eat. Ash set their table up and dished up the salad while Ryan added the Mango Salsa to the fish plate. It looked great and tasted even better.

They toasted to each other and then ate their meal slowly. "You know Ryan, if you can't make it as a pilot, I think you could make it as a Chef. This fish is delicious. Congratulations on a job well done."

They spent the evening watching the boats sway back and forth in the harbor. The future was ahead for both and in their own ways they were looking forward to the challenges it would bring to them.

When it was time for bed, Ashley told Ryan to meet her in bed. She would be out in a minute. When she came out of the bedroom, Ryan could not believe his eyes. She had on a red bra with matching G string. It was an outfit that left nothing to the imagination. "Ash, you look amazing, Ryan said."

"Thanks, big guy. This red outfit is meant to signal the beginning of one long hot summer. My plan is to make it so hot you will never forget it."

All Ryan could think was "What a way to go."

CPSIA information can be obtained
at www.ICGtesting.com
Printed in the USA
LVHW091022221020
669312LV00069B/464/J